SKELMERSDALE

Brought to Book

BROUGHT TO BOOK

A Tale of Lust, Cunning and Deceit in the Book Trade

Ian Norrie

Elliott & Thompson
London & Bath

Also by Ian Norrie

Next Time Round in Provence
Next Time Round in the Dordogne
Next Time Round in Tuscany
(all with drawings by Michael Floyd)
A Celebration of London
Hampstead : London Hill Town
(both with photographs by Dorothy Bohm)
Sabbatical: Doing Europe for Pleasure
The Book of Hampstead (co-editor with Mavis Norrie)*
The Book of the City (editor)*
The Heathside Book of Hampstead and Highgate (editor)*
The Book of Westminster (editor)*
*(with photographs by Edwin Smith)
Writers and Hampstead (compiler, with calligraphy by George
Simpson, photographs by Keith Wynn)
Hampstead, Highgate and Kenwood: A Short Guide.

Publishing and Bookselling (with Frank A Mumby)
Mumby's Publishing and Bookselling in the Twentieth Century
Sixty Precarious years: A Short History of the National Book League
A Hampstead Memoir: High Hill bookshop, 1957-1988

Novels
Hackles Rise and Fall
Quentin and the Bogomils
Plum's Grand Tour

For all those friends, colleagues, customers, adversaries – and the categories sometimes overlap – who made life in the book trade, exhilarating, memorable and rewarding; and to the memory of Mavis, my darling wife, who shared the experience and sealed, for us both, many of the friendships.

Blanche Ardbuckle felt seriously affronted. The end, though undoubtedly nigh, was being botched. Her power of command, rigorously asserted for most of eighty years, had been severely eroded. She, who had hired and fired on whim, imperiously beckoned lovers to her bed and, when it suited her, rejected them as summarily, now lay dying attended sporadically by only a nurse.

From her bedroom high above Rustrock Common, Blanche watched house martins swooping against a pale blue sky, then darting in and out of the eaves. Darting was the word used, about her eyes, by the only lover she had not rejected. 'They are never still,' he had said. 'They are probing eyes, eyes that find out everything. Sometimes they frighten me.' They had frightened many but had now lost authority. So, why did she not contrive to take an overdose, arrange a lethal injection, demand a goblet of hemlock, or delivery of an instant asp?

She had left it too late. 'Bridget,' she called in a weak voice, 'bring me a cyanide pill.' She lacked conviction. Anyway, Bridget did not hear her. To distract herself she tried to imagine 'their' faces when the legatees heard the terms of her will.

Near the lower end of the Common, the Editor of the *Rustrock Gazette & Herald*, anticipating an imminent need, tapped out the obit of a distinguished citizen, on his beloved, ancient, metal-cased Olympia portable. Should he liken her to Margaret Thatcher or select, as might seem more appropriate, an essentially literary figure? In which case, who? Agatha Christie? Barbara Cartland? They were exemplary success symbols but didn't have quite the stature he sought. He needed someone who epitomised what drove readers into bookshops today. Inspiration hit him in the index finger. It had to be the blessed Delia.

Rustrock Spa, with a university more concrete than red brick, was in 1990 almost unique among southern British towns for lacking retailers whose fascia boards proclaimed adherence to nationally familiar chains. This was because Blanche Ardbuckle, by then the octogenarian owner of the borough's only bookshop had, almost half-a-century earlier, bought most of the estate of a destitute duke. She owned all but a few dozen square feet of freehold property within the central square mile of a watering place never fashionable, although Beau Nash had once paid it a visit.

The Duke, whose ancestral death duties Blanche in effect had paid, detested her all the more because she later allowed a distant cousin of his to preside over her poetry book department. He retired to sulk on a Mediterranean shore, with the residue of his former heritage, but derived some satisfaction from knowing that the exquisite house overlooking Rustrock Common, in which Blanche lived, was not hers. He had contrived to sell it, prior to the appointment of the Official Receiver, to the very man who had become not only the lady's lover, but also the general manager of her business.

On a mid-May morning in Blanche's eighty-first year, some staff at Ardbuckle's had arrived by the time John Ogglethorpe (Manager, Fiction & General), was ready to unlock the main recessed, and uninviting, door, which was flanked by several listed, and impossible-to-dress, neo-Gothic windows. John, mid-thirties, six-foot plus, plump to portly, dark, curly hair, observed to an assistant whom he dimly recalled having previously encountered – but they came and went with such frequency, it was impossible to remember – 'I wonder if the old bat lasted the night?'

On the first floor Maimie Perkes (Art), an emaciated spinster who knew much about painters but little of business, crossed herself and spoke, in hushed voice, to Amy Thresham (Travel), 'Mother of God, bless us, I have a feeling she'll not live out the day, rest her soul', phraseology she employed only when speaking to catholics. Amy, a fellow communicant at Holy Joe's, who, having escaped her family in Alberta, spent much of every day in a genealogical trance thinking about her English forbears, sighed 'Amen'. Truly, she likened Blanche to her wicked cousin Ruth but Brownie points were to be had for charitable thoughts.

On the mezzanine, Daniel Drybrough (Paperbacks) took a broom with his good arm and deftly swept a small heap of detritus, ignored by Nell Pickett (Cleaner), through gaps in the banisters, onto a section of Fiction & General below. To himself he admitted his indifference about whether or not 'She' had seen the sun rise. It was something he had not experienced for yonks.

In one neo-Gothic turret near the roofscape Lord Terence Absolom (Poetry) ruminated about whether to stay or withdraw when Blanche died; in another, Fergus Welch (Science & Technology), a stroppy Ulsterman, gifted as a sculptor and a womaniser, pondered on how long it might take a new management to rumble the rackets he operated.

On the higher second floor, necessitated structurally by the grand central hall created by an exuberant Edwardian architect, Adrian Thomson (History), baby-faced, brushed-back hair, looking eighteen but in his fortieth year, spoke of obituaries. He predicted that, in the nationals as well as the local, they would be sickeningly conventional and not mention Blanche's appalling record as an employer; in the adjoining department, round-shouldered little Gerda Kohl (Foreign books), with hair that was something between Struwwelpeter's and a traditional corn dolly's, shed tears, in expectation, because a boss was a boss, and loyalty was a discipline.

On the lower second floor – Ardbuckle's was an edifice of intricately eccentric design – Kim Mahon (Sport), herself intensely unsportive but in love with the gear, wondered, would trainers and a track-suit be acceptable attire for the funeral?; on a third floor tower, reached up an unroped, stone, circular staircase, Jim Woodstock (Philosophy & Religion) told his unheeding junior that the next management would be well-advised to play down some of the clapped-out ancient beliefs and embrace Mind,

Body & Spirit; in a sub-mezzanine semi-undercroft, Mona Darling (Children's and Young Adults) exclaimed to her absent-minded, part-time assistant, 'I don't wish Miss Ardbuckle any harm but when she goes I do hope this department will come up out of the basement. None of the mums can get a push-chair down here, let alone a pram. And when I told her these were the readers of the future, all she said was, 'When they grow up, Mona, they'll be able to manage the stairs'.

In a partitioned lower lean-to, sited between enormous buttresses and added during World War Two, book-keeper and accountant, Jawarharlal Deolali, advised his sidekick, Denis Sandlethorpe, that because Ardbuckle's was a private limited company, in the unhappy event of the proprietor's demise, there would be no moratorium on payment of invoices to suppliers, or of wages to staff; on the further side of the hard-board 'wall', Audrey da Costa (Mail Order), once described by Terence Absolom as 'a black and female Falstaff', informed herself, though not the three partly cowed and nervously giggling girls who daily submitted to her tyrannous authority, that the new management would be obliged to double her salary. Failing that she would take 'her accounts' to another bookseller because the customers with whom she dealt were loyal to her, not to Ardbuckle's.

In the cavernous and dry cellar, immediately above the ample founda-tions which, when they were laid, may, or may not, have disturbed Roman remains (prying conservationists were not so thick on the ground in Edwardian times), Maurice Watkins (Caretaker, also, when needed, Packer) found the timing perfect. He was ready for retirement, state pen-sion due any day, all his perks from Blanche nicely sorted away, so he didn't want to know who might take over 'when she slipped orf the 'ook'. Beneath a cumbersome stone flight of steps, beside a wing which rambled off on a designer whim never satisfactorily realised by the successor to the first architect, who had died in harness, Norwood Butling (Security) was writing his letter of resignation. A sleek, smart, six foot ex-police sergeant, he would be retiring to his own bookshop, at a south coast resort, to which for many years, he had been filtering volumes belonging to Ardbuckle's.

Rumours of Blanche's condition reached staff in the annexe, a remote area behind a pergola, reached through an approximation to a tube-train tunnel. They meant little because the proprietress had not visited this outpost, comprising the departments of Education, Music & Drama and Social Sciences, for some years and none there had worked for Ardbuckle's for longer than eighteen months.

In a central office, above the vast entrance vestibule, where Blanche Ardbuckle's private suite, including her bedchamber dominated by a four-poster, had once been located, Hugh Mattingson (General Manager), author of iconoclastic treatises on the Christian religion, and sometime professional thespian, awaited a call to the dying lady. A tall, broad-shouldered man, with a refined swagger, he tended to dominate all gatherings which he graced. Should he attend Blanche's bedside wearing full papal regalia, or the simple habit of a Franciscan?

He owned both. His wardrobe was all embracing.

· 2 ·

Blanche once again watched a house martin dive from the eaves of her bedroom window and disappear across the Common, only to fly back into orbit seconds later, presumably overcome by agoraphobia. Blanche loved birds, flowers, trees; she was less fond of human beings. She disliked dogs because they fawned upon her and cats because they didn't. And, at this moment when she ought perhaps to be thinking of eternity, she was having uncharitable thoughts about Hugh Mattingson who hadn't sold her Ridge End.

Ridge End was a breathtakingly exquisite early nineteenth-century villa, three storeys high, with a balcony at first floor level and demure, bow-windowed bays, two of them to the left hand side of the porched entrance. One bow had doors opening onto a small, immaculately mown lawn. Trailing plants had freedom to range at will. The tiled roof of the first floor balcony fell short, by a few feet, of the storey above, which itself was fractionally lower than the level it surmounted. The slight but studied lack of uniformity bestowed distinction on proportions that would, otherwise, have been too perfect.

Blanche chuckled as she remembered the will she had recently made. Four men and one woman were to be the main beneficiaries. How surprised they would be; what consternation would be generated by the conditions she had laid down. How Mark Ampersand, her solicitor, had disapproved. At one moment she had thought he would refuse to act for her. Heigh ho, she reflected, solicitors, like everyone else, are in business.

Blanche was sole owner of the bookshop bearing her name. It was said to be on the site of a Roman forum, although not a shred of evidence – not so much as a tile or a coin dropped by a passing centurion – had been unearthed. The spa was of eighteenth-century origin, at a time when it had sought to appeal to royalty and attendant gentry, to architects, landscapers, courtiers and all the riffraff required to minister their needs. Its other raison d'etre was a spring of repellently-flavoured iron water, bubbling perpetually, and flowing into a conduit connected to bottling arrangements. Rustrock, closer to London than was Bath, despite its magnificent common never acquired the same reputation. It was less popular, in its brief prime, than Tunbridge Wells, or Hampstead, yet its water still enjoyed modest sales when marketed in small phials and stocked by health food shops.

It was Blanche's grandfather who had in the late nineteenth century converted the derelict pump room of the spa into a veritable temple of books. His son succeeded to the business in 1904 and added numerous floors, wings, attics, outbuildings, cellars, turrets and conservatories, mostly in the Gothic style, to create a twentieth-century folly to which Pevsner devoted several enthusiastically witty paragraphs in his Buildings of England volume on *Wealdshire.*

Blanche's more prosaic approach to the property market came much later and had saved the business from bankruptcy.

· 3 ·

The day wore on.

At her command no bulletins were issued officially about Blanche's condition, but rumour reported she had had a remission.

Customers at Ardbuckle's, some unaware that the founder's grand-daughter lay at death's door, were eager only to complain about why the books they had ordered were not to hand; others, family friends or clients of long-standing, entered the premises as though treading upon a hallowed sanctuary, in a few cases going so far as to look about them for a box in which to contribute to whatever fund might be thought appropriate. Many enquired, in hushed tones, excruciatingly amplified by imperfect acoustics, 'How is she?'

'She is holding her own,' they were told, by an ageing maiden who had been seconded to the front of the shop from Miscellaneous, a department reached by a spiral staircase, and situated below the cupola, where determined antiquarian booksellers often disinterred bargains hidden in the woodwork.

Many employees felt as similarly remote from sorrow at Blanche's impending demise as Daniel Drybrough (Paperbacks) did, but there were those who grieved. And not only the devout R.C.s, Maimie Perkes (Art) and Amy Thresham (Travel); there was also Gerda Kohl (Foreign).

'Little Gerda Kohl', as she was patronisingly known to her colleagues, was of German origin but had spent her youth in Australia, whither her parents had fled from the Third Reich. They were non-Jewish liberal Bavarians. Klaus Kohl had closed his bookshop in Munich after declining to display copies of *Mein Kampf* in the window. He was just in time. It was August, 1936. Gerda was in Rome, doggedly making copious notes about every antiquity in sight; Wilhelm, her brother, was at Cambridge University, on a summer course, perfecting his English. Both were warned by friends not to return to Germany. From England, where the family was reunited not only with one another, but also with funds previously deposited in the City, they sailed to the Antipodes.

After the war Gerda was the only one of the Kohls to return to Europe.

She resumed bookselling, first in Oxford, then in Rustrock Spa. At her interview, she fell instantly in love with Blanche .

Miss Ardbuckle found the little German woman, who spoke English with a slight Australian accent, repulsive but was soon impressed by her unusual honesty. No one in the Foreign Department, let alone Gerda, had to be sacked for embezzlement. The fraulein had given Blanche absolute loyalty but now, aged sixty-nine, past the retirement age and without a private pension, Gerda was concerned lest the next management should dismiss her. She had never understood why most people were so antipathetic towards her.

Maimie Perkes also feared losing her job. She had an encyclopaedic knowledge of her subject but ought to have become a reference librarian in a college of art. She lacked all business sense but adored selling and, although she amassed bulk orders from itinerant sheikhs casting around for stately homes to line with bookshelves, her stock grew inexorably. Her criterion, when buying, was, 'if I like it, so will the customers.' She bought as for a perpetual Christmas and, because books from one department could be paid for in another, and sales were not analysed, it wasn't possible to measure a stock/ turnover ratio. Blanche often had a gut feeling that

Maimie overbought and protested, on several occasions, 'You have too many books, Perkes', only to be told, 'I don't have sufficient shelves, Miss Ardbuckle.'

Blanche suspected a false argument but, as always when on the shop floor, her mind was concentrated upon apprehending thieves.

Maimie, well into her fifties, had no idea where she would go if sacked. But Blanche had been good to her, so she said a prayer.

Amy Thresham, about to be forty, had for seventeen years been grateful to Blanche, even though she likened her to her wicked cousin Ruth, she who had strayed. In 1973 Amy had been dismissed from Foyle's for persistent lateness, having spent what should have been the first half-hour of her working day pouring over family histories in the basement of another bookshop. Out of work, she had hitched a lift to Rustrock Spa because that was where the driver who responded was bound.

Amy's flaxen locks betrayed German ancestry which was emphasised by her incipient obesity. As she walked, she flung herself along, flaunting her lower limbs in a manner which should have been sexually provocative, but wasn't. On the day she applied at Ardbuckle's for a job, the Travel Department manager had been summarily ejected for the usual reason. His deputy was on holiday, his second assistant was in the loo, smoking. At that moment when Gauleiter Framley, Blanche's henchwoman, who resembled Harpo Marx dressed in a belted blue tweed suit, had shown her into Travel Amy had sprung into action, briskly selling a *Michelin Green Guide to Italy* and commenting admiringly on the wisdom of the customer's choice. In fact, until that moment, Amy had never heard of Michelin. Her total knowledge of travel literature was confined to air company handouts perused on her flight from Edmonton, Alberta, to Heathrow, five months earlier. The dreaded Framley was impressed. She reported the incident to Blanche who made Amy manager, at the same time as sending the second assistant packing for prolonged occupation of the loo.

In his top floor tower, known disparagingly to colleagues as 'The Garret', Lord Terence Absolom (Poetry) wished he had a written contract. There was only a gentleman's agreement by which he worked for what it cost his chauffeur-driven Bentley to convey him, five days a week, between his family seat and Ardbuckle's.

His income derived from the House of Lords and the National Trust. He was a lord of limited means. Ironically, he was not paid for the only actual work he did. In the basement, Maurice Watkins (Caretaker & Packer), accepting a batch of returns from dextrous Daniel Drybrough who deposited it neatly, with one arm, on a bench, commented, 'reminds me of when old Bugger Bognor died before the war. The wireless kept repeating, over and over, "the King's life is ebbing slowly away." Dad boxed me on the ear for giggling. Now my wife got a feelin' for Bognor when I told 'er that. So that's why we're goin' to live there when…' He signalled eloquently upwards with one index finger…' The ole dear's certainly takin' 'er time. Probably tryin' to sack the bleedin' doctor.'

· 4 ·

In fact Blanche was feeling better. She rang for her nurse. 'Bridget!' She commanded. 'I have turned the corner. Bring champagne.'

Bridget knew better than to argue, but before filling the order phoned the doctor, who said it could do no harm. Blanche reflected wryly that in so many matters she had always had her own way. In fact, in most, though not all.

Blanche, born in 1910, encouraged her father's architectural excesses to divert him from the bookselling operation to which she gave herself singlemindedly once her 'education' was complete. In the process she saw off her two sisters by persuading Father to settle generous dowries upon them. As she again gazed out on Rustrock Common she thought of Pauline and Annie and compared their tragedies with her own. Her sisters had enjoyed brief, childless marriages, become war widows, then lost their lives on a shopping expedition (with black market coupons) to London, in 1944, when a doodlebug landed on a bus in Kensington High Street.

Blanche's personal life was also destroyed by the war, but she had trained herself not to think of it.

· 5 ·

At Ardbuckle's, the news flew round. 'She is asking for champagne!' 'A sure sign she's going,' commented Hugh Mattingson, who had decided to attend her death bed clad as a druid.

It was closing time. Few of the staff were eager to go home. They sensed that a significant moment was upon them. The three grieving women departed for dowdy bedsits. Accountant Jawarharlal Deolali also went home, to the four-bedroom house where a dozen relatives of his wife occupied, uncomplainingly, a windowless attic. Most of the male staff opted for a drink in the Duke's Head where they were greeted by Gordon Ruffle, junior reporter on the *Rustrock Spa Gazette & Herald,* a spiky-haired youth who specialised in having flair, which others described as cockiness.

Blanche Ardbuckle was good copy for the *G & H* whose editor, Jeremy Basker, liked to refer to her as 'Our very own duchess'. She owned the property where the two papers – *Herald* on Wednesdays, *Gazette* on Saturdays – were printed, written and administered, but wasn't the proprietor, although she had shares in the company.

Gordon Ruffle had been told by Basker to get something for the midweek edition. Basker liked to play the tough Fleet Street editor, which he had been for twenty strenuous years; Gordon, the statuary six-two in height of the orange-juice generation, with high, shining cheekbones and swiftly diminishing acne, expected to last for longer at Canary Wharf, but relished the treatment. 'I hear she asked for bubbly', he said to John Ogglethorpe.

'What else can you tell us, Gordon? I suppose you have Ridge End bugged?'

'Seriously blokes,' said Gordon, once they all had drinks, 'The boss wants something for the *Herald*. What are the staffs' reactions?'

'She ain't dead yet,' Alec Tremlett pointed out. He was number two to Fergus Welch who cried, 'Give the boy a break. Listen, Gordon, in the staff room, bets are being laid on how long she'll last.'

'Who's the bookie, Ferg?'

'I cannot reveal names but you know, Gordon, what a meanly paid lot we are? How could any of us afford to run a book?'

'That, of course, would not apply to the Rev Hugh Mattingson?'

'I have not said a word. No fucking utterance whatever. Mind you' – Fergus leaned forward, his nose almost touching that of the reporter – 'We are having to be ultra gentle with the punters. We are having black armbands prepared for them – tastefully monogrammed in gold braid with her initials, B.A.'

'For some,' observed Adrian Thomson (History), the boyish, clean-shaven graduate, 'B.A. signifies academic achievement, but not in her case.'

'Will you be expecting to go to Oxbridge then, Peter Pan,' asked Fergus, of his thirty-nine year old colleague, 'if you get your A-levels?'

Gordon took it all down.

· 6 ·

Blanche had only a few sips of champagne, then refused further sustenance of any kind. She fell into a reverie. She might not be as much recovered as she supposed but she could still programme her memoirs...

Life had treated her both generously and unkindly. The only man she had loved was long dead, the only child she had borne had probably also perished. To compensate, she was rich, more from the property she owned than from the sale of books; she had power over those who worked for her. She liked that, and enjoyed being a tyrant. For most of eight decades she had been in rude health, with a finely tuned digestive system and a strong head for alcohol. She was intelligent though not intellectual, liked reading biographies, playing the piano, and going to the opera. She had no religion and was not subject to nervous disorders. She was only ever unselfish when the wishes of others reflected her own inclinations. Wasn't she perhaps being unfair on herself?

Wasn't she?

No, she thought, she was not. 'I don't think I would have liked me,' she mumbled to herself. 'Well, not altogether...'

She reflected how wise she had been, following her father's death, in 1951, to concentrate on the property. George Ardbuckle had bought whole streets of houses in Rustrock as tenancies fell in and freeholds became available. Much of it was now classifiable as slum. Blanche had been interested only in pocketing the rents; her eye was on commercial property which could not only be let at unrestricted rents, on full repairing leases, but had the added advantage of keeping out competing booksellers. Large areas of Rustrock Spa belonged to the Dukes of Bidborough until the 1950s, when death duties struck the family not once but thrice. Blanche scooped up most of the estate to give Ardbuckle's ninety-five percent of the town centre. She then turned her attention to the handsome terraces also owned by the Bidboroughs. She had become so absorbed in what she saw as her own private Monopoly board that she neglected her emporium until the appointment of Jawarharlal Deolali as accountant. What a blessing the man had been to her! (And how well she had rewarded him!) He had come as an audit clerk, brought to her notice improprieties in the running of the business, then accepted her offer to become Financial Adviser to the company.

As soon as she had tired of playing Monopoly – there was little left to buy, she recalled, apart from Ridge End and Woolworth's – she turned her attention once more to selling books, and clinched a deal with the university Vice Chancellor to supply the faculty and students until the year 2000. She told him that by the terms of the Net Book Agreement she was legally forbidden to offer the university a discount but promised a donation of ten per cent of annual turnover. (This also contravened the Agreement but he, the Vice Chancellor, was not aware of that.)

Next she transformed several acres of land she had bought bordering the Common into a site for a yearly book jamboree. The origin of this lay in disposing of overstocks at the shop but it soon developed into an annual fair with secondhand and antiquarian dealers clamouring for pitches. This was how Hugh Mattingson had first come into her life.

Ah, she had still been a handsome woman then. Tall but not inelegantly so, straight-backed, slim, auburn-haired, with finely pointed nose, perfectly formed high cheek bones, slightly dimpled chin, famously darting blue eyes, high forehead and firm bust. All that, well into her seventies. Hadn't she been, she asked the swooping house martins, something of a goddess amongst women? A squawking magpie answered for them, disparagingly. She ignored it, 'Let's face it' she whispered to herself, feeling weaker and weaker, 'I was a beauty. And the energy I had…'

In her heyday, every morning, following an early breakfast, she was on the move around her ever-expanding empire, walking briskly as a nurse, taking stairs three at a time, running from place to place for the sheer pleasure of it (also, for the chance of discovering a malefactor) and, every day, taking two short swimming sessions in her private pool. She expended so much nervous energy (some called it hysteria) that she did not put on weight despite eating heartily three times a day and drinking a bottle, sometimes two, of wine each evening.

She was not sorry that she had had few real friends. Away from the mattress she was much attracted to her own company – people could be so boring. Herself, she never found anything but totally absorbing. She loved to convey her thoughts onto tape which could not answer back except disruptively when the technology hiccuped. It was a shame that she had pressed a wrong key and destroyed, at a touch, all those confidences.

Yet, for all that Blanche liked to be alone, she also enjoyed being waited upon. She bathed and dressed herself, but that was all. She had never cooked so much as a fried egg, nor carried out the most elementary of household chores. In her garden she dead-headed roses, slashed back over-hanging branches, pruned intensely, drastically. She thrived on acts of destruction. They were as satisfying as sacking incompetent employees, but she never dug, planted, sowed or swept.

She laughed – and nearly choked – when she remembered how she had refused schooling and been taught by a succession of tutors, none of whom tolerated her for more than a year, although all found her rewarding to teach on such days as she deigned to pay attention. Finally, they were discouraged by her indifference to their advice on how to pass exams. She did not pass because she did not sit them. She made her own rules; she sought no letters after her name.

At seventeen she had travelled extensively in Europe and America with a companion; at eighteen she took cruises to other continents, attracting, as she floated on international waters, ardent admirers – also acerbic comment from elderly passengers; at nineteen, no longer a virgin, she swanned back to Rustrock Spa and began to dominate her father's business, ruling and over-ruling in a prefectorial style which earned her the hatred of most staff. A few dared to oppose her. Sometimes she listened to them but invariably concluded that their advice was wrong. Yet she remembered from the dim past, that there had occasionally been a tiny core of doubt in her mind, though she had always triumphed over it. Then she thought about her lovers and, for the last time, began to enumerate them, emitting little gasps of recollected joy. Yes, some had afforded her deep pleasure, although none had been favoured for long....it had been better that way...and at least they had not lost their heads, as had the victims of Turandot, with whom, she had been told by one of them, she was often compared...

Drowsily she watched a house martin... a mist seemed to be forming over the Common... that Common which had never suffered the indignity of being transformed into a tidy park... she tried to find the champagne glass but knocked it from the bedside table...

'A pox on Bridget...' she muttered... 'you're sacked...'

· 7 ·

The general manager of Ardbuckle's, the Very Reverend Hugh Mattingson, who claimed dubious theological credentials procured in the midwest of the United States, burst upon Rustrock Spa in the sixties, when he hired a stall at the book carnival. At this he displayed a range of religious tracts colourfully adorned in purple and orange wrappers, featuring the faithful submitting to their beliefs in a lusty manner. Although physically attracted, Blanche resisted him because it was a time in her love life when queueing for her favours had become imperative. Hugh was an exciting prospect but would be none the worse for a spell in the deep freeze and, anyhow, he was infatuated with a woman he called his 'priestess.' Until he got over her Blanche treated him as an entertainer, revelling in his self-proclaimed elitism. He told her he wanted millions spent on opera, theatres and orchestras but nothing on football, schools or hospitals; his sermons, public and private, embraced all subjects. He was, he declared, ecumenically expansive and expensive. Blanche made his stall a feature of the fair, which was in need of a publicity boost.

Most of the tracts on his stall were written by Mattingson, who had given them such titles as: *Prayer is Mirth, The Belly-Laugh Catechism, Fun with Post-Coital Hymnology* and *The Stand-up Comic's Book of Revelation*.

The person in charge of running the carnival objected that the booklets, as he dismissively referred to them, did not qualify for inclusion at the fair because they were neither secondhand nor antiquarian.

'Don't be stuffy, Henry,' barked Blanche. 'They're remainders, aren't they, Mr Mattingson? It is time the carnival extended into remainders, especially as we now have the use of Half Acre Meadow.'

Hugh protested they were not remainders. They were first English editions of books which had done well in America. He had over seventy-five titles but would display only one of each, and soil them individually, so that they appeared second-hand.

'Seventy-five doesn't make much of a stall,' complained Henry, who sensed his days were numbered.

Hugh, as a gesture of conciliation, said that he would make space for his selection of bibles, missals and commentaries on the gospels. He solemnly crossed himself. 'My mother's maiden name was Bray,' he told them.

The ruse worked. Hugh constantly had to replace volumes he sold with others carefully thumb-marked or cornered. Business was so brisk he found it difficult to keep pace with demand, so he hit upon the device of showing mint copies impressed with sticky labels, swiftly supplied by a local printer, suggesting they had been first sold by Foyle's, Hatchard's or Heffer's. Other dealers became suspicious so he found it expedient not to replace at once all of his own works, but to augment them with books by Malcolm Muggeridge and other 'divines'. That got him through the first carnival. In the following year he returned, still accompanied by his 'priestess', and hired a much larger space. He displayed a notice stating that due to popular demand he had scoured the country for copies of all his books, and found an abundance in theological bookshops lying unsold behind stacks of prominently displayed Lent books, ghosted for various bishops. All, he claimed, were genuine second-hand copies. No one believed him but little could be done against the combined forceful personalities of Blanche, Hugh and his 'priestess', who now had her own pulpit beside the stand. At the same time, such was the demand for Hugh's books in secular shops that they became minor bestsellers, appealing to a public which liked the notion of having its religion, but also getting a laugh out of it.

Mattingson became a cult author who amassed great wealth. He bought what little property local agents could offer. One of them, acting for the voluntarily exiled Duke of Bidborough, kept certain properties from Blanche's grasp. That was how Hugh acquired Ridge End, which he leased to his employer, to the fury of the 'priestess'.

Hugh became a familiar figure in the town, striding about in colourful garments of all periods. He favoured ponchos, saffron robes, gaudy pantaloons, eighteenth-century tailcoats in rich corduroy, doublet and hose, Oxford bags, plus-fours, brocaded smoking jackets, Russian peasant blouses, mandarin Chinese coats with voluminous sleeves, cowboy hats, cardinal's hats, top hats, deer stalkers, stetsons and every other kind of headgear. Some days he might appear in medieval armour, on others in a World War Two siren suit. He had togas, Greek tunics, dhotis, kaftans and, on one memorable occasion, he even 'wore' the Emperor's new clothes. His fingers, arms, ankles were adorned with rings of all sizes; his hair sometimes changed colour thrice in the course of a morning. He reckoned to have a costume for every day of the year and another for every evening. It became a favourite pastime for shoppers to linger in Town Square just for the sake of observing what Hugh was wearing as he performed his way, like an itinerant player, across Rustrock, stopping to talk to this citizen or that, as often as not giving them a blessing relevant to whatever faith he supposed them to favour.

In due course he rented a disused Elim Tabernacle (from Blanche) and opened a place of worship where he sold his own books, undercutting Ardbuckle's. When guide books to Wealdshire were reprinted he was featured in them. The inhabitants of Rustrock became inquisitive about his background. Was there a wife? Children? What was the status of the 'priestess'? The *Gazette* ran stories about him.

Hugh, the local paper reported, had been brought up in a Methodist family in a Midlands town. He had found his experience of religion so intensely cold and unfriendly that he had rebelled against what he saw as an oppressive non-conformism while retaining, he averred, his belief in Christianity

He had attended drama school and spent many years as an actor without becoming a star (though he was seldom out of work). He was given a small role in a long-running West End play. As a part it was not significant, nor did it attract notices, but the impresario who bought it for Broadway insisted he must have 'the guy who plays the butler.' American audiences were crazy for English butlers. It was an extension of the Jeeves syndrome. So he must have Hugh Mattingson. There were arguments with the American counterpart of Equity but they were resolved. Hugh made his debut on Broadway. The play ran for three nights.

Having crossed the Atlantic, the suddenly resting actor thought he should enlarge on the American experience by exploring the hinterland of New York. The terms of his engagement allowed for a return passage but he risked that, packed his bag and headed west not, as so many young actors before him had, for Hollywood, but for adventures, probably spiritual, perhaps mystical.

During the long London run Hugh had spent hours in his dressing room (he had ten lines soon after curtain up and another two just before the end of act three) analysing his Methodist childhood, which he recalled as cheerless. To pass the time he added spicy stories to the religious tracts he had endured, jotting them down and continuing them mentally as he answered his call for act three, performed his two lines, and took the final curtain. These later formed the basis of his religious writing. In the United States, a country committed by all but the actual constitution to extreme versions of Christianity, he found an immediate public for his books, not least from sects who spent nights on bare mountain tops joyously awaiting Armageddon,

He settled in Pennsylvania, following a few months on the road, had his first booklets published and began to draw crowds to open air meetings. It was then that he ordained himself. Nobody questioned his credentials and, under the influence of Ella, a nineteen-year-old student who left college to become his devoted amanuensis, he developed an unusual approach to spreading the gospels.

'You're so funny, Hughie,' she told him, 'you'll bring about a religious revival. You'll have Billy Graham demanding your deportation. What you gotta do is make yourself a national figure before he gets his big guns loaded against you.'

'How will he do that, dear child?'

'You don't have one million bucks?'

'I do not.'

'Don't worry. I'll think of something.'

It didn't take Ella long. She studied the programmes broadcast by all the leading stations. She discovered a slot which had fallen vacant through someone dying of drugs, or not getting backing, 'or sump'n'. She engineered Hugh into it. Ella was one of that monstrous regiment of American women who, without taking a single shot, are on a permanent high. They set out with innate resolution to fatigue anyone standing in their way into total submission. Either that or they get themselves strangled. Ella, in a high-powered nasal drawl, whined and nagged till she got her way. (She would probably become the first woman president.) Hugh hit the big time.

Audiences loved Hugh's deadpan humour, delivered in his English butler accent. "'Laughter", he told them, quoting the playwright Christopher
Fry, "is the surest touch of genius in creation." It was an English author
who wrote that. My message to the world is based upon it.' And he proceeded to find humour in every book of the Bible, even in such unlikely
theological works as *Christ, the Life of the Soul*, and the *Confessions of St.
Augustine*. He developed a theory that laughter is actually mystical thera-
py. 'Go to your Maker,' he ended one programme, 'with a dying chuckle.
Eternity will be hilarious.' They believed him because they liked the sound
of it. No hell fire, no angels moaning everlasting motets as they moved
from one silver-lined cloud to another. No souls in perpetual torment.
They could hardly wait to be despatched.

It was while he was in the States that Hugh began to indulge his sartorial whims. He loved dressing-up. It was why he'd become an actor and it
also fitted the religious life. Church leaders, he mused, tended to be far
more showy than actors, who dressed so quietly they might as well be
insurance clerks. Costume meant much to him. He would love to have
been Lord Chancellor, or a cardinal, or even a town crier. Only in costume
would he be fulfilled. So he was agreeably surprised that being a pam-
phleteer and broadcaster offered the same opportunity.

But the Billy Graham factor was too much for him. The old hand evan-
gelists who had led the born-again market for decades didn't tolerate
Hugh. They soon had him off the airwaves on the grounds of blasphemy
and obscenity. Ella reacted without wasting time. 'We had fun, Hughie.
We made a lotta money. Time to pack it in and go home. I'm making for
Capitol Hill, bud. I guess that's where my destiny lies.'

Hugh wasn't too upset. He had begun to find Ella wearing. She would
talk when he wished to. In fact, she rarely stopped. So he recrossed the
Atlantic, first class, and settled into a small Somerset town where he
amended his books for the English market, then braced himself for further public appearances.

· 8 ·

John Ogglethorpe (Fiction & General), a man concerned that life was passing too quickly and uneventfully, opened the front door of Ardbuckle's, remarking to his newest assistant, a limp creature of indeterminate gender, whose name eluded him (and its appearance gave him little clue), 'I understand she's gone.' He was greeted by the posturing figure of Hugh Mattingson, clad in the saffron robes of a Buddhist monk, chanting:

'La reine est morte. Vive la reine.'

'And Om mani padme hum to you, Hugh. Was there a last minute conversion?'

'My dear fellow, I sleep in these blessed garments on hot nights, and I was called suddenly from my slumber.'

'At least they are more becoming than pyjamas.'

Hugh ignored him. 'Call the staff together. I will inform them personally.'

'I doubt if there's more than half-a-dozen in yet. I can hear Maurice hawking away below stairs. And that sounds like the twitter of Maimie Perkes.'

Gordon Ruffle flung open the door and shouted, 'Is it true?'

Hugh looked pained. 'You have been awarded a Companionship of the late lamented British Empire for Total Vulgarity in the face of Death.'

'I accept. Where's the body?'

Hugh, remembering he was presently representing a meditative order, drew a small elephant bell from beneath his robes and gazing placidly, even forgivingly, at the junior reporter, tolled it melodically.

The staff drifted in and received the tidings stoically. Their jobs had always been at risk. Were they now more, or less, so? Was today to be proclaimed a holiday, a total shut-down or Business as Usual?

'It would have been the wish of our late lamented proprietor, and of the founding fathers before her,' declared Hugh to a slowly gathering group of booksellers, 'for the customers not to be incommoded.'

'Especially,' commented Fergus Welch (Science & Technology), deafeningly sotto voce, 'if they happened to find themselves on the aforesaid commode at that specific moment in time.' He twinkled his deep blue eyes at Maimie Perkes (Art), not because he fancied her but from habit, because she was a woman.

Hugh looked placid again and tinkled his bell. 'We shall, therefore, remain open but anyone who wishes to express their grief may like to join me immediately, in the turret of Religion and Philosophy, for a brief service.'

'Forgive the interruption,' said Jim Woodstock (Philosophy & Religion), 'but I've got a black mass going on up there at the moment. I always let the witches touch down on Thursday mornings on their way to the University Occult Seminar. They find it a good primer.'

'Then, I will conduct my meeting here,' said Hugh, 'but please protect us from any low flying broomsticks…'

'Dear colleagues and former servants of the departed Blanche…'

'For fuck's sake,' cried Fergus and strode away to his department.

'… I have to tell you that the business will continue and will be administered, for the time being, by Mr Mark Ampersand of Trotter, Lamb and Ampersand, solicitors.'

Gordon Ruffle, who should not still have been present, registered that information.

'…he is calling a meeting of the beneficiaries of the will, the contents of which will be published in due course.

'For the moment, let us experience a moment of silence in memory of our dear Blanche Ardbuckle.'

The silence had barely commenced when Nell Pickett (Cleaner) was heard, below stairs, screeching, 'Maurice, you 'aven't put out the bleedin' wheelie bin.'

· 9 ·

The death of Blanche Ardbuckle was news at national level because during the six decades or so that she had dominated the family business in
Rustrock Spa she had become known for her annual book fair, or carnival, as she preferred to call it. This increasingly lively event attracted not
only Hugh Mattingson and other dealers but the general public as well, to
a bonanza of bargains displayed in temporary, waterproof booths erected
over a ten-acre site to the west of the Common. There was, also, a rau-
cous, small, traditional fair, complete with steam organ which clanged
away merrily for twelve hours a day.

Later, the carnival came to include unique author signings at which
writers autographed second-hand copies of their own books. On occasion
they found themselves inscribing first editions which already bore their
signature. Blanche laughed this off. 'It makes them twice as valuable,' she
declared. (In the long watches of the night some authors asked themselves, 'Twice as valuable to whom?')

Many articles were written about Blanche and her annual carnival. Most
included references to her ever-expanding bookshop, once described as 'a
bewildering maze of rooms on five, six, or is it seven, floors, descending
to who knows how many dungeon–like basements, and soaring (no lift!
no escalator!) to turrets and domes? It has grown with the speed of con-
volvulus, threatening to oust the town hall, municipal gallery and
St.Cuthbert's church from Town Square. Only the university seems invulnerable beside it but it is rumoured that Ardbuckle's even owns the freehold of the land over which that spreads.' (*The Breast-Packers Guide*)

Blanche promoted herself and her business in individual style. She did
not establish book clubs or literary luncheons, à la Christina Foyle, her
more famous London counterpart. Instead, she sponsored quarterly
banquets at the University where distinguished principal guests made

speeches live on radio and BBC-2. The banquets provided good copy for the media. One author denounced his hostess as 'a squalid and illiterate shopkeeper who had grown rich from the work of creative artists forced into the gutter'; another guest vilified a bishop, who was talking about his memoirs, as a hypocrite, threatening to drive him from the high table, 'just like your Mr J effing C threw the traders out of the temple'; sometimes fruit and bread rolls were hurled at speakers, at others good claret splashed their fashionable attire. There were many who believed that Blanche's publicity manager, incited by Hugh Mattingson, who later incorporated that role into his own portfolio, fixed it all.

When they reported her death the media speculated on who would inherit Blanche's wealth, a subject soon to engage their collective attention to the exclusion, for a day or two, of the undercover activities of minor members of the royal family.

· 10 ·

When the letter arrived from Mark Ampersand, Monty Devereux's fortunes were at one of those cyclical lows to which life as a backbench Tory MP had accustomed him. In fact, so low that he didn't currently have a seat.

Publicly he blamed his defeat at the '87 election on boundary changes, but, on the surface, where he was wont to operate, he knew that his pro-Europe tendency had not endeared him to the hierarchy of his local party. It had not re-adopted him. In fifteen years in the House no office had come his way. He had not been invited to appear on a television chat show or a radio discussion, no newspaper had sought his views – apart from freebies distributed in his suburban constituency – and he had not become an expert on anything. All that attracted attention was his shrill

laugh over which he exercised no control. It burst from him instanta-
neously when anyone paid him the slightest attention and, the higher his
degree of non-attainment, the more frequently was it heard. Far from
sparkling, his political career had barely even flickered.

Monty was lobby fodder, occasionally permitted to ask a question, usually formulated by the Whips' Office. He wasn't even a qualified lawyer,
making him almost unique in his calling. Moreover, his business was
verging on insolvency.

The solicitor's letter reminded him of his happiest time in the book
trade when, although miserably underpaid, he had received unlooked for
rewards from the boss woman of Ardbuckle's.

Blanche gave him a job, in 1960, after he had failed to get a degree and
his parents, who were confectioners, had turned sour, saying he must now
fend for himself. At university he had skipped tutorials, neither bought
nor read the set books, and spent too much time carousing and woman-
ising. He swore to make amends. He would learn bookselling, get backing
to start a chain, then care for his parents when they reached old age.

He became Blanche's mistress, or that is how he recalled it. In practice,
during the short period when he shared her bed, she continued to pay
him a derisory wage and neglected to give him a latch key to her flat in
the penthouse over the shop. He was ordered to leave before daylight,
drop the catch and not let on to his colleagues, all of whom, apart from
Gerda Kohl, had already guessed. They also forecast imminent dismissal.
That invariably happened and they counted themselves lucky not to have
been chosen. They were wrong. It was Monty who gave notice when, having been offered a publicity job, by a publisher, he told Blanche and asked
for a rise. She refused. She already had her eyes on another young man.

After a few months at the publisher's, one day Monty spotted potential in the trash pile of unwanted and unreturned typescripts accumulating on the editorial director's floor. He began to read an unloved brain-
child while waiting to see the director, who 'was in a meeting'. Most peo-

ple in publishing, he had soon learned, spent ninety per cent of their time in meetings. Monty observed that he didn't.

He took the typescript to his tiny office, publicity having been allocated the ex-Hoover cupboard beneath an elegant first floor staircase. He read with growing interest, excited that the firm might reward him for discovering a bestseller. He was interrupted by a command to present himself to the managing director's secretary. She told him that the board had decided he must go. He was about to tell her about his 'find', but thought better of it, accepted dismissal and absconded with the unwanted typescript in his brief case. He contacted the author, a scrap metal merchant with literary aspirations, EC connections and an exotically fraudulent past. Maurice happily provided the capital for the company Monty formed to promote the book and this marked the start of his career in vanity publishing. His instinct proved correct. The book reprinted many times but Maurice hankered for real riches, so his subsequent works were sold at auction for huge sums with which Monty could not compete. Thereafter he took tens of thousands of pounds from eager novelists and poets who seldom received their share of the profits because there were none. Then, in 1972, having won a by-election, he kept his company afloat in case he should lose the seat. Anyway, being merely a Member of Parliament was not, in his view, a full time occupation.

Since leaving Ardbuckle's Monty had had little contact with Blanche but they had resumed friendly relations. He had asked a question or two for her in the House and, generously, for old time's sake, not charged her the full going rate. In return she had invited him to some of her summer and Twelfth Night gatherings as one of her privileged non-paying guests.

Now here he was, about to become a millionaire, from what he could read between the lines of Ampersand's letter. There were conditions, unstated, but, as a politician, he was used to there being strings attached. Deirdre, his current partner, enquired with some belligerence about this Blanche. Monty calmed her, saying she was about 109 years old and so far into his past as to be prehistoric. He also indicated that the bequest would ease their financial tensions. Deirdre relaxed. (Monty was unaware of her current credit card balances.) 'I just hope it won't be a liability,' he said, 'the last time I saw the shop it looked pretty tatty, but the solicitor chap does say "a substantial bequest." He must know.'

'Doesn't he say how much?'

'Nope. Only that there are four other major legatees and we all have to meet at his office and hear the conditions.'

'Maybe I will marry you, after all.' Deirdre kissed him. He was rather a darling and they did have fun. Well, sometimes.

Monty was short for Montelimar, where his parents had met at a nougat summer school. It was a name he had surppressed; it didn't suit his image. He was of medium height, plump without any suggestion of obesity, neither too tall nor too short, and with a slight downy blonde moustache. He dressed correctly, in the strict sartorial sense, but also incorrectly, regularly wearing club and regimental ties to which he was not entitled. In fact, Monty was as decent as a Tory MP is likely to be and was only a Conservative because he had worked out that their party was in power over longer periods than was Labour. He found most of the chaps he met in the House agreeable, apart from the extremists on both sides but even some of them were good for a laugh, which, regrettably, he was only too ready to provide.

· 11 ·

'The old sweetie!' was Dickie Klute's reaction to Ampersand's letter. 'Butch!' She bellowed at her husband who was battling with a coffee grinder. 'I'm going to be a millionairess.'

'Have you won the Booker?' He enquired.

'Wrong time of year', she snapped, going into verbal overdrive, 'you should know that. There's been enough nail-biting when I was on the short list. But you never take notice of what's happening to me. You and your cricket, and your share prices. And your interminable lists of all the things you've forgotten to do...'

'We've run out of beans.'

'There're plenty ground in the cupboard, don't tell me it's not the same... AND', taking up her theme again, 'your epics and sagas that never won anyone any prizes...'

It was common knowledge, in literary circles, that the only reason why Dickie continued to live with the man she called Butch, who had been her official husband for twenty-four disputatious years, was that he was her copy, the central character of all fourteen novels she had written. He was Butch, the faker of masterpieces in oils, Butch, the drunken Celtic poet, Butch, actor-manager, Butch, secret agent. Also, Butch, a light-hearted philanderer who endured endearing mishaps with alluring upper-middle class ladies – the readers liked a bit of variety so long as he was still identifiable as the incomparable Butch. He was Butch, maddeningly unpunctual, victim of his own incompetence, Butch who was scholarly yet stupid, Butch who was invariably wrong-footed by other characters, but Butch who, for all his faults, was basically decent and loyal. The readers adored Butch. What he would get up to next they were agog to know. Increasingly, there were moments when Dickie herself wondered, because, as inspiration, he was flagging.

In the daily grind Butch, whose true name was Donald, drove Dickie to such distraction that she escaped for long periods to the Dodecanese where she wrote her books and had an easy-going liaison with a Greek who kept a wife and family on a neighbouring island. She had tried to breathe fictional life into Kristos but it hadn't worked. And it wasn't working any more with Butch. She had pushed their relationship to the limit. She could scarcely bear to be in the same room as him.

Butch worked for the B.B.C., had done for decades, adapting formidably long narrative poems for dramatisation, serialisation and, often, mystification of the listening public. Much of his time was spent at Lord's cricket ground, or in taverns in Fitzrovia, where he always hoped to encounter old buddies from the wartime Ministry of Information days. In a detached way he was fond of Dickie. He had even enjoyed sleeping with her when they were first married but he was a straightforward sort of chap and didn't always go along with what she wanted to get up to. He'd never been a gymnast. So, he tended to say about her, 'She's all brain, you know, amazingly clever, can't think what she sees in me.' A candid friend had once replied, 'You're her cake, you're her bread-and-butter, you're the cream in her coffee... the tops... the Mona Lisa'... he couldn't remember how it went on...' But you're definitely not her Prince Charming.'

Butch smiled vaguely, wiped egg yolk from his lapels and sought to engage his cruel friend in discussion of early epic verse, an aspect of national culture which he thought – perhaps correctly – might strike a note of truth among African listeners in the more undeveloped regions.

On the day the Inheritance Letter arrived Dickie had just returned from her Greek island and was planning to depart, almost at once, for the cottage, near Piddletrenthide, Dorset, to battle with the final chapter of her novel. Should she be forgiving, and invite Butch for the weekend? No, he'd hate it, so would she. And soon, thanks to Blanche Ardbuckle, perhaps, they would be able to part amicably. Or thanks to Booker. After all, Iris had won it, and Ruth, and Bernice, and Penelope, and even the *other*

Penelope, for God's sake! So, it must be her turn soon, or was she in the same boat as poor Beryl?

Dickie, who was christened Hilda May, had worked at Ardbuckle's for a rather longer span than was usual for a junior assistant, arriving shortly after Monty had departed. She was a graduate searching for someone to support her while she achieved fame as a writer. She adopted a policy of total friendliness, flirting openly with colleagues and customers of both sexes, maintaining a witty stream of comment to all, and lending an ear to everyone's private troubles, mainly because she wished to memorise their speech rhythms. In doing so she found herself genuinely interested in the problems related and thus became the in-house agony aunt, particularly for Gerda Kohl, whose personal attractions were minimal to most of those who encountered her.

Blanche shrewdly judged Dickie's potentials and, in 1963, appointed her Personnel Officer, a designation then almost unheard of within retail bookselling. This did not relieve Dickie of her other duties on the shop floor, nor did Blanche raise her wages. It just meant that whenever the proprietress wanted to part company with an employee, without facing them, she relied on Dickie to be the intermediary who did the sacking. Dickie understood and used each instance to deepen her research for the basic character she needed to be the touchstone of her success as a novelist. One day Donald Klute mooched into the department where she was at work.

Dickie stayed at Rustrock for a few more weeks while Donald/Butch researched papers, deposited at the university, allegedly throwing new light on Piers Plowman. Then, when he returned to London, she followed. In the intervening decades she had not lost contact with Blanche. She, like Monty, was present at many Ardbuckle events. Dickie, with her elegant, twelve-inch long cigarette holder, her extended eye lashes and a monocle in both eyes, was very much part of the occasion, especially when she chose to arrive in a vintage banger. Photographers worshiped her.

· 12 ·

Dean Phillips jogged determinedly, resolutely, but with little actual enjoyment, along footpaths between allotments, then down lanes with high hedgerows where he was a nuisance to himself, and to passing cars, and finally into the drive of the shabby semi-detached house in the nondescript southern village where he lived with Phyllis, once his wife, now his partner. They had had their marriage officially annulled, although they were still as deeply in love as they had been forty years previously. They believed it more honest to be unmarried.

As Dean raced, more than jogged, towards the kitchen door and the bacon, sausage and eggs awaiting him, a twinge of conscience pricked him. He should have been breakfasting on muesli and crunchy nuts, washed down by pure orange juice, but somehow, to get him through his working day, he needed a traditional square meal before mounting his bike to ride the three miles to his business. He was a powerfully built man, six-one, broad shouldered, large featured. At sixty-five, he was still handsome, with a mop of pure black, wiry hair, craggy jaw, classical nose – 'I'm descended from the Greeks,' he told new acquaintances, eyeing them deadpan, 'in a direct line from Theseus.' He had always been fit despite a penchant for fried breakfast.

He fondled Phyllis's buttocks as he passed her – she was attending to the pan on the hob – spied post on the kitchen table, and opened an envelope of cream laid stationery with an embossed heading – Trotter, Lamb and Ampersand, Solicitors.

'Trotter, Lamb,' he exclaimed. 'I don't believe it. Straight out of happy families.' He read what lay below the heading. 'I don't believe this, either.'

Dean, who was of Quaker stock, had spent much of his life attempting to reconcile left wing convictions with commercial practice, something which more famous followers of William Penn had not found an insurmountable barrier to acquiring wealth. He had a clear, mathematical brain, admired organisation and efficiency, and understood the essential requirement that business must be profitable. He wished, though, that things were ordered differently. When he entered the book trade, in 1952, at Ardbuckle's, having found teaching literature to large classes of boys, unrewarding, he was soon confronted by evidence that there were many books essential to the economic well-being of the trade, which offended him. He also told himself, uneasily, that he was not a censor.

Another significant, testing moment of Dean's life, after his forced return to teaching, came when he inherited two thousand pounds. He ought, he knew, to make this over to famine relief, persecuted minorities, or the elderly. Instead, he bailed out an ailing bookshop, in the market town of Loamfield, whose owner was thus able to pay his rent and settle overdue accounts with publishers. Dean wished he could exchange jobs with the tired old shopkeeper but, instead, remained at his teaching post attempting to instil a love of Shakespeare and Milton into boys whose compulsive reading was limited to motor car manuals. Then the bookseller obligingly died, in advance of his grievously sick shop. Dean, encouraged by Phyllis to act on impulse, bought the business from the old man's grateful daughter.

Dean and Phyllis supplied the prestigious Loamfield School but also vowed to become community booksellers. They refurbished an outhouse, attached to the shop, as a gallery where artists, charged only a nominal commission on sales, could exhibit their work. Dean acted with the town dramatic society and provided free box office facilities in the shop. The couple established a string quartet in which Phyllis played viola. At the bookshop various societies held meetings on payment of a paltry sum. Dean served on the town council as an Independent. All the councillors were Independents but most were Tory. The bookseller, so as not to appear unnecessarily contentious, announced that he was a pragmatist, thus paving the way for radical achievements which gained him the respect of many fellow citizens.

As he was served breakfast, Dean told Phyllis, 'The old battle axe has left me part of her business.'

'Blanche?'

'Who else?'

'It was on the news that she'd died. Didn't I mention it?'

'I saw it in the paper. There has to be a catch.'

Phyllis looked alarmed. 'It's not the whole caboodle, is it?' She thought with horror – suppose we had to move to Rustrock Spa? All their friends, their social life. It couldn't be.

'Apparently I'm one of five. There is to be a meeting at the solicitors, where we will learn the conditions.'

'Perhaps they won't be acceptable?'

Dean laughed, patted her knee. 'We'll come through.'

'Well, it may be a bigger shop than ours – it's the largest I know anywhere, except for dreadful old Foyle's... but ours is nicer. Perhaps you'll be allowed to sell your share. When's the meeting?'

'Several dates suggested. Early next month.'

'*Next* month! Today's the thirtieth.'

As he cycled into Loamfield, Dean thought, swerving to avoid an oncoming, overtaking Mini, this might solve the pension problem. He hadn't seen Blanche since they met at a booksellers' conference a few years previously. They had indulged in chitchat, within a small group, each knowing that no one else present was aware they had slept together.

· 13 ·

It was the early 1950s. The nation was beginning to recover from the effects of war, shedding its shabbiness, all but rejecting rationing and moving towards the benefits of a consumer society. Dean was glad to leave London, and the secondary modern where he was teaching, but dared not return to the southern country town where he had been reared. He feared being dragged back into the Quaker net. They were lovely people – most of them – but he no longer shared their beliefs. He needed to find his own way, uninfluenced. In *The Times Literary Supplement* there was an ad, from a bookshop in Rustrock Spa. 'Experience not essential', it read.

As he approached, passing the bubbling fountain on Town Square, he was impressed by the scale of Ardbuckle's. There were law courts and civic offices on one side, the theatre on another, a Victorian Gothic church on a third, the Duke's Head on a fourth, while, on the fifth – for it was not a conventionally shaped square – was Ardbuckle's, with its pastiche embellishments from many periods, looking as imposing as a royal residence. It floated between grandiosity and grandiloquence, to Dean an abomination of a building but one, like Leeds Town Hall, which could not be ignored. Yet there was only one entrance, up a short, gentle ramp to what was surely, outside central London, the largest bookshop in Britain? Not for Ardbuckle's the wide, plate-glassed double doorway suited to a major store but a solid, single piece of oak painted, in tiny letters and numbers, with the details of the opening hours. Entering it called for the intrepid spirit of a Livingstone or a Freya Stark. Having reached the top of the ramp it was necessary to exert the force of a rugby forward to open the formidable door.

On either side of the entrance were heavily mullioned windows displaying, apart from items of the emporium's stock in trade, many carcases of long defunct insects. The fly and the wasp predominated, lying overexposed to sunrays, on volumes, Dean noted, about the subject of a promotion of the moment, Oriental Cuisine. Possibly the incinerated creatures were included in the recipes?

Ardbuckle's faced south, so most books on show had suffered severe heat stroke. Wrappers had faded, bindings had warped. Distributed amongst them, apart from solar-fried insects, were particles of cheap necklaces and cuff links belonging to members of staff who had been instructed to reclaim from the window books required by customers. Dean was warned later that only assistants with experience of jungle warfare were capable of recovering volumes intact and, that amongst those who had been successful, there was high mortality from incurable tropical diseases.

Once inside, Dean was confronted by a choice of several passages, all dimly lit, leading from the grand entrance hall. Prim, handwritten signs pointed, one way to TEXTBOOKS, another to NEW TITLES, a third to ADMIN OFFICES. The prevailing colour, on floor, wall and ceiling, was bottle green.

Up on a mezzanine floor, reached by a semi-circular stone stairway, Dean met a man in a shabby suit who was carrying two large tomes. He asked him for guidance. 'I've come for an an interview with Miss Blanche Ardbuckle.'

'The dragon herself! Up that flight of steps to the big, mahogany door. Mind the treads at the return. Left at the top, then second door on the right. Christ, this is heavy!'

Dean thanked him and asked if he could take one volume to lighten his load.

'Thanks no, this is my leaving present.'

'Except,' said Norwood Butling (Security), a sharp featured youth who worked part time when not on official police duties, materialising, apparently from the actual woodwork, 'that you're leaving without it. No prosecution? Right? On your way!'

'Sure you don't want me to put it in the boot of your car, Mr Butling? Always supposing there's room.' The man in the shabby suit scuttled off.

'It can be a mistake,' said Butling, 'this policy of never prosecuting staff.'

Dean continued to climb, noting that the steps had carpet and there was now dark red paper on the walls. He entered a waiting room where several people sat, with the air of those waiting hopelessly for travel visas. He took a spare chair.

An inner door opened and a tall, ungainly woman, dressed in a patterned, dark grey, tweed two-piece, emerged and glared at him. She had high cheekbones and lips which swirled over her chin.

'You've just come,' she said, accusingly.

Dean affirmed this was so, and gave his name.

'Phillips. Yes, she wants to see you. Go in.'

The others waiting looked aggrieved. Wasn't this favouritism?

The woman in tweeds ushered Dean into a room heavily furnished with solid Victorian tables, bookcases, cabinets and, on the floor, an intricately patterned carpet in varying shades of dark red and dark green. Behind an enormous desk sat Blanche Ardbuckle, upright and unsmiling, watching him intently as he approached. He wondered if he should sit down in the unoccupied red plush chair. As no one spoke, he smiled and said, 'Good morning, Madam,' and was about to be seated when Tweedy snapped, 'Wait till you're invited.'

Blanche said, 'You may go, Framley.' She continued to stare at Dean, reminding him of a massive cat in its prime. Gradually her look became more benign.

'You wrote an interesting letter, Mr Phillips.'

'Thank you.'

'You said…' She motioned him to sit… 'you think that bookshops need modernising, and that you would welcome an opportunity of expressing your ideas on the subject. I wonder why you wrote that to me? We are known to be traditional here, some would say old-fashioned, but we do know what we are doing. And also what we want our assistants to do. Which is… to sell books. It is a salesman I require. Not a designer.'

'I thought perhaps the roles might be combined, Ma'am.'

'What is your experience, Mr Phillips?'

Dean blushed. 'As a bookseller, none.' He laughed. 'Nor as a designer. But I have been using bookshops all my life.'

'Are you one of those who read the stock in bookshops, but never buy?'

'Not as a regular practice, though I have been guilty of it. But I've been buying books since I was six. For Christmas and birthdays, I have always asked for Book Tokens. I have a large library.'

Blanche said, severely, that staff were not expected to read the stock except in their own time. The fact that so many chose to ignore this rule had made her chary of employing bookworms. 'If they're always reading, they don't have time to tidy shelves and look after customers. So why do you wish to be a bookseller?'

'Because I don't like being a teacher.'

That appealed to Blanche. 'Which department would you like to work in?'

'History or Philosophy for preference… Politics, perhaps…'

Blanche thought that a dangerous reply. People interested in politics spelt trouble. Yet there was an openness about this black-haired young man which she liked. She was also attracted by his clear blue eyes and strong jaw. He resembled the favourite film stars of her youth.

'I can pay you five pounds a week,' she said.

'Not more?'

She shrugged her shoulders 'Five ten.'

'I accept.'

'Start on Monday. Report to Miss Framley. Don't be late.'

'Thank you, Miss Ardbuckle.'

'As you go, tell Framley to clear the waiting room. I shan't see any more today.'

· 14 ·

When, the following week, Dean reported promptly at 8.30 a.m. to Miss Framley that person took him firmly by the right wrist and said, 'We're going down here.' They descended stone steps to a deep dungeon, designated Goods In Department. It reminded Dean of a visit he had once made to the chateau of Loches, in the Loire, where political opponents of the powerful might be held in the bowels of the earth, often for decades.

Approaching a dimly lit area Framley bawled, 'Watkins, this is Phillips. He'll help you this morning.' She turned to Dean and snapped, 'Insurance card, P45. Bet you haven't brought them.' He handed them over, wondering why she should hate him so much. As she snatched the documents the venom in her look intensified. He knew she was out to get him. He smiled. Her eyes bulged. She was surely about to have a seizure but the man Watkins came towards them out of the gloom, nodded at Dean, and said to Framley, 'I'll need more than our two pair of 'ands to get through this lot. I suppose, dear Miss Framley, you don't 'appen to 'ave taken on any Indian goddesses this week, 'ave you?'

Framley glared at him with incomprehension. She was rarely happy about young Watkins, already at twenty-seven the longest serving employee. She suspected dumb insolence lay behind his remarks. Who were these Indian goddesses?

Dean enquired where he should hang his raincoat. They stared at him pityingly. 'I suppose,' remarked Watkins, 'you'll be asking next, which counter 'ave you been allocated to sleep under at night? Well, we've given that up at Ardbuckle's, 'aven't we, Miss Framley? Security don't like it.'

'You shut up, Watkins.' Framley walked away.

'Excuse me,' Dean shouted after her, 'I was engaged to work in History… selling books. History, or Philosophy.'

'You'll find plenty down 'ere to be philosophical about,' Watkins told him. Dean spent the remainder of the day unpacking parcels, learning to allocate their contents to this department or that, and clearing up wrapping paper and cardboard cartons, all the while listening to a running commentary from Watkins about the iniquities of Ardbuckle's and the lady who owned it. Dean asked why he stayed.

'She's got me by the short'orns, 'asn't she?'

'How has she?'

'When I come 'ere, just after the war, I'd been invalided out of the army. Mind you, I'd 'ardly got into it before I was across that bleedin' Channel and getting shot up in Normandy. I got married a month before D-Day. 'Ad to get special leave.' He gave his prodigious wink, known to generations of staff at Ardbuckle's. 'Didn't do not to be married then. And while I was copping it at flippin' Cong, my little lady was bein' doodlebugged in Bermondsey. She never wanted to go back. The memories was bad. Lots of friends killed. Bloody marvellous she wasn't. Miss Blanche, as we 'ad to call 'er, was finding things difficult, getting staff, wartime restrictions, all that caper. So she's pleased to find me looking for a job and exempt from the regulations.' He screwed up his eyes, patted his chest and nodded profoundly. 'So what does she do, the bleedin' bitch? Offers me a tied cottage to go with the job and, bloody fool that I was, I says, "Oh, thanks, Miss Blanche," and accepts. And she says, "I can't pay you more than two ten a week, Watkins, because it wouldn't be fair on the boys who are still doing the fighting…" And me 'avin' just been invalided out! Mind you I was lucky not to be sent back. I never 'ad no after effects, felt bloody marvellous but I didn't let on. I often wonder if my papers didn't get mixed up and some other poor sod, with only 'arf a 'ead, got sent out again instead of me. Any'ow, we 'ad to 'ave somewhere to live, and there was no rent to pay. So 'ere I am, and 'ere I stay for another year or two. But, he gave another wink… 'I've got something put away. 'Aven't missed opportunities, you might say.'

Dean asked if most staff were employed on this basis. 'Naow, the others 'ave got too much sense, or someone warned them.'

'But, of course,' he added with intentional irony, 'they don't 'ave the security I 'ave. They comes and goes but I'm the silly sod 'oo goes on doing all the 'ard labour down in this bleedin' pit.'

Watkins returned to his bench and worked concentratedly for an hour or more, before letting off further steam.

'When you go upstairs, as I do from time to time for a breather, or on some official query like, there's never the same people there for two weeks running. She keeps sacking 'em. Takes a 'ole lot on this week, sacks 'alf of them the next. Says they're all cheating 'er. They'd be bleedin' mad if they wasn't. You'll see, mate. What's your name?'

'Dean Phillips.'

'Dean? Don't think we've 'ad one of them before. You'll see, Deanie.'

'You'll 'ave to survive, same as the rest of us. Once you've learnt 'ow, it's not such a bad racket. Now get these fucking parcels unpacked, wot you think you're bleedin' doin', standin' 'ere chatterin'…'

At closing time, Dean, tired beyond anything he had previously endured, picked his raincoat from the floor and plodded to his digs, wondering how long it would be before he sold a book. Next morning, at the bench, unpacking only his third parcel, he was hailed by Miss Framley bellowing, 'Phillips!' He had already learned from Watkins of an incident on the shop floor. One of the departmental managers had been reprehended for misconduct. 'So 'e's gawn. No prosecution. She's very fair like that. But straight out on yer ear, and no reference.'

'She wants to see you,' said Framley. 'In her office. Urgent.'

'Shall I just finish this parcel?'

'URGENT! I don't think you're going to last, young man.'

''Oo does?' reflected Watkins. 'Only me.'

· 15 ·

'Now Phillips,' said Blanche, 'You said you were interested in history. Well, we have an unexpected vacancy. In fact we have several. You'll be in charge for the time being. I want you to go there right away.'

Dean found he comprised the entire staff in the department. The former manager's three assistants had been unmasked as conspirators at the same time as his misdemeanours were discovered, so all had been dismissed immediately. Blanche did not tell him this; he learned it from the manager of the Foreign Department, Gerda Kohl, a wan little lady, wearing a drab, fawn overall. She had been silent witness to the whole short episode when Blanche, followed by Framley and Norbert Butling, had marched in, made accusations, delivered judgement, then marched out, with Butling escorting the villains from the premises, and throwing a few volumes into the boot of his car.

'I should not say so to you,' – Gerda looked even more haunted than usual – 'but it reminded me of the Gestapo. You must not say I said this. I am a great admirer of Miss Ardbuckle.' She became suddenly aggressive. 'And what do you know about history books? I suppose I must help you.'

'Well… I am a history graduate. If I had been sent to manage Sport I would have been in trouble. But I know nothing of bookselling.'

'Ach,' said Gerda, 'it is commonsense. If you need help, Mr…?'

'Phillips. Dean.' He smiled at the sad little woman. She seemed to need it.

'I think we do not yet have first names, *Mr* Phillips.'

'As you wish… *Fraulein.*'

Then the phone rang, the intercom buzzed and three customers entered the department. Dean picked up the receiver of the outside line. Did they have Toynbee's *Study of History*? That should be easy. 'I'll just make sure.' As he passed the intercom it buzzed again, so he answered it.

'Is Harry there?'

'Harry's gone.'

'Well, Bob then?'

'Bob's gone.'

'What about Liz?'

'They've all gone.'

'Who are you?'

'I'm Dean. I've just come. Hold on. I'm dealing with a query.'

Dean searched for Toynbee. It was a large history department. He realised it could take hours since alphabetical order appeared not to have reached Ardbuckle's. He returned to the phone. Speaking with quiet authority he said he was sorry that he could not immediately locate a copy but he would ring back when he had. 'I thought it was out of print,' said the enquirer.

'We have ways of obtaining out of print books. May I take your name?'

Having bluffed his way out of that one, he returned to the intercom.

'That was pretty good,' said a voice at the other end. 'I wouldn't mind having you in this department. I'm Tim, in Literature. Buzz me if you need help.'

Framley then arrived, dragging into the department a timid, teenage girl. 'This is Pearl,' she said. 'She's come to help you. She's the post girl's assistant.'

'I don't know nothing about books,' said Pearl. 'Please, Miss Framley. I won't know what to do.'

'That will make two of us,' observed Dean. Framley threw him her venomous look. 'For a start. You could answer the phone.'

Pearl burst into tears. Framley thumped her.

'I'm afraid,' said Dean, 'I can't deal with your request just at the moment. Our entire staff has been rushed away… Yes, it's an emergency, and there is no one here who knows the stock. Will you give me the title, please, and your phone number.' The caller, mollified, complied. Dean, who had been brought up never to lie, began to feel corrupted.

Blanche had come in and overheard the incident. 'That was good, Phillips. Most tactfully dealt with.'

'Isn't there anyone,' he asked, 'in the entire shop, who has worked in this department?'

'No one. We thought of the people who have just walked out...' She neatly shifted the responsibility... 'as semi-permanent. One of them had been here for more than a year. They all knew their books very well. YOU must get to know the books, Phillips.' She turned and walked away.

Dean learned quickly, acquired a couple of assistants, with no more experience than his own, and began to feel on top of the job. But, was he the manager or not? At the end of his second week he felt sufficiently confident to find out. He asked for an interview with Blanche.

'You have to fill in a chit,' said Miss Framley who had become civil to him since he had not reported her for striking the girl Pearl. (He had not actually noticed.) Framley handed him a piece of orange-coloured duplicating paper headed:

REQUEST FOR INTERVIEW WITH MISS ARDBUCKLE
SUBJECT OF INTERVIEW
NAME /DEPARTMENT

Under SUBJECT, Dean wrote – Job Specification.

Blanche sent for him. 'What does this mean?'

'I just want to know where I stand, Miss Ardbuckle. I was engaged as an assistant in History, or Philosophy. I spent the first day unpacking books in a cellar, then I was suddenly placed in charge of History because the staff had walked out...'

'I sacked them. They were thieves.'

Dean looked piercingly at her with his honest blue, no nonsense, Quaker eyes. 'I only wish to know, now that I have two people newer here than myself, am I the manager or not?'

'You are the temporary manager.'

'And does that entitle me to a temporary higher wage?'

She smiled. This one was different. 'It could do.'

'May I ask how much, Miss Ardbuckle?'

'It will not be less than a pound a week. But only until your replacement is appointed.'

'May I apply to replace myself?'

'I'll consider it.'

'Thank you, Miss Ardbuckle. Would it be possible to talk to you about the department after we've closed, please?'

Such a request had never before been made to her. All her staff, past and present, made a point of keeping out of her way unless it was unavoidable. This one was noticeably different. He was growing on her. To her amazement she heard herself saying, yes, he could come back at five forty-five.

'Thank you. Or would you like a drink? It's been a warm day.'

Her state of amazement heightened. 'I don't keep drink here.'

'We could meet at the pub on the corner, the Duke's Head.'

Amazement turned to admiration. He wasn't frightened of her, he wasn't even in awe. 'Yes,' she said, 'that's a pleasant idea.'

· 16 ·

Standing at the saloon bar of the Duke's Head, Dean thought, here am I, at the end of the third week, in a new job, buying my employer a drink for the sake of suggesting ways in which she could improve the running of her business. People don't do this sort of thing. He ordered a G & T, and a half of bitter.

Blanche Ardbuckle, spinster of forty-two years, seated on a fixed, cushioned bench in an alcove, a glass-topped table before her, had never before been in this building. It was one of the few in this part of the town which she didn't own, because the brewers' had refused to sell their freehold. A Duke, around 1800, had given the property and land to the then landlord out of gratitude. The publican had saved his life when he was about to fall in front of a runaway carriage.

'Cheers!' said Dean, feeling awkward. Blanche did not respond. The bizarre nature of what was occurring had also struck her. She must extricate herself from this untenable situation.

'Your good health, Phillips,' she said, eventually. He clenched his teeth. He hated being addressed by his surname alone.

'It was cheeky of me to invite you for a drink…'

'It was unusual.'

There was an uneasy silence.

'Do you think,' asked Dean, 'it was a responsible act to push me into the History department on my own, without any help?'

'What else could I do? Anyhow, you have coped very well. The takings are good. It's a shame I may have to sack you…' she allowed herself a roguish smile… for insolence.'

They looked at each other and laughed.

'Miss Ardbuckle, will you allow me to change things in the department?'

'I shouldn't think so. What things?'

'I would like to introduce stock control.'

'What's that?'

He started to explain; she started to listen. Her attention wandered. 'It would be too expensive. I'm getting hungry. Let's go up to my flat for a bite.'

Blanche had an expansive penthouse, concealed from the street by enormous pediments, at the top of the rambling building. It luxuriated over the multi-level roof and was equipped with every labour-saving device that had been invented by 1952. Dean, at that time, had never lived in a house that had a fridge, let alone a freezer, wall-to-wall carpets, concealed lighting, central heating, a dish washer, a washing machine, and every other gadget taken for granted by later generations of all classes. Blanche lived alone because she valued her privacy. She would like to have employed a maid to dress her and keep her clothes in order, and a waiter to serve her meals, as well as a cook to prepare them, but they would have been an intrusion. Instead, she ate food prepared at a local restaurant. It was delivered in her absence to a maid, Jean Roper, who cleaned and tidied while Blanche was at work. She rarely met her, this person who washed-up, cleared-up, swept, dusted and performed all her household chores.

It was, therefore, simple for Blanche to provide a three-course, pre-cooked meal for herself and Dean. She always had sufficient for four people and discarded what was left uneaten. This latter information outraged Dean but he remained silent. After supper they sat on a voluminous, deeply cushioned settee taking coffee. She began to seduce him. He resisted, but not for long. The experience overwhelmed him. It was every bit as good as he had heard. He achieved manhood. And about time. He was almost twenty-six.

Blanche, content to have ended a prolonged period of abstinence, was ready to respond to Dean's post-orgiastic mood. For him, guilt had not yet set-in and he was thinking that if she would allow him to be her lover, she would surely permit him to modernise her disgraceful old muckheap of a shop. She listened, drowsily, to what he was saying, and made murmuring sounds of approval. He told her about beautiful bookshops he'd read about in Finland and Sweden and the United States. She agreed that Ardbuckle's should become finer than any of them.

Then she became totally awake, sat up, and said, 'You shall be the shop manager. Not just History.'

'I've only been in the trade for three weeks.'

'That will make your approach all the fresher. No pre-conceived notions.' Blanche said she had always worked on impulse. 'Don't come in tomorrow. I have to prepare the ground. Come here at eight in the evening. Then we'll sort it out.' She felt invigorated as well as satiated. This young man was the best thing that had happened to her for years.

They lay together again. Before it was light she bade him leave. He was so exhausted he felt relieved that he didn't have to be at work later. Blanche took a bath, during the course of which her elation drooped. Did she really want dear old Ardbuckle's transformed? No, she would make him go at it gently but at least it afforded a good opportunity of ridding herself of a manager who was buying too much and probably swindling her. He was fired at midday, and felt fortunate to be given four weeks' wages plus a certificate of employment. He had been expecting dismissal anyway. Dean never met him.

That evening Blanche invited Dean to write her a paper on his proposed improvements, and then settled to enjoy a brief relationship with him, away from the shop. She calculated that she could delay decisions on modernisation until she had tired of him in bed but this took longer than she had anticipated because he became unusually interesting to her. One night they were lurching around and not getting anywhere, and she was thinking, what has gone wrong – have I lost my allure for this young god? Suddenly, she found they were in such a tangle of limbs, that she began to wonder if she had grown extra legs, a thought which made her giggle.

Only momentarily because, audaciously, he rammed in from behind, and below, with what seemed to her the longest erection of all time, penetrating her exquisitely.

'Who taught you this?' she cried.

'I just did it,' he panted, as his member gave a final jerk.

'Phillips!' she exclaimed, 'you've been studying the *Kama Sutra.*'

Then she was overcome with hysterical shrieks. He responded politely, proudly, accepting his prowess but unable to perceive the joke, utterly unaware that his performance had placed him in line for a potential fortune.

· 17 ·

Years later, in that same group at the Booksellers' Conference with Blanche and Dean, had been ace-whizz-kid Abel Farmer, the entrepreneurial force behind a fast-growing chain which had opened sixty bookstores in thirteen years. Abel was now having similar thoughts to Dean's after carefully reading the letter from Ampersand, and was wondering if it were true that Blanche had slept with every attractive man she had employed. To him she was a lady who had known how to make things whirl – when she was in the mood. If only her occasional joie de vivre had been more abandoned, and she had been prepared to take risks, they could have gone places together. Then he would have had no need of city finance which was easy to raise but liable to be withdrawn at short notice when return on capital was deemed inadequate.

Abel glanced across the kitchen at his current wife who stood moodily, waiting for the toast to pop-up, and compared her unfavourably with Blanche. That was another problem. When would he attract the woman who really attracted him? None seemed to go along with what he thought of as his essential daring, either in business or in bed. He had no misgivings about himself as a man. He had been named in the public print as 'the broad-shouldered, trim-bearded, blue-eyed six footer with an enviable waistline, suggestive of under-indulgence. Yet, at the numerous publishers' launch parties he attends, he emanates conviviality and amiability even to the extent of actually listening to what others are saying...' Abel went along with that. What the gossip columnist had omitted was reference to his ruthless streak. It concerned Abel that the writer had not thought this worthy of mention. He reverted to recalling an image of Blanche who had enraptured him at a time when Doreen, so nearly his first wife, simply bored him.

Abel, on coming down from Oxford, had been torn between the diplomatic service, commerce and the navy. The navy had won. After three years spent reading English and foreign languages, he was surfeited with study. To Doreen, a fellow student, with whom he had shacked up, he declared, 'I'm full up to here with knowledge. What I now want is experience.'

'Won't you teach, then?' she asked.

He knew he had made a mistake, fallen for a lovely girl of middle-class dimensions who expected that they would share a safe, well-planned life. What he had taken for love was infatuation and a need for orgasms. He extricated himself from the relationship by exercising the ruthlessness of which he later became proud but which, at that moment, appalled his then more sensitive nature. Doreen burst into tears but actually felt relieved. She was already attracted elsewhere. 'We'll stay friends,' he said, scarcely able to register his good fortune. They never met again.

Abel took a temporary job with a merchant banker, for once accepting parental assistance. Father, heavily and affluently into life assurance, breathed sighs of relief. The boy was going to be one of them after all.

The boy was not.

Abel found himself stultifyingly indifferent to the city's obsession with percentages, foreign exchange rates and stock market indices. He wanted a *raison d'être*. Not political, not spiritual, something somewhere in between. Too young to have done National Service, he regretted that his country did not need him but decided it should, nonethless, endure him. He applied to the Royal Navy, and was accepted.

He went through Dartmouth, was commissioned, served in foreign parts on an aircraft carrier which rode over waves it no longer ruled, called in at Hong Kong and Gibraltar, then delivered him home, on a long leave, to his parents' architecturally abhorrent mini-mansion, reached up a private, rhododendron-lined driveway near Esher, Surrey. Here, to everyone's astonishment, this seemingly healthy, six foot-plus hunk of young manhood suffered a coronary.

As Abel lay convalescing in the Duke of Connaught Hospital for Naval Officers, erected on the site of a Roman villa on the South Downs, he considered what he should do next. The navy invalided him from the service, and he wasn't too upset on that score. The buggery had not appealed to him, nor had the flag waving. A few days before his discharge from hospital he walked into the nearby market town looking for something to read as an alternative to the blockbuster novels and ghosted autobiographies of showbizz celebrities, which was all the Duke of Connaught library had to offer.

'Is there a bookshop here?' He enquired of a policeman on traffic duty. The officer knew where the nearest loo was situated, and the bus terminus, or how to get to Tesco, but he was not accustomed to being asked where there was a bookshop. It was a hit below the belt. Remembering his badge of office, he rallied. 'You mean Smith's? It's over there.'

Abel did not mean Smith's. But the constable had sown a seed. Farmer's first shop was opened in that very same Sussex market town four years later. By then Abel had gained experience with the celebrated Ardbuckle's of Rustrock Spa.

That had been fifteen years ago. On the last night that he slept with Blanche, Abel had experienced a moment of vision, not sexual, but commercial. The orgasm preceding it had been entirely satisfactory to him and also, he supposed, to Blanche. He had got up to pee. When he returned to the bed chamber she was sitting up against a billowing fraternity of pillows, her hair incredibly well-groomed, her face shining with recollected ecstasy. Or that was how he saw it; actually, she was about to command him to fetch her powder compact. He, his member already reactivated, sat on the bed beside her, tickled her left cheek with his beard, then kissed the tip of her nose. But his zest for commercial achievement had become inextricably intertwined with his primitive sexual needs. He enthused about the potential of her business while attempting to enter her again. He poured out words of what, together, they might attain nationwide, worldwide even, how they would dominate the global book market. She had pushed him away. Enough was enough, and he was beginning to repel her. How unperceptive of him, she thought, not to realise that there was room for only one person at the head of Ardbuckle's. And why confuse business with carnal pleasure? A pity. Prior to that he had been fun.

Abel attempted to return to her side but she advised him to leave. Soon it would be light. Juliet, he thought bitterly, had phrased it rather better.

Abel worked on at Ardbuckle's for a few more weeks of 1975 but the bar was up. If he met Blanche on the floor of the great warren of her bookshop she either looked away or issued some petty instruction. He took the hint and, while waiting to secure premises of his own, gained experience in the increasingly active world of charity where he worked alongside charming duffers who had been found wanting in commerce, education and even publishing, or been declared redundant from the commissioned ranks of the armed forces. All were assisted by bands of eager but undirected and unpaid volunteers. He toyed with attempting to organise this disparate group into an effective work force but they seemed happy within their own fantasies, having convinced themselves they were doing their bit for the Third World by coping with vast intakes of clothing, depleted sets of china, buckled cutlery, unplayable shellac gramophone records, scratched LPs, weeping cassettes, hordes of out of date yearbooks and travelogues and mountains of dog-eared, grubby, paperbacks. He knew he could not lead them to higher peaks of achievement.

But Abel learned much about human nature during this two-year interlude while he doggedly persisted in raising the necessary finance for his chain of bookshops. Eventually, the City took to the personable young man with the naval background, capitulating to the slightly messianic quality of his blue eyes, to the carefully coiffeured beard, the disarming smile, as the City always does, when it seems to be onto a good thing.

Now, in the fourteenth year of his enterprise, Abel remained buoyant, immodestly proclaiming himself, at the suggestion of his PR consultant, 'the saviour of British bookselling'. Yet he was frighteningly short of capital. What he had achieved in thirteen years was, in his estimation, nothing short of stunning. The City was less convinced. The returns were just not good enough.

Rustrock Spa was one of the places Abel had failed to crack because of Blanche's grip on the property market there. She had made it clear she would stop at nothing to prevent his opening on what she saw as her territory. Now it seemed, when he received the letter from Trotter, Lamb and Ampersand, she had had a change of heart, although he would have to contend with other legatees. But it would surely be possible to buy them out? Then the future of the Farmer chain would be secured on what was left of the Ardbuckle fortune, based, as he was aware, on real estate more than books. He would be able to send the financiers in the City packing until it was his turn to summon *them*. Abel made himself available to Ampersand on any of the days suggested for the crucial meeting when the will would be read.

· 18 ·

Stanley Brooke-Forster did not receive the letter from Mark Ampersand until three days after it had been posted because he was on tour in yet another revival of *Private Lives;* it had to be forwarded to Aberdeen. The granite built city on Scotland's oil coast was not responsive to Coward and the first thing that Stanley read on that Friday morning was a review in the *Aberdeen Evening Express.* The critic of that paper dismissed his performance by saying he would have been more suitably cast as Elyot's grandfather – a part not written into the play.

'Elyot's father I could have borne,' Stanley muttered into his coffee cup, 'but this is too unkind.' The Ampersand letter was a palliative. Having been short of the ready for most of his theatrical career Stanley was open to all offers; that, after all, was why he was playing Elyot at the age of fifty-five, though his closest friend had insisted he didn't look a day over forty, the age Gielgud had last played Hamlet. He had to admit it was different for great stars. Sarah Bernhardt had not only acted Hamlet but played it after having a leg amputated. Perhaps one day he would amaze the world by appearing as a headless saint. As the son of a Roman Catholic bishop he had implicit belief in all saints, especially those who carried on regardless after being deprived of vital parts of their anatomy.

Stanley was brought up far across the Irish Sea, well away from his father's diocese, by his English mother who had adored the pomp and costume of the church. She set her sights on several cardinals during Stanley's boyhood but ultimately became the wife of a baritone with the Carl Rosa Opera. Thus Stanley spent much of his youth, before and after RADA, on tour and now, in middle age, he longed to settle as he had once before, for a few months, in Rustrock Spa. His first professional engagement had been with the repertory company there at the Theatre Royal. He had made quite a hit as a dashing juvenile with natural, mouse-coloured curls and a ready smile. Indeed, he had given the doomed Palace Players an unexpected last lease of life. The maidens of Rustrock Spa were to be found, after performances, waiting for him at the stage door. He seemed assured of a dazzling career but the rep's days were numbered; the dreaded box had entered most homes. When the last season folded, Stanley, who had enjoyed the stability of living in Rustrock, decided to use it as a base from which to audition for film and TV parts. When they were not forthcoming he began to work, on Saturdays, at Ardbuckle's. He enjoyed acting the role of bookseller and accepted Blanche's offer of a permanent position in Philosophy. Like many a resting actor he temporarily convinced himself that he had put the stage behind him. Blanche, who didn't expect staff to stay long with her, did not object to employing thespians who might leave at a moment's notice. And he was charming, though, she thought, having slept with him, probably queer.

Now, with the Ampersand letter before him, Stanley again felt a strong attraction to Rustrock Spa. He really would renounce his precarious profession. Should he walk out of *Private Lives* this very night? No, that might be interpreted as funk in the face of a belittling notice. He would play, at least, the following week at Brighton, because the inheritance wouldn't be paid that quickly. And Brighton was nearer to Rustrock than Aberdeen so the fare would be cheaper. He wrote to Ampersand that he could be available on any day when there was not a matinee.

· 19 ·

Thanks to Jeremy Basker, editor of *The Gazette & Herald*, the citizens of Rustrock Spa had twice-weekly opportunities to discuss the goings-on of their 'Queen of Books' and, now that she had died, they were eager to know what would happen to her company and her property. Many were her tenants, others enjoyed spin-off, in their businesses, from the carnival. Blanche Ardbuckle was a vital factor in the economy of Rustrock. Jeremy knew this and catered for it in his columns.

A wider public than that represented by readers of the *G & H* also became interested in the future of Ardbuckle's because of rumours of what might be revealed when her will was read. These rumours became 'informed leaks', thanks to Gordon Ruffle.

At Rustrock Grammar School (founded 1618) Gordon had sailed effortlessly through 'O' and 'A' Levels and was languishing in the upper sixth debating the desirability of this university or that when, to the horror of his parents, their only child became influenced by the views of his uncle Claude, a retired newspaperman who had worked on the long defunct *Reynold's News*. Claude's tales of Fleet Street fascinated the boy who quickly developed a nose for what was newsworthy. Not only could he, as a child of his age, cope with the hardware, and the software, he also knew, instinctively, the stuff of journalism which was out there, so Claude had taught him, on the streets, 'along with the painted ladies, my boy, but don't tell your mother I said so.'

When Blanche Ardbuckle died Gordon sensed that the particular stuff of it, in this instance, might be something his ex-school chum, Ellis North, could throw light upon. Ellis was now working temporarily in the offices of Trotter, Lamb and Ampersand while waiting to hear if he had found a place at Exeter, Sussex, Durham, or wherever. Gordon phoned him to enquire how he was making out. 'Why don't we have a drink?'

Ellis reacted positively. Life in a solicitor's office was humdrum.

Most of his old chums were doing Voluntary Service or backpacking in distant parts. He was flattered by Gordon's attention, Gordon, an awesome figure at school, one who might have even made Oxbridge but who had opted for the local rag.

They met at the Duke's Head. Gordon insisted on buying all the drinks. 'It's on the paper. Expenses,' he said, grandly.

Ellis protested. 'I must pay my whack. I'm not a story.'

Gordon talked about his work on the *G & H*, exaggerating the responsibilities he had been given, and making a romantic case for the role of small town reporter. Then, very earnestly, he began to probe, as one deeply absorbed in the lot of his fellow men, into Ellis's daily life as a solicitor's clerk. 'Everything to me, you see, is copy. To be worthy of my vocation, Ellis, I have to *know* what other people do.' Soon, he casually mentioned the death of Blanche Ardbuckle.

'She was a client of Mr Ampersand's.'

Gordon evinced exaggerated surprise.

'Oh yes, Mr Ampersand is very much involved...'

'Do you have to call him that?'

'Mister Ampersand? Yes, the law is very formal. I don't think the partners know one another's first names.'

'I'm told Miss Ardbuckle was a bit like that with her staff. I reckon she's left a pile. Here, have a drink.'

'They're all coming to see Mr Ampersand next week. No, no more, Gordon, thanks.'

'Who? The staff?'

'No, the people in her will. I shouldn't tell you this.'

'You haven't.' Gordon did his open smile. 'I wouldn't think there's much of a story in it anyway.'

Ellis looked affronted. 'Some of them are quite big names.' He grinned and blushed. 'I didn't say that either. These are professional secrets. Now let me get you a drink.'

Gordon let him. We're getting there, he thought, but he was wrong.

While at the bar Ellis reminded himself he mustn't get squiffy, must not reveal any names. But he might tease Gordon a bit. He returned with two halves of bitter and said, 'My lips are sealed from everything except this. Cheers!'

'Cheers! That means, either you don't know, or every lawyer has his price…'

'Then it's a high one,' said Ellis. 'You should see the bills they send out.'

'I'm silly not to be taking up law…'

'I'll say. I can tell you this Gordon, without revealing any secrets…'

'Since we pledged everlasting friendship in school milk.'

Ellis chuckled. 'I can tell you this. One of the beneficiaries…' he kept his voice low, looking conspiratorially around the bar… 'one of them is a very, very famous actor.'

'Is he a knight?'

'I can't tell you that.'

'What's his name?'

'Walter Plinge, you fucker.'

'Very witty.'

'Well, of course, I'm not telling you…'

'No, of course…'

'Another is a very, very famous woman novelist. She almost won the Booker.'

'That could be a lot of them. How many times short-listed?'

'Fifteen.'

'Liar.'

Ellis went on. 'A third legatee – that's what they call them …is a politician who lost his seat at the last election, or maybe the one before…'

'Tory?'

'Your guess.'

'And the fourth?'

'Don't push me mate! The other two are in the book world. That's all I can say. And I shouldn't have said that.' Ellis congratulated himself on having recognised what Gordon was up to, and on having dealt enigmatically with a tricky situation. For fun, he added, 'Will your paper pay me?'

'They would if you… you know…'

'No can do. Must go. Mum puts my supper in the oven because Dad won't wait to be fed for a minute when he gets home. She gets angry if it spoils. Good to see you, Gordon. Let's meet up again.' He suddenly felt superior to this boy of whom he had been so in awe.

'These book people, are they publishers or booksellers?'

'You're talking over my head. Bye.'

· 20 ·

The fax which Gordon sent through to news desks in Docklands, Farringdon Road, High Street Kensington and elsewhere read:

> Strong rumours in Rustrock Spa that Blanche Ardbuckle, who died on Monday, left her immense fortune to be divided between five people of differing backgrounds. One is a knighted actor, another a leading lady novelist, a third an ex-Tory MP who lost his seat for being pro-Europe, a fourth is, probably, the best-known bookseller in the U.K., the fifth is a mystery figure also believed to be in the book world.
>
> The actor has played at the National and RSC… Gielgud and Michael Hordern are known to have been close friends of Ardbuckle's. The novelist may be Margaret Forster or A.S.Byatt, the politician could be Chris Patten. Leading booksellers who fit the role are Christina Foyle – herself said to be worth mil-

lions – Julian Blackwell, of the famous Oxford dynasty, and Tim Waterstone. The name of Lord Weidenfeld has also been bandied about. All five are due to meet next week at the Ardbuckle solicitor's. His name is Mark Ampersand who can be reached at…

By the time gossip columnists had interpreted this in their unique styles many eminent names featured in accounts to be found as much in the holier-than-thou prestige press as in the tabloids. Speculation about the identity of The Five varied according to the supposed tastes of the journalists' readerships.

· 21 ·

At Ardbuckle's newspapers became the exclusive reading matter of the staff.

In the poetry turret Lord Terence Absolom digested a story on the front page of The *Times* which had doctored Gordon Ruffle's description of a 'mystery figure in the book world', to read, 'an up and coming entrepreneur.' It must be Tim Waterstone, mused Absolom, or was it the other chap, the one who ran Dillon's? Yet neither had ever worked for Ardbuckle's in the Lord's recollection.

Terence held the newspaper close to his aristocratic nose and closed his right eye. That way he could read the newsprint with his left. Absoloms never wore glasses; they didn't believe in them. At once, inspecting the page before him, he saw his riddle solved when the name of Abel Farmer was put forward as a legatee. 'Could be,' he remarked to his assistant, Poppy Dukes, 'I recall Farmer well. He and Madam A. were very thick for a short while. I wonder if the other bookseller is Hugh? He'll be livid if he doesn't feature in the handout. It'll wound his amour propre. Mind you, he doesn't need the cash. Unlike us poor old landowners.'

Poppy had no idea what he was on about and was, anyhow, one hundred per cent immersed in applying for a job elsewhere. She had let it be known, in the staff canteen, 'I shall be the rat who leaves your ship and won't be served up for lunch', a comment that some of her colleagues thought obscure.

Terry Absolom called himself, 'a serious dilettante'. He edited a poetry magazine, underwriting its production costs, and had once published a thin volume of verse, *Exterstices*, with Chatto and Windus. It had sold 248 copies. Blanche believed his presence in the shop added cachet but she offended him by refusing to permit the holding of poetry readings after hours. She had heard of the drunkenness at Fitzrovian-style pubs when Terence's friends foregathered to lament the declining status of verse.

On the ground floor, John Ogglethorpe (Fiction & General), once his own boss until massive rent increases had forced him to close his bookshop, and now on the brink of embracing failure, enjoyed the snide innuendo of gossip columns in the *Guardian*. 'So why weren't you included in the best of the bedworthy, Dan?' he enquired of a colleague. 'I'm sure I've seen you hot-footing it up to Ridge End.' Daniel Drybrough (Paperbacks), one-armed and a black patch over his eye socket, took the ribbing well. 'I showed her a thing or two, John, but she complained about you. Said you couldn't get it up.' A browsing customer coughed loudly.

Maimie Perkes (Art) who had had an unrequited crush on Blanche, frowned at the *Daily Telegraph* which a customer placed before her. Hitherto, she had never supposed that Miss Ardbuckle had shared her inclinations. Who was the lady novelist? 'I hope,' remarked Mrs Winthrop-Moore, the customer, 'that it isn't Anita Brookner. I do so love her books.'

Maimie, a devout RC, with so overpowering a sense of guilt that she had relinquished painting for bookselling because, at the Slade, she had discovered great gifts as a forger, now felt wicked for harbouring unclean feelings for Blanche. Maimie was fifty-five, with red hair, veined cheeks, and a body so slim some thought her anorexic. She did not wish to discuss the novelist with Mrs Winthrop-Moore. 'I wonder if I ever worked with any of the five?' she mused. 'More to the point,' commented Roger, her assistant, 'did you ever sleep with any of them?'

Maimie ordered Roger to take early coffee. 'You should dismiss him for insolence,' said Mrs Winthrop-Moore. 'The law prevents it,' replied Maimie. 'He's. a protected species. He's been here for more than six months.'

'Miss Ardbuckle didn't bother about the law. She would have flouted it. She seems to have been a very *flouting* sort of person.'

'I never heard of it spelt like that before,' said Roger, as he left.

In Mail Order, Audrey da Costa was drooling over the *Sun,* which was assessing the chances of the political legatee, inaccurately named as a cabinet minister. 'I think it'll be good for business,' she prophesied while eating her fourth cream doughnut of the morning. An ex-nurse, who had arrived in Britain from the Caribbean in the early fifties, Audrey had been forced, through gluttony, into a sedentary job. She had made herself indispensable in her role at Ardbuckle's, deliberately filing the records of many of her customers in her head. There they peopled her world to the confusion of everyone else she encountered. They were the only real people in her life. She was speaking and listening to them at all times so, when any actual, four-dimensional person confronted her, they were regaled, through whatever mouthful of confectionary Audrey was masticating at that moment, with tales of what these mail order customers had said, or written.

'Heard from old Beth this morning,' she would say to a colleague, 'she wants anything we've got on hydrotherapy. Do you know what she told me about her sister…?' Her colleagues learned to turn her off and to get on with their own work, but it was disconcerting for newcomers. Audrey never took holidays, didn't embezzle, and ran her department with a rod of steel. Her three terrified assistants were longing to read both the *Sun* and the *Mirror*, and were whispering seditiously.

'You three artful dodgers, you get round the store with my customers' orders. They want their books.' The downtrodden girls trailed out of their passage-like office, each with a list of requirements which departmental managers would almost certainly refuse to supply because they anticipated over the counter sales for them. This led to guerilla warfare with the da Costa girls who were sent back, when managers were absent, to filch the books. Audrey always got Blanche's backing because, 'a firm order is a firm sale.'

In the annexe, that deprived area beyond the pergola, occupying part of the site of a former wartime RAF camp, matronly Lisa Fry (Education) said to pretty little Dilys Biggs (Drama & Music), 'This could mean there will be light at the end of our tunnel.'

'Or at least, some up-to-date posters to decorate it.' Dilys, with pony tail and pronounced, firm nipples, had transformed the two battered Nissen huts housing her stock, into a colourful department alive with arresting photographic studies of contemporary musicians and actors. 'I hope I have a picture of whoever the actor is.'

'You soon will have, darling, if I know my stage people,' replied Lisa, whose own department, once the sergeants' mess, was furnished with trestle tables and shelving made from orange boxes. Most of its tatty stock was bought back from graduates to be re-sold to enrolling students.

In the staff room, those who got to first coffee before Roger, (Art), were being hectored by Fergus Welch (Science & Technology), the disputatious Ulsterman of innate charm, no qualifications (he left Queen's, Belfast, in mid-course to pursue a colleen over the border), multifarious talents (he could sculpt, service a car, change a nappy) and wild, leftish political views (he was still inclined to the belief that Stalin had been misunderstood). He wished to know from present company, stirring its powdered

Maxwell House, why he was not among Blanche's chosen. Those present, spinsters Amy Thresham (Travel), Gerda Kohl (Foreign) and Mona Darling (Children's & Young Adults), were too embarrassed to respond. Amy, who suffered from CGS, (chronic genealogical syndrome), was absorbed in thoughts about her ancestors; Gerda had been traumatised sexually in childhood, and froze at mention of the subject; Mona lived in a full-colour fantasy world, where the Flower Fairies cohabited with Ant and Bee to propagate exotic creatures, of innate purity. They ceaselessly roamed forbidden territories from the Never-Never-Land, to Oz, prowling behind cupboards, beneath carpets, across time and cultural barriers, into middle planetary, inter-earth domains, only endurable to children not yet on hard drugs. (And adults in a state of post-Christian ecstasy.) Mona, a flat-chested, birdlike creature resembling a hen with arms, came of a background she cherished, where 'we never discussed politics, religion or sex,' from all three of which she believed herself to be safely distanced.

Mercifully for Fergus, Lester Constantine (junior assistant, History), a gangling, second generation immigrant, born in a back-to-back in Bristol, was also present. 'Wasn't she a bit past it, Fergie, by your time?'

'Hugh Mattingson may have thought so. Indeed, he told me just that.' (Which was a lie.) 'But, man, she was a game old bird, and she taught me a thing or two.' Amy surreptitiously crossed herself. Gerda Kohl rebuked him – 'You should not talk so in front of the young'; Mona Darling took all heat out of the occasion, or hoped to – 'I think Miss Ardbuckle was a real English lady who would have liked nothing better than to serve us all tea from a bone china service...'

'Yeah,' sneered Fergus, 'probably with a tea bag past its use by date.'

· 22 ·

Mark Ampersand, a well-preserved forty-five-year old (clean-shaven, own hair, no paunch, black-framed glasses) stood in the ground floor oval reception room of his offices, overlooking a sloping swathe of common beyond a private road, once the entrance to the ducal mansion. It was Tuesday in the week following Blanche Ardbuckle's death. Men, some with cameras, others with notebooks in their hands, or protruding from their pockets, had taken up positions on the pavement. Mark said to Ellis North, 'Are these what are called paparazzi?'

'Yes, sir,' replied the young man who had become aware that he was under suspicion as the source of the press leak. 'I believe they are.'

'Then, they will be disappointed when they see who turns up for the meeting, won't they, Mr North?

'Isn't Stanley Brooke-Forster well known? He was in that soap about lawyers on Channel 4.'

'And that was a farrago of misconceptions. But he is not, as I am aware, a knight. Nor has he appeared at the National Theatre.'

'Perhaps when he was a child actor, sir?'

'When he was a child there was no National Theatre. And why are you so keen to justify the gossip writers, Ellis? Are they friends of yours?'

'No, sir, the only journalist I know...' He fell silent, aware he had blundered.

'You know journalists, do you?' Ampersand did not care for the sadistic streak he was revealing; he thought of himself as essentially humane, a decent, happily married family-friend sort of chap who tried not to harm others.

'Not real ones, Mr Ampersand. I was at school with a bloke who is on the *Gazette*...'

'Don't go on. Fortunately you are not intending to take Law at university.' Ampersand said no more. Ellis North did not deny he was the culprit. Instead he wondered where he might find another temporary job. Or should he eavesdrop on the forthcoming meeting and sell the story to

Gordon? He sighed. Adult life seemed to be as potentially corrupting as school.

The photographer representing the *News of the World* addressed the others. 'Ask me, this is a bloody waste of time. Nothing in this for our bleeding punters. Fucking actor-managers aren't up our street. Or sodding lady novelists.'

'Stanley Brooke-Forster was in that soap about the law.' Gordon Ruffle felt an entrepreneurial pride in this event which he had set-up.

'Who the fuck are you?.'

'I'm the *Gazette and Herald*.'

'The bleeding what?'

'It's the local rag,' said the man taking pictures for the *Independent*.

'Not bad as locals go.'

'It's my story,' said Gordon. 'I started it.'

'So it's all your fucking fault,' said the *Sun*. 'I can't see the lady novelist being all tits and bum…'

'You're such a bloody snob, Ron,' observed *The Times,* 'just because they have brains doesn't mean they lack tits…'

'When you achieve our circulation I'll ask our boss to give you a bonus.'

'Who's this fucker?' asked the *News of the World*.

A mini cab was slowly approaching, pursued by a young *London Weekend* cameraman, desperate to emulate what he had so often seen on the box. It was his first assignment. As the cab slowed he aimed his lens towards the heavily tinted glass. A door on the opposite side opened and out swept Stanley Brooke-Forster. It required an actor of some talent to achieve an effective exit from the back of a low saloon. Stanley's rated at least eight out of ten.

'That sod's not Gielgud, nor bleeding Guinness,' said the *Guardian* with venom. 'and I've mug shot them enough for my bunch of highbrow commies.'

'It's Stanley Brooke-Forster,' shouted Gordon. The actor relaxed, enjoying the situation, then put up his arms in mock alarm when faced, at close range, by the youth from *London Weekend*, who bawled, 'Hold it! The film's jamming.' The pressmen all jeered.

The *Scotsman* reporter asked, 'D'ye expect to come out of here a millionaire, Mr McKellen?'

Stanley made a camp gesture and, with an extravagant wink at "the Gallery", replied, 'actually I'm Anthony Sher.' That got him a good round. 'My agent', he went on, 'said not to settle for less than a billion,' which raised more laughs than he had squeezed out of the previous evening's audience, at Brighton, in the whole of Act Three. Then he faced them without a blush and said, in a resonantly low voice, 'She was a dear friend. I shall miss her.'

'Who's he fucking lost?' asked the *News of the World*.

The *Scotsman* persisted. 'My apologies. Sir... Sher... er... but will you be keeping it all? They say it's a tidy fortune.'

Stanley assumed the posture he would have adopted, had he ever been cast as Lear, for "Attend the Lords of France and Burgundy," and gagged, 'Charity begins at home. Sometimes, it becomes housebound.' That got another round.

Gordon pushed himself to the fore – after all, it was *his* scoop. 'Have you ever played Rustrock Spa, Stan?'

'I have indeed, young man.' The actor turned to Gordon, gave him the most disarming of smiles, dissolving into a steely glint of the eyes, and added, 'I was here so long ago in rep that, in those days, cub reporters addressed me as "Sir"!'

'That was before fucking theatres had roofs,' bawled the *Mail*.

'Gentlemen, you will excuse me,' said Stanley, about to enter the offices. He turned and asked, 'I may need a pocket calculator. Can anyone lend me such a thing, please?'

'Nice one!' shouted Gordon, 'SIR Stan.'

At that moment *London Weekend* was sprinting dementedly again, attempting to mount the running board of a pearl grey Hispano Suiza which had entered the private road. Dickie Klute made a habit of hiring this prestigious vehicle from a Lincolnshire farmer who had diversified into veteran and vintage cars. Once again, the *Weekend* was on the wrong side of the vehicle and focussed unsteadily on a view of the Klute backside as its owner emerged. Dickie was adorned in an exquisite two-piece in deep purple and a hat which had, admittedly, already been seen at Ascot but she guessed it would be new to Rustrock Spa. Her trademark cigarette holder, loaded and afire, was ahead of her, and her new monocles, one silver, one gold, gleamed in the sunlight.

'I've come across this old bird before,' said the *Mail,* 'I think she's the fucking novelist.'

'We were promised Beryl Bainbridge,' complained *The Times.* 'Now she's good copy. Worth the packet of fags it costs to keep her talking, but a lovely lady. This old cow looks as though she only smokes *Gauloise.*'

Dickie, smiled shyly and paused for each and every cameraman, all of whom obliged because it was their practice to use dozens of reels of film. No matter that Dickie Klute wouldn't be news – unless she won a major prize, or wrote something libellous – you had camera, you took film. The *Birmingham Post,* a kindly, courteous, person who still believed it was possible to be a journalist and a gentleman, half-bowed, smiled, and said, 'Welcome back to Rustrock Spa, Mrs Klute. We met at one of the Ardbuckle banquets.'

'Of course.' Dickie made an extravagant circle with her twelve-inch long holder, allowed both monocles to drop, caught them cleverly and replaced them in the wrong eyes. 'I remember it well, Mr...?'

'Dingle.'

'You got there before me. Dear Mr Dingle.' She exchanged her monocles. 'Those were happy days. How *are* you?'

'If I'd known you were to be here, dear lady, I'd have brought along my copy of your last novel to be signed.'

'Makes you puke,' said the *Mirror* to the *Independent*.

'Have this one on me,' said the *Tatler*, retching.

'Were you,' asked Gordon, navigating around the cigarette holder, 'a great friend of Blanche's?'

'I think…' Dickie drew herself up in the way she had learned long ago from actresses in drawing-room comedies '…I think I must have been if it is Miss Ardbuckle to whom you refer.' At the same moment she thought, no one in my books ever talks like that, so why do I? Aloud, to the eager young man in the loosely-tied tie, revealing at least two undone shirt buttons, she added, 'I can't quite place you. Are you *France Dimanche?*'

At that moment the BBC arrived in three massive pantechnicons which effectively blocked all access to the private road. A squad of cheerful chaps, dressed casually but expensively in anoraks or leather jackets, and all wearing ties, emerged and began to strew miles of cable in every direction. Cameras were set-up on trolleys, executive chairs were distributed profusely, the press corps was amicably greeted in response to a battery of insults and someone, presumably a producer, said, 'We thought we'd look in; we happened to be passing.'

Gordon muttered, 'I bloody phoned you.'

A helicopter flew low overhead, prompting *London Weekend* to leap onto the bonnet of a parked Rover to try a close-up. He damaged a wing mirror.

'It's landing on the Common,' someone shouted.

'It won't make it. The gradient's one-in-four.'

The helicopter disappeared from view. Shortly after, a trimly-bearded face and head appeared above a gorse bush and Abel Farmer strode confidently towards the media.

'The politician!' cried the *Sun*. 'Is it Hezza? No, too young.'

Several reporters began descending the steep hill of the Common, outstripped by the *Weekend* cameraman who tripped and fell into a thicket where there proved to be insufficient dock leaves among the nettles.

Abel made the pavement with a swift pincer movement around the advancing reporters, and vaulted over a single railing.

'That's not fucking Hezza,' said the *News of the World*, clicking frantically just the same, because it might be royalty for all he knew.

'Must be one of the booksellers,' pronounced Gordon. Interest at once evaporated. Booksellers were never news, just boring people defending retail price maintenance and whinging if any government so much as aired the idea of VAT on books.

Abel passed through the throng of pressmen, looking agreeable…all publicity was good publicity.

'Are you attending the Ardbuckle meeting?' asked the *Daily Telegraph*, politely, hoping he might give a lesson to the vulgar young man from the local paper.

'I am.'

'Then you must be Mr Blackwell?'

'I am not.' In the presence of the press Abel kept a low, respectful demeanour. He was wary but always ready to hold open the door.

'Mr Heffer?' queried the *Independent*.

Abel shook his head.

'And he's not bleeding Christina Foyle either,' said the *Sun* to the *Mirror*.

The *Daily Telegraph* persisted. 'You wouldn't be Tim Waterstone?'

'I wouldn't mind being. He's got more shops than I have.'

'So tell us who you are, clever dick,' murmured the *Guardian* to Gordon.

'I'm Abel Farmer and I think I'm a bit late.' He paused to pose. This could be a historic moment. 'I really must go in.'

The Beeb producer approached. 'Hi, Abel! Just one for my lads.'

'Basil!' Abel greeted his old prep school mucker. 'Where have you been all my life?'

They were interrupted by the arrival of Monty Devereux in a pony and trap which was, after tense negotiations, manoeuvred around the pantechnicons.

'Prominent fucking politician, my arse hole,' said the *Mirror* angrily to Gordon. 'Time you grew up, laddie.' The *Telegraph* winced and approached Monty who had recently attracted publicity by not getting selected for a safe seat in the shires. 'Is it true,' he asked, 'you are joining Labour?'

'Too far to the right for me,' joked Monty, contributing his hyena laugh.

'What about Libdem?' enquired Gordon.

'Too far to the left.' He knew how to get quoted. Monty tethered the pony and went inside.

'Not worth waiting for those buggers to come out,' announced the *Observer.* 'There's a boozer down the end of the road. Sonny boy will tell us when something's happening.'

Gordon blushed but did not respond. One day he'd be in a position to hire and fire. He'd remember. Meanwhile there was the contingent from the Beeb to be chatted-up.

Dean Phillips had also been admitted to Ampersand's offices. He had quietly chained his bike to the railings and walked inside without attracting attention.

· 23 ·

The five legatees sat uneasily in the oval reception room each trying to pretend the other four were not in the same situation. Stanley Brooke-Forster reflected how much more comfortable it was than the average outer office of a theatrical agent. Dean Phillips wondered if he should introduce himself to Abel Farmer, reminding him that they had met. Monty smiled 'cheese' at one and all, and drew embarrassed smirks in response. Dickie Klute noted what everyone was wearing. Abel Farmer was occupied with devising a plan for getting something on account.

A secretary emerged through an elegant, crescent-shaped Regency door and said, 'Mr Ampersand apologises for keeping you waiting. He's had to take an urgent call. May I offer anyone coffee? Tea?' They all murmured, 'Thank you, no.' Then Dickie Klute, who never liked to waste potential copy, remarked with a dazzling smile, removing her monocles and beaming at each of the others in turn, 'That seems to settle that we are all here on the same business. I'm Dickie Klute. I write books. I've done my best to live up to the gossip and look like someone famous, such as Ruth Rendell, but the press wasn't deceived. Now which of you gentlemen is Sir John Gielgud in disguise?'

Stanley rose and bowed. 'I understudied the great man once when I was young. Will I do? I'm Stanley Brooke-Forster.'

The others stood and introduced themselves, exchanging names but little else. No one liked to say, 'Wonder why she chose me?' Monty cleared his throat and asked Dickie, 'How well did you know Blanche?'

'How well did anyone?' Dickie replaced her right monocle and examined the politician. Monty screeched, the others winced, then Abel commented, 'You speak as a novelist, Mrs Klute. I knew her pretty well, for a time…'

He was interrupted by the appearance of Mark Ampersand apologising profusely for keeping them waiting. He offered no explanation but had, in fact, been sitting at his desk in a funk for nearly two hours, unable to concentrate on anything beyond the thought of having to deal with these people. At this moment he deeply loathed Blanche Ardbuckle and wished he'd had the courage to refuse to act for her. Instead he had taken it out on Ellis North, nagging him to tidy chairs and sweep the floor of the office. But the dreaded moment could only be delayed, not denied.

'I am required by law,' began Mark, 'to read you the precise words of the last Will and Testament of Blanche Clarissa Ardbuckle, deceased lady of this borough of Rustrock Spa in the County of Wealdshire. I must read it without making comment. You will understand, lady and gentlemen, that the words you will hear are those that Miss Ardbuckle required me to write down on her behalf, and that I exercised no influence over her whatever.'

The five sat motionless, intrigued, unsmiling.

The solicitor read:

> *I bequeath £5,000 to my maidservant Jean Roper, of 44, Arkley Buildings, Rustrock Spa...*

There followed a number of smaller bequests, some of a capricious nature, to persons and charities. Four of the five listening to Mark were restless, shifting on their buttocks; Abel lay back, closed his eyes and deducted, by mental arithmetic, each sum announced from the figure of five billion pounds, at which he asssessed the Ardbuckle fortune, and then divided the amount by five. The bequests so far declared were the merest petty cash compared with the capital sum.

> *The bulk of the remainder of my estate after death duties if any I bequeath to one of the following five legatees each of whom will receive an initial payment of £50,000...*

Stanley, who had been enacting the role of disinherited son, swapped it for that of mourning cousin and cleared a lump in his throat which, had it been a close-up on the box, would have been a moving moment. Abel registered, despite himself, disappointment. Monty allowed himself a small grin (£50,000 for a start was not to be sneezed at). Dean looked apprehensive (there was some catch). Dickie looked pleased (it was better than being shortlisted for the Booker and then losing).

Ampersand read slowly through their names and addresses, reluctant to proceed to the next paragraph, but the moment had to arrive.

> *In selecting these five from among the thousands of friends made during a long life, I have been guided by this consideration above all others...*

Mark paused, cleared his throat, looked truly miserable, removed his spectacles, wiped them, replaced them, lowered his head and, in a very low but just audible voice read...

> *...of all my lovers they... were the best... in bed.*

Mark hesitated and flushed more furiously even than before, informing the company, again, 'I am bound by law to read out this further passage...' Why had he agreed to this monstrous will?

> *...I think of them all with affection. Dickie, a well of gregariousness, Dean, who seemed to have more limbs than is customary, Monty, that commando of sex who must surely have been born in the Spanish town of Peniscola...*

Abel guffawed appreciatively, hoping for something as good about himself.

> *...Stanley, the gayest of you all, in all respects, and Abel, who pretended that any orifice would do...*

Monty smirked, feeling rather chuffed, Dean blushed, Dickie pursed her lips, Stanley acted being impassive, thinking, 'It's only a month since I came out', but Abel released a bellowing laugh, jumped to his feet, and cried, 'Has she given us ratings?'

'Please be seated, Mr Farmer, I have not finished.' Mark Ampersand read on, blushing deeply:

> *Apart from their performance in bed, the five named persons impressed me during the time they worked at Ardbuckle's by their idealism, a quality with which I have perhaps not been unduly identified. Each of them extolled to me the value of worker-management control, partnership, co-operation. I rejected their advice at the time because I was management and they were workers. However, I now recognise the need for change, so, if the five accept the bequests, none of them for the present will become managing director, or chief executive. All will be equal and earn the same annual salary…*

On Abel's face there was a wry smile; he believed in delegation but this was ridiculous. Monty was unmoved; he was accustomed to committees, and thought he knew how to take charge of them. Stanley and Dickie looked perplexed. Dean sighed. He felt depressed.

> *…The trading name of the bookselling business, the annual carnival and of the property company shall continue under the umbrella of Ardbuckle Limited, in perpetuity, or for as long as it takes clever lawyers to break the trust…*

Mark looked at them shyly and smiled. Abel commented, 'I think you're being got at instead of us'. There was a lowering of tension. Mark resumed:

> *The company must not be sold while it remains solvent.*

Mark paused, took a sip of water and wished it were whisky.

'Is that all?' asked Dean who had resolved not to take part in this charade.

'I'm afraid, not. I will continue.

Initially the shares of the company will be held in a trust administered by my solicitor, Mark Ampersand, of Trotter, Lamb and Ampersand, and my accountant, Aubrey Winters, of Frobisher, Day and Potter, of 4, Little Lane, Rustrock Spa but, on acceptance of the terms of the will, each legatee will receive, in addition to the aforementioned £50,000, a contract entitling each one of them to an annual salary of £30,000 for one-and-a-quarter years…

Stanley ceased acting his crowd role and allowed himself a small gasp.

Monty made a vulgar thumbs-up gesture (in financial terms it would be almost as good as being an MP), Dickie and Dean appeared bemused. Abel muttered, 'Not enough.' Mark read on:

At the end of one-year-and-a-quarter from the date of acceptance one of the legatees will receive from the Trust the entire share holding in Ardbuckle's.

They stared at Mark in disbelief. He must be inventing it.

…Three weeks prior to the termination of the contract, all those who have been employed at Ardbuckle's, with the exception of the five legatees, or how so many there may by that time be, for a period of twelve months or more, will be invited to vote in a ballot for that legatee whom they believe to be best-fitted to continue to run the company. The four legatees who are not elected will receive a further £50,000 each but will not, thereafter, have any entitlement to employment within the company…'

'The old bitch!' Abel guffawed. 'What a Byzantine mixture of malice and generosity. What fun she must have had...'

'May I finish?'

'Is there more? Sorry.'

> *Despite the salary they will receive, if the terms are acceptable to them, the legatees will be at liberty to pursue their own careers in the interim period with the proviso that none of them owns part or the whole of any business of any nature whatsoever operating within the borough boundaries of Rustrock Spa in the County of Wealdshire. Given this day...*

Ampersand, whose clothes were sticking to his body, and whose face had become, he was certain, permanently scarlet, heaved a massive sigh and told the legatees, he had never before had to read out so embarrassing a will.

'Is it legally binding?' asked Monty.

'Would I have...?'

'No, no, no, no offence...' Monty monitored in his dreadful laugh.

'Why,' mused Dean, aloud, 'one year-and-a-quarter? Isn't that a curious period? Does it have legal significance?'

'I believe that Miss Ardbuckle supposed...' Mark grinned, already feeling better '...probably not incorrectly, that there would be some legal hold-up for technical reasons, and she wanted the five legatees to enjoy a full year of, as she would have seen it, exposure...'

'Lovely double-entendre,' commented Dickie.

'...to her staff. I think that was her intention.'

'You read it very nicely, Mr Ampersand,' said Dickie, 'with real feeling. I am sure we are all indebted to you but I think we shall need a break to consider it. May I suggest tea... laced perhaps, with a drop of green chartreuse?'

· 24 ·

They all felt uneasy, shattered even, and mooched about the room. Dickie asked if she might step into the garden. Stanley, following her, said in jocular tones, 'I'm for accepting now. A guaranteed one hundred and thirty thou – wow!' He added, 'I suppose you're going to prune the calceolarias', a line he recalled from another Coward play, to which Monty responded, 'Gorg- eous colour aren't they? Of course, with our ever-changing climate, you get so many flowering seasons don't you?' He screeched again, hoping his observation made sense in context. 'I think the – er – laugh is involuntary,' Dickie observed to Stanley. They moved around the garden until Mark ordered the resentful Ellis North to tell them tea was served. 'Ask them how they like it.'

'We haven't any of that green stuff the lady mentioned.'

'So you were listening at the keyhole.?'

Ellis glowered at his erstwhile employer. He had not joined the partnership, even temporarily, to become a waiter. He had already swept the floor, something he had never done at home. (Nor had his father.) He recovered his composure, remembering that there might be some advantage in dallying at this gathering, poured tea as graciously as he could, and as slowly as he dared, eager for the business of the meeting to be resumed. When it was, Mark's eyes told him that he should leave, but he knew that Mark knew he might eavesdrop again.

Abel was the first to speak once they had re-settled themselves.

'Before we get too excited about this extraordinary bequest we ought to know precisely what sum we are talking about. Over half-a-million is accounted for immediately. What is likely to be in the jackpot? I mean, will it be serious money such as would build and equip a royal yacht, or pay for a season at the Met, or is it just a few million? I cannot imagine that any of us will want to spend a year loitering around here, trying to make a good impression on the staff, for peanuts. The salaries, for a start, are not over-generous…'

Dean could not believe what he had heard. Two handouts of fifty thousand plus another of thirty and a bit, for a part-time job! At present, he and Phyllis got by on twenty, some of which they gave to charity.

Ampersand thought Abel was being greedy. Coldly, he told him, 'The properties, which comprise large units of the former ducal estate, were valued in the last balance sheet at over two billion.'

Dickie tried to remember when millions became billions. Stanley supposed he had walked into an Aladdin's cave. His first problem would be, should he tell his agent?

'The annual carnival,' Mark went on, 'nets about quarter of a million, the retail business, from the shop alone, sometimes makes a loss, so far as can be told. You'll have to ask Winters, the accountant, about that. Sometimes there's a profit. You write stock up, you write stock down. It's all above board. There's no laundered money or anything like that.'

'Can you tell me exactly what laundered money is?' asked Dickie.'It would be useful to me, as a writer, to know. You don't actually iron it, do you?'

Mark, who wasn't certain either, smiled. 'What I mean, Mrs Klute, is that there is no mafia. The Ardbuckle accounts are properly audited each year.'

'What's the stock worth?' asked Abel.

'It's in the balance sheet. It's been agreed with the Inland Revenue. I have Mr Winters' assurance… There will be little in the way of death duties, which may surprise you, but the company is registered, absolutely legally, in the Bahamas. And, as I said earlier, the shares are being held in a temporary Trust.'

Stanley laughed nervously. 'I wish I'd known about the Bahamas. I've never toured there. Sounds the sort of tax haven actors need.'

'And writers,' said Dickie.

'May I go on?' Mark asked with some assertiveness. 'If you accept the terms of the will one of you is certain to become a millionaire; the others will have more than their expenses paid. It is for you, lady and gentlemen, to decide.'

Dickie asked, 'If I refuse to take part in this rather macabre lottery, will the terms of the will still be made public?'

'I'm afraid so.'

Dean said he must have time to talk it over with Phyllis. Abel, attempting to conceal impatience and anxiety, asked how long they would all need. Mark threw in that the contracts of employment would commence on the day they all agreed, or opted out.

'I don't need to sleep on it,' Monty told them. 'I'm for it now. I have made up my mind.' Then he spoiled his bid for leadership of the group by emitting his laugh. How, wondered Dean, had he ever got selected as a parliamentary candidate? Aloud, he suggested, 'Let's meet in seven days.'

'Great,' shrieked Monty, 'I'll bring the bubbly.'

'When you do,' advised Dickie, 'don't let it be shaken about in that pony and trap of yours.'

'No prob. I'll have the BMW next time.'

'*My* prob,' said Stanley, 'is that I'm on tour. This week it's Brighton. I can get here without trouble when there's not a matinee. Next week we're playing Newcastle-on-Tyne.'

'UP-on,' corrected Dickie, an obsessive sub, 'UPON-Tyne.'

'Yes, it's right up there, a long way,' replied Stanley.

'And the week after, dear chap?' Monty felt himself in command.

'Liverpool. I could make the Sunday…'

Monty asked if expenses were payable. 'I'm not asking for myself…'

He screeched a bit and nodded towards Stanley. 'There must be some petty cash. Who's in charge in this interim period?'

'Hugh Mattingson,' the solicitor told him. 'He's the manager. The general manager, I should say, but not the managing director. He's responsible to the Trustees.'

Stanley looked disdainfully at Monty and declared, in a lordly way, 'If you have problems, my dear fellow, let me help. I doubt I shall turn down this one. I've taken some unsuitable parts in my time but this seems promising…'

Monty threw back his head and shreiked again. 'Well said! Sans arbitrages, sans patronages, and all that.'

'What does the stupid prat mean?' Abel whispered to Dean, who ignored him. He had not sought to be associated with this bizarre will but every man, he thought wryly, has his price.

Mark then interrupted saying he didn't wish to be uncooperative but he was about to go on holiday. 'I'm off this coming weekend for a fortnight. I can't alter the arrangement. There are too many people involved.'

'When do you go, Mr Ampersand?'

'On Sunday, Mrs Klute, at noon.'

Abel took control. 'Do you have a matinee this Saturday, Stanley?'

''Fraid so. Don't you?'

'Every day, including Sundays, but my public is happy with understudies. If my heli picked you up at first light and returned you to Brighton in time for the matinee…?'

'Done, dear fellow.'

'Does that suit everyone?'

'It will have to.' Dean registered Abel's authority. 'But one thing before we leave… all that in the will… the press…?'

Mark regarded him compassionately. 'I'm sorry. I thought I'd made that clear but it won't be in the public domain immediately.'

He was wrong. Ellis, the tea-maker, had his revenge. He was also Ellis who was required to deliver documents, buy stamps, collect packets from other solicitors. When the pony and trap and the Hispano Suiza had departed and the helicopter had zoomed over the Common, when the reporters and photographers had dispersed, with the Beeb convoy making for a rumoured scene of disaster on Salisbury Plain, there were still a few foot-bound journalists in the Duke's Head. On an errand, Ellis looked in and found Gordon among them. Afterwards, he reflected, he had done no harm. And a hundred quid was a hundred quid. Next morning the five legatees read in their morning papers variations on the theme:

BOOKSELLING QUEEN LEAVES ALL
TO HER FAVOURITE LOVERS

· 25 ·

When they learned the names of the legatees, the staff at Ardbuckle's again compared newspapers. Sitting late over second coffee, John Ogglethorpe (Fiction & General), Maimie Perkes (Art) and Terence Absolom (Poetry) mulled over the conditions of the will. Amy Thresham (Travel) brooded about the nature of second-cousinhood and didn't listen until John Ogglethorpe began speculating about Stanley Brooke-Forster's sexual prowess. Then she left. Terence stayed but looked pained. He did not discuss the subject because he was impotent, which was why his two wives had left him. He was strikingly handsome – at forty-five he passed for thirty – although his tummy was becoming very slightly pronounced due to over-consumption of wine. He had also developed a slight stoop through short-sightedness and his refusal to wear glasses. The Poetry and Belles-Lettres section, in its Gothic tower, reached by exceptionally worn steps, trodden by most major poets of the century, was his pride and joy. The thought of having to defend his long-standing right to run it in his highly eclectic manner, and bow to the wishes of some group-minded tycoon, appalled him. 'If Abel Farmer takes over I shall resign,' he said. John Ogglethorpe bore this threat with fortitude. It offended his left-wing principles that Absolom worked without payment. Even an aristocrat should be worthy of his hire. There was further friction between the two men because, although Blanche had maintained an official belief that poetry did not sell, and retained Absolom's services for reasons of prestige and cost-effectiveness, when a fresh offering from Ted Hughes was published, or a new anthology from Oxford University Press, Ogglethorpe was permitted to cream off the majority of sales in his ground floor department. Absolom resented this but Blanche insisted that bestsellers belonged on the front counter, greeting customers as they entered. In her way, she *had* embraced modern retailing techniques.

'Would the National Trust allow you to have a stall at your castle?' John asked Terence. Maimie quickly intervened to say that they should all stick together. As a devout Catholic she was shocked by the terms of the will although she had to suppress feelings of jealousy for Dickie Klute. All the while she had supposed Blanche to be purely heterosexual (and staff room gossip provided sufficient evidence of that) she had been able to quell the guilt she felt at being attracted to her. Now it was different. She calmed herself by observing that the three of them were all most experienced booksellers and any incoming management would be proud to employ them. She was dimly aware that her department was grossly overstocked, but if Blanche, who made the quip about there being too many books, had tolerated her, so surely would others?

At another table, Fergus Welch (Science & Technology) lectured Lester Constantine (History) on the virtues of a management buyout. Lester asked what they would use for money.

'We'd get a loan. The banks are falling over each other to back new enterprises. That's how Abel Farmer got his funding.'

'I heard he's in difficulties. One of the reps told me. These banks lend you money O.K., but if you don't do well, they get tired of you, and call their loan in.'

Fergus thought Lester could be right and changed the subject. 'I can't think why I wasn't chosen by Blanche.'

'Oh, not again, Fergie.'

'I was one of the last to have her. She had style.'

'Well, man, you do have a reputation for not being choosey.'

Fergus flirted automatically with almost all women. He was unfaithful to Dolly, the mother of his two children, spending three nights a week with Muriel, a teacher with a mission to persuade him to develop his talents as a sculptor.

· 26 ·

Although, after the meeting, the legatees had left the office in a group, Dean Phillips did not attract attention from the paparazzi who had fixed their already dwindling interest on Monty, Dickie and Abel, none of whom offered much of a lead. Dean bade farewell to Abel, who was wondering where they had met before, unchained his bike and set off for Ridgeley. He loved cycling but on this occasion he rode automatically, his road sense operating like radar while his mind surged with troubled ruminations about the meeting. His first instinct was to refuse the bequest. But could he afford to turn down a certain £130,000? It would provide for retirement. Then they could move to somewhere secluded, near to the children.

The bequest was like a reward from on high and, had he still been a believer, Dean might have thought of it as such, ignoring all relevance to that camel and the eye of the needle. A more worrying aspect of the inheritance was the flippant reason for it. He had certainly slept with Blanche. That wasn't on his conscience. It had happened before he met Phyllis, though why, considering their almost obsessive cult of openness, he had never mentioned it to her he could no longer remember. He supposed it was because she hadn't asked him. When they met, Dean and Phyllis were instantly attracted to each other and never looked back until that moment when they decided to divorce because married status did not seem suitable for them.

The brief affair with Blanche was not recollected with pride but Dean felt no guilt. It was an experience common to numerous young men and Phyllis would not be hurt to learn of it. And she would learn because, when he told her the names of the other legatees, it would be natural to reveal the common denominator. Phyl, though, might well be against accepting the money. Then, he thought, with a chuckle, we shall have A Dark Night of the Soul, and probably end up agreeing to take the loot for the sake of the children.

Phyllis greeted him fondly. 'Pour us a drink. Then tell me all about it.'

'So, as I say…' Dean was in an armchair with Phyl snuggled about him in that easy, feline way that those who have been long together acquire… 'my initial reaction was, I want nothing to do with this. I admire Abel Farmer but we're not on the same wavelength.'

'Did he say anything to you?'

'I don't think he remembered me. Why should he? All the people he must meet…'

'You're too modest.'

'Come on, Phyl…'

'So then you had second thoughts. All the nobility in your soul, was suddenly dispersed…' She giggled. 'I know how it happens.'

'We don't have pension arrangements, we don't want to go on here for-ever and ever. Just the first fifty thousand would see us all right.'

Phyl shook her head. 'If we take that, might as well have the lot.'

'I won't argue.'

'But you'd have to work at Rustrock for a year?'

'Some of the time.'

'You'd hate it.' She de-snuggled herself, got up. 'You must give it a go. If you don't, darling, you'll always regret it. I know you. And there is no real

problem. With that salary we can pay two people to do your work here…
or as much of it as you will delegate' She cleared away the glasses. 'I'll look
after the shop on Saturdays. You might even bear the luxury of a minicab.
  'But it's a lovely bike ride.'
  'Yes, especially in the rain.'

Next morning when he came in from his jog the bacon was cold and over-
cooked. Phyllis looked unaccustomedly bleak.
  'It's in all the papers.'
  'But the will hasn't been published yet.'
  'Look!' She held up the *Guardian*. 'All holier than thou, as usual.'
  'How do you know it's in the others?'
  'It was on the radio. I don't like to think of you with that old woman.'
  Dean laughed. 'She wasn't that old then. Do you want to know how it
happened? There was nothing obscene about it. It was the most natural
thing in the world. I lost my virginity. That's all.'
  'You didn't love her then?'
  'I don't think she was loveable.' He gave Phyllis a hug, a lingering smile,
then got on his bike. 'Next year I may have a chauffeur.'
  'But no peaked cap.' She shouted after him, then waved till he turned a
corner. They were still in love, a fact their children found curious.
  When Dean returned that evening from Loamfield, Phyllis asked if he
had made up his mind. He had. But he didn't expect to be the outright
winner. That would be Abel Farmer. 'The point is to get the money and
buy an annuity, or whatever. Then we won't be a drag on the kids. I certainly don't want to run Ardbuckle's'
  'Were the press on to you?'
  'Only the local. I'm not news for the nationals. None of the reporters
there yesterday noticed me. And that's a good thing…'
  'So long as you don't feel snubbed… I'll get us a lovely supper. You go
and sit in the garden. Have a drink.'

He reminded her he didn't drink alone. 'I'll wait for you. See what needs doing out there.' But he couldn't concentrate. He could think only of Blanche.

· 27 ·

Butch Klute, whose baptismal name was Donald, emerged from his second storey hidey-hole where, according to Dickie, he spent whole days devouring statistics from *Wisden,* of which he owned a complete set. It was nearly ten o'clock. Was it the day Lorna came or wasn't it? Had Dickie returned from Greece, or was she in Dorset? He couldn't remember but, if it was one of Lorna's days, she might have laid his breakfast.

It was. She had. A smell of coffee pervaded the room. That was good, except that Lorna was staring, lips pursed, giving him her old-fashioned look. He bade her good morning and became engrossed in his perfectly cut grapefruit, at the same time as tuning into Classic FM. He knew that would deter Lorna from talking to him, stop her from airing whatever grievance lay behind the look. A movement from a Mozart symphony was followed by the pizzicato piece from *Sylvia,* which gave way to a Schubert impromptu and then part of a rousing Rossini overture. By which time he had finished the grapefruit, eaten the freshly made wholemeal toast and drunk his coffee, leaving only half of the now soggy shredded wheat for the trash can. Why did she never learn that he preferred corn flakes? He took his umbrella, waddled gently out of the house, down the steps, onto the pavement, turned left and headed for Lord's where, however often rain stopped play, he proposed to spend the entire day. On a seat in front of the pavilion he would probably be joined by Jeff, Jonty, Jumbo and, among others, both Alec and Alan Fishguard (A.J.A and A.J.B., in the good old amateur days). From time to time they would retire through the

Long Room to the bar. Butch could think of no more agreeable way of passing a day once he was on schedule with his endless task, of adapting epics for Radio 3. He was permitted to work from home, although he had a room at Broadcasting House, 'for the look of the thing'. At present, when not at Lord's, he was adapting *Orlando Furioso*.

Butch settled into his favourite seat, three rows up from the gate through which the players came and went, and soon satisfied himself, from the supine way in which bowlers and batsmen were behaving, that there would be nothing to warrant undue attention for some while. He found these uneventful spells soothing at the beginning of a day. Then Jumbo joined him.

'How's your lady, then?'

Butch frowned. They didn't usually enquire after one another's wives.

'What? She's in splendid shape,'

Jumbo looked surprised. 'Glad to hear it.'

Silently they watched an over or two; the score did not progress.

'Not too put out by those headlines, then?' Asked Jumbo.

'Who?'

Jumbo, embarrassed, coughed. 'Your good lady.'

'Should she be?

'Say no more.' Either Butch had not seen the papers or he didn't wish to talk about it. Pretty cool, though.

Butch idly watched the six-foot-four giant return to the bowling mark, about a quarter-of-a-mile away, before running at least eighteen paces and hurling the ball at high speed in the direction of the batsman who, unmoved and unmoving, watched it pass him.

'Sensible to leave that one alone,' commented Butch. Jumbo grunted, privately exploring the possible alternative of the batsman leaping out of his crease and clouting the ball to the boundary – as they once had... in the old days. Butch, as the giant began another unproductive run-up, said ruminatively, 'Dickie get a good review, then?'

Jumbo forced a hearty bellow. 'You always had a good sense a-yumour.'

'Don't get the joke. Anyhow, her book's not coming out till the autumn.'

They lapsed into further silence. Then Jumbo trotted off, leaving his *Daily Telegraph* on the seat. A batsman was bowled and made his way, disconsolately, towards the pavilion. Members clapped politely as he approached them. Butch, sensing the embarrassment of the man, looked away as he passed. In so doing his eyes fell on a headline in the *Telegraph*.

DEAD BOOKSELLER'S AMOURS
MALE AND FEMALE LOVERS

Even the *Telegraph*, he thought sadly, had become vulgar. Then he noticed the name, Dickie Klute. So that was what Jumbo had been on about. He became aware of louder applause. The new batsman was already out and on his way back to the dressing room. Butch preceded him up the steps and made his way quickly to the back door of the pavilion, stepping out on to unconsecrated territory. From the bar Jumbo saw him walking briskly towards the main gates and thought, 'Dear old chap. I should never have mentioned it. What a thing to happen.'

When Butch reached home, Dickie was on the phone. So she was not in the Dodecanese or Dorset. (Now he came to think of it he faintly recalled seeing her the previous evening.) She was saying, 'I really have nothing to add. It all seems very trivial to me. I don't actually wish to discuss the matter. Goodbye.' She switched off her cordless. 'You're back early. It's not raining is it?'

He stared at her. Had she really slept with a woman? He knew she was a bit kinky but hadn't realised it was as bad as that. It had been a funny old marriage… so far as he could tell. It was the only one he'd had.

'Dickie, old dear, I think we must talk…'

'You've seen the papers, I suppose…' The phone rang. 'That'll be another of them. Let it ring. Or say I'm not here.'

But Butch could not let a phone ring and ring. Ignoring the cordless, which never worked for him, he picked up an instrument on the hall table. 'Hello. Daily which? No, I'm afraid she's not available for interview. No. I'm sorry. I don't know. I am not anyone of importance... sorry... goodbye...'

'Well done, Butch. You could have said you were a passing hermaphrodite.'

'Dickie, that's very offensive.'

'Now Butch you mustn't be upset about this. It'll be good publicity for the book and, anyway, it's the sort of thing that everyone's up to nowadays.'

'Not at Lord's.'

'Wait till you have women members.'

Butch paled at the thought. 'Why did you sleep with her, Dickie?'

'Copy. A writer has to experience everything.'

'Oh? Who have you murdered?'

Dickie laughed, and caught a monocle as it fell. 'That's not relevant to my work. No one gets murdered in my books, as you would know if you ever bothered to read one.'

'I hate reading about myself.'

'Why don't you go back to Lord's? The sun's shining. And I've told Lorna we're both out to lunch. I'm going to Piddletrenthide to finish my book. Don't make any statements to the media.'

When Dickie opened the front door she noticed a cameraman at the gate. 'Hell! I shall just have to face it. Good morning! 'She cried, as she walked briskly to the garage carrying her weekend case. 'Can't stop now.'

She drove off, pursued by the young man from *London Weekend* who took many shots of her side and back windows while motorists swerved to avoid him.

Butch decided against Lord's and mounted to his hidey-hole to commune with *Orlando Furioso* in which epic, in his view, people behaved rationally, normally.

· 28 ·

The media soon lost interest in the Ardbuckle story. There were no out-raged husbands, wives, paramours, mistresses, who would bite. Those who were contacted regarded the affair as rather a lark and were more exercised about the precise size of the fortune that might, one day, come their way. Butch Klute, when at last located, made such circumlocutory reference to the *Divine Comedy*, the *Lusiads*, and other lesser-known epics, that his interrogators became, at first uncomprehending, then shatteringly bored. Monty, easier to contact, was suavely evasive, taking the line that anyone of any consequence had sown wild oats, dropping names such as Edward VII and Lloyd-George, and adopting a man of the world stance. Abel could not be traced – he was said to be between branches in his helicopter – and his wife of the moment was quoted as saying his past was no concern of hers, and vice versa. Stanley could not be drawn beyond an obscure statement that, 'for every one who came out, another went in.' Dean relied on a proven formula of deterrence involving a recitation of *The Lay of the Last Minstrel*, guaranteed to drive any reporter, or phone salesman, off the blower by the sixteenth stanza. As none of the legatees was a pop star, a bishop or royalty, their news value soon waned.

So, when the five next met at Mark Ampersand's office not even Gordon Ruffle was present on the kerbside to monitor their arrival. Abel's helicopter touched down on an accommodating thin flat stretch of Common, delivering himself and Stanley. Dickie didn't rate it an Hispano Suiza occasion, and cadged a lift from a grateful fan; Monty drove in by secondhand Rover; Dean, as before, cycled to the rendezvous. Mark enquired if a decision had been reached. This was a matter of form. All of them had been in contact already to tell him that, whatever misgivings they had, they would accept the conditions of the will.

On the flight from Brighton Abel had impressed Stanley by his grasp of the situation; he had also implanted in the actor's mind suggestions about combining the carnival of books with a festival of theatre – 'You would obviously be the one to get that off the ground.' Stanley was relieved. It was long since he had done any bookselling and this put him on firmer ground. Instantly, he began to choose plays. Abel then fell silent, musing on how to lure the other three into accepting deployment into activities which would leave him in charge of the shop.

Monty saw political possibilities. The sitting member for Rustrock Spa was seventy-five. No age in politics, but he couldn't last for more than another three elections. This would give Monty time to ingratiate himself with the electorate under whatever policy seemed most opportune. Something deep down told him he was certain to win the Ardbuckle jackpot. Then the seat would follow and he would probably become Minister for the Arts. The future had to be rosy.

Dickie, inevitably, saw copy in the situation. Butch – if it became essential to stick with him – had not yet been placed in a commercial context. She envisaged him in sub-Maxwellian machinations that would send him floundering into agonising depths of false impropriety from which he would emerge, as always, a shining example of the triumph of soiled rectitude. Or just being at Ardbuckle's might provide a wholly new character. After all, it was at Ardbuckle's that she had met Butch.

Dean was looking solely for a pension substitute, of modest dimensions, but also regarded the inheritance as so bizarre an intrusion into his life that he could take it or leave it.

Only Abel was living on a razor's edge. He had to find fresh backing, within days, for his beleagured chain. There had to be a way of persuading Ampersand to find a formula for buying out the other four, using Ardbuckle finance. Lawyers, he believed, could always bend matters when the money was there. If the others were offered a quarter of a million immediately they would surely take it?

But it soon became clear to Abel that there were fresh obstacles.

Ampersand delayed asking each of them to sign their formal agreement to the will, while telling them that a sixth party, a certain Reverend Hugh Mattingson, had come into the picture. Mark explained that Hugh was the only person, apart from the company secretary, Jawarharlal Deolali, whom Blanche had trusted. 'He's been with the company for a long while, twenty years or more. Only a general factotum named Watkins has lasted longer.'

'I know Watkins,' said all five, in unison.

'Then perhaps one of you can give me his private address. Miss Ardbuckle left him her second best bench.'

All of them found this a riot. Ampersand was rather put out. 'I'm serious.'

Abel, amused but tense, said, 'I know Hugh Mattingson. He wears fancy dress and was once a witty letter writer to the trade press. I thought he must have left Ardbuckle's.'

'He is very much still there. He's general manager. I thought I'd mentioned him previously,' said Mark. 'He believes he should be a legatee.'

Abel asked why.

'Because, so he claims, he was Miss Ardbuckle's common law wife for thirteen years.'

Some gasped, some took deep breaths. Only Dickie, who sensed a plot to be used, spoke. 'Can he substantiate the claim… I mean, legally?'

'He is challenging the will.'

Abel thought he should leave at once and search for other backing. Clearly there would be no ready cash from this source in the foreseeable future, as Ampersand confirmed when Monty asked if distribution of funds would be held up.

'So there is nothing more we can do until his appeal has been heard?'

'I think not.'

'How long have you known this?' Abel blurted out.

'Since yesterday.'

'You could have told us.'

'As we were meeting today…'

Abel gave Mark an agonising death-look he would never forget, and said, 'Tell us where we stand. Is the appeal likely to be upheld?'

Mark took time to compose an answer, thus further irritating Abel. He played with his hands, stared out of the window, glanced down at the floor, moved documents around his desk, sipped a glass of water. Finally he spoke:

'In my years in the law, lady and gentlemen, I have perceived that it is never safe to assume that the wildest action may not succeed. I don't believe Mr Mattingson has a case but I am not counsel. I must advise that you wait and see.'

'Is he approachable?' Abel enquired. 'Could we not meet him and hear his views, even perhaps…' (He became aware he was sweating and that others were watching him) '…see if we have some common ground?'

'You mean buy him off?'

'I didn't say that, Mr Devereux.'

'I did.' Monty screeched.

Dean intervened to say he didn't see why it should come to that, six wasn't much more of a crowd than five. 'And it is unlikely that any of us was with Blanche for thirteen years.'

'Surely, surely,' pleaded Dickie, 'we have to know more about this man. I think I just remember him in my day… didn't he start off in Art? Doesn't anyone remember?'

No one did. And Dickie was wrong. She and Hugh had not overlapped.

Abel said ominously, 'From all my legal knowledge, and I admit I am not qualified, I don't believe he can stop settlement of the will at this stage…'

'That could be, Mr Farmer, but I don't quite understand the urgency.'

Mark outstared Abel. 'And I cannot think of beginning to authorise payments from the estate at this moment, excepting what is needed to keep the business trading.'

'I understand. Will you excuse me?' Abel walked quickly from the room, forgetting his obligation to fly Stanley back to Brighton for his matinee.

'That young man has financial problems,' said Monty with a screech.

Mark said he would take counsel's advice but not until he returned from his vacation. 'I will be in touch with you all within a month.'

Stanley realised he had lost his lift. 'I'm on in two hours,' he wailed.

'I'll give you a lift,' Monty offered, 'if I can have a ticket for your show.'

'How kind. It's Saturday, but I doubt if we're quite sold out.'

'Better be off. Tell me, which pier is it?'

'It's the Theatre Royal! Do you mind?'

It was too late for them all to sign agreement to the will. Mark proposed it should be held over until the next meeting. His holiday beckoned.

· 29 ·

In Mark Ampersand's absence it was necessary for Ardbuckle's to continue normal trading, so Hugh Mattingson was confirmed as general manager with authority to sign cheques, countersigned by book-keeper, Jawarharlal Deolali. This undoubtedly enhanced his status but it did not compensate for the wrong Blanche had done him. Mattingsons were not for spurning.

'So there's some sort of hold-up,' noted Terence Absolom (Poetry) to John Ogglethorpe (Fiction & General), in the staff room where his lordship was taking mid-morning cranberry juice as a gesture towards dieting. 'What I heard,' said Alick Tremlett, (number two, Science & Technology), 'is that grand Sir Hugh is being difficult.'

'That's because he's not a beneficiary of the will,' John told him.

'I wonder why she never fancied me,' Alick, a handsome six footer, reflected ruefully, and John, devoted to his Jane, wondered if he were the only male at Ardbuckle's, apart from the gays, who had not been attracted to Blanche.

Lord Absolom did not deign to consider the matter of why Blanche had not invited Alick to share her bed but Kim Mahon (Sport) offered her opinion that it was because he was too much of a tough guy. Alick, flattered, did not demur but observed, 'Now we know there is another side to the lady, did she never make a pass at you, Kim?'

'I don't sleep with geriatrics. I have a Humbert-Humbert complex.' She bellowed with mirth and choked over her cigarette. Kim, who hailed from the Aran Isles, was overweight, short-sighted, ran her department through a nicotine fog and had never in her life kicked, batted, bowled, thrown, handled or netted a ball, a weight, a disc, or a tiddleywink. She had never been to Lord's, Wembley, Wimbledon, Twickenham, St Andrew's, or any venue staging the Olympics, but she had lived vicariously, every great sporting event of the past two hundred years, by virtue of books, radio and Sky TV. She had not actually read through any of the books which she sold in impressive numbers, but she knew the names of the authors, she knew the titles of their books and their subject matter, and she indiscriminately recommended everything, with overpowering enthusiasm. When anyone complained she replied, disarmingly, 'Didn't you like it, my love? Never mind. Swap it for something else. I know the very person who is just waiting for this one.'

'I heard another rumour,' John Ogglethorpe informed them. 'some long lost daughter of Blanche has turned up. That awful reporter chap told me.'

'What he told me,' replied Alick, 'was that she's Sir Hugh's daughter as well. Could all go back to that great day after the carnival. You were here then, Terry. Remember? When I came it was one of the first stories I was told. By Maurice Watkins, I think. The other one was about dreadful old Framley who actually chained the new recruits to the post table until they handed over protection money. The folklore was very vivid then. I'm not sure it didn't include an occasional crucifixion. Those were the days.'

· 30 ·

By the time of his third Rustrock Book Carnival, Hugh Mattingson had become the acknowledged star draw, bringing increased trade to the legitimate dealers and attracting paragraphs in national newspapers. He soon ousted Henry as manager; he also rid himself of his 'priestess'. Half-Acre Meadow, under his direction, became a philosophical and theological book fair in tandem with the original antiquarian event. So far as the Christian religion went it was broadly non-evangelical. Catholics and high Anglicans were welcome but encouraged to wear rich vestments. 'Bring all your up-market church camp,' Hugh entreated them, 'let your stall be a tribute to pageantry, but you must stick to books. I won't have any relics. Absolutely no bones or shrouds. And no statues of the Virgin, or any of those chocolate box illustrations from old Bibles.'

Given such strictures the orthodox preferred to be represented in the longstanding antiquarian division, although the Catholic Truth Trust maintained a vigil in Half-Acre Meadow, beneath a green bay tree. Gradually, more and more eastern faiths came to take stalls on the main site. In stature, and international prestige, the fair-cum-carnival became a major event in the book world calendar.

For many years, following the departure of the 'priestess', Blanche, who was not short of admirers, deliberately kept Hugh at a distance, so valuing his contribution to the prosperity of the company that she didn't wish to risk losing him should he be found wanting in bed. He continued to entertain her by expressing outrageous views, also by pretending concern for her immortal soul, insisting that he would lead her to salvation on an avalanche of hilarity. Inevitably, they grew closer, until at the conclusion of a spectacularly successful carnival, Hugh stretched the meaning of religion to include a Bacchanalian orgy on the Common on the final evening. He, of course, played Bacchus, and was enthroned on an ox-cart laden with grapes on the vine. As the revelries drew to a climax, he announced,

'We will pay homage to the monarch of the carnival. Lead us to Ardbuckle Towers!', meaning Ridge End, which he had already acquired from the Duke and leased to Blanche.

The young people attending upon Hugh, including some in Tarzan outfits, dragged the cart up the steep bank to the house where Blanche was lying on the balcony of her bedroom enjoying the balmy evening and considering, not for the first time, how she was to contrive to buy this idyllic residence from her manager. She was also rejoicing in the provisional takings for the carnival which had been shown to her an hour before, sent in a sealed envelope by Jawarharlal Deolali. The noble-nosed, handsome, tall Hindu accountant from East Africa, had ordered his heavily subjugated wife of several decades to deliver them. She, although nominally European, was enjoying none of the privileges for which feminists had campaigned on her behalf. 'Go wife,' said Jawarharlal, to the mother of his two emancipated sons, and of his three rumblingly rebellious daughters, 'give her this message. Do not unseal the envelope. You will not be able to read it, anyway, without your glasses… give them to me… and do not trip as you climb. Now, go, please.'

This message had been safely delivered by a terrified free citizen of the European community some while before Hugh placed a long ladder against the balcony leading to Blanche's bedchamber. He ascended with the agility of a superannuated teenager, clasping a libation of champagne, which slurped over the side of a golden cornucopia. In his silver grey beard, grown especially for the carnival, he resembled an Old Testament prophet. With imperious skill he coped with both ladder and horn of plenty.

Blanche called out, 'Mind the wistaria!'

'It isn't in flower, great lady. I will make it flower for you.'

'What are you, a horticultural Canute? It will do so anyhow; it has two flowering seasons. Neither of which is scheduled for tonight, you absurd man.'

It was not possible to deflate Hugh. 'Great Queen of Literature,' he cried, 'I come to you', and, into the word 'come', he introduced whole syllables of double-entendre. This was a night of conquest. He had been abstinent for too long and he felt certain of his prey.

Blanche, on this still, warm evening, when everything in her particular garden was blooming, when her particular business was booming into what, in her journal, she called, 'the persistent promptings of nature', considered how she had never lain with a religious man, though she did not think of Hugh as essentially holy. He was a showbizz priest, something out of *Carmina Burana*, or a play by Shaw.

She welcomed Hugh onto the terrace, accepted his garland of grapes, waved him towards a chaise longue.

'Think of me,' he declared, 'as Dionysius of the Spa.'

'I think of you as some kind of debauched cardinal.'

He chortled. 'It's all the same, Gracious Madam, Countess, High Priestess, Duchess, Goddess… Titania, Isis, Osiris…'

'Surely Osiris was a man?'

'You are all things to all people…'

'How common!'

'…I have brought you offerings beyond the divine products of the grape. I have brought you my most newly conceived work.'

From beneath his billowing robe, coloured in alternate folds of chocolate brown and French blue, he drew a book, on the cover of which embedded scarlet lettering, against a clerical grey background, spelt out the title – *The Alternative Ten Commandments*, or, *Making Your Last Supper Last*.

She giggled and said, 'I think you may have gone too far.'

'That is the whole purpose of life.'

From below, at the foot of the ladder, there came sounds of cheering.

'Our public,' said Hugh, and led Blanche to the balustrade to acknowledge the applause. He made the sign of the cross, then bellowed, in his resonant bass, 'On such a night as this, God cried, "Stand up for bastards!"'

The crowd roared approval. Hugh and Blanche beamed down upon it, graciously saluting. What more could be done to extend the magic into the small hours on this ecstatic night? Hugh called for silence. 'GO – ODD.' He roared. 'GO – ODD is LO – OVE – ove...' He swept Blanche into his arms and carried her, triumphantly, to the bedchamber.

'You're sacked,' sang out Blanche as Hugh gently lowered her onto the outsize bed.

'No,' he replied, 'it is I who will sack you.'

The relationship endured for some years, during which Hugh remained too important to the business to be dismissed. Blanche resented, but understood, this. One evening when he was preening himself in her presence, she said, 'Don't think you are invulnerable, Hugh Mattingson.'

'Madam,' he replied, 'I am the owner of your house but,' he added, rubbing an index finger gently around her right ear, 'you shall have a new lease of Ridge End.'

That wasn't good enough, and why couldn't he remember that it was her left ear she liked having stroked? 'I can afford,' she asserted, 'to pay one thousand times the present rent. And how dare you, my employee, dictate terms to me!'

'Lovely lady,' he replied, tickling her, 'there are terms and terms.'

She pushed him aside. 'I want nothing less than the freehold.'

He grasped her body. 'It is not for sale.'

She again rejected him. 'Then I shall dismiss you.'

'If you do, I shan't renew your lease.'

'I have squatter's rights.'

'Not by the terms of our lease, honey bee.'

'Stop pinching me. It hurts.'

'As does your indifference... sweet child.'

Blanche gave his erection a karate swipe. He howled. She squeezed his crotch and said, 'OK, you're my landlord, I'm your moll. Now let's have coffee and go to the shop.'

He rolled extravagantly about the bed, nursing his member, yelping, 'I am dying, Egypt, dying.'

'Reincarnation may help. And another thing, don't be so damned literary.' She went to the shower.

The relationship continued for some while, which was why Hugh was so piqued at not being named, as one of her preferred lovers, in Blanche's will. It was not the money; he was already a rich man in his own right. It was, as John Ogglethorpe and Terence Absolom had surmised, Hugh's sexual amour-propre that was wounded. When his rejection from Blanche's bed occurred he sought comfort elsewhere but he believed she had simply become too old for the game. Yet, during all those years when she was his mistress, she had led him to suppose he had been her favourite man. Stirrings of revenge arose in him....

· 31 ·

Following the second meeting in Ampersand's office Abel, having forgotten his commitment to Stanley, flew his helicopter to the City of London, relishing the grim irony of being within grasp of a fortune whilst knowing that the Official Receiver was awaiting a call to protect his creditors.

Abel was chief executive of a company with sixty outlets in southern England. His venture had quickly taken wing, bankers had backed him enthusiastically, greedily, believing in this young man's clout. But he hadn't done quite as well as they had forecast so, with a recession biting, they were rectifying their mistakes. Abel had over-traded, lavishly filling his shops with thousands of slow-moving, and even non-moving, titles, believing they created a literary ambience which would be paid for by the swiftly turned-over bestselling cookery, gardening, and DIY titles. His buyers, though, had not judged correctly and publishers were demanding prompt payment not only for shelves of unsold back-list, but also for bestsellers.

Abel's destination was a discreet mock-Georgian terrace in an alley not far from the Mansion House, the Bank of England and the Royal Exchange. In John Stow Lane was the European headquarters of a private bank whose expertise in the manoeuvrability of both funds and man-power had outwitted the Nazis, the Bolsheviks and even the Swiss. The bank had not obliged Abel when he first approached it. Then he had been seeking a six figure sum; now he needed at least seven. This gave him con-fidence. 'They' were such financial snobs about lending so-called small sums. If only 'they' could be persuaded that his was a long term project, founded on vision.

In John Stow Lane Abel encountered his old school chum, Harry Watts who, that very afternoon, was toying with the problem of having too much under-employed capital. Who could be trusted with a vast loan? He listened to Abel.

'I know it has to work, Hal, because it's already working in the places where I've opened. Sixty of them, all across the country! They're doing well but I'm stretched for capital. And those sods round the corner who backed me are threatening to foreclose. Just at the very moment when I'm about to break through. I've spent thousands on a new stock-control sys-tem which is being introduced into every branch. It will cut out so much wastage. I'm on the brink of something even bigger and better than Waterstone's... why doesn't the City show more acumen?'

Harry Watts looked calmly at Abel, endeavouring to ascertain if he had what it takes, in City terms... a quality indefinable, unanalysable, not to be detected by bar-coding, carbon dating, hormone relating, blood group counting, genetic grading, brain scanning, body scanning, or even urine testing. He looked unwaveringly at Abel for all of fifteen seconds... and he decided.

That settled, Abel relaxed and began to tell Harry about the Ardbuckle situation but his friend was not in the mood for small talk. 'I have some calls to make. Come to the Jamaica Wine Bar at six. That's when I unwind for my version of the happy hour. Hang around. In a bit, my secretary will bring you papers to sign.' He shook Abel's hand, pleased to encounter a firm grip, then was suddenly immersed in talking and listening to several cordless phones at the same moment.

At the Jamaica Wine Bar Harry allowed himself ten minutes complete relaxation before gently taking a sip of the one large Bourbon on the rocks he permitted himself before returning to the office for the evening stint. He paid total attention thereafter to Abel's story of the Ardbuckle will and Hugh Mattingson.

'…then there's this stylish old bird of a novelist, Dickie Klute, who just laughs off having slept with Blanche, on the grounds that she must give her characters verisimilitude… I've heard it called a lot of things, for God's sake… and this real prat of a politician who makes you understand why democracy just doesn't work, although we all have to pretend that it does…'

Harry thought, is he a compulsive talker, or is it just the excitement of getting backing? Have I made a mistake?

'…and there's a wonderful old poofter of an actor who just hasn't made stardom… he still could if the right part came along on the box but at present he's touring in *Private Lives*… it's all a wonderful charade and I don't doubt that when the moment comes, I do not doubt it at all, Hal, I'll get the Ardbuckle loot, even though I have Hugh Mattingson to contend with…'

By then Harry was feeling so relaxed by his one Bourbon and the burr of Abel's pleasant speaking voice, that he had momentarily ceased to pay attention but his vibes trembled when he heard mention of Hugh. Abel broke off, fearful of boring his backer. 'I talk too much.'

Harry was reassured. No compulsive talker ever admitted that.

'Abe, you need to have this guy on your side. Cherish him.' Then, he added playfully, 'so how come you were so high in the ratings for this lady? I remember you as a randy old sod but I didn't realise you were world class.'

'I suppose I just flattered her vanity.'

'C'mon, mate.'

'It's a very strange experience to lay your boss so soon after handing over your P45.'

'Did it happen under the counter, behind the Bible showcase or in the shop window?

'No way. She was incredibly discreet. I was invited to visit her at home. Not invited. Commanded! When I told my colleagues – I'd been there all of two weeks – they guffawed. They knew what it meant. If Miss Ardbuckle invited you to Ridge End, her mini-mansion at the top of the Common – which actually belongs to Hugh Mattingson, but that's another story – well, it wasn't to discuss business. If you were a virgin when you arrived, you wouldn't be by the time you left. I had become one of the few and favoured. So I was subjected to much badinage because, from experience, my workmates knew my days were already numbered. La Belle Dame wasn't entirely lacking in mercy but there was more than a touch of Jezebel in her behaviour. "Start applying for jobs now," was what one of them advised me.'

'And did you?'

'I lasted one month.'

'So what happened?' Harry had a quarter of his Bourbon to finish.

'I was young, Hal. And she wasn't my first conquest. I was married to my second wife at the time and had no problems sexually. But I was ambitious to get my ideas across… about modernisation of bookshops, and hers in particular…'

'You must have been a great lover.'

'Piss off.'

That's good, thought Harry, that's how you should talk to backers.

'So, in between having it off… and she liked to talk as well… she wasn't a nympho or just prick crazy… I was able to put my suggestions… introducing credit cards, refitting, holding author events, signings, parties, poetry readings, all the things we now take for granted…'

'And you gave her a good fuck in between suggestions?'

'Not each one.'

'And she didn't listen, or didn't want to know?'

'It got me nowhere. In the middle of the night, well just before dawn, she clapped her hand and said, "Now you must be off. On the shop floor I shall ignore you unless I have occasion to rebuke you. Don't expect any increase in your wages." She gave me a quick peck, and added, "I've enjoyed it, I think you've got something." Whether what I had was business acumen or sexual prowess I was left to think about. That is, until now, when I am one of five legatees who may become a billionaire, thanks to her. And it's going to be me because I'm not the losing sort…'

Harry coughed discreetly, satirically, raising amused eyebrows…

'…Given adequate capital, I know, I know.'

'I believe you, Abe, but don't overlook Hugh Mattingson. You may need him. Come to my office tomorrow for the cheque.'

'Thanks, Hal. Have another?'

'One is my rule. Do you have a rule?'

'Yes, I never eat on a full stomach.'

· 32 ·

Having settled the immediate fortunes of his company, Abel determined to bring matters to a conclusion at Rustrock Spa. Harry was right. He must get Hugh on his side. As he stepped into the jacuzzi it came to him. The jacuzzi was of even greater inspiration to him, he believed, than the steam bath had been to his forebears

Abel called Hugh. 'I don't know,' he began, in a jocular way, 'what you have to say about all this sub judice lark but wouldn't it clear the air if we had a talk?'

'My dear fellow,' responded Hugh, 'forgive me, but I can't quite place you, or what it is that is sub judice.'

'I find it difficult, Mr Mattingson, to believe that you don't know that I am one of the five legatees named in Blanche Ardbuckle's will. Even if you don't read the papers it must have got around amongst your staff. And I did work at the shop back in the seventies, when you were already running the carnival.'

'One meets so many people but now that you mention it I did see your name in the *Mail*.'

'And I am aware, Mr Mattingson, that you are contesting the will.'

Hugh trumpeted a great guffaw, which was unpleasant for Abel. 'I'm sure it is quite improper for me to be speaking to you.'

'But kicking over the traces is not exactly alien to your nature?'

'I could hardly quarrel with that assessment.'

'So how about lunch?'

'I'd be delighted.'

'Would that place at Bray, near the river, be convenient?'

'Bray-ay?'

'You don't know it?'

'I am a simple country bookseller, Mr Farmer. Bray-ay sounds like something five star.'

'It is.'

'We have a quite excellent little trattoria here in Rustrock… I don't like to be away from Ardbuckle's for more than a long local lunch. It's important to keep my eye on everything that is happening in the store. Forgive the Americanism. It does not seem inappropriate for so large an emporium…'

'What's the name of the restaurant?'

'It is the Trattoria della Brocciolacchio.' Hugh sang out the words, swinging the base of the phone in his right hand, like a censer.

'I know it. It's in *The Good Food Guide*'

'I use it because it's in *Michelin*. I never eat anywhere that's not in *Michelin*.'

'Tomorrow, twelve forty-five suit you?'

'*Impossible*' Hugh pronounced it in French. He then pronounced it in Italian. 'Not on,' he said in English. 'I have to be in London to see my lawyer.'

'So who will mind the shop, Mr Mattingson?'

'The accountant wallah. Jawarharlal Deolali. He is utterly reliable, he never slept with Blanche.'

'Could you lunch with me at my club?'

Hugh believed he could.

When they met next day at Kemble's, a building almost as overpowering and rusticated as a Renaissance Florentine palace, and situated in an alley in Covent Garden, Hugh was dressed in a Romany outfit with a tasselled night cap that drew envious glances from actor members of the club. He greeted Abel ecstatically when they met at the top of a steep flight of dangerously broken steps, and handed him a copy of his book, *The Giggle Factor in Genesis*. 'My dear sir, do let me draw your attention to what Melvyn Bragg was kind enough to say about it.'

Abel, thrown by his guest's appearance, told him there was a club rule which did not permit 'papers' being studied on the premises, thanked him for the book and shook his hand. He would read the book with great interest later.

'But, my dear sir, I am not trying to sell it to you.'

Abel could not face taking this 'gypsy' to the bar and, after that, into the august dining room, so he pretended he had been unable to book a table. 'But I've got one at au Mange-Tout, across the road.'

At au Mange-Tout, where food was twice as expensive as at Kemble's, and the wine four times the price, Abel tried to assess his guest. He was hampered by Hugh's scarcely concealed fury at being denied entrance, in his magnificent costume, to the Kemble's inner sanctum. He sublimated this in a show of noisy eccentricity, first talking loudly about his work on *Genesis*, then demanding dishes beyond the artifice of the international chefs employed in the kitchen.

'What I would really relish,' Hugh advised the maître d'hôtel, when waiter after waiter had retired in confusion, 'is just a simple, gently battered, baby otter, prepared in the Vale of Evesham style. Is that too much to ask?'

The maître d'hôtel lamented, histrionically. 'If only the gentleman had given us advance warning. Then nothing would have been too difficult.'

'How unsophisticated this once great city has become.'

'I think this may be the close season for otter hunting.' Abel suggested.

'I'm so passionate for it that I would accept it even out of a tin. Never mind.' Hugh sat back, bowed his head and seemed about to pray. Then he looked up pleadingly at the waiter and asked, in a subdued voice, 'would it be possible to request a very lightly boiled egg, with a mottled, deep brown shell? NOT FREE RANGE! I should like it served with pain rustique spread with Normandy butter from the Evreux region. And, perhaps, as an indulgence, because I am so impressed at what I notice on other people's plates, I will have it accompanied by just a single radish. That will be more than adequate.'

The order was accepted without demur. Abel offered his guest a drink. Hugh inclined his head slightly, seemed to be about to protest total abstinence, then said, 'For medicinal reasons, I am quite unable to digest food unless it is served with vintage Bollinger which, I am told, extraordinary as it may seem, is not available on the National Health.'

'I don't think this is an NHS restaurant,' observed Abel, a tart remark which drove Hugh out of his huff at not being at Kemble's. He changed his mind about the boiled egg and said he would settle for steak au poivre washed down with Gevrey Chambertin. They exchanged banter about whether the sweet should follow the cheese, or vice versa, and agreed to differ. By the time Hughie, as he had become, was devouring a massive portion of Stilton drenched in port, the two men had begun to savour each other's characteristics.

'So when, mon ami,' enquired Hugh, 'did you enjoy the lady's favours, if I may put it so brazenly?'

'I cannot give the precise date but… about late '75.'

'Ah! After Monty Devereux but before Lord ffloppy de Prycke?'

'Hughie! You made that one up.'

'That's what they called him in the staff room.'

'To his face?'

'My dear Abe, to his prick!'

'I don't believe you.'

'It's a good line. I say, this *is* a splendid lunch.' Hugh made a show of savouring his port. Abel took the hint and summoned the waiter to bring more, then they reminisced about Blanche, each exaggerating his own moments of triumph, and Hugh relating how he came to buy Ridge End from the Duke of Bidborough.

'She'd had her eye on it for some while but couldn't induce His Grace to part with it. This irritated her. She was used to getting her own way, as you know. There she was owning the most enormous chunk of Rustrock yet she couldn't get her hands on one of the best houses overlooking the Common. *The* best as far as she was concerned. That's when she set her cap at the Duke but he wasn't having any. I forget what his particular vice was… something to do with game birds, which was what made it so difficult for him… and that's why he was so depressed and frustrated. He called her a whore, on her own shop floor, even though he was already bankrupt. That's when I stepped in. I paid his debts, bought Ridge End, on condition I didn't sell it to her… *Sell*, note, not let… My dear boy, it's very stuffy in here. Shall we walk down to the river?'

Abel would have liked to amble but Hugh set the pace. Traffic lights and motor car horns were nothing to him. Out of breath, Abel joined him on the Embankment, below Charing Cross. Hugh was standing, militarily erect, revelling in the scene. Abel felt sure he was about to declaim Wordsworth. Instead he bellowed, 'I am basically riparian. I suppose that could be attributed to the fact that I was born beside a millstream. During my Christian period I always referred to myself as Jordanian.'

'And to what have you been converetd?'

'Mainstream humanism. That's why I gave up running the carnival for Blanche. I'd had my fun with theological treatises… that one I gave you is a reprint. They still sell amazingly. They've made me a small fortune but once my belief had gone, I couldn't write another. It would have seemed insincere. So I turned to property. Really I did His Grace a good turn. The poor old bugger bought an annuity with what I'd paid him and toddled off to Provence, or somewhere. Died last year. Oh, I've come a long way since I played that butler… I told you about that?'

Abel, though not incurious, said firmly that he had.

'I was never much of an actor.'

'Hughie, you never stop being one.'

'It's much easier off stage. Anyhow, the lease of Ridge End has some months to run. Must be worth something to the estate?'

'You know the estate doesn't need it.'

'Don't get ratty, dear boy… it was a splendid lunch.'

'Hughie,' said Abel, still just sober enough to know his judgment might be impaired, 'I have a proposition which I think may appeal to you…'

They sat on a bench for a while. Hugh listened attentively. 'I'll sleep on it,' he said, finally. 'Why don't you put it to the other legatees and call a meeting to which, if you choose, you could invite me.' Then he rose, as though the matter were already decided and declared in a thunderous voice, 'I am a riparian! I am, quite simply, Old Father Thames.' He adopted a magnificent stance, his head profiled against the river, and held it for what seemed to Abel an eternity.

A passer-by said to her companion, 'Whose statue is that then, Freda?'

Hugh then terrified both ladies by moving abruptly. He bestowed the most genial of smiles upon them and, swiftly producing a book from his pocket, said, 'Please accept, dear ladies, my treatise on...' his voice sank to a sexy throb... '*Genesis*.'

Freda's companion drew her away. 'Don't take it, dear, he's a religious nut case. It may explode. He looks a bit Irish.'

'How roight y'are,' cried Hugh. 'I am an IRA riparian devil incarnate.'

The ladies hurried away. Hugh turned to Abel, feeling sobered, 'I should tell you, dear boy, reverting to Ardbuckle's, I've had the most interesting suggestion made to me for a signing session. From a publisher. Let's sit over there, beneath dear old Shell Mex House, if that's what it still is, and I'll tell you about it.'

· 33 ·

As soon as Mark Ampersand returned from holiday Abel phoned to ask when he would be calling a meeting to sort out the problem of Hugh Mattingson. He told Mark most of what had already passed between him and Hugh, omitting the idea for a signing session which he was thinking of filching for his own chain. Ampersand complained mildly that he was only just returned from his vacation. He had a mountain of work awaiting attention. Abel was insistent that the meeting should have priority.

'Very well, I'll get in touch with them all as soon as I have a moment.'

Abel asked if he might have permission to call the meeting, 'But I will say it is on your authority? It will relieve the pressure on you a bit. Which days are you free?' Mark, knowing that there had to be a meeting, accepted the suggestion.

'Ideally,' said Dean, when Abel phoned him, 'we should sit at a hexagonal table so that no one is seen to be in the chair. But I'm quite happy for you to conduct the meeting.'

'Not better to draw lots?'

'That has a sinister quality. No, you preside. Now, before you ring off, just how much rein do you think we should give Hugh Mattingson?'

'We're not obliged to give him any rein, we just need to agree terms with him, to buy him off, as it were.'

Dean winced and Abel felt his distaste when he said, 'We'll play it by ear… no need for unpleasantness… I hope,' adding, on a firmer note, 'I'm glad you've taken the initiative, Abel. None of us wants this situation to continue indefinitely. If I had made proper pension arrangements I would have refused the legacy in the first place but Phyl and I talked it over, and it does seem sensible to accept the initial offer. I have no ambitions for the jackpot, though. That's yours.'

No problem there, Abel told himself. If only Dean were younger he'd give him a branch to manage. Now he must tackle Monty.

The hyena laugh was followed by, 'Now don't get me wrong, old chap but who's supposed to be in charge of this meeting?'

'None of us is allowed to be in charge, Monty, by the terms of the will, but it's necessary to implement some action. And Ampersand has called the meeting. I'm just helping him out because he's busy, and we ought to get on with it. Please don't imagine that I'm making a power bid.'

'Good God, no!' bellowed Monty.

'We have to keep things moving. It's essential if the business is not to suffer.'

'I do agree, Abel. But one doesn't want to be shoved around.'

'Who's shoving you around? Do you think I am?'

'I didn't say that.'

'But do you?'

'My dear Abel, of course not.'

'So what are we arguing about? Will Tuesday the 20th be convenient for you, in the board room at Ardbuckle's?'

There was silence while Monty riffled through his diary where there were numerous virgin pages. 'Yes, yes. I believe I can make it. Where is the board room?'

'In that old penthouse where she used to live. Before she moved to Ridge End.'

'My God!'

Abel guessed the reference. 'Is that where she taught you the facts of life?'

'I wasn't exactly a teenager at the time.' He chortled at the memory, his chortle being a strangulated version of his screech. 'As a matter of fact, Abel, I tried to teach her some facts of life about managing staff. I was always pretty progressive, you know? I wanted her to start a pension scheme, give senior staff shares. She wouldn't have any of it. That's when she lost interest. And do you know that all the time that I was, well *seeing* her, as you might say, she didn't raise my miserable wage by so much as a penny?'

'That fits. Now you've got another chance. If you get the jackpot.'

'Not much likelihood I'll get that. But, Abel, we'll make it a clean fight, eh? No dirty stuff?'

'I promise you, Monty, I'll polish my daggers every day, until they're gleaming.'

'Shake on it, so to speak.' Monty wished he had eyeball contact. He wasn't sure where he stood with Abel. When he spoke he asked, 'Do you think we can trust that actor chappie?'

'I don't think we should discuss our fellow directors. We're all in a curiously invidious situation. We wouldn't be human if we didn't wish to win but we must bear in mind *the needs of the business.*' That was good electioneering talk; if only this idiot, Monty, would get himself a safe seat it would divert his attention from Ardbuckle's.

Monty determined to stay close to Abel. 'I shall propose you take charge of the meeting,' he said.

'Before you say another word,' yelled Dickie, having registered it was Abel on the line, 'I have to thank you, darling, for having such a lovely girl running your Wimborne branch. She wanted to know about my next book, and promised me a big display. And a signing! You just don't know what this means to an author. At the moment I've got a block but her atttitude really will help me.'

'Reputation counts for a lot,' countered Abel, mentally flattened by this outburst. 'I wanted to get in before bloody Waterstone's got you on their circuit. You're quite a name, you know?'

'Darling, am I really?'

'Don't be so modest.'

Dickie sighed, but with utter contentment. 'Well, you see, we just scribble away in the dark, and our royalties aren't paid for absolutely months after they've been earned, it's terribly…'

Abel joined in '…lonely being a writer.'

'Now don't spoil it.'

'I think the lighthouse keeper approach to creativity is a bit played out, Dickie. Booksellers, publishers, writers, we're all in the same game together... Signing sessions, author tours, chat shows, gossip columns... if we, meaning you, as well as me, don't get involved in the whole razzmatazz the books just don't move off the shelves. Simple as that.'

Dickie felt marginalised... but only marginally.

'Now what I was really phoning about, Dickie, was this meeting with the Mattingson man.'

'Remind me, darling, who is he? Is it important?'

'He's the one who is making the counter claim to Blanche's will.'

'*That* man!' (If only she could remember why he was so crucial.)

'We have to persuade him to give up his claim to the will. I have had this idea...'

'Explain it in very simple language. I am not a business woman.'

When Abel had finished she said, 'But it can't be essential I should be there. I am deeply into a book, on the brink of breaking a terrible hang-up.'

'I'm afraid it is, indeed, essential. You remember the wording of the will? We all have to agree.'

'Couldn't I have a ... you know?... a poxey-doxey?'

'A proxy? No. Unless you want to lose sight of all that loot you really must come. We must be a team.'

'You're rather a bully. And yet when you came on the blower I couldn't have been thinking sweeter thoughts about you.'

'I'll make up for it when we meet again.'

'One thing you can do for me... tell me how it was between you and Blanche. For the sake of my work...'

'I suppose there may be something gained by going public before the media invents its own story.'

'I've just had the most exciting news,' said Stanley when Abel rang him. 'Do you watch *A Wink or a Nod?*'

'No, what is it?'

'An upmarket soap about life in an auction house. But it is on BBC-1, just before the news. Randolph Pottersby, who plays the eccentric senior partner, has had a stroke. He'll be out for some weeks. They've asked me to audition for it. It's urgent because they film only three weeks before screening, to keep it topical.

'That's great, but you must come Stan, to meet this Mattingson man. We must all be present because we may need to apply the veto. We have to stand up to him. He was an actor, too, before he became some sort of clergyman, not to mention a compulsive show-off, to boot.'

'I think I once played with him.'

'We need a bit of star quality to quell him.'

Stanley would love to have thought he had star quality; well, if Abel believed so. 'You really feel I have that?'

'Of course.'

'OK, I'll come. Remind me about this Hugh? I think we did *The Importance* together. I put it like that. Nowadays we have to be team spirited. He, in fact, was only the butler but I treated him as an equal off-stage.'

· 34 ·

'Before I even think of withdrawing my objections to the will, I ought to know something more about these people who propose to extend my terms of engagement, of whom, I am told, you are one. I hope you are prepared to be thoroughly indiscreet.'

Hugh and Abel were in the saloon bar of the Duke's Head. It was where the former reckoned he had the best chance of being overheard by someone who would spread his words on the local grapevine, though latterly, he was aware, some of the citizens of Rustrock were becoming impervious to his exhibitionism. It just showed how public taste was deteriorating. Memory of the splendid meal Abel had provided were fading fast; Hugh was not certain as yet how he would deal with Abel, while Abel was concerned that the proposals he had put to Hugh after lunch at au Mange-Tout had not borne fruit.

As Hugh moved to the bar to buy the other man a drink Abel noted that he was clad in an exquisitely pressed I Zingari blazer and tie, straw hat to match, and immaculate white flannels. The youngest descendant of the original Rustrock Spa idiot, who understood nothing which was not closely related to the game of cricket, instantly recognising Hugh's outfit, could scarcely believe his luck. At the bar he confronted Hugh and demanded an autograph. Happy to oblige Hugh was less pleased when the idiot followed him back to his table in the alcove, chanting statistics, learned by heart from *Wisden,* with all the singleminded piety of a medieval monk. He only succeeded in ridding the alcove of the idiot's presence by threatening to pour champagne over his autograph book. Having seen the poor deranged creature off, he presented Abel with a bottle of Moët et Chandon.

'I may not,' cried Hugh, 'be a legatee but I feel myself to be an inheritor.'

He released the cork which skimmed over Abel's scalp and crashed into an "18thC" warming pan, all of five years old, hanging from the low-beamed ceiling which, when the inn was erected, had been several inches higher. Abel asked himself what Hugh meant by declaring himself 'an inheritor.' It was unnerving for the pace-forcing, chain-bookselling legatee who was intending to dominate the market against all opposition. He endeavoured to pull himself together, sipped the champagne very slowly, then began to talk, also very slowly. Wine did not usually affect him so swiftly. Perhaps he should have eaten. Or was it a result of the break-up of his third marriage? He told himself to watch it. And also to watch Hugh. Harry Watts had been right. 'I can assure you. Hughie... the staff will eat out of your hands. They have correctly judged the situation, and they are all delighted by the rumour of your appointment. They feel safe with you; they *know* you.'

Hugh pushed aside his glass. 'My policy has always been to play one off against another. I'm a great carrot dangler.'

'Shall we have this corked up? You don't seem to be drinking and I've had enough.'

'I can't stand fizzy drinks,' declared Hugh. 'They make me burp.'

'I love your originality. One vintage tomato juice, please, for Sir Hugh. And don't spare the Worcester sauce.'

'I think I can get along with you, my dear Abel.'

'And I with you... Hughie.'

'Suppose you win, and I think you are certain to, would there be a place for me in your set-up?'

'Your advice would be invaluable.'

Abel reckoned he could deal with that situation when the time came. In any case he might well need him. In the adjoining alcove the inevitably present Gordon Ruffle made notes, observed by a raven-haired young woman, in backpacking gear, who was sipping coke. Their eyes met when Gordon closed his notebook and glanced up. She threw him a slow, confident smile and said, 'You a wrider?'

'Yeah. You a Yank?'

'Sure. You know this burgh?'

Gordon was mesmerised by her probing, dark eyes, her smooth, deep-coloured skin. Most Americans, he told himself, were mongrels. 'Yep,' he said, 'I know this burgh intimately. I was born here. I'm on the local papers. I'm a features editor,' he lied. 'What brings you here?'

'I've bin in Israel, Idaly, Parr-ee… working in bookstores. When I got off the ferry at Noohaven, a guy gave me a lift.' She rose, walked over to Gordon. Her anorak and jeans did little for her lithe young body but Gordon noted the slim hips.

'Why did he drop you here?'

'He said he was goin' to the country. I'd get a train here for London. And I liked the name. Rustrock Spa. It's cute and it kinda rings a bell. I dunno why.'

Gordon felt himself seriously smitten. 'Where will you stay?'

'A youth hostel? You got one of those? I don't have a lot of cash. My purse got pinched on the boat. But I got my air ticket and my Visa card which I keep in my pants. Say, we haven't introduced ourselves. I'm Margitte Einstein.'

'I'm Gordon Ruffle.'

'Great to know you, Gordon.'

He bought her another coke, offered her his parents' spare room for the night, and said his mum would give her supper.

Mrs Ruffle, who didn't care for foreigners, offered guarded hospitality. Mr Ruffle, his wedding gear instantly aroused, was more welcoming. Over supper Margitte disarmed both parents with stories of her travels, yet Gordon's mother was relieved to hear that the young woman's flight was booked, the following evening, from Heathrow. 'I meant to spend longer here in England but I got so fascinated by Parr-ee.' Mrs Ruffle didn't like to ask where that was.

Next day Gordon insisted on lending Margitte some money, 'To see you through until your flight leaves. You can pay me back when I come to New York.' And he meant it.

· 35 ·

Some staff at Ardbuckle's were not pleased with the rumoured elevation of Hugh Mattingson. Fergus still thought they should demand a management buyout, and threaten to strike if it was refused, but his plans to walk out had been postponed because the company to which he was going had folded. Led by Maimie Perkes (Art), Gerda Kohl (Foreign) and Audrey Thresham (Travel), most female members of staff pledged loyalty to the memory of Blanche, and to working under Hugh. Fergus was disgusted and called them blacklegs, adding, in an aside to Alick Tremlett, 'and that's the first time anyone's referred to *their* legs.' Lord Absolom (Poetry) said striking was not part of his code of practice, which led Fergus to further observe to Alick that Britain would never have a revolution because the workers were a load of softies. Alick, ever the realist, replied that he would hardly classify Lord A as one of the workers, adding, 'anyhow, I can't afford to strike. I have three mouths to feed.'

'Do you suppose,' asked Daniel Drybrough (Paperbacks), during second coffee, 'that if Sir Hugh becomes managing director we shall all have to wear fancy dress?' Mona Darling (Children's & Young People), recalled a fancy dress party to which, as a girl, she had gone attired as the Ugly Duckling. No one commented. Dan said, 'It was easy for me. I always went as a pirate.' That also caused embarrassment because no one ever mentioned his black patch. He laughed. 'I've always worn it. My mum was marvellous. She used to say, "If you're a bit more soiled than some of the others, why should it matter?"' Dan beamed from his good eye and they all felt better. Adrian Thomson (History) replied, 'I can't understand the fuss about Hugh. He's effectively been manager for years. Ever since she stopped coming in every day.'

'Ever since he was banned from her bed,' remarked John Ogglethorpe.

Mona Darling hurriedly finished her coffee and left. It was time to return to the rational, decent world of children's fantasies. Even the disreputable

William Brown was preferable to the company of her colleagues. Kim Mahon (Sport), blowing a final cloud of smoke before stubbing her cigarette commented, 'Perhaps we could petition Sir Hugh for segregated staff rooms. Or would a barracks be more suitable for the gentlemen?'

John apologised for upsetting her sensitivities; Daniel said, 'Some of us might opt for a mixed non-smoker.'

· 36 ·

On their way to Ardbuckle's, Stanley Brooke-Forster and Dickie Klute met at the railway station, then shared a cab. They became gridlocked into a traffic jam caused, quite simply, by the fact that about two hundred too many cars were bent on parking in the inadequate space provided by the municipality. In the twenty minutes it took to get them flowing again towards the outskirts of the town from which they had come, Stanley and Dickie found themselves tête-à-tête, even coeur-à-coeur.

'Dear Stanley,' said Dickie, who was surprisingly philosophical about such situations, 'I must ask you this. I know, as an artiste, that you are aware of the paramount significance of verisimilitude...' She narrowed her eyes to look at him with penetrating intensity through her monocles, quite his most frightening experience since, as a young actor, he had played the Messenger to a great actor's Macbeth.

'It is my starting point,' he replied, not being one hundred per cent certain of the meaning of her last word, also wondering whether she had ever thought of wearing pince-nez; there was something downright peculiar about two monocles.

'Good. So you will not mind my asking, even though I find it embarrassing, did you, dear Stanley, do it for the sake of your art? I mean you are... you... er... came out recently, did you not?'

Stanley allowed himself an old maidish trill. 'I wasn't being presented to Her Majesty.'

'No, no, darling, I mean with Blanche when…' she kept her voice very low because of the cab driver… 'you slept with her.'

He gave one of his more convincing stage laughs. 'I was very, very fond of Blanche.'

'Weren't we all? But, in my case, I did it for my art. I'm not at all that way inclined, even with a husband like Butch. And I must confess I was hoping that sleeping with her might also help me to a managerial position because my books weren't earning me anything then… and I was also very interested in staff welfare.'

'That wouldn't have won you any Brownie points with Blanche.' He hoped this might change the subject. He did not wish to discuss the intimacies of the bed chamber with Dickie. Blanche had roused him by asking his opinion of famous actor queers such as Noel and Ivor, and it had worked.

'Did she sack you?'

Stanley again felt relief. 'Yes, I lost her a lot of lolly. It was hilarious.' This was not what she wished to know but she'd better go along with it. 'What on earth did you do? '

'I persuaded her that it would be of great advantage to the carnival – you know, the secondhand book spree she holds every year – it was in its infancy then – if she presented a pageant about Rustrock Spa, as a background feature. I put this to her one time, when… how shall I put it?'

'You were in bed.'

'What a splendid feed you are. I do admire your timing. Did you ever think of the stage?'

'Never. Stick to the point. You were in bed.'

'That's right. And it wasn't half bad.' He beamed with recollected ecstasy. It was Ivor that night.

'So why did you come out?'

'Fashions change. And I've always been… er… ambiguous.'

She would have to choose a fresh approach. She had this hang-up concerning Butch and her bisexual protagonist and it was essential to the plot that he should sleep with an heiress. She must know what Stanley had experienced when he slept with Blanche. She couldn't quite believe in this character she had part created, but she'd almost got him. 'What happened to the pageant then?'

'I went over budget. Also it rained. It poured! Every single day of the carnival. And the dealers and their customers were only interested in finding bargains. They didn't want sideshows. We were no sort of incentive.'

'Thank Christ for that!' shouted the driver, and slammed his foot down, throwing Dickie and Stanley against the dividing panel. 'Sorry, lady, sorry, sir.' The traffic had magically disappeared. Soon they were at Ardbuckle's where they were shown to the board room. Although they were late, others were later.

'So,' Dickie returned to her theme. 'How do you think Blanche regarded you while you were together?'

The damned woman was at it again, 'We didn't discuss th… ah… parameters,' he said, loftily. Then he changed the subject. 'Dickie, have you never thought of wearing pince-nez?'

'Certainly not. I'd look absurd. Now, Stanley, I am a professional writer. I have to know about people. I need to know about you and Blanche. You will tell me won't you.' She removed both monocles and programmed her seductive look.

Stanley was aghast. Was there no stopping her? 'The Sundays haven't been on to you, have they?'

'I would never sell my story to them.'

'Every man has his price. I wonder what they'd pay?'

He was saved by the arrival of Mark and Abel, followed shortly after, by Monty and Dean. At the end of the meeting he planned to give Dickie the slip.

· 37 ·

The room designated for the use of the board which, despite the fevered protests of Jawarharlal Deolali, never met during Blanche's lifetime, except in the imagination of her financial advisers, had been the lady's boudoir before she moved to Ridge End. On the dais where the great bed had stood was a throne of medieval design. On the floor below it stood a hexagonal table.

'I think,' said Abel, proudly, 'that it will be difficult for any of us to claim we have precedence seated here. Friends,' he smilingly addressed them, 'before we proceed there is an important item of business. Mr Ampersand reminds me that we have not yet formally agreed acceptance of the will, so the fifteen-month probationary period has not begun.'

They meekly accepted his authority, and agreed.

'So where does Mr Mattingson sit when he joins us?' asked Dickie, Mark Ampersand having taken the sixth place at table.

'Could he not,' suggested Dean Phillips, a twinkle observable in his eyes, 'be enthroned, looking down upon us? Presumably there is some reason for placing that historic piece there.' He felt totally relaxed now that he had opted – or so he thought – out of the race for the jackpot.

'It's symbolic.' Dickie giggled. 'It's where her bed used to stand.'

'Perhaps it is where the Chair should be.'

Mark rose, climbed slowly to the dais and lowered himself, a figure of dignity, onto the throne, secretly enjoying the nonsense of the occasion because, *they* did not know that, thanks to an inheritance beyond Blanche's control, he was not going to be part of the law for much longer.

'Attend the Lords of France and Burgundy!' Stanley declaimed that line, which lay so often at the top of his consciousness. Only Dickie recognised the quotation, although Dean found it faintly familiar. The others looked surprised, apart from Mark. He was ready for anything from this lot. He called upon Abel.

'Although the five of us are equal in authority, and none of us may be chief executive or managing director, by the terms of Blanche Ardbuckle's will, I think there can be no objection to our being, as it were, Leader of the Opposition, but in strict rotation.'

'Oh, very witty,' hyenaed Monty. Stanley subdued him with A Look.

'Are you agreed?' enquired Mark from his throne.

'Am I permitted to enquire if we are?' Abel was determined to ridicule the protocol, as the swiftest means of disposing of it.

'Should we take a vote?' asked Stanley.

'What, on whether or not he is allowed to ask if we are in agreement?'

Dickie was entering into the spirit of the occasion. Monty intervened to say he was in favour of a secret ballot.

'We have only one scrutineer,' Abel objected.

Stanley said impatiently, 'Chairperson, Mister, Missus, Mooz, Whatever! *Who*ever! I must be in London at three to meet the cast of *A Wink or a Nod*. I've taken over from poor Randy Pottersby.'

'Then shall we begin?' Abel assumed command before anyone could object. 'You will recall that, at the last meeting, we were thrown into some confusion when we learned that the general manager, who styles himself the Reverend Hugh Mattingson, claimed that he was entitled to benefit from the will because he had been Blanche's common law wife for many years.' He looked at them sternly, in the way he had learned in his brief career as a naval officer. 'I have to tell you that he will withdraw his submission if certain conditions are met...'

They regarded Abel solemnly. There was not so much as a squeak, even from Monty.

'...Hugh Mattingson is, and has been, effectively, for the last several years, manager of Ardbuckle's, although dear Blanche, typically, never appointed him as such, in writing. You may be surprised to learn that, until we gave him our temporary backing at the last meeting, he had no job specification.' They relaxed and laughed. 'Yet his longevity of service is unrivalled, except by Maurice Watkins whose carriage clock, or whatever, is due any day.

'It is possible that Mr Mattingson's length of service may be due to the fact that he was also Blanche's landlord, as well as her employee. An unusual coupling. But,' he dared, 'we are used to those.'

Dickie wondered if she should explain that one to Stanley.

'The terms of the will preclude any of us from having authority over the others…'

'You're not doing badly,' Monty pointed out.

'Would you care to take over? I'm perfectly willing…'

'No, no, please.'

'I would remind you, Mr Devereux, that Stanley is anxious to get away. I'll go on. There is nothing, I believe, which prevents us from appointing someone outside our group as managing director, or chief executive…'

'Why should we wish to?' Stanley was baffled. 'I'm just a simple actor man. I don't understand these subtleties of business… it's rather like Pinter… but surely that would cost a lot?'

'It's the price we have to pay for getting him to drop his claim. He is by no means certain he can win it but it could delay the proving of the will for months. Even for years. During that time the business would be greatly harmed. *And*, we should not receive one penny of our inheritance.'

Stanley thanked Abel and looked downcast at the prospect of being deprived of his lovely loot.

'Also,' Abel continued, 'it will be of benefit to us all to have someone running the place who is already familiar with the business. Mr Mattingson is sufficently aware that his chances of winning the claim are slim, and he's prepared to settle for a certain fifty K.'

'How much?' Dickie was flabbergasted.

'Who is to pay him that?' asked Monty.

'We are. Who else?'

Monty saw his perks disperse before his eyes. 'There must be another way.'

'You do not have to accept the proposal I have made. I have a successful business of my own to run. I'm not dependent on Ardbuckle's…'

Dean allowed himself a slight frown. Every publishers' rep to whom he had spoken recently had told him Farmer's was up the spout. But he decided not to rock the boat.

'No, no,' cried Monty. 'Don't misunderstand me. I'm sure we are all deeply indebted to you for what you have done.'

'Hear, hear,' from Dickie. 'Someone must decide whatever the will says.'

Ampersand looked pained on behalf of the law. Stanley wasn't quite sure how much fifty K was worth.

Abel remained calm. 'I do not believe I have done or said anything that is against the spirit of the will. I am laying before you a plan. It is for you to accept or reject it.'

Stanley asked precisely how much it would cost each of them.

'I was going to suggest five thou a head from your annual salary. That would double Mattingson's present remuneration, part of which is derived from the property. He not only manages the shop but collects rents from half the buildings in Rustrock. And it is those rents which will pay our handouts. The bookshop makes very little.'

Stanley was happy with that. He was expecting thirty grand – was K the same? – but twenty-five would be more than he had ever earned except for one vintage year. Anyhow, he had landed this plum character part in the soap and he was not a greedy man. Dickie wasn't listening. Her protagonist, still stuck somewhere between Butch and Stanley, was not shaping-up. Only Monty demurred. 'Does he really need to earn so much?'

Dickie came to, and suggested a vote.

'The terms of the will forbid it. We must be unanimous.' The others regarded Monty with varying degrees of hostility.'

'I agree! I agree! I just wanted to make the point.'

Abel could not resist mimicking Monty's screech. He blushed. 'I do apologise. To revert to business. The crucial reason for having Hugh as managing director is that there's nothing to prevent *him* from taking majority decisions. But – influenced by us.'

Monty thought this a clever move and shrieked in support.

Dean said it could be dangerous.

'Not really, as long as he recognises that we should help him to decisions. If he fails to, we can dismiss him. But the strictures of the will don't apply to him…'

Mark gave Abel an admiring look. So did Dean.

'Approved,' said Abel, 'by spontaneous expression. I'll call Hugh.'

The Reverend gentleman had decided on monkish attire. He entered wearing a rich habit of gleamingly brushed brown cloth, with an orange girdle. The cowl lay on his back revealing a plaid lining. He wore open sandals but no socks. On each finger he had placed, inappropriately, a topaz ring. He swept in, smiling broadly, bowed to the legatees, and to Mark Ampersand, then took the empty chair, watched in amazed silence by Dickie who found herself totally overcome.

'I have read so much about you all,' declaimed Hugh. 'It is delightful to meet you at last offically.'

'But you surely know Mr Farmer?' Dean was a stickler for truth.

'Only unofficially.'

They laughed, then were silent. Dickie was bowled over by this man. He had to be Butch's successor. Abel nodded at Hugh.

'I believe I know why I have been summoned here.'

Dickie recovered, chirruped, removed one monocle and beamed at him. 'And I think we know too, Mr Mattingson, but why don't you tell us? Then I'll know if we are right.'

Abel wondered why she had become soppy and resumed authority.

'We know that Stanley Brooke-Forster has an urgent meeting in London, so may I speed things up by formally proposing that Hugh Mattingson, at present general manager of Ardbuckle's, be appointed managing director for one year and three months at an annual salary of £50,000.'

All were in favour, with Monty seconding.

'Do you accept, Mr Mattingson?' Dickie removed the other monocle.

'Ma'am, I do. Let's hope it will be a happy marriage.' He gave his girdle a whirl. Dickie hoped so too, but she was thinking of a different liaison.

Abel continued,' May I suggest we ask Mr Ampersand to draw up a simple service agreement and also propose that, during the fifteen months ahead, we conduct ourselves as being subject to Hugh's authority when we are in the presence of staff?'

'But not,' roared Hugh, approvingly, 'in the privacy of this ex-bedchamber, eh?' There were grunts of approval.

'Hugh,' enquired Dickie, moving around him admiringly, 'why are you dressed as a monk? Is it your usual shop uniform?' She touched his arm experimentally. She liked the feel of him. She squeezed his wrist. He let it go limp and replied, 'Dear Lady, no. I have a different costume for every day of the year. I am the saviour of the rag trade. I thought this appropriate for today because it is the anniversary of the death – by hanging and quartering – of Saint Elderby, the martyred Jesuit whose secret hideout, until he was sprung was, at Rustrock Hall. I am not RC; I am not even Christian anymore, but I like to observe historical anniversaries. It brings colour to life. It can also be good for trade.'

'Now, as you have all consented to be my directorial colleagues may I suggest we make dates for individual meetings so we can get to know one another? But first, should not the occasion be celebrated in a glass of something?' He opened his habit and revealed a bottle neatly held in the lining. 'This is brewed by the monks at Beaverbury Abbey. It is 80 per cent.'

'I hope,' Dickie gurgled, feeling already thirty years younger, 'that you will go on as you've begun.' She whispered to Stanley, 'Isn't he gorgeous? I wonder if I should come to work dressed as a vestal virgin?'

· 38 ·

After the meeting had ended, Dickie floated out from the room, feeling transparent, translucent, transmogrified… she would decide which later. She did not care how she might appear to others; she was out of this world, yet on top of it. She was ethereal but also three dimensional. She was to receive fifty-thousand now, and an income of twenty-five thousand for the next fifteen months. It far outstripped any literary prize. And no gnawing pains to endure between publication of the short list and the award dinner.

She found herself outside a minicab office. Why not? Dorset wasn't that far off. Anyhow, money no longer mattered. The hire car firm was delighted and promised a car within minutes. Once installed in the back of the saloon Dickie concentrated her thoughts on this new man in her life. She felt herself on the verge of liberation from Butch. Then she thought the inspiration might be a fusion of Stanley and Hugh, because there was no way in which Hugh could be anything but flamboyantly heterosexual. She immersed herself in 'her people', as she liked to call them, muttering their thoughts, laughing, sighing, groaning, weeping, with them, experiencing one emotion after another. It was exhausting but all in low key, all inaudibly expressed, all extravagantly mimed, until she became aware that the driver was watching her in his mirror. By then she had emitted a burst of manic laughter, and he was wondering what sort of lunatic he was transporting. He saw the old bat relapse into the upholstery, a contented smile spreading over her face as her monocles dropped to her breasts.

As she lay back Dickie believed she had found a solution. She began to feel these two, Hugh and Stanley, with their different personalities, as her own creation. She recalled, when she had slept with Blanche, how she brought on an orgasm by imagining she was Horatio Nelson, as portrayed by Laurence Olivier and, later, Blanche had confessed she had come by invoking Robin Hood, alias Errol Flynn. Possibly, her bisexual hero, whilst lying with the heiress, would see himself as Michelangelo and have balls as heavy as chunks of Carrara marble.

Dickie vented a cry of total submission. Christ, thought the cab driver, I hope she's not soiling my upholstery. His property was, in fact, unblemished. Dickie had instantly transferred her thoughts to how she should conduct herself, as a director, at Ardbuckle's. She would not go to the shop every day. She did not wish to over-expose herself. There should be an element of mystery surrounding her – after all, she was a short-listed Booker novelist. She had forgotten that not all bookshop assistants automatically adore all authors....

She decided that, when at Ardbuckle's, she would have a weekly surgery, such as politicians had, when the staff could come to her with their problems. That's how they would get to know her. That way she might win the jackpot, although it seemed unlikely. She sighed extravagantly. What she needed was not a husband but a companion, a friend ever ready to be at her side. Her thoughts turned again to Hugh Mattingson. He was powerful stuff. Could she really fuse his image with Stanley's and come up with something of her own? Perhaps she should abandon the present book and start a new one.

· 39 ·

In the second floor turret housing Philosophy & Religion, manager Jim Woodstock looked disconsolately at the notebook in which he recorded the departmental figures. Despite the publicity Ardbuckle's had received from the media, takings were not good. This affected his lifestyle, not because he received commission on sales – no one received commission – but because poor trade made it unwise to intercept the flow of cash from his till to Jawarharlal Deolali's accounts office. Woodstock, bald-headed,

middle-aged, attired like the manager of a minor branch of a major clearing bank, was wont to sort away one hundred pounds a week from his
takings – 'not a penny more, not a penny less', as he boasted to his partner. He was an ardent salesman with a willingness to pretend to any religious belief, or philosophical doctrine, if it boosted sales. Now takings
were so lean it seemed inadvisable to remove even so little as a tenner a
week. If this went on he would require social security. He enquired of
Mona Darling (Children's & Young Adults), 'How are you doing?'

'It's a little quiet,' she replied guardedly. Mona avoided explicit statements with the skill of a politician. She had confided only with Blanche.
She did not trust Hugh. How could she when he dressed in so bizarre a
fashion? Once he had burst in on a children's party she was holding wearing a Babar the Elephant costume. It had wholly distracted attention from
the worthy historical novel, set in the time of Hrotha, a tenth-century
swineherd, which she was promoting. The anthropomorphic element in
children's literature had gone too far. She was so outraged that she
became willing to think even Peter Rabbit as ripe for the pot.

Jim remarked to Mona, 'I hear the reason Sir Hugh's been placed in
charge is because the five legatees, as they call themselves, have to make
unanimous decisions, but he is not bound by this ruling.'

'I don't know. I keep myself to myself.'

'Your stairs was filthy this morning,' announced Nell Pickett, trailing
her grimy mop.' I suppose it's 'aving all those kids up and down.'

Mona glared at Nell and sighed. It was well known that the cleaning
lady's methods were not conducive to the removal of dirt. Once, a sympathetic departmental manager watching the old girl (Nell had always
been old, even older than her hat) bent double, dragging a plague-ridden
rag across the line of his territory, had cried, 'It's disgraceful you don't
have a mop, Nell. I'll get you one tomorrow.'

She had replied angrily, 'I don't want no mop. Filthy things. No good to
me they're not.' And she had continued to wield her rag, making smears

which, in the course of time, came to form a not unattractive pattern on the ancient linoleum.

Jim Woodstock wondered for whom Nell might vote, at the end of the fifteen months, because she would certainly qualify, and thought it likely that marking an X was probably the limit of her literacy.

· 40 ·

From early in his career Stanley Brooke-Forster had proved to have a temperament suited to his calling. He was an optimist, not a worrier. Every post, every telephone call, every visit to his agent's office was a possible prelude to a long and lucrative engagement. If it were not, then the next would be. In 'the profession' you did not necessarily begin at the bottom with a walk-on, then work up to stardom. You might have your name in lights at twenty-one but be playing one-liners at forty. And sometimes you had to earn a temporary living away from the boards. Survival was all but, when the call came, whatever you might be doing to make ends meet, you must be disloyal to the employer of the moment, blow him a kiss of thanks, then be on your way to the next touring date, film set or broadcasting studio. There were no pensions, no redundancy payments, no paid holidays or paternity leaves. You were on your own, with Equity in the background. That was how it was when he left RADA, in the early fifties, how it was today, how it would ever be. Old timers told him he was lucky. When they had embarked on their careers radio was only just beginning, the cinema was still silent, there was no telly, no commercials, no fees for repeats. So many had fallen by the wayside. But it was the same for Stanley's generation. He could think of only three from his RADA class who were still regularly in work.

Stanley was not without talent. He quickly became a polished pro, sufficiently sensitive to sympathetic direction to transform a small part into 'a little gem'. And it was the little gems, after the first ten years, at which he aimed. He became aware he couldn't sustain a major role unless he made a copy of another actor's' performance; in little gems he could create his own.

He had 'rested' very little. He wasn't bankrupt or in debt but he had no savings and didn't own a house, flat or car. He had been through a dismal marriage, fathered a child and had relationships with men and women. But he was getting old, and competition for parts was fiercer than ever, so the Ardbuckle windfall plus the TV soap couldn't have come at a better time. They would tide him over until the big break came; he never doubted it would.

At Ardbuckle's Stanley felt in awe of Abel, a confident being who knew his way around a strange world, and overshadowed by Dickie in whom he recognised the qualities of another 'pro', while Dean was a steady rock of a chap and Monty was a pain. He returned to Rustrock after meeting the cast of *A Wink or a Nod,* all of whom had welcomed him effusively. Meanwhile, he was determined to play to perfection the part of a bookseller. He'd done it before, he'd do it again, and he had this plan to place before his fellow directors, though first he must ascertain if the theatre where he had acted in rep still existed. This was simple. The Theatre Royal had been metamorphosed first into a bingo hall, and later a warehouse. At present its future was again uncertain because, the estate agent he consulted told him, the lessee was not paying his rent. 'Between ourselves. He's scarpered. There'll have to be a repossession. Trouble is it belonged to that Miss Ardbuckle, like half this town does – or did. So can't help you.'

Stanley took pride in being sort of part-owner of this decrepit building but did not let on to the estate agent. He booked a room at the Spread Eagle, then took a seat in the bar, keeping a wary eye open for possible company for the evening. He did not enjoy being on his own; he preferred an audience. In extremis, he was even willing to be one. The barmaid asked, off-handedly, if he knew Rustrock. 'Got an idea I've *seen* you, *some-where*,' she said, in her fashionably soppy accent.

'I once acted at the local rep.'

She didn't know what he meant. 'Reelly? Selling things?'

'My dear child! I was acting in rep, at the theatre. I wasn't selling.'

'I see.' She left him to serve another customer, bored by this faintly distinguished looking man whom she couldn't understand. Stanley doubted that the barmaid was a devoted viewer of *A Wink or a Nod*.

Monty was also in Rustrock that day. He, like Stanley, felt compelled to identify with the town. His overtures to the local Tory party had been coolly received. As he had foreseen the sitting member aimed to remain for several more Parliaments, provided his particular vices were not rumbled. Monty might have made a better impression had he opened his cheque book but that was something he dared not do.

On this visit Monty had his mind focussed on the Libdems. He admired Paddy Ashdown and thought the Tory/Labour stranglehold on the Commons needed loosening. He sauntered about the town, built on three levels with much of its heritage intact, impressed by its quiet dignity and variety. Rustrock, he found, had a symphony orchestra under a professional conductor, a municipal art gallery strong in pre-Raphaelites and Italian mannerists (its one Pontormo attracted scholars in modest numbers) and the university was widely respected for its English department. Its current head was a fashionable, iconoclastic novelist who bought all the books he wasn't given for review from Blackwell's because he detested Blanche. Monty felt an affinity with the town. If the Libdems adopted him, he was sure he could win the seat; by the time he had located their headquarters he was certain they would.

The offices were closed. On the door was a faded, typed appeal for voluntary helpers.

Although Dean Phillips had decided not to compete actively for the

Ardbuckle staff votes, neither did he intend to be a sleeping partner during the probationary period. He proposed to push for generous staff pensions and stock control and hoped he would have Abel's support, although he was aware that the other bookseller had a reputation for saturation-level stockholding and for demanding extended credit from publishers. They were in different camps and much would depend, he supposed, on the stance Hugh adopted.

Abel resisted temptation to ride roughshod over the other legatees. He despised Monty yet dared not under-estimate his abilities, although he would have been hard put to have listed them. And weren't all politicians untrustworthy? He felt confident of jollying along Dickie and Stanley, nice, naïve types and not at all greedy. They had not looked for this inheritance; they would settle for what they got and be grateful. So would Dean, but Dean was slightly worrying. He was a man of integrity which could be a dangerous quality in business. He was also the only one of the four who was an experienced bookseller. He must play his cards very openly with Dean; his motives would have to be seen to be utterly impeccable.

Publicly, Abel declared to Gordon Ruffle, when asked about the new management structure, 'We hope to bring Ardbuckle's out of the nineteenth century before we find ourselves on the threshold of the twenty-first, and preferably a few years earlier. Everything in the way of furnishings, fittings, decorations, now coloured chocolate brown or bottle green, will become sky blue or shimmering yellow. We shall transform it in the way that Hugh Mattingson brought new life to the carnival all those years ago.'

'I don't recall that being in the minutes,' commented Dickie, reading it aloud to Stanley, who replied, 'I cannot study parts *and* read minutes.'

· 41 ·

The prospect of a guaranteed fifty thousand a year commended itself to Hugh, who was about to buy a Bentley. He had agreed to drop his claim to the will but his amour-propre was still grievously harmed. How could Blanche have preferred those people – one a woman, another a gay, two of them shopkeepers and the fifth, worst of all, a politician – to him! He was no snob but it was surely necessary to maintain standards? This was Hugh talking to imaginary reporters for the sake of his ego. What bothered him was the slight inflicted by Blanche. They had regularly enjoyed wondrous times together following the night he had climbed, Romeo-style, to her balcony. On innumerable occasions they had climaxed together, after romping ecstatically around her vast bed, sometimes at night but more often on what was called Early Closing Day, a custom long since discontinued where the actual shop was concerned. But Blanche, on Wednesdays, still chose to retire to Ridge End, in the afternoon, for a light lunch, and a discussion of the state of the business, after which champagne and smoked salmon became the precursor to bed. How was it that any of these people she had named in her will could have been preferred to him? She must, he concluded, have forgotten to alter it, probably supposing herself to be the first immortal. No, that was not Blanche. It was her impetuosity. He remembered the fatal, unromantic early closing day when she had lost interest and pushed him aside. 'No more, Matty. I'm finished. I'm old.' Yet she was only seventy-five!

'Nonsense,' he had cried and leapt upon her. She had pushed him away.

'It's all over. It happens to everyone. I'm now going to slip into tranquil old age.' He tried to laugh convincingly but felt a chill which had nothing to do with the temperature. She meant it. They never slept together again, but he did not believe he had been supplanted. So how could she treat him so shabbily in her will? He was determined to discover, from the five, what had been so special about them. He would invite each of them, in turn, to Ridge End, where he had unofficially taken up residence – well, it was his house! – and wine and dine them, boasting so much of his own triumphs that they would have to respond and, in so doing, reveal details of their intimacy with Blanche.

· 42 ·

Largely on sentimental grounds Hugh's first guest was Stanley. Years before they had acted together, although Stanley had not, so far, given any sign of remembering this. Mattingson wore his actor-manager suit for the meeting, at Ridge End – morning coat, high collar, brocaded waistcoat, spats. Plus a silver knobbed cane to hand, for appropriate gestures.

Hugh's recollection of Stanley dated from a tour of *The Importance of Being Earnest* in the early fifties. Stanley was playing Algernon Moncrieff, (poorly, in Hugh's opinion); himself had the role of Lane, the butler, the one who reports on the lack of cucumbers to be had at the local market, 'even for ready money'. Hugh had already gravitated towards playing servants; he was also Stanley's understudy and, as such, longed each day for a call informing him the leading man was indisposed. Before every performance he arrived three hours early at the stage door, hoping that the doorman would say, 'You're on.' It never happened. Stanley never missed a performance but he was ever aware of the menacing presence of Hugh in the wings. The butler/understudy watched him, night after night, on the excuse that he was keeping himself au fait with Stanley's moves… 'just in case'.

Stanley was determined that Hugh would never be called upon to deputise for him, but the man acting Merriman, the other butler, was more fortunate. He was understudying John Worthing and the actor playing that role sprained an ankle. Hugh was deeply envious, a feeling which was transmuted to fury when he learned that he would have to double

Lane and Merriman because the assistant stage manager, who would normally have stepped into the latter part, was also incapacitated.

'How can I be the same butler when one works in London and the other in Bunburyshire?' complained Hugh, to the company manager.

'We'll give you a bald wig and moustachios for Merriman and you can play it cross-eyed.'

Hugh was forced to comply but the resentment showed. There was a pecking order for stage butlers. Crichton, of course, was at the apex but Lane rated higher than Merriman. For the few nights when the latter played John Worthing, Hugh gave his usual polished performance as Lane but adopted a different accent on each appearance as Merriman in the hope of unnerving the other actors. One evening, while deciding whether to be Dublin Irish or scouse, he forgot his lines and instead of announcing, as Merriman, that the dog cart had again come round, he said, 'The cucumber sandwiches are at the door, Sir.'

Stanley, as Algernon, rallied with admirable sangfroid and replied, 'Tell them to call again next week when I will have ready money.' The audience, well acquainted with the play, howled. When the curtain fell, Stanley congratulated Hugh on getting him the loudest laugh of his career.

All these years on Hugh also could laugh.

Technically, Stanley was still a rung or two up the ladder, but for how long? He prepared himself for their meeting. 'Having been born with such good taste,' he declared to Colin Bateson, his manservant and dresser, 'it's as well I have the means to live up to it.'

'Let's 'ope we don't 'ave another Black Friday, then,' replied his lugubrious servant, another resting actor who was capable of sounding his aspirates but enjoyed playing the part of an uneducated lackey. 'And which poncey outfit we puttin' on today, yer Grace?'

'Today, Bateson, you will be fabulated. We have a true artiste coming to see us, one with whom I trod the boards decades ago, one of whom you may actually have heard.'

'Wot, ole Stan-down-the-pan, as we used to call 'im when we was with the Court Players?'

'Why did you call him that?'

'E was always drying. No good at weekly rep. Couldn't keep more than one play in is 'ead at a time.'

Hugh told Bateson *The Importance* anecdote, adding, 'I don't think there will be any need for you to recall that you worked together.'

Bateson bowed himself out elaborately, recalling his Wolfit days when he had played a courtier, when he wasn't playing a messenger, or a Gentleman, or a First Citizen, or being nine-tenths of an angry mob.

Hugh offered Stanley coffee.

'Thank you, no. Tea, perhaps, if I may?'

'Earl Grey? Juniper? Camomile?'

'If you have a Mazzawattee '85?'

'I'll get the kitchen to ring through to Assam.'

Stanley felt relaxed to be with a kindred spirit. 'I must tell you, my dear fellow, I dined out on that cucumber sandwich story for years.'

'So you do remember me?'

'Yes, but you had a different name then?'

'I was young. I thought Beerbohm Macready would impress agents.'

Bateson swept in with a tray, and began serving. 'This is Colin Bateson,' said Hugh, 'He was a great hit as Caliban at Scunthorpe.'

The three men corpsed. Bateson set down the tray just in time. Hugh spilled tea over himself; Stanley slopped his on the carpet. There is nothing so riotously funny to theatre folk as a reference to Scunthorpe.

Recovered, Stanley admitted, 'In fact it's good to be away from those bookselling people, and that woman writer who's *so* inquisitive. The camaraderie of the theatre is blissfully different.' He prattled on about his first visit to the town and his subsequent employment at Ardbuckle's.

'I was going to ask you about that,' said Hugh.

Stanley's day was instantly ruined. Hugh was as nosey as that damned novelist. But he must keep calm. 'I discovered the old rep is still there, nearly opposite the bookshop, in the square. The theatre is just a shell but it could be rehabilitated. I would like to make that one of my aims as a director.'

'How very interesting. How quite stunningly fascinating.' Hugh had a rather old fashioned approach to acting sincerity. 'You know the university now has a Chair in Drama? Yes. A great thing. That's why we've enlarged the department. Now it so happens that the manager has just left. I must confess... entre nous... the turnover of staff is alarmingly high.'

'Why would that be?'

'The wages. Blanche was awfully mingy, you know.'

'But the business is worth millions.'

'That's because of the property.'

'Tell me about the drama department.' Stanley was scared the subject would return to Blanche and bed.

'I will... I do find this tea utterly disgusting... Bateson!'

'It's not a bad idea to boil the water but, as an actor, I have drunk so much cold tea.'

Bateson appeared and was duly rebuked.

'I was saying,' Hugh sat himself on an elegant conversation piece and motioned Stanley to join him. Balanced on this quaint and delicate item of craftsmanship, their noses all but touched when either leaned forward to emphasise a point. 'It would be a golden opportunity to have someone of your experience, dear Stanley, with your knowledge of theatre, to have you to supervise drama and music. Even if you can't be here all the time. Your name would count, also. Stanley Brooke-Forster, adviser to our drama department! It would look most impressive. *And*, if you get on well with the staff, *And*, if they like you, they'll pass word to their colleagues in other departments, so when it comes to voting time for the jackpot... ber-BOOM!'

'That won't be for a year or more.'

'Can't start campaigning too soon.'

'But you said the staff is always changing…'

'They only get a vote if they've completed twelve months service. Those are the ones to go for. Now, while you're here…' He gave a throaty chuckle… 'I must show you the bed chamber. I'm sure you'll have an attack of the old déjà vu.'

Stanley groaned inwardly. They were all at it, but he was forced to submit and followed Hugh upstairs where the spurned lover threw open double doors and proclaimed, 'There's the venerable old war horse.' He sat on the enormous bed under its red and gold canopy, and bounced up and down vigorously. 'I've never known a mattress like it. You must agree?'

'I'm afraid I can't remember.' Instead Stanley went into raptures about other furnishings and Hugh took the hint. So what was it, he thought irritably, about Stanley that had appealed so positively to Blanche, some quality, evidently, lacking in himself. 'Were you always gay?'

'I must have been always inclined that way, but I was also attracted to women when I was younger, especially if they learned my little secret. Which is something, dear Hugh, that you are not going to be told, although you seem so inquisitive.'

'Stanley, I am being utterly intrusive. A terrible fault of mine. It is none of my business.'

'Yet,' Stanley ruminated, plaintively, 'I have a daughter.' They were silent for a moment. 'What I would really enjoy talking about is the theatre. If we could arrange to reopen it, and run it with the university drama department, it could benefit both of us. I hate to see a theatre dark.'

Hugh changed tack, and decided to encourage Stanley's ambitions as an impresario. They would almost certainly lead to financial disaster, as they had once before, and that would benefit the grand plan he was evolving. He smiled engagingly at the actor. 'I'll introduce you to Barnum K. Wright… American, of course. He's just published an edition of Marlowe which has such prolific footnotes that, in *Tamburlaine*, the actual text disappears completely for several pages at a time. 'There is a long analysis of precisely how Tamburlaine came "to entertain divine Zenocrate" … if you get my meaning dear boy?'

Stanley did, and thought miserably, why do they all, always, come back to that?

· 43 ·

Despite failing to draw Stanley on the details of his relationship with Blanche, Hugh was happy to fall in with the actor's plans for the Rustrock Theatre Royal. He knew he would not have an easy passage running Ardbuckle's for fifteen months, so it was his intention to play it dangerously, if necessary bringing the company to the brink of disaster. The legatees would be made to pay for Blanche's renunciation of him as a lover. But, he would need allies. Dickie and Stanley seemed the most likely. Abel, clearly, intended to use him as a puppet ruler for his own ideas and, in bookselling terms, Abel was the most experienced and ambitious of his new bosses, the only one with a defined aim, which was to make Ardbuckle's part of his own group. Monty was also ambitious but wanted to use Ardbuckle's for his political career. Hugh did not trust either man but the other three should prove malleable. He would go out of his way to win their support.

Dickie had come up with proposals for an Ardbuckle's Children's Book of the Year and a local history of Rustrock. Hugh was enthusiastic about both and suggested she should announce them at the party he was proposing to throw. He would encourage Dean to concentrate on his concern for the tenants of what 'the Quaker', not inaccurately, called 'Ardbuckle's slums'. He would also foment potential differences between the two booksellers. The future promised to be diverting.

Hugh's first major happening was to be an evening reception at Ridge End to which the entire staff would be invited, along with the Mayor and councillors of Rustrock, the Editor of *The Gazette & Herald*, the Vice Chancellor and faculty of the university (even the fashionably iconoclastic novelist), prominent citizens not belonging to those categories and the media. Hugh adored organising parties and no expense was to be spared on this one. The legatees would each be allocated a room where they could meet the staff. The said legatees willingly gave their assent.

The invitations to staff were accompanied by letters stressing the importance of the occasion where there would be 'Announcements of Significant Concern to Them.' They were posted to arrive on a Monday morning and became the only topic of conversation in the staff room, and on the shop floor, for several days.

Adrian Thomson (History), one of the longer serving employees – all of four years, though his appearance suggested he might be about to sit A-levels – climbed the turret steps to his department and burst in upon his colleagues, announcing, 'I have received the Royal Command. Bow, bow, ye lower middle classes!'

'We've got them too,' said Sandra Stokes. 'Lester is terribly impressed.'

'Are you going?'

'Of course. What have we to lose but our jobs? As the axe falls the bubbly will flow. And I've always longed to see the inside of her house.'

'Me too. It's my period.' Sandra had a deferred place to read history at Leeds. Nobody knew why; none wished to risk a lengthy explanation.

Lester insisted on reading the invitation aloud. He was six feet-two, as thin as a pin man and of Jamaican origin. 'This is really something. How do they get all those little mouse bites on the card? Is it called rodentation?'

'No! Deckle-edging,' Sandra informed him. 'Where were you brought up?'

'In a back-to-back in downtown Bristol. That's why I couldn't get a place at Bayley Hole.'

'You've just got a chip on your shoulder.'
'A whole deep fry pan of them, Sandra. Sometimes the weight is unbearable.' The flashing smile he awarded her made her wonder about going to Leeds after all. 'Just listen to this, for Chrissake:

THE BOARD OF ARDBUCKLE'S LIMITED
REQUESTS THE PLEASURE OF THE COMPANY
OF

Lester Constantine Esquire

'Esquire! That's me!

AT A RECEPTION WHERE THE MEMBERS OF THE
RETAIL TEAM WILL HAVE THE OPPORTUNITY OF MEETING
THE FIVE NEWLY APPOINTED DIRECTORS AND OF TALKING
WITH THEM IN A RELAXED AND INTIMATE ENVIRONMENT…

'Which one you want to be intimate with, Sandra?' Lester read on:

CHAMPAGNE, 18.00. BUFFET SUPPER, 19.00.
CARRIAGES AT MIDNIGHT.

'Should be twenty-four hundred.'
'You didn't read the bit about the tragic demise of our late benefactor.'
'I can't see it was tragic at that age, poor old bat.'
'You're just jealous, Adrian, that she never asked you to sleep with her.'
'And how can you be so sure?'
'You said yourself you have never been to her house.'
Adrian laughed. 'Sleeping with great-grandmothers never appealed to me.

'Now what about some action! Medieval and Middle Ages hasn't been dusted for weeks.'

Lester said he hadn't wanted to disturb the patina. 'It gives the department credibility.' Sandra complained of a lack of dusters. 'Lester had to use his very own man-sized Kleenex yesterday before he could sell a set of Runciman. It was touch and go. I shall give my vote to whichever of them says we have to undergo a facelift.'

'Or the one who offers a double economy pack of tissues,' said Lester.

· **44** ·

In Art, Maimie Perkes was trying to stifle her wicked thoughts about the likelihood of actually visiting Blanche's bedchamber, by wondering aloud what she would wear to the reception, inevitably drawing fire from Roger, her bolshie assistant who suggested, 'what about going as Botticelli's Venus? I could lend you a huge cockleshell I picked up on a beach in Greece...'

'If you hadn't already told me that you are leaving quite soon, I'd demand your dismissal. Actually, I shall miss you, wretched youth. I suggest you come to the party as something out of Bosch.'

The invitation caught Amy Thresham (Travel), the other practising RC, in mid-absorption with her most recent genealogical discovery, that a great-great-great uncle, seven times removed, had been hung for stealing a sheep. She offered a quick prayer lest he be still in purgatory, and told Maimie she would attend the reception, although she had yet to decide how to vote. 'I have an open mind,' she said. 'I'm in favour of Dickie Klute.' Returning to her obsession, she said aloud, 'stealing a sheep must be an unwieldy business', a remark which nonplussed Maimie who was not privy to the inner thoughts of Amy.

'Do you have your own loom?' enquired Maimie.

'No,' replied Amy, pursuing her recklessly streaming consciousness to Maimie's further mystification, 'I shall wear my scarlet nightie.' She relapsed into silence. Of course, it was the very thing. Ankle length, short sleeves and it was emblazoned with a surrealist motif described in a mail order catalogue as, 'enigmatic'. It was shapeless by intent and Amy had noticed customers wearing similar garments during the recent heatwave. Once at the reception, she would talk about Madagascar because she was reading Dervla Murphy's account of that place. Which should get her through the evening. She had no small talk. As she approached Ridge End she would be talking to herself and would continue to air her thoughts aloud, about Madagascar, regardless of whether anyone was listening.

Lord Terence Absolom was not bothered about dress. He would attend the reception in his suit of grubby, fawn corduroy. He was especially interested in attending because he wished to embark on influencing his colleagues' voting intentions to the detriment of Monty Devereux and Abel Farmer, both of whom he found unspeakably vulgar.

John Ogglethorpe accepted the invitation in a carefree spirit and was unworried by sartorial considerations. All that mattered to him at that moment was that Jane's morning sickness meant what they had supposed. He had promised to look for work in London where, amidst the affluence of urban pollution, she wished their baby to be born.

'I just want to see where she got fucked,' said the deplorably single-minded Kevin Marden (also Fiction & General, the most junior of juniors in John Ogglethorpe's department). He had a two-one in English from an ex-poly and was talking to his neighbour Gordon Ruffle. Kevin's foremost motivation in life was to shock his parents, who numbered amongst Blanche's purely platonic admirers. Gordon had encouraged him to take a job at Ardbuckle's, 'Since you are not qualified for anything else.' A year or two hence Kevin would settle for a six figure income from derivatives, futures and other imponderables, and his mother would be quoted as saying, 'He was always a lovely boy, always a credit to us.' A little later she would take buns she had baked to his cell. On the night of the party he arrived home drunk and claimed to have lain with a girl 'On Blanche Whorebuckle's bed.' His father thumped him, stating angrily, 'That woman was a saint. What she did for literature!'

The invitations arrived in the annexe a day late. Denys (Drama & Music) was thrilled at the prospect of meeting Stanley Brooke-Forster, whose portrait was already on the wall above her desk. Lisa (Education), but also stand-in manager for Social Sciences, which was housed in the former RAF cookhouse, with psycho-analysis laid out on a vast ex-chopping table, said tartly, 'They should have held the party at this end of the tunnel, and called it an exercise in Field Sociology.'

Audrey da Costa (Mail Order) opted for a long mauve smock embossed around the breasts with lines of orange lilies. Some, unkindly, likened this garment to a petticoat. Wearing it, Audrey felt it gave her massive body freedom. She sought the approval of Amy Thresham who happened to be passing through her department. Amy, emerged momentarily from her own genealogical ruminations and replied, 'I think old Beth would approve', which was good enough for Audrey, although she could not recall, at that moment, when Amy could possibly have encountered Beth who was one of her customers in the southern hemisphere. The party garment was silk and had proved impractical for use in Audrey's so-called office, which constituted a wide passage between other offices, a leftover space for which the Edwardian architect had had no use. Audrey presided there at a long trestle table surrounded by incoming orders, a carton of cream cakes and her three cowed underlings, whose invitations to the reception she had intercepted and destroyed.

Fergus's sole object in attending the party was to consume an entire case of Moët et Chandon, or whatever might be on offer. The future of the company no longer held much interest for him unless his colleagues opted for a management buyout. He would attend wearing jeans and a tee-shirt, both spotlessly clean. He, also, was miffed that he did not feature in the will because, despite what Blanche had told Hugh, she had reverted to her former Wednesday afternoon habits when he, Fergus, had arrived at Ardbuckle's.

Audrey was not known to the bookselling public of Rustrock Spa, nor was Jawarharlal Deolali, now the company secretary, who fought valiantly to stamp out shoplifting, and to circumvent shrinkage from staff pilfering. Jawarharlal and Indira, his wife, who walked three paces behind him at all times, were much gratified at receiving their invitations. It would provide an opportunity for meeting important local citizens and members of the university faculty. Despite the watertight contract he had insisted on having from Blanche, Deolali felt nervous about the new management, with its actors and writers and such people, so he was seriously thinking of setting-up a consultancy to act for his, and his wife's, mega-throng of relatives, all of whom owned pharmacies, corner shops or minimarkets. It was appropriate, he decided, for him to attend the reception attired in formal Hindu garb, and for Indira to wear her most gorgeous peacock-blue saree.

· 45 ·

As befitted their status the Deolalis approached Ridge End in their company car. Jawarharlal would take one glass of champagne, out of politeness, and sip it, bubble by infinitesimal bubble, throughout a long evening; Indira would have one, possibly two, fruit juices. Yet trying to approach so close to the house was a mistake. The way to Ridge End was blocked by the BBC pantechnicon which had, again, descended on Rustrock Spa. News-wise it was a silly season, between test matches, and with a short lull after Wimbledon. There were rumblings from the Gulf, sporadic shootings at various trouble spots from Belfast to Beirut, but for foreign news desks it was a quiet week while, for home news editors, violent outrages had not occurred even at anti-war demonstrations. No high ranking member of Government or Opposition had been found behaving indecently in a public loo, attempting to pass an out-of-date credit card or lying under oath, although there were numerous, undetected instances of all these misdemeanours. Members of the royal family, and the aristocracy, who were enjoying clandestine romps were, for once, being discreet. There had been no earthquakes, terrorist incidents, air disasters overnight, or, so far, during the course of a singularly uneventful day. No one of note had died, absconded with pension funds or a Renoir, carried out a coup, or murdered his mistress. Tapes and phones at news agencies were silent, fax machines were experiencing catatonic depression, web sites were still in their infancy and there were rumours that a satellite had become broody and was refusing to transmit.

That was why the Beeb pantechnicon, manned by a posse of reporters, technicians and cameramen bored beyond endurance trying to photograph disguised criminals in black-glassed vehicles, had arrived at Rustrock Spa in search of a good story, as promised them by Hugh Mattingson.

The Deolalis, joined, with dignity, the crush of guests, at which juncture

Indira was compelled to stand beside, not behind, her husband. Soon after six at least one hundred and fifty guests were present – two-thirds of them staff – quaffing the bubbly. The reception area was festooned with Ardbuckle memorabilia. Photos of every member of the family who had worked in the business, including those who Blanche had ejected, rejected or otherwise suppressed, were on display. The shop and carnival were depicted at every stage of development. A rostrum had been erected at the foot of the elegant staircase, emblazoned with press cuttings, past and present.

Abel Farmer was first to arrive at the house, well in advance even of those guests who had interpreted punctuality as a command to be early. He found Hugh directing operations with military precision but willing to be interrupted.

'I'm told you are making an anouncement of special importance, Hugh?'

'That, dear sir, is true.'

'There was nothing about it on the invitation.'

'I wanted to let it be known at the last moment to make sure no one would forget. I knew you'd be on time. You see, Abel, there is great dissatisfaction among the staff. They are unsettled by all the publicity, and by the new set-up. I just want to reassure them that they have every reason for staying.'

'Do we want all of them to stay?'

'I certainly want most of them to, for the time being, anyway. Until we can engage better replacements. Business is not good. I've always thought all publicity to be good publicity but the figures don't reflect this. I'm not sure why.'

'So what are you going to tell them?'

Hugh essayed a Henry the Eighth laugh, in keeping with his costume, holding his arms akimbo. 'I want that to be a surprise, even to you.'

'I can't wait.' Abel savagely disturbed a plate of canapes.

Monty and Dean arrived. Abel enquired if they knew about the announcement. They did not. Dickie and Stanley, who turned up next, did.

'It's to be a morale booster,' said the novelist, 'nothing more than that.'

Stanley looked smug, adding, 'He has some very interesting proposals to make. I was talking to him earlier.' Abel felt some qualms that Hugh had not revealed them to him.

They were then all distracted by Amy Thresham's appearance, wearing her ankle-length scarlet nightie, her flaxen hair tied in a bulging knot partly kept in place by an enormous pair of dark glasses. She was in mid-flow about Madagascar…

'…the thorns in the trees were gigantic, sufficient to tear off an arm… Dervla Murphy had to protect her young daughter…'. She talked incessantly, though her mind was occupied with the problem of how her sheep rustling ancestor had broken the news to his wife, until Hugh mounted the rostrum to be received with a great cheer, for his costume. He was the very picture of Henry, in short tunic, slightly longer coat, with bulging shoulders, and a round, flat cap set at a rakish angle. He beamed regally upon the crushed horde of reporters with microphones, crouched on the floor below him. Television cameras began to whurr, lights flashed. Hugh not only looked like royalty, he felt and acted the role.

'My Lord,' he began, bowing at Terence, 'your Worship the Mayor, Vice Chancellor, Ladies and Gentlemen, nay, friends and colleagues, and the two categories are not mutually exclusive, I am about to make an announcement that is, I believe, of historic importance in the annals of our company. It is one such as our dear departed Blanche Ardbuckle never made in her life. I honour her memory…'

Hear-hears merged with a low grumble of dissent.

'…She developed a great bookshop, handed down to her by her father, and his father before him. She started the great carnival which enlivens the Common every summer, and where once I had my stall. She enriched

Rustrock Spa.' He held a pause commandingly. 'She enriched herself.' He held up his right hand to forestall comment. 'She did not enrich her staff.'

There were many cries of surprise, and several pained looks from the more patrician customers. Surely, this was bad taste?

Some reporters began to make notes. Gerda Kohl registered deep shock. She believed implicity in the master-servant relationship. Viewing at home, the iconoclastic novelist wished he had accepted the invitation.

'Well done,' bellowed Fergus Welch. 'Time someone said that.' The legatees maintained impassive expressions. Monty and Abel tightened their grips on the banister rail.

Hugh continued: 'The new Board, the members of which you see here, behind me...' He turned and doffed his cap at them, then replaced it at an even more rakish angle, 'The new Board proposes to change all this.'

There was enthusiastic applause.

'For the first time...' Hugh, forgetting his costume, became Churchillian... 'There will be an actual wages structure. It will compare favourably with that of every other bookselling chain in the whole United Kingdom... even with that of Mr Abel Farmer.'

Abel forced himself to smile as the cheering broke out. Above the din the voice of Fergus asked, 'Do we know what he pays?'

'I will tell you more. There will be twice yearly bonuses.' (Cheers.) 'Provided that turnover and profit warrant it.' (Jeers, but friendly ones.) 'There will be a pension fund. Commission will be paid on departmental turnover. It will be Ardbuckle's finest hour.'

'Good old 'Enery,' cried out Daniel Drybrough, who had decked himself out as Nelson for the occasion, his devoted mother having taught him not to flinch from his disabilities, but to flaunt them. He adjusted his black eye patch, used his empty glass as a telescope and said, 'I see no pay rise. Who's paying for all this?'

'The few, perhaps,' observed Lord Absolom, 'who have always been owed so much by the many.' The cameras were trained on him.

'I didn't know you were a socialist peer, Terry,' shouted Fergus.

'I am what I am,' Terence replied, smirking at the cameras.

'An existentialist peer! Kiss me, Terence.' Daniel collapsed at his feet.

Hugh called for silence. 'The money will come from greater efficiency. And effective promotions. We are a famous international company. We shall build on this reputation. We shall also become a tourist attraction…' Aware that he was losing them, he added, '…And I may become your next prime minister but one! I've learned all the patter.' They liked that. 'More seriously, I do have many ideas for improvements. One of your number – I daren't reveal who – has put to me the idea of a staff uniform.'

Gerda Kohl clapped, beside herself with approval. Now they might all have brown overalls such as she had worn in Munich. The rest roared their disapproval.

'Wait! WAIT! I knew you would react like that. I am not going to suggest those drab garments that assistants in continental bookshops favour. The proposal is much more imaginative. Indeed, it is innovative. The clothes you now wear out during the course of your duties will be replaced by others provided by the company. I envisage you all dressed as characters from fiction and drama…'

Fergus asked if he might have use of Hugh's wardrobe. Non-staff guests felt distinctly marginalised. Hugh ignored Fergus and claimed, 'It will be fun for the customers identifying who you are representing. Won't it, dear customers?' A few smiled thinly and shifted their feet.

'Not when I'm being Fagin,' shouted John Ogglethorpe, who then, like Daniel, collapsed. Jane, who was on tomato juice, called a cab.

'I leave you with that idea,' said Hugh. 'But I will not keep you from the splendid buffet-banquet laid out in the dining room. Eat your fill and, afterwards, mingle with the new directors, each of whom will be holding court – if I may so put it – in a different room. They want to get to know you, customers as well as staff. I'm sure you want to get to know them. Bon appetit.'

While the guests devoured gargantuan quantities of smoked salmon, grilled salmon, trout fillets, sea food compote, cold silverside, topside, ham, chicken breasts and legs, quiches, crostini, salads of every description, cheeses, pates, trifles, fruit tarts, fresh fruit, cheesecake, zabaglione, and countless other titbits, all washed down with vintage Burgundy, white and red, fruit juices and sparkling mineral water, Abel was observed by Hugh convening a hasty meeting of the legatees in a corner of the green sitting room.

'This is all new to me,' Abel told them. 'What about these proposals? How can we possibly afford them?'

'Well, there are the rents,' suggested Monty, emitting his screech and drawing all eyes onto their seditious looking group.

'But has he costed the operation?' Abel complained.

Dean said that he doubted anyone at Ardbuckle's knew what that meant. Stanley was sure, 'Hugh had worked it all out. We must trust him.' This comment aroused instant suspicion in the others except for Dickie, who agreed, 'He does seem to have a very good business brain.'

It was now three against two, Abel calculated, concluding that Hugh was playing the veto game, à la United Nations, but for reasons he could not at present fathom.

Monty was practical. 'We can't go back on it now. He's announced it and we'll have to play along with him.'

Dickie supported this. 'I might as well tell you all that I am going to let the staff know about my plans for a children's book prize. I've written a little paper on it. I'll give you all a copy after.' She was on top of the world. Stanley had followed Butch into the waste basket. Her new hero was a thinly disguised Hugh, a clerical rogue surpassing in iniquity all his thousands of predecessors of all denominations. Stanley confessed that Hugh had been responsive to his suggestions about reviving the local theatre in co-operation with the drama department of the university.

Abel began to get the pattern. 'So, there's a great new ball game,' he remarked. 'It looks as though supper is over. I shall go to the summer sitting room to await my interlocutors. May I have a word, Monty?'

Stanley set off for the master ballroom. He did fervently hope they would not harp on about the bed. Dickie repaired to the Blue Drawing Room, Dean to the Aquamarine Bedroom. The five legatees spent the next two hours talking and listening to changing groups of guests. What had been planned as a PR exercise to get to know staff and customers became more like the hustings as each of the five proclaimed their programmes.

Dean Phillips, at his meeting, talked only about the slum property owned by the company, and said it was more than a disgrace, it was a crime. Before anyone drew higher salaries it should first be ascertained what the cost of converting it into decent accommodation would be. 'So,' enquired Fergus, Adrian and Alick, at different moments of the evening, 'will you forego your directorial fees until this has been done?'

'Yes,' said Dean, and meant it but, circumstances, as in politics, were against him.

Abel, feeling wrong-footed by the man whom he had thought of as his ally, determined to announce his own reforms. 'There will,' he told each group that gathered to hear him, 'be total modernisation. We shall reshelve, change the interior where necessary, and permitted, open seven days a week, and all night if it seems appropriate. And we will stock every book in print if it can be turned over in twelve months. Also, we shall go on line as soon as the internet is opened. Ardbuckle's will at last enter the twentieth century.' He spoke with conviction and enthusiasm. He didn't know where the money was to come from and, at that moment, he didn't care but, if the others were into making wild promises, he was not going to be caught out. His image was in peril. Monty, briefed by him to outline the same policies, did so with less authority but felt he had made a breakthrough.

The enthusiasm, aided by the wine, was infectious. Suddenly everyone was expressing the type of starry-eyed idealism associated with New

Year's Eve. They were moving – indeed, had moved already – into a brave new world where wages would rise, living conditions improve and business boom. So they all had several more drinks, apart from the Deolalis who carefully made their way to the gate, manoeuvring over, or past, recumbent bodies, and withdrawing from the revelry.

Hours later, when the final guest had finally gone, Hugh, not entirely sober, retired to Blanche's bedchamber. Before getting onto the bed, it took him some time to cast off his royal garments. Whilst doing so he made the task more difficult by lurching involuntarily about the room. In removing his tights he fell against a wall, sprang a catch, and a drawer opened, revealing a cavity. He thrust his hand into it and pulled out several heavily bound quarto journals with handwritten entries. After a quick perusal he wisely decided to leave reading them until the morning, but he didn't replace them in the cavity. He was sober enough to register the possibility of not being able to spring the catch again.

· 46 ·

Next day, most national papers carried pictures of Hugh as Henry the Eighth. His speech got a whole minute on BBC 1, and ninety seconds on ITV. He, and others, were reported on every radio channel.

One tabloid had a banner headline reading:

MILLIONAIRE BOOKSELLER DENOUNCED AS WHORE

Another, in only slightly smaller type, proclaimed:

LOVERS HEAR FORMER MISTRESS DENIGRATED

The posh papers were slightly more restrained, and marginally more accurate. The *Guardian* gave it most space:

> The colourful figure of Hugh Matterhorn, dressed for obscure reasons as Henry VII, drew roars of approval at a lavish champagne reception in Rustrock Spa last night, when he told staff and customers of Ardbuckle's Bookshop that, under the new management their pay would be doubled, generous pension schemes would be introduced, they would all receive commission on sales, have longer paid holidays, and an overall security never enjoyed while their recently deceased employer was alive.
>
> Mattinghorn, a former actor, and author of tracts sending up the Christian religion, has been confirmed in his position of Managing Director by the five legatees of Blanche Ardbuckle's will. They earned their bequests because the deceased named them as her favourite lovers. It is rumoured that this enraged Hugh Matterhorn who thought he should have been included, having been secretly married to her.
>
> 'Who, or what, is to pay for all this?' He bellowed at his audience which included the Mayor, the MP, and most of the Weald University faculty. 'I will tell you. Ardbuckles' owns acres of this town, it is rich in rents. Tenants will pay for it.' Local businessman listened unbelievingly. Mattinghorn also told staff that they would earn their increased wages by greater publicity. One method would be to make them dress as famous characters in fiction. Many roared their disapproval.
>
> Members of staff, who asked not to be named, said, 'Grand Sir Hugh – that's what we call him – is crazy about dressing up. It's the actor in him.' A colleague said he would not be prepared to work in doublet and hose but pointed out that there were plenty of characters in contemporary novels who habitually wore scruffy jeans and torn tee-shirts, and that he'd settle for them.

The *Daily Telegraph* dwelt on other speeches at what it called 'fringe meetings in various bedrooms', ending by quoting Abel Farmer: 'The entire shop will be gutted. All that will remain is the fascia. That's listed.' Asked how long the shop would be closed, he said it wouldn't be. It would operate from dozens of portakabins at the carnival site on Rustrock Common. *The Times* reported that ex-Tory MP, Monty Devereux, one of the named lovers of Ms Ardbuckle, had claimed all the ideas announced by Hugh Mattingson were his. Asked about the cost, he said, 'We shall expand, we'll be more efficient.' Asked if there would be redundancies, he said he thought there might be 'some de-peopling'.

There were further reports about the lavish buffet supper, 'when the finest wines were served', turning into a drunken orgy. 'Swaying figures staggered home across the Common. Many spent the night under bushes, or on park seats. It seems unlikely that Ardbuckle's can open for business today.'

The principal book trade journal summed it up, a week later, in the words of its weekly gossip columnist:

Any publisher present at the Ardbuckle rave-up in Rustrock Spa last Friday, would have turned bright green with envy at the sight of so many representatives of the media taking notes and pictures. Even 'Auntie' was there with one of her gigantic mobile caravans the size of a studio. Most publishers' (none was invited to this razzmatazz event) parties are ignored even by the trade press. Abel Farmer, one of the caretaker directors of the company, revealed modernisation plans for the time-warped bookshop. They might have been flown across the Atlantic that very morning.

Gordon Ruffle had not been present at the reception. He had crossed the ocean in the opposite direction and was chatting-up Margitte Einstein, the young woman who had once received his mother's grudging supper.

Since then he'd made several transatlantic calls of which his father was still unaware. Gordon believed himself to be madly in love, so when Rustrock's travel agent, FLEE WITH FLIGHT, offered a five-day return, Gatwick-Kennedy, for a fare so ludicrously low that the airline participating went bankrupt one month later, he took a week's holiday.

In a dowdy, downtown, New York apartment, reached up six steep flights of stairs, in a nineteenth-century block without an elevator, Margitte returned Mrs Ruffle's largesse, with interest. She found herself taken by this cocky young Englishman who was bursting with love and ambition.

'You know, sumthin', Gordie, I am THE original, cosmopolitan woman. I've even got English blood in my veins.'

'My god, Marg! Don't tell me it's blue?'

'I guess I haven't bin litmus-tested yet.'

They made love in a wild, puppy-like style, though Margitte insisted they take precautions. 'Mom didn't teach me much, Gordie – in fact she didn't teach me anything. I got it from dear old Gran who hated the sight of her.'

'She hated her own daughter?'

'Mom wasn't her daughter.'

· 47 ·

Hugh slept soundly, as was his custom after a heavy evening's drinking, and woke after five hours. He instantly recalled his discovery in the wall of Blanche's bedroom. *His* bedroom. There were six of the bound quarto journals, each two hundred pages thick. Opening one of them at random, his eyes fell on this:

> *H2O gave me a blissfully funny time. Before he joined me, he stripped and emerged from the bathroom with as massive an erection as I have encountered – at least in the western world. "Isn't it ludicrous?" He cried gaily, "I feel like a knight on a charger." And he whooped around the room, naked, unashamed, while I collapsed on the sofa with laughter. "Now would you," he went on, rather as the virgin man did years ago," have arranged such fundamental things so absurdly, if you had been father of the universe?"*
>
> *"You won't father anything if you don't come inside me soon." I said. "I wasn't meaning to," he replied, "but I'll aim directly at you. Char-arge!" He bellowed, just like whatsisname in the Henry the Fifth film. But he controlled himself. I can't think how. And we came together, with him shouting chivalrous remarks all the time. It was such fun.*

Hugh wondered which of her lovers this was. The date was 5 March,1960. Who would have been around then? He pondered this while he broke off and went to the kitchen for coffee. As he drank, and devoured a plate of canapés which the caterers had neglected to bin, he riffled through more pages. Then he closed it abruptly. This was a treat to be rationed. He would go through the volumes systematically finding, with luck, the answer to many conundrums about Blanche and her behaviour. He would begin that evening. He phoned his mistress, whom he was anxious to offend because he was deeply bored by her, to say he would be delayed and would she make a cold supper because he didn't know what time he would be with her. And she needn't wait up. On second thoughts, he added, she could put the bolt on the door. He'd stay another night at Ridge End; he'd got something in the fridge. When she raged at him he hung up. That, he thought, is a hint she can hardly ignore.

· 48 ·

Written into the agreement between the legatees and Hugh was a clause giving the right to any two of the Directors to call a meeting of the Board at seven day's notice. Abel, sensing that Dickie and Stanley were still in cahoots, and wishing to be seen to be forming an alliance with Monty, phoned Dean, at the Hotel Bristol, on the morning after the party. (Abel, of course, was at the Rustrock Spa which had high rating in every guide from *Michelin* to the *AA*.) Dean agreed there should be a meeting. 'But must we wait seven days?'

'You mean we may have to call in the Receiver before then?'

'It can't be that bad. I just think it's commonsense for us to have the meeting while we are all here.'

'Hugh could object. He knows we'll be getting at him. He may wish to buy time.'

'If he doesn't agree we can have an unofficial board meeting. An informal talk, we could call it. Just the five of us.'

Abel approved Dean's thinking. He'd be a sound ally.

Dean offered to ring round. 'Monty is where you are. Dickie and Stanley are at the Connaught, which sounds very grand.'

'It has only one little house in *Michelin*. I'll ring. I've got the number.'

Abel was anxious to remain in command.

'As you wish. I can stay over another night if necessary. In any case, I want to look at more of the slum.'

'I think it's very good of you to take that issue to heart. If Hugh agrees, should the two of us have a short meeting first, rough out a sort of agenda?'

Dean said he would rather play it by ear. He was not anxious to become part of a faction headed by Abel, especially as he had put his perks from the company on the line. He hoped Phyl would applaud the self-sacrifice.

Abel did not press him, 'I'll get on contacting the others. Can you be paged where you are?'

'If they shout loud enough from reception I shall hear wherever I am.'

'I hadn't realised the Bristol was a tent.' Abel rang off with a crisp, captain of industry, 'Bye now', too soon to hear Dean's rejoinder – 'Yes, but the flaps are draught proofed.' Dean reckoned he could get on well with Abel, though a small voice cautioned him to keep his distance.

Abel was surprised when Hugh made no demur about having a meeting that day. 'Since we are all here, it would be foolish not to but, I warn you, I can't run on into the evening. I have an important engagement. How about fourteen-thirty? At the emporium?'

'Fourteen…? Oh yes, that's fine.' Abel, who thought of himself as a European, was annoyed that he could not adjust to the twenty-four hour clock, even though he'd been a sailor. 'I don't think we need an agenda…'

'No time, dear boy. And we all know what we wish to discuss. Quite an evening wasn't it? I promise to behave. I shall wear black.' And so Hugh did, getting out of mothballs a sombre morning suit said to have belonged to Rustrock Spa's most revered undertaker. Hugh allowed himself one pale yellow carnation as a buttonhole, to lighten the gloom. Abel supposed that the quick wink which the managing director threw at Dickie on arrival was a portent of mischief.

'Lady and gentlemen…' Hugh tapped his gavel gently '… this meeting was convened so rapidly that there has been no time to make an agenda, and the minutes of the last meeting are still marinading. I do apologise. Shall we move straight on to Any Other Business?'

Monty shreiked and said Hugh was incorrigible. 'Whoever heard of a meeting starting with that item?'

'We must all move with the times.'

'I certainly think,' Abel began on an ominous note, 'the meeting should get down to it at once, and the business, as I see it, is to endeavour to salvage what we can from the chaos we created, between the six of us, at the party. For a start, I think the MD should be asked why he did not inform us that he was proposing to revive all the extravagance of the welfare state for the benefit of those we employ.'

Dean was not pleased.

'Dear boy,' said Hugh, 'it was spontaneous. It was of the moment. From the heart. It was the commedia dell'arte in me.'

'I would have thought,' said Stanley, on cue, 'that we might equally ask Mr Farmer why he didn't tell us in advance that he would commit us to a vast rebuilding programme.'

'Or,' added Monty, 'why the honourable lady member didn't tell us beforehand about her prize.'

'Come to that,' Dickie smiled sweetly, 'the gentleman bookseller from Loamfield promised that slum clearance would take priority over all else.'

Hugh did his Falstaffian laugh. 'You might as well condemn Mr Brooke-Forster for advancing his plans for a theatrical revival that would cost millions. Good souls! Do not let us worry. Let us think positively. Maybe we can carry out all the things promised last night – if we all agree.'

Dean said sternly, 'As a matter of practical common sense there is no way in which we can go back on your proposals, Hugh, and may we please stop referring to each other in this pompous, pseudo-parliamentary fashion? The staff were promised higher salaries, commission, pensions, everything that is the norm in most humanely managed companies. I hope we can afford them. We certainly can't refuse to pay them now. It would be breaking faith.'

Stanley said he would not agree unless his theatre project went ahead, and Dickie said she felt similarly about her prize.

'Don't you think that I feel strongly about slum clearance? It's just a question of not being irresponsible.'

'You're too good to be true,' sneered Monty.

Dean flushed. 'I thought *you* might have recognised that as practical politics.'

'He's out of training,' Stanley pointed out. '*We* call it resting.'

'Order! Order! Shall I mention something that may make you less antagonistic to my proposals?'

They stared at Hugh with mild hostility.

'You are aware that Ridge End, where we made merry last night, where Blanche lived for the last thirteen years of her life, belongs to me? She had a fourteen year lease which still has seven months to run. We were discussing terms for renewal when she died. Had the dear soul lived she would have remained there – at an increased rent, of course. As things stand there is no problem about the lease reverting to me, unless you wish to negotiate to keep it in the company. If you do you will have hefty dilapidations; Blanche was careless about maintenance. But I am prepared to forego my statutory due because I would like to live in the house myself. As you are aware, it is a gem.'

'Must be worth a bomb,' Monty commented.

'I make this offer as a gesture of goodwill, although I think I could claim it anyway since I wish to live in it myself. If you would like me to leave the room while you discuss it…'

Abel said brusquely there were more important matters to consider.

'Can we take this issue later? What is essential to discuss now is the updating of these shop premises. We need not only a refit, better lighting, escalators, lifts, new floor coverings, window seats for customers… things that are now taken for granted... and there must be computerised stock control. Those shabby old manually operated tills have, for decades I am told, provoked serious mental breakdowns in National Cash Register salesmen. We have to go on line and move Ardbuckle's into the world of terminals, disks and other contemporary sophistications.'

'Is sophistications a noun?' Dickie wondered aloud. Dean told her, 'Anything goes nowadays.'

'How many times, Hugh, have you fired someone for embezzlement, or for nicking stock?' asked Abel.

'My dear fellow, I'd need a computer to calculate that.'

'Precisely. It can't go on.' A steely glint came into Abel's eyes. 'UNLESS I have the board's approval to gut and modernise this neo-Gothic monstrosity of a shop, I shall veto every other proposal made.'

'Two can play at that,' said Stanley. 'If I'd a gauntlet to hand I'd throw it down. I feel exactly the same about my proposal. To an actor, theatre takes precedence over books.' He switched his voice to Gielgud mode. 'I see here the chance to refurbish that lovely little playhouse where I once performed, and to make it part, the living part, of a university dra-ar-ma department. It will bring glory to the bookshop, it will bring purchasers ... wealth untold! I have to insist, dear friends, that you vote for my-ee plan, also.'

Dickie said the same went for her. Monty wished he had a hobbyhorse of his own. Dean repeated it would be irresponsible to take decisions at this stage. 'I was all in favour of having this meeting today because we were all here, and there seemed to be a crisis. Now I should like to go home and think about it. We should all do that.'

Abel was for an instant decision. 'The press are on to this, thanks to last evening's exhibitions... to which we all contributed, I know, I know. The staff is restive. It's been promised a lot. They know we are meeting.'

'You cannot wish to resolve so complicated an issue with this small degree of thought and discussion. You must not bully us, Abel.' Dean said that, in the last twenty-four hours, they had been faced with so many fresh proposals they must not decide anything immediately. 'I suggest we each produce a short paper – one side of A4, no more.'

'What's that?' Stanley asked Dickie, more voce than sotto.

'Foolscap, I think,' she replied, 'but I send mine to a typist.'

'We should each – thank you, Dickie – circulate our paper. No more than three hundred words. Then meet again in a week.'

· 49 ·

Members of the board descending singly from the penthouse where Blanche Ardbuckle had once lived had no option but to pass through some departments of the shop before leaving. Inevitably there were encounters with members of staff, who had nobly come to work nursing severe hangovers.

'Hi!' Maimie Perkes greeted Dickie affably as she passed through Art.

She had first fancied her when she saw her on a book programme on BBC 2, and there was every reason now for being well disposed, after the promises the author had made the previous evening. Dickie thought it diplomatic to be effusive. 'It was lovely meeting you. I was so interested in your comments on Francis Bacon. You quite sold him to me.' She flapped her hands hopelessly, looking for the exit, and wandered off towards Poetry, encountering en route Terence Absolom who said how happy he was to see her again. 'What I wished to enquire of you at the reception, Mrs Klute, was, did you have a copy of *Pearls in the Market Place*, that I might add to my personal collection, please?'

'However do you know about that?' Dickie was genuinely startled. No one, in the last thirty years, had mentioned to her the slim volume of verse she had published soon after graduating. 'Not only has it been out of print for most of my life, you could say it was never really in print in the first place.'

Lord Terence looked grave. 'I have handled two, possibly three, copies during my time here. I neglected, I regret to tell you, to add one to my own collection.'

Dickie had heard that pilfering was rife amongst the staff but did not like to comment on what seemed like a confession. 'I believe I have one at home.' She was flattered. 'To whom should I address it?'

'How kind. To Lord Absolom, if you would.'

'Of course. I hadn't remembered your name.' She assumed his first name was in the tradition favoured by circus and theatrical persons to enhance their billing. Rather vulgar but, apparently, it gave them confidence, though he would have done better to choose Earl. She went down a further flight of steps, was glowered at by John Ogglethorpe who had discovered, during afternoon tea, that he was still drunk, and was nearly knocked down at the front door as Amy Thresham barged in with a king-sized packet of alka seltzer. Amy tittered and said, 'I do hope your prize is a huge success.'

'How very nice of you.' Dickie felt she may have picked up a few votes. She congratulated Amy on the scarlet dress. 'You should wear it on duty.'

'I don't think Mr Mattingson would like me to.'

'Well, so long as he doesn't wear one.' She adjusted her monocles and strode out feeling she had made definite progress.

Monty lost his way and found himself in Science & Technology.

'Hallo to you!' He was beamed at by Fergus Welch. 'That party gave us a lot to think about. As well as drink about. How was your meeting?'

The politician rallied, always available for an on-the-spot interview. 'I think you could say we covered a lot of ground. Interesting ideas were floated. Some meaningful stuff.'

'Will we see it reflected in our pay packets this week, Mr Devereux?'

Monty was thrown. Were they really paid weekly? And wasn't this man a departmental manager? 'Takes a little time for things to filter through the system, Mr... er... ah.'

'Even when we're paid in cash?'

'What did you say?'

'Most of us are paid in cash. We can't afford bank accounts.'

'You'll need one soon. I can promise you that.' Monty extended a hand which Fergus ignored.

Rejected again, Monty scuttled downstairs. Fergus looked contemptuously after him. 'He'll not be getting my vote,' he declared to Kim Mahon (Sport) who was walking gingerly past him carrying a copy of *1000 Best Cricket Stories*. 'Don't speak too loud,' she pleaded. 'Bouncers are battering my brain at two second intervals. Darling! What a party! Was it worth it, now?'

'Probably not. They'll wriggle out of it. I'm an Ulsterman. We're used to being offered new deals. They never come to anything.'

'It's a pity you can't all become Christians,' said Kim.

Stanley Brooke-Forster also ran into Amy Thresham who greeted him smilingly. 'Remember I asked you about the chances of transferring to drama, Sir Stanley?' (She had just discovered that Joanna Baillie was a long lost, great, great, great aunt who had written plays, and she wished to research her.)

Stanley did not remember. 'You were the lady in the – ah – scarlet gown. Very becoming. Do you ever wear it here?'

'You think I should?'

'Unless there are rules about it.'

'I don't think it would be right in Travel. But it might suit Drama. I'm told that Denys is leaving. I think a change would be good for me, over there, the other end of the tunnel.' (She was thinking it would be easier to get on with her own research in a less busy department. And she was bored with recommending holiday venues she'd never visited; it would make a change to recommend plays she'd never seen.) 'Would you put in a word for me, Sir Stanley, please?'

'I'll see what I can do but, dear young lady, I am not a knight. Please don't "Sir" me. It could be unlucky.'

Abel, who knew his way out, sped swiftly through departments nodding affably at members of staff. They, according to their disposition, courteously returned the greeting or stared at him with not quite hidden resentment. He was THEM; they were US. If and when the twain met, to whose advantage would it be?

Dean left the board room with Hugh, of whom he enquired, 'I hear you have some other publicity project in hand?'

'It needs to be kept absolutely confidential.'

'Then you had better not tell me.'

'You're right. I won't for the moment.'

'After last night's party, it could be anything. I wouldn't put it past you to stage a nude orgy on the Common.'

'You're almost there. See you next week, dear Dean, with your protective sheath of A4.'

·50·

Hugh was glad that Dean had not been more inquisitive. He could not wait to return to Blanche's journals, which he decided to approach systematically and chronologically. He found the early volumes naïve when they were not downright tedious. Her blinkered comments on international affairs indicated that she approved of both Nazi Germany and Soviet Russia. Dictators had an undoubted appeal for her. After all, in their own interests, she argued, people needed to be told what to do; it was the only sensible way of dealing with them. There were pages of indignant comment about this but nothing of her love life.

It was the same in the volume dealing with World War Two, which had left Rustrock virtually unharmed. She recorded the bombers, some way to the east, droning towards London. Once a doodlebug dropped near the bottom of the Common, destroying one of her properties. Books boomed; business was excellent. She was not called-up and gave no explanation. Hugh supposed she had fiddled it. Then, in the third volume, the mood changed. The war was over. She began to record having lovers, to write about them. The entry for 21 June, 1950, by which time she was in her fortieth year, read:

> *Such a well-spoken and beautfiully mannered young man came to the flat tonight. I have been fancying a virgin for some while, and he was one, but he performed with exquisite grace, reminding me of my dear Alphonse. Then, afterwards, he began to laugh uncontrollably. It was infectious. I laughed too. Then I asked what was funny. "It's so absurd," he said, "I don't mean to be rude. I don't think you are absurd, Miss Ardbuckle, but what a strange piece of human organism to have evolved for reproducing the human race. Don't you think so? You really would think nature could have thought up something less complicated and messy." I saw what he meant, but I said to him,*

"Isn't it bound to be messy? If the seed were a little pebble, or a piece of grit, it would hurt." But he was right. Although Alphonse would not have thought so. Then my young man became serious and we talked about evolution and his Quaker upbringing, and the way he had distanced himself from it trying, at the same time, not to offend his parents. After a while he was roused again. I watched his member rising slowly, nobly. It was comical. We both laughed. It was a jolly night, though I think I prefer my sex with someone older. But it has reminded me of my lovely Alphonse. People think I had a lucky war. They don't know.

Hugh found himself quite moved. Who was the Quaker? Were the staff and wages books stored from that long ago? Jawarharlal might dig them out for him. But what about Alphonse? He had stumbled on something there. Had he skipped an earlier reference in the wartime journal?

Hugh, who had moved into Ridge End without waiting for a decision from the Board – after all, he argued, it was *his* house – went to the kitchen, took a lasagne from the freezer, heated the oven, washed a lettuce, poured sauce vinaigrette into a salad bowl, uncorked a Californian Chardonnay to have as aperitif, helped himself to nuts, listened to an enraged message from his mistress on the ansafone, deleted it without replying and retrieved a volume of the journal from the study. He turned to 1940 and was soon further mystified:

June 5
A call from Paris from J. We couldn't stay long on the line. There is rising panic at the prospect of a German breakthrough. J and Yvette have loaded their car with clothes and a few precious things. They will leave during the night. They are making for a place in Perigord. They have no news of Alphonse. Will I ever hear from any of them again?

September 7
The blitz on London has started in earnest. We could hear the bombers
in the distance all night. No word from J, none, therefore, from
Alphonse. Were J and Yvette machine-gunned on the road from Paris?

Hugh found no further references before he served himself the lasagne.
Later, as he finished a generous portion of Roquefort, over two glasses of
vintage port, he dipped again into the journal but soon became drowsy.
He laid it aside. It was still an experience to savour. He needed to keep
alert. He must not skip a word.

· 51 ·

For the Ardbuckle staff the period immediately after the party was
euphoric. The future seemed brighter. The directors had held a meeting
and were expected to announce decisions beneficial to all. The feeling was
that they couldn't go back on what had been promised. Some staff gave
interviews and were inaccurately reported at national level. Ardbuckle's
remained in the news, yet business was slack. By the day after the day after
the party nothing had altered. That was when Fergus Welch asked loudly,
in the staff room, 'What are the bastards up to now? If only,' he said to
Maimie Perkes, 'you weren't such a snob about trade unions.'

'*Trades* unions,' she said, pedantically.

He ignored her. 'We could call everyone out now, and shut the shop.

'You are so vulgar, Fergus. I have undertaken to work for this company
for the salary…'

'Wage!'

'SALARY. I have always been salaried. I am a gentlewoman. I get my
cheque on the twenty-fifth of each month.'

'Yes, in arrears, you silly…'

'Fergus!'

'Any sane person takes cash every Friday.'

'I can resign if I don't like company policy. Otherwise,' said Maimie, 'I stay and fight my own battles.'

'When we get a union shop, you'll be out, I promise you that.'

'You are so out of date, Fergus.'

To avoid becoming involved in such encounters, Hugh absented himself from the shop as often as possible. (He also disconnected his ansafone.) He went straight to his office on arrival each morning, bullied Jawarharlal to search the archives for old wages books, otherwise spent every available moment engrossed in Blanche's journals. When he came upon the entry for 13 September, 1954, he felt a frisson in his spinal cord:

Tonight I took me to bed, as Pepys might have said, an actor man who is "resting", as they say, and therefore working for me at the shop. I suspect he may be queer, although he told me he had once been married, and was keen on a young actress in our rep, at the time it closed, only recently. He talked rather too much, and struck poses, but that was the actor in him. I suppose they have to. He told me funny stories about things going wrong during performances and he became a little hysterical. I think he was trying to work up a desire for me. I helped him by telling him I am attracted to queers because they always tell risque stories and want to entertain one. His reaction was immediate. We had a very jolly romp, which I always enjoy. Sex is a strange business. I like it to be fun.

Hugh recognised that one but what was it they had done which was such fun? What sort of risque stories had turned Blanche on? He didn't altogether believe in what Blanche had recorded. Why hadn't she described this 'jolly romp' in detail, and how did it qualify Stanley for being one of the chosen few? What had given him precedence over Hugh? He sighed, turned his attention to pre-1939, searching for something he must have overlooked first time through. There had to be references to Alphonse. Further reflections were interrupted by calls from Monty, Stanley and Dickie, all soliciting his support for various projects.

· 52 ·

The directors each circulated their memos, all admirably brief, on one side of A4. Dean stated he wished the staff to be rewarded in accordance with Hugh's promises; so, without any reservations, did Dickie and Stanley; Monty thought the increments should be linked to profitability; Abel was against commission.

Abel wished to separate the property business from the shop and to sell it as a going concern. So did Monty but Dean thought this unwise because it was probable that the shop was subsidised by the rents from the property. He also thought that if any part of the property were redeveloped the present occupants should be rehoused and compensated. Neither Dickie nor Stanley commented specifically on this aspect but both supported what others had recommended in general, and both firmly insisted that their own pet schemes should go ahead – even the History of Rustrock, which was Dickie's other main idea.

Dean was against both the rehabilitation of the theatre and the children's book prize, as priorities, and Abel agreed with him; Monty thought such schemes should be paid for out of funds accumulating from the sale of property.

The exercise had achieved little except to clarify on paper what each had already said in words. When they met again, Dean observed, 'I see that Any Other Business is again the only item on the agenda.'

'That is because I am an obsessive traditionalist,' explained Hugh who, for reasons known only to himself, was garbed as either Athos or Porthos, but no one was willing to pander to his absurdity by asking.

Abel took control. 'May I suggest that instead of each of us arguing points written into our schedules, we concentrate on those areas where we agree?'

'If any.'

'Not true, Monty. As you must all be aware it is only about major policies that we have to be in unison. We have delegated day-to-day management of the shop and property to Hugh…'

Hugh nodded sagely, glad to have this point confirmed; he had plans which had not been revealed to anyone but Abel.

'…but if he were to implement, for instance, the refurbishment of the theatre without consulting us, then…'

Hugh agreed. 'I think we all know where we stand.'

Stanley, surprisingly, made no comment. His mind was on his Soap. The public had taken to him, but how long would Pottersby remain sick? Dickie sulked and said she didn't see why she should lose her prize.

'Dear Dickie, it is only postponed. We must be realistic.'

Dickie pouted. Dean suggested, 'Couldn't we agree that whoever gets the – what is it called? – the jackpot should put in hand the prize during their first year in office?' Abel and Monty both thought this unenforceable but the latter, with a squawk, declared it, 'a master stroke.'

'So,' declared Abel, 'we are all agreed that raising salaries and modernising the premises are essential to the health of the business?'

There was a rumble of assent. Abel went on: 'It is my belief that Ardbuckle's must be gutted. Everything except its awful Victorian-Gothic frontage which is, unfortunately, listed, has to go. And whilst this is happening the shop has to carry on business elsewhere. I had thought the obvious temporary site was on the Common, with the carnival out of the way for the winter, but maybe we could go into the old Ritz cinema instead?'

Dean asked if that would mean purchasing it but, before Abel could answer, Hugh said they were unlikely to get it. 'I have,' he said, 'on my desk this very morning a brochure from a company which says it is negotiating the purchase of the Ritz. Not only the Ritz! Also the few other properties not owned by Ardbuckle's, and asking if we would be interested in selling our entire estate.' He drew a poniard from his belt and swore, 'There's villainy in heaven! Did you know about this, Abel?' It was more an accusation than a question.

'I did not but I do know that there is a huge discrepancy in our cash flow.'

'The managing director...' As he spoke Hugh threw his poniard above him – they all caught their breath – and deftly snatched it from the air as it came down '...is not only aware, but has taken appropriate action.'

Dickie begged him to sheathe his weapon. 'What action are you taking?'

'I have sacked the rent collector concerned. He was miserably paid by Blanche. She said she wouldn't raise his money because he was bound to be on the fiddle, but that there was no point in sacking him because his replacement would do just the same. That was what I was up against. But who told you about it, Abel? Actually, it concerns only a trickle of our cash. The rest flows with the same joyous ripple as Schubert's salmon quintet.'

'Trout,' corrected Dean.

'One freshwater fish is much like another.'

Abel said, 'Never mind the fish, what about the cash?'

'Do not panic. A few lost rents are not the end of the world but, lady Dickie and gentlemen, it is true to say that business is very poor indeed, as at this moment of the old tempus, so I have plans to boost it. They will become apparent next week.'

Monty asked, 'So what about this property offer?'

Abel said that it should be left on the table until the succession had been determined. 'Anyhow, we are not authorised to sell company assets. Meanwhile we must gut Ardbuckle's, refurbish it, and, if the Ritz site is not for renting, carry on business in an array of super portakabins. And the staff get a rise. Any objections?'

'But what about that splendid idea of costumes for the staff?'

Dickie again sulked when told this also was out of the question at the moment.

Hugh said it was important there should be a further meeting next day to pass the minutes of the current one. 'The company will arrange accommodation.' Dickie came out of her sulk, and eyed Hugh, to suggest, 'We could all tuck-up in Blanche's great bed. Rather appropriate, don't you think?' Stanley turned pale.

They parted in good humour, Hugh to hurry home to Ridge End for a further instalment of Blanche's journal.

· 53 ·

18 Oct. 1968

I've never attempted it before with a woman but I do like variety in my sex. Jay and I spent a long time working out what it was we should actually do, neither of us being natural lesbians. We both recalled that old limerick about who does what, and with whom, and to who. That reduced us to helpless mirth but we were determined to make a go of it because, as Jay said, it would be useful experience for her as a writer. A little later she complained she'd dislocated her index finger and that, again, made us collapse with laughter. She reckoned it was worth it. I used a big toe. I was glad I'd cut my nails. So was Jay. It was all most complicated but hilarious.

Hugh easily pinned that one down. His systematic approach already abandoned, he flicked over pages until he read:

Tonight I tried doing it in the bath.

The phone interrupted him. It was Abel. 'I know you only want this meeting tomorrow so that we can pass the minutes, but I really feel we must get on with the refurbishment...'

'Yes, Abel, my dear, you see it as a vote winner. I can't blame you for trying but you could be wrong. Have you thought what it will mean for the poor staff? It's going to be a nightmare trying to run a bookshop in a clutch of portakabins. And it will be winter. I'll have to wear galoshes.'

'That should turn you on.'

'Yes, it's funny about galoshes, isn't it?'

'I wouldn't know, Hugh.'

'You're such a prude. I'll lend you a pair. Anyhow, this portakabin idea could lose you a lot of votes. If I were you I'd wait till after the election.'

'I'll sleep on it.'

'Before you go, do I have your approval for the naturist signing?'

'I can't give you authority. You're in charge. Just don't involve me.'

'Oh, Abel! I was hoping you'd agree to be billed as The Most Erect Man About Town.'

'With you present the competition would be too great.' Abel rang off, thinking, if he goes ahead with that it could be the end of him. Hugh returned to what he called his blanchisserie:

18 August, 1975.
Today, DJ surpassed himself. He ought to be on the box. "Have you," he asked, "ever done it in the bath?" Cheeky young,man! It was my sixty-fifth birthday. "I'm not at all kinky," I replied. He put on an outrageous American accent, "wanna bet?" "Don't go too far," I warned him but I hoped it would amuse me. I need diversions. He's very attractive, less than half my age, according to what he told me at his interview (he's working in Literature) and it could be I'm lucky to

have him. He said he liked to do 'IT' standing up in wardrobes, with,
for preference, a smell of mothballs thrown in. Or, under the bed, with
a potty to hand for the overspill. I told him to get out, he was being
crude, I wasn't like that. "ME!" He cried. "Crude! I'm respectable
enough to have it off in a pulpit in mid-sermon. If they'd let me, I
could bring back the masses to church, and I don't mean the sung
ones, or the black ones." On that note we got into bed and he began a
sort of ritual chant, which reminded me of an RC service I once
attended:

I shall come up your left nostril,
I shall come up your right,
I shall delve into your left ear.
I shall delve into your right,
And I may poke about, poke ABOUT, PO-OKE about!
PO-oke about, in your mouth.

He pretended to do all these things, repeating the chanting as his great
member waved around – I wish I could remember the tune – it was a
sort of dirge – and I knew he would end up in the right place, it was
gorgeously erotic and funny, as he tried out the alternatives.

There were a few more entries about DJ who, alas, never succeeded in
amusing the lady to such an extent again. After what she told him had
been a memorable performance, he grew over-confident, and suddenly
became serious about plans for expanding the bookshop, opening
branches, modernising, giving Ardbuckle's a facelift, introducing "SYS-
TEMS".

I pushed him out of bed. "You're supposed to make me laugh," I said.
"You're the jester. Sod the books." His reaction was marvellous. He

leapt onto the bed. "I agree," he shouted. "Sod all books, and f… all
booksellers. Would you like to hear my Max Miller songs?" And he
lulled me to sleep with music hall ditties, penetrating me very, very
gently, as he sang of Mary, from the Dairy." When I woke, he'd gone.

It clicked for Hugh. Abel, it must be. He only had to check with the wages
book. After that it would become merely a matter of how to use the mate-
rial to advantage. Blackmail did not appeal to him but the proceeds from
a Sunday newspaper serial did. Meanwhile the entries he had read had
made him horny, so he phoned Dickie at her hotel.

'Dear lady, it is not too late, I hope, for me to suggest I carry you off to
what is the Rustrock Spa equivalent of the Boul' Mich?'

'You must be joking.'

'No, truly. Will you join me in a nightcap?'

'Very well, as long as you don't arrive wearing one.' The book was coming along swimmingly. Rarely had she written with such élan and speed.
To have drinks with Hugh would be a form of revision.

Over a cognac he convinced himself he fancied her; it had been a long
time since… He engaged her vanity by asking about her working methods, 'When the creative feeling comes over you…'

'Oh, come on, Hughie…'

'What form does it take? Do you lock yourself in a garret?'

'You've hit it. Clever man. And it is what I have to do at this very
moment. Just talking to you has loosened something.'

'Dear lady, I had hoped…'

'Well, it wouldn't do, would it? Everything is quite complicated enough
already. No, you must excuse me. See you at the meeting.'

No man likes to be rebuffed but there was worse to come for Hugh.

Returning to the journals it occurred to him that Blanche surely must
have commented on *their* times together. His attention began to wane as he
read through pages recording book trade trivia, then he came upon this:

Last night, for a brief spell, I was treated like royalty, and I adored it. That absurd mountebank (Ajax, I'll call him) who plays an increasingly important role in the company's prosperity, literally came over the top. It was the end of the carnival, which is a greater success this year than ever before, and partly due to him. Ajax – perhaps I should call him Romeo, but no one could take me for sixteen – or was it fourteen? – even in a bad light – climbed to my balcony at Ridge End (which he owns and I'm determined to get it from him), on a ladder placed against the wall by revellers. He was dressed outlandishly, as usual – I forget if it was meant to be anyone in particular – and he serenaded me before coming up over the wistaria. He made abundantly clear that he was bursting with notions of conquest. It was gloriously exhilarating. The crowd hung about and cheered, went on cheering long after we had retired to my room and closed the shutters. It was like I imagine an old style bridal night, only I never had one. He was unexpectedly gentle with me, made a long, lingering approach, exploring my body, asking what I liked to do best. He was not the bombastic, swashbuckling, rather brutish man I had known for some years. We reached our climaxes together after much playfulness. Then he took me so gently into his ample embrace, and we slept for a while...

Hugh felt restored. Then he read on:

Later, we made love again, with somewhat less finesse – and I wished we hadn't – but he was urgent for it. Men are like that. Yet something was wrong with the experience, I realised, as I was lying comfortably, drowsily, on my luscious cushioning. It was only much later in the day that I realised what it was. Ajax had made it all too solemn, too reverent. And I like it to be fun. That's my forte.

The bitch, thought Hugh. He said it aloud. 'The old bitch. I gave her a wonderful time and there she was lying, analysing it.' He read on, looking for further mentions. There were many, at irregular intervals. She had not recorded every night they spent together but once she wrote:

Ajax seems very attentive but I don't think his mind is on me… Ajax for me was much too passionate. I thought he would tear me apart. I will not be treated like a whore, although how do I know how they are treated? Yet, afterwards he was charming. And he made me laugh so much. If only his lovemaking did…

So that was it. In a way it served him right. He had treated religion as a subject for hilarity; Blanche had seen sex in the same light. He lay brooding about it. Fancy that rather upright Dean Phillips giving such a polished first performance. And his sense of the risible in it had earned him a possible fortune. And what about Monty and his rollicking youthfulness? She'd liked his approach also. How the man had changed! Hugh reckoned she would not have enjoyed his screech of a laugh, so he couldn't have acquired it by then. What politics does to people! The Stanley episode didn't count too much and he couldn't understand why the actor had been so favoured, but Abel he could. Threatening to poke his member into the lady's lughole! Right up her street. 'In a manner of speaking,' he added aloud. 'Must keep *my* sense of humour, even if it is too late.' Though it might not be. He wasn't one of the five legatees but he could not be entirely ruled out from winning the jackpot.

Hugh considered whether he should publish the journals. There would surely be a market? But who owned the copyright? The five directors? The trustees? No literary executor was mentioned in Blanche's will but that was not surprising because she had not been a writer. Should he consult Mark Ampersand, or a literary agent?

He then allowed his thoughts to be interrupted by the publisher Fred Brill, who was awaiting him by appointment.

· 54 ·

Fred Brill had an alternative philosophy list with a forthcoming title on naturism. He had come from Harringay, in north London, to discuss it with Hugh. At Harringay he had gambled successfully on the dogs to provide the capital, Ronnie, his boy friend, needed to publish books about aromatherapy, then in its pre-fashionable phase. From herbs and rose petals, processed in gleaming copper alembics emanating arresting odours, they soon branched out into health farms and dietetics. It was less than a quantum leap from there to naturism.

'Forgive me, dear Mr Brill,' said Hugh, who was dolled up as a Red Indian chieftain, and finding his moccasins were squeezing his toes, 'the true nature of naturism eludes me at this precise moment. The faculties, as one gets older... you know how it is?'

'It's what used to be called nudity, Mr Mattingson.'

'I once visited a nudist camp when I was a youth.'

'Yeah, but I expect that was for carnal reasons.'

'Not at all. I was a member of the concert party provided to entertain them. *We* were all clothed.'

'I see,' said Fred, who had a singleminded, businesslike approach to naturism which, for him, was something to be tolerated only in bed, or in the bath. He was not certain how to deal with this oddball. Why was he dressed up as an Indian? What was his game? In his twangy London whine, he said, 'My author, Armand de Tancarville, now he sees naturism as a religion.'

'You've come to the right man. I, too, have written numerous religious books.'

'Well, he's not attracted by any particular religion. He's more into your actual nature. It's not what the sun means, or the moon, or the planets... the stars... that sort of thing. He takes it all very serious. That's why he believes people should go to his camps by the Mediterranean – it's all legal,

Mr Matt – and expose theirselves in total nudity. For therapeutic sessions with the elements.'

'When you say "total nudity", Mr Brill…?'

'Stark bollock naked.'

'Spectacles? Hearing aids?'

'They're allowed.'

'Fig leaves?'

'No fig leaves.'

Hugh warmed to the idea. It might be just what was needed to point Ardbuckle's in the direction he wished it to go. The human body was, after all, extremely attractive, and not only in the dark. It was also essentially provocative.

'What do you have in mind then, for this particular event?'

'The usual signing, preceded by a short reading.'

'From this gentleman's book?'

'Right. He likes to do the reading hisself. He has quite an appealing sort of French voice. He's French, you see? Then he'd give a little lecture on the value of naturism, like he says it is in his book. Mr Mattingson, you've got to think of it mystically. That's why he has his alokytes.'

'His alokytes?'

'Yeah, these women.'

'While he's reading?'

'Yeah, it gives it the religious content.'

'You mean, they actually… while he's reading?'

Brill laughed. 'No, Mr Matt, of course not.'

'What do these … acolytes? … what do they do?'

'They stand there taking orders. Acolytes. That's right.'

Hugh had a sudden vision. 'And they are in their…?'

'They haven't got nothing on, neither.'

Hugh felt a restricting heave of desire. 'How very interesting. What happens then?'

'They lift up their arms and look imploring, and utter these imbrocations?'

'I suppose we'd have to make sure the heating was on?'

'I think you'll find it very moving.'

'And none of them has anything on?'

'No one. Just like it was at Stonehenge, so Armand says. He says you get this tingling of the skin, and a feeling that all sorts of liquids are rushing about in your veins… he says it's very spiritual.'

Fred always felt embarrassed when he explained but Ron made him do it because, 'You sound so sincere, Fred, that's what counts.' What counted for Fred was that people bought the book.

'And he sits there signing, stark…?'

'That's it.'

'With the acolytes also…?'

'Starkers.'

'Couldn't we be prosecuted?'

'No way. It's a religious ritual, you see? That brings me to my next point. We think the signing will have maximum effect if your staff, on the floor, also become naturists… just for the signing session.'

Hugh nodded. A scheme was evolving.

'Also, you might ask your customers who wish to attend… you might ask them to be naturists too…'

'What stark…?'

'Yeah.'

'All the way from their homes?'

'Na-ow. We thought you could provide changing rooms. Somewhere they could strip.'

'And we don't have to clear this with the police?'

'No need. Remember that play with all those rugger types? It was on in Shaftesbury Avenue. And the curtain goes up and there's these fifteen great blokes all stark bollock naked, having just got out of their ordinary clothes, and before putting on their togs. And you had all these polite people sitting in the stalls and the circle. They tittered a bit, some of them, but that was all. Too well bred to do more than laugh nervously, yet none of them had ever seen the like. I mean some folk, Mr Matt, don't even see their partners. They put the light out first. Anyway, this play went on, night after night, with these actors starkers in front of several hundred people, showing off their pricks like prize stallions.'

Hugh found himself thinking, suppose they had been female rugger players. Fred Brill, not a frequent theatregoer, had been happy that they weren't.

'And,' said Brill, slowly, impressively, 'there was no prosecution. Why not? Because those actors, pretending to be rugger players, were performing a ritual… religious, if you like… and all those people in the audience were celebrating a communion with them… metaphorically sucking their pricks, that sort of thing.'

Hugh took off his head dress, scratched his cranium. 'I wonder if my board would agree?'

· 55 ·

At the board meeting next day, Hugh, garbed as a commissionaire from a posh Kensington store, swamped in gold braid and buttoned to the neck, determined to mention neither the journals nor the signing. The sole business was to pass the minutes of the previous meeting, but Abel was not to be deflected. He had lain awake much of the night trying to decide if he should opt out of Ardbuckle's and devote attention to his own still partly fragile group. If he did, he might later make a killing in Rustrock when the inevitable opening occurred. Or should he plump for redeveloping Ardbuckle's now because he was the favourite to win the jackpot?

He knew, also, that Ardbuckle's needed a firm, experienced, guiding hand. The gutting of the existing building and the establishment of a pre-fab township of portakabins on the carnival site would afford him an opportunity of proving his qualities as a leader. He saw himself urging the bookselling staff to glories of self-sacrifice and personal realisation, each and every one of them, beneath his flag, a hero of the hour. Then they would return to premises which, he would tell them, 'Will be so luxurious and harmonious, that you will not want to go home of an evening. You may not even have to! I may arrange for en suite bedrooms beneath cen-trally-heated, air-conditioned counters.' What wit! That would surely win him their votes?

Abel did not regale his fellow directors with these fantasies. To them, he insisted, 'Time is of the essence,' a catch phrase then popular in the finan-cial sections of the quality press. Dean was disturbed by the fanatical gleam in Abel's eyes. So surely would the employees be? Abel might well dig his own grave. Then who would get the prize which he, Dean, was now not certain he would reject if it came his way? Were any of the others capable of doing the job? Perhaps not, but many become victors by default. He resolved to stay for the sake of the staff and the tenants. Phyllis would back him.

Stanley was confident that the fame *A Wink or a Nod* was bound to bring him would influence the staff in his favour, especially as the por-takabins were bound to make Abel unpopular.

Monty also smelt defeat for Abel over the portakabins and, while he had no coherent idea of what his own line was, instinct told him it was sensi-ble to encourage the young tycoon towards his doom.

Only Dickie was outspoken against it. 'We really should wait until after the vote. I don't believe it about all these alarm bells. I don't hear them ringing. The shop looks nice and busy to me, and the staff are all terribly pleased about their rises, and pensions, and things.'

Monty opposed her, pointing out that the benefits had not yet been conferred. 'The honourable lady...' (They all groaned) ...'Forces me to appeal to the managing director whom we appointed to deal with this very situation. *We* have to be united in our decisions. Hugh, you will know what best to do, and you are authorised to act for us.'

Hugh looked grave. 'I believe I know my duty.' He knelt at the foot of a small desk and pretended to pray.

He really is marvellous, thought Dickie, he makes rings round all of us. Her new draft was complete. She couldn't wait to get back to Piddletrenthide to make one last revision. She would take a minicab again. Money meant nothing to her nowadays. Then she had a startling idea. Wouldn't the book make rather a good play?

Hugh rose and rejoined the meeting, which he reminded the directors was taking place solely for the purpose of passing the minutes. However, he had received guidance to work towards Abel's proposals.

'You mean the Lord is into Any Other Business?' asked Monty.

'Bless you, my son,' said Hugh, with a wicked twinkle in his eyes.

Next day, however, he was obliged to convene another meeting at the command of Mark Ampersand, who had learned of the possible intentions of the new directors. All but Dickie were present to be informed that, although the business must be run positively, during the interim period, no major changes such as were envisaged could be undertaken until probate was granted on Blanche's will. 'That may take several months.'

'Longer than a year?' asked Dean.

'I would hope not.'

'So, Mr Ampersand, you are saying we must put things on hold,' said Hugh, 'while we wait for the inevitably protracted processes of the law to take place. It won't be simple, I can tell you, to keep the staff from seething. They don't want the portakabins but they do want some certainty. And I thought I was just about to make a breakthrough with them.' He removed his ankle length Wehrmacht greatcoat to reveal blue jeans, with uneven patches of white, and a tee-shirt reading CATCH ME COMING THROUGH THE RYE.

'At least,' commented Stanley, 'your trousers aren't actually out at the knees. That's something.'

'I wondered about offering you a nose ring,' said Abel.

The managing director ignored them. 'We must give them all another rise now, and promise the earth when probate is granted. That may do the trick. And a major publicity stunt, should boost sales. You must allow me to keep details of that to myself for the moment. I want to break it to you and the public at the same time. Also, I feel I owe it to you to make it absolutely evident that none of you is involved. So, just in case it back-fires, which I assure you it won't, you can't be blamed.'

Abel, who thought he knew what Hugh was up to, decided to recommend playing along with him. Give him sufficient rope, was his policy, though he kept that to himself. Dean argued that surely, as directors, they ought to know but Abel replied sternly, 'We must trust Hugh, and wish him luck. And you will, of course, know before it happens because there will have to be time for the public to respond.'

'I don't wish to appear prudish,' said Dean, 'but will you please record in the minutes that I declined to back a scheme about which nothing was revealed to the board.' Dean blushed, felt square and left the meeting.

Abel felt he must play along with Hugh, at least until he worked out the other man's tactics and aims. Possibly Bonaparte had felt similarly about Wellington?

· 56 ·

Dickie Klute's book was finished, but the idea of dramatising it wouldn't go away. She hadn't written a play since adolescence. Dare she now? She felt sufficiently on top to give herself a break and to pop into Dorchester to do some shopping, thinking that Thomas Hardy probably had the same reaction after a major bout of work. She called at a bookshop where she was known. 'Oh, Mrs Klute,' said the proprietress, 'I was just reading something about you in *The Bookseller*. It's to do with Ardbuckle's. Did you know about it?'

'What is it?' She had not been paying attention to her directorial duties.

'This signing they are having for a... naturist book... by that dishy looking Frenchman. Haven't they told you?'

Dickie read the trade journal with increasing interest. When she returned home she phoned Hugh. 'Would you like me to come to the signing? It sounds fun.'

'Dickie! I'm so pleased you've got in touch. Business is very bad. This is a desperate effort to improve the situation.'

'As bad as that? You mean I won't get my lovely lolly Blanche left me?'

'I hope you will. Yes, I would like you to be present.'

'I shall know what to wear,' she simpered.

Hugh enlisted Gordon Ruffle's help in interesting the media in the signing, and the first response, at least, was promising. The trade press announced it two weeks ahead in its gossip columns and, when Gordon (who was finding it irksome to attend to his duties because he had heard that morning that Margitte Einstein was flying into Heathrow a fortnight hence) encouraged one or two ladies of Rustrock Spa to make shocked comments, items appeared in various newspapers, and on the radio. A slight compromise was reached with Armand de Tancarville, through his publisher. It was agreed that fig leaves might be optional, Hugh making the point to Fred Brill that, in fact, many of the customers might find the event more erotic that way. Fred did not pass that onto the author. He told him there was a local by-law.

'But, I myself, m'sure, I shall be… in the old *comme ci*, as it were, and the local by-laws do not apply to you because you are a naturist. It is your religion.'

'That is so. Thank you, Monsieur Brill. I am very pleased that, at last, you 'ave been able to find a bookseller willing to 'ave a signing on my conditions.'

'After this, Armand…' The Frenchman looked pained. '…M'sure de Tancarville, I mean, we'll be in demand all over the country. A reprint is in hand.'

· 57 ·

On the Thursday chosen for the signing the ground floor of Ardbuckle's, or most of it, was transformed to resemble a Mediterranean beach, with a simulated deep blue sky and plenty of soft sand spread over every square inch of floor space. On the stroke of ten, Armand de Tancarville, his heavy brown locks covering his head and shoulders, his penis dangling in a ring of more bushy hair, took his place at a dais and introduced the philosophy behind his book. For the next three hours, he signed copies while his acolytes moved gracefully around him, posing statuesquely for half of every minute.

Male customers, most of whom opted for fig leaves, were so taken by the acolytes, while the female ones, many of whom had decided on total nudity, were so enraptured by the author, that there was a remarkable lack of self-consciousness. The staff had been bribed with promises of double-time pay, so few had refused to be on duty. Terence Absolom had sent apologies because his presence was essential that day in the Lords to vote against a government bill upholding an EC measure to introduce metrication to the traditional sonnet form. Most of his colleagues had their private parts concealed by belts made of printed leaves from damaged books. Dickie Klute was enchanted by this idea of Hugh's and insisted on adorning her lower regions with illustrations from *The Story of Art*. She dashed up to the old penthouse to undress, noticing as she went, Daniel Drybrough clad only in his black patch. 'I must have one of those,' she cried. 'Hugh, send to the chemist, please.' Instead Hugh asked Daniel to remove his and hand it over. This embarrassed the young man who said, 'I shall feel naked without it.'

'That is what you are supposed to be.' But Hugh relented, and Dan thought, if Mum could see me now! He brushed against Dickie and the life force threatened to overflow. Mum, he further reflected, would be so proud.

Two long queues – one for men, one for women – moved slowly, because the author liked to chat to each client. Two young women assistants from a nearby shoe shop blushed and giggled to one another as they noticed some of their customers in the line. ('I've never only seen 'er bare feet before, Sandra.' 'Shut up, Sharon.') 'I always knew you had lovely breasts, Miranda,' remarked Mrs Fabian, wife of the senior lecturer in geography at the university. 'Don't be personal, Diana,' replied her companion, 'or I shall mention that mole on your rudder.'

Gordon Ruffle overheard and noted that his fig leaves were rising to a horizontal position. He had de Tancarville's book in one hand, his notepad in the other. His neighbour whispered, 'Try and think of something else.'

'How can I fucking think of something else when I'm surrounded by naked women?' (Each one of whom made him think of Margitte.)

'Might be just as bad if you were gay, like me. Fortunately – or unfortunately – there's no one here I fancy.'

Fred Brill and Ron, his partner, who were wearing belts made of illustrations from de Tancarville's book, overheard, and looked hurt. Then everyone's attention was distracted by the descent of Dickie Klute, on the staircase, wearing her Gombrich girdle and an eye shield.

'Look at 'er!' someone muttered. 'She's like that pop star who always has a black eye.'

'Mrs Klute!' cried Mrs Fabian. 'What a lovely picture you make. That centrepiece on your belt is surely Cranach's Adam?'

'That's correct, darling. I always feel he looks so like Alan Bates. That's why I put it there.' She turned round. 'You may like to see the impressionists, too.'

'A Renoir on each buttock. How clever of you!'

'You could call them *post*-impressionists,' observed Daniel.

Then a stentorian voice was heard, belonging to a smartly dressed elderly lady who had just entered. 'Mister Mattingson! Whatever is going on?'

'Mrs Winthrop-Moore! How lovely to see you. Do get undressed and join the queue.'

'You must be out of your mind. I was told this was going on. I've never seen anything like it!'

'Come on lady!' remarked an elderly man, clad in the smallest of fig leaves. 'At your age?'

'This is absolutely disgusting. I shall send for the police.'

· 58 ·

Meanwhile, in the Gothic turret housing Science & Technology, Professor Ellstein, Head of the Physics Department, of whom it was said that his world was divided into Uncertainty and Complementarity, found himself distracted from perusal of a new edition of *Excited States of Nuclei*. It appeared to him, that the young man who usually served him, Mr Welch or Woolf, or some such name, had forgotten to dress, apart from a belt made of sheaths of paper through which a pink membrane was distinctly visible.

Fergus Welch, for it was he, was not overjoyed to be taking part in the 'nudist parade' but he needed the money, now he also had stopped fiddling the till because takings were so poor. He was disconcerted when he felt his member stirring. It couldn't be that dotty old prof; he'd never had leanings that way. Was it because Muriel had rejected him? No, it must be because the paper for the sheath was a bit rough. He moved quickly to a shelf with his back to Ellstein, who then returned to his studies. After a while the professor, who had transferred his attention to *Dysfunctions of Solid-state Particles* and decided to buy it, approached the assistant, the manager, or whatever he was, who, he now realised, was more or less nude.

'Are you finding it too warm, Mr er… er?'

Fergus blushed. 'No, it's a stunt, professor. Not my idea. It's for publicity.'

'Not many people seem to have noticed.' Ellstein thought that remarkably witty. He might repeat it at dinner at high table… if he remembered.

'It's all happening downstairs, professor.'

But something else was happening here, in the turret. Fergus was having a massive erection. He bent below the counter, pretending to search for something, willing his organ to flag. It wouldn't. He tried standing sideways. That made matters worse. He took the Professor's credit card and processed it. Mercifully, Ellstein's attention had been attracted to another book. Fergus rushed to the loo on the nearby landing and ran a cold water tap on himself, drenching his costume in the process.

In Art, Maimie Perkes felt chilly and wondered if she might cheat by donning a scarf which was lying beside the counter. Or would that disqualify her from overtime payment which she desperately needed for her phone bill. She had promised half of what she received to her church collection, so her priest had sanctioned her taking part in the 'parade'. She opted for exercise and walked swiftly about the department, swinging her delicate boobs and buttocks, to the delight of two browsing students, one of whom sketched her.

On the ground floor, John Ogglethorpe, whose belt was made from a defective copy of *The Times Atlas of the World*, the pages of which were larger than other books, sat unhappily between the signing author and the two publishers. He had promised Jane he would keep his head lowered and not look at the ladies but, sod it, he told himself, I can't help being normal.

Trade could not have been more brisk. de Tancarville seemed to be tiring but was regularly sustained by mugs of black coffee. Camera bulbs flashed. A cassette was introduced playing catchy tunes by Offenbach. 'What fun if we all did the can-can,' said Dickie who was about to retire upstairs to make changes to her art gallery, when Mrs Winthrop-Moore, a formidable flint among Rustrock battleaxes, returned with a police sergeant accompanied by a smirking young constable. The latter reckoned he would be the envy of his section house that evening when he told them about this lark. Cor, he'd say, you never saw such a lot of cunt in one place, and nothing to pay for lookin at it. Unless you wanted the book.

Mrs Winthrop-Moore withdrew. 'For the sake of my dear, late husband, I cannot stay here. It would have shocked him that I should witness such a sight.' (Didn't he have one, then, wondered the young constable?)

Sgt Johnson addressed Dickie as, 'Miss Ardbuckle', whom he vaguely remembered having met at the scene of some petty felony, and said, 'We had a complaint, Ma'am.'

'Yes, sergeant.' She decided to be Blanche.

'Well, about this carry on, Ma'am. A lady says "it's disgusting".'

'And does she come from Tunbridge Wells?'

The people in the queues laughed.

'She comes from Rustrock Spa, I reckon, Ma'am.'

'And do you think, Sergeant, that the human body is disgusting?'

'It's not what I think, Miss Ardbuckle...' (But was this Miss Ardbuckle? Hadn't she popped off...?) 'I'm just a police officer.' Then he noticed Gordon Ruffle making notes. 'Does your editor know you're dressed like that, Gordon?'

'He will do, when the photos are developed.'

Johnson looked at Dickie. 'May we go somewhere more private please?'

'Certainly. Come to the board room. Hugh, will you join us?'

Hugh, whose belt was appropriately illustrated with pages from Kenneth Clark's *The Nude,* followed them upstairs where, once seated, Dickie asked the policeman, 'I suppose you've been on a beach at the seaside, Officer?'

'Yes, Ma'am, I have.'

'Even to the extent of being what is called topless?'

'No, Ma'am, not me personally. The daughter...'

'Then what is all this fuss about?'

'I'm only telling you, Miss Ardbuckle... if you are Miss Ardbuckle...' Dickie didn't flinch... 'that I'm investigating a complaint. And Mrs Winthrop-Moore is a very well-known member of the community...' Whoever he was talking to was still quite dishy, and he was aware of a stirring between his thighs, which wasn't fair, he was only doing his duty...

'What is the exact nature of the complaint, Sergeant?'

'Mrs Winthrop-Moore thought that what she had seen was disgusting.'

'And did you?'

Hugh beamed at the policeman. 'You surely would not think that Miss Ardbuckle would be indecent... if she were here?'

'I think this lady's behaviour is unusual, Sir. So, if I might say so, is yours.'

'Take that down,' Hugh ordered the constable. 'Anything you say, Officer may be used in evidence against you. I must warn you of that.'

'I have nothing to say, Sir, at this moment, except, you may be hearing from my inspector. I'm only here to investigate a complaint.'

The policemen left and passed through Religion & Philosophy on their way out. There, Pete Service, the assistant on duty in an otherwise empty department, was gazing pensively out of the window, his fig leaves around his ankles, absent-mindedly masturbating.

'Shall I book 'im?' asked the constable.

'I've seen nothing,' replied the sergeant. 'Dirty beast!'

'AND in the religious department!'

'You've seen nothing,' said the sergeant.

Mrs Winthrop-Moore was awaiting them across the square. 'Have you charged them with gross indecency, Sergeant?'

'I'll make my report to the inspector, Ma'am.'

The policemen walked away. Sgt Johnson sighed, genuinely dejected. 'I've done murder cases, arson, GBH, robberies of all sorts, motor offences, you name it, I've done it, but when it's anything to do with sex, I don't like it.'

'Would you call that sex, Sergeant?'

'What would you call it, Constable?' He hoped his wife wouldn't notice the stain on his underpants.

· 59 ·

During a short lunch break when Armand de Tancarville drank a gallon of black coffee and ate several slices of quiche which was as good as any he had tasted in his native land, and far superior to any served on his naturist reserve, Fred Brill and Ron suggested that the through-put of customers ought to be accelerated. The queues were getting longer.

'What is this through-put, please?'

'The number of copies you sign, m'sieur,' said Ron. 'There are still long queues. Perhaps you could sign the books and just smile, not talk to them?'

'That would not be polite.'

'Most of them are in a hurry,' Fred told him. 'They've got to get back to work. And they have to get dressed first.'

'How many have been sold?' asked Armand, haughtily.

'To date, m'sieur,' said Ron, 'four hundred and four. If you'd just smiled and said, "thank you", it could have been a thousand.'

'You wish me to be on a treadmill?' But Armand was impressed. He had the gift of mental arithmetic and his royalty was twelve-and-a-half percent. His haughtiness became less marked.

Up in Art, Maimie had quite enjoyed being drawn by three young students, two male, one female, who had settled themselves on a section of carpet (the sand didn't extend to the upper floors) set before a low display stand. 'We thought we'd have our *dejeuner sur l'herbe*, here,' one of them announced cheerfully. Another uncorked a bottle of wine, a third distributed morsels of food.

'Feel free,' said Maimie, 'but try not to spill anything on those Hockneys, though I don't mind if you upset sauce vinaigrette on the Dali calendars – they're 1986.' They all laughed, then ate and drank. When replete, they lay back, patted their own bare bodies reassuringly, then slapped each other tentatively. It was fun being in the nude, as it had been in the paddling pools of early childhood. Each of them felt an inner glow of sophistication which was transmuted to Maimie until she happened to glance at her desk diary.

'Christ!' She exclaimed, then crossed herself instantly, uttered a Hail Mary, and amended her expletive to, 'Bloody hell!'

'You have to get dressed?' asked a student.

'You're right. I've got a class coming from St.Augustine's at half two. The entire A-level sixth. They're coming to choose prizes. What will the sister in charge make of all this nudity? And, of all of you! Please get out quickly. I must find Hugh.'

Maimie fled downstairs, clutching her belt of *Pictures from the Bible*, stumbled over copulating couples, their signed copies abandoned at their sides, and, on the ground floor, met Maurice Watkins (Maintenance) who was keeping vigil, wearing Bermuda shorts. He had refused to go further than that, though he wasn't displeased to show-off his suntan, carefully built-up, year after year, on the old Costa Brava, then topped-up in his backyard. The missus liked him to relax till he was cooked to the point when she found him well and truly done, but he winced at Maimie's panic-stricken call. He liked women he could fancy, however unattainable they might be, though not women as skinny as this one.

'Maurice!' she screamed, 'you must help me. Get rid of all these nudes, I've got a class of catholic schoolgirls coming in an hour. No, less than an hour. And with their teachers – two nuns. They've never seen naked bodies.'

'I wouldn't be too certain of that, Maim.'

'Where's Sir Hugh?'

Maurice responded with a boilerman's megarumble of a bronchial laugh, which went on for unfathomable levels of phlegm. ''E was last seen going up to the pent 'ouse with his girl friend.'

At that moment a crocodile of smartly uniformed gals, many about to burst into womanhood, was seen advancing across the square upon Ardbuckle's, escorted by two nuns wearing headgear similar to that of a state registered nurse.

'Lock the doors,' shouted Maimie.

Hugh appeared, as though by royal command. 'You should have warned me, Maimie.'

'You can't confront a nun looking like that.'

'You forget that they are more used to God than we are.' He flung open the front door, made an impressive imitation of a blessing in Latin, beamed powerfully on amazed students and nuns, and proclaimed, 'Rejoice, for the Lord is with us.' The nuns were not into denying that, though some students wondered about it. But they were all well disciplined and knew the response. 'Rejoice, for the Lord is with us.'

Nuns and pupils filed politely in. Hugh explained that a lunchtime life drawing class had overrun, suggested they should walk quickly past it, and then mount the stairs to Art. He waved them away, turned to Maimie, ordered her into the refectory where she was to quickly dress and told her, reassuringly, 'It will all work out', at the same time as exchanging winks with the younger nun whom Armand was regarding lustfully.

One hour later, Maimie buzzed Hugh. 'Is it safe for my party of girls to come down?'

'Yes, if you blindfold them.'

'Have your nudists gone?'

'They'll be here till we close. If you get through the tunnel to the annexe you might make your way out by the old cookhouse door in Anthropology. Try reaching it from the fire escape.'

In desperation Maimie did. The senior nun, worried because she seemed to have lost Sister Bonaventura, was open to all suggestions. Maimie led the way down stone steps to the ground floor emergency door. There she stopped in horror. The exit was blocked by a nude couple in post-coital slumber. 'I've made a mistake,' she announced. 'We'll try that door,' pointing to one in the wall. They all trooped down further stone steps and into the boiler room where Maurice, dressed now in dungarees, was enjoying a mug of char.

'Maurice,' said Maimie, signalling desperately, 'we couldn't get out the other way.'

'Then you'll 'ave to go up through the shop, Miss Maim.'

'What's it like up there?'

'A norgy.'

'Girls,' announced Maimie, 'I have another treat in store. Sister Mary, don't you think it would be useful for the girls to have a lesson in life drawing?'

'How clothed is the life, Miss Perkes?'

'I will ascertain.'

Helped by John Ogglethorpe, Maimie settled the girls in a ground floor annexe, beyond Paperbacks, where they were confronted by three tired assistants who were instantly recruited to become models. Sister Mary looked relieved that they were female and asked, 'Where is Sister Bonaventura?'

A brief search revealed the young novice, unclothed, standing before an appreciative Armand de Tancarville who was inscribing a copy of his book to her.

'Sister Bonaventura,' said Maimie to Sister Mary, 'appears to have – er – leaped over the wall.'

'At last,' replied Sister Mary, fervently, 'Mother Superior will be so relieved.'

· 60 ·

There were no prosecutions. This irritated Hugh, leading him to wonder what he should do next to achieve his ends. The media had a short field day, treating the naturist signing as a comic incident. Trade improved. The legatees neither officially approved nor condemned the action of their managing director. Abel booked similar signings at two of his shops but failed to attract as much publicity or as many sales. Gordon Ruffle, who had transferred his international phone expenses to the *Gazette & Herald,* borrowed his father's ancient Cortina to drive to Heathrow and meet Margitte.

On the journey back to Rustrock, Margitte said, 'I got some very, very, exciting news for you…'

Gordon felt a momentary chill. 'You're not…?'

'Didn' I tell you about my gran's advice?'

'We can all make mistakes.'

'Not me, Gordie. But I bin finding out a lot of things about myself. And I need your help.'

He leaned over and kissed her passionately as the Cortina swerved onto the M3 filter road, accelerating as it went, until Margitte said sharply, 'Would you mind taking holda that steering wheel! You Brits all drive too damned fast.'

'You've put me into overdrive, Marg.'

'Not in this crappy old banger, I haven't. Where'd it come from?'

'Originally, Marg, from Detroit.'

'I guess,' she philosophised, 'we're all descended from Columbus.'

Following the signing, Hugh and Dickie repaired to the boardroom where, as Dickie put it, 'It's like old times.' They let it be so. She was feeling totally relaxed, having solved the problems presented by dramatising her novel, and having dispensed, at last, with Butch. Hugh realised, yet again, that enforced abstinence had not agreed with him, also that Dickie might prove a useful partner in more than one way in his fight to frustrate the terms of Blanche's will.

Hugh's next move was to make a list of those members of staff, including himself, who would be eligible to vote for the one legatee who was to inherit the crown. John Ogglethorpe had the identical intention. No one with less than a year's service, at the date of Blanche's death, would qualify. It would not be a long list…

In fact, the list amounted to twenty-three persons out of a total staff of one hundred and twenty-four, including part-timers, who did not, anyhow, qualify. This meant that any director backed by twelve or more voters must win but, supposing that four of the candidates each received four votes, the fifth could win with only seven. And, if one candidate withdrew, and three totalled the same number, of six or seven, then there would be a tie, for which there was no provision in the will. Yet, if any of the twenty-three left, or were sacked, before polling day, the winner could take all with fewer than seven. Hugh studied the list he had made and checked for length of service with the wages records. He would vote for Dickie but it would be safer to reduce the numbers of the electoral college. Similar thoughts had occurred to Fergus Welch who had committed himself to an unholy alliance with John Ogglethorpe – for the time being.

The twenty-three included the boyish-looking Adrian Thomson (History), and his assistants, Sandra Stokes and Lester Constantine; Lord Terence Absolom (Poetry); Amy Thresham (Travel), immersed, as always, in familial distractions; Fergus Welch, unofficial head of the unofficial branch of a union Blanche had not recognised; John Ogglethorpe, his unofficial but neither convinced nor convincing deputy; Maimie Perkes (Art) a lifelong entrenched anti-unionist; Audrey da Costa (Mail order) still enfranchised, yet remote in her closed world of mail-order customers she had never met, although once 'dear old Beth' had phoned from the Cape; accountant Jawarharlal Deolali and his sidekick, Denis

Sandlethorpe; Kim Mahon (Sport), who, having a basic residue of anarchy in her genes, did not believe in the finality of any umpire's decision, on or off the field; John Woodstock (Philosophy & Religion), whose sales had not been boosted by the naturist signing; the afflicted but indomitable Daniel Drybrough (Paperbacks); Gerda Kohl (Foreign), over retirement age but still in work because she had nothing but her state pension; Mona Darling (Children's), so devoted to her calling that she sometimes saw her young customers in the guise of rabbits and kittens; Alick Tremlett, deputy to Fergus; Nell Pickett (Cleaner), with her trademark filthy mop, and Maurice Watkins (Maintenance) but he was not planning to stay. The list did not include the bullying Miss Framley whose protection racket, reducing the miserable wages paid to juniors by twenty percent, had, long before, been uncovered by Hugh Mattingson, or Denys, who had left to have a baby, or Lisa, her colleague in the annexe, who was catering for students with a secondhand textbook service run from her front room.

Didsbury Jackson, the stooge in charge of the carnival, a little mouse of a man, who spent part of the winter on half-pay in the Luberon, planning the next annual event on the Common, did not qualify, but there were also Hugh himself and three others: Katie Pimple, Amy's assistant, allegedly a foundling left half-a-century before in Gardening & Natural History; Alouette Mendes, Gerda Kohl's deputy, who spoke English with a Maurice Chevalier accent and soothed customers offended by Gerda's vituperative, intellectual condescension; and Amy Finchingfield, who prepared, cooked and served the repellent dishes, offered at nominal prices, to members of staff willing to eat in the canteen. Amy was employed on a small retainer, plus a share of the profits, and had kept her clientele on the verge of food poisoning for two decades. She reckoned to net as little as 1p on every plate of beans on toast, and wastage was prodigious. It was supposed she stayed in the job only for the sake of feeding her numerous grandchildren who came to the kitchen door, like furtive alley cats, to devour the customers' leftovers.

· 61 ·

The staff received the message that there would be a delay in implementing the new order, apart from nominal pay increases, with a mixture of resignation and annoyance. The collective response, as conveyed to Hugh by John Ogglethorpe, was that they had never been taken in from the start. 'Promises. Promises,' Hugh was told, 'kindly direct me to the next party political conference.' To his colleagues, John said, 'I knew Sir Hugh had overshot the mark. Then all the other silly buggers had to commit themselves to policies even wilder than his.' He was talking to Fergus Welch and Adrian Thomson during a prolonged afternoon break, while their underlings gasped for tea but dared not leave their posts.

Adrian, caressing his chin and feeling distinct evidence of stubble for the first time in a fortnight, said, 'We are getting a token rise. That's something. And they have apologised.'

Fergus forced a belch. 'You'd be fucking useless at the barricades.'

'I've never understood,' Adrian reflected, 'how they contrived to dig up the paving stones on those occasions. If I tried, I'd just break my finger nails.'

Fergus, who had nothing much in the way of policy to offer, commented bitterly, 'What have we got to lose?'

John agreed. 'That's a point. If a really good job turned up, I'd take it. So would you both. But we do have a little power between us. You do realise that?

Do you know the precise terms of the will?'

'Well, ye-es…' from Fergus.

'Well, no-o…' from Adrian.

'I wasn't sent a copy,' jeered Fergus.

John said he'd come across one on Hugh's desk. 'It confirmed what the local rag said. The five directors are on trial. One of them has to be elected as sole winner by such staff as qualify as an electoral college.'

'We know that, for Christ's sake. It includes us three.'

'Right, Fergie, but no one qualifies who hadn't put in one year's service at the time she died. How many does that make in the electoral college?'

'It's probably a question of how few.'

'Right again. Twenty-three, that's all.'

'So what do we do, exterminate everyone who doesn't agree with us?'

'That may be a little drastic, but you're getting there.'

Maurice Watkins trundled in, whistling tunelessly and stating that he was gasping. 'Me kettle's broke. Mind if I 'ave a cup 'ere?'

John asked him what he thought of the message from the management.

'They'll wriggle out of anything, won't they? They always 'ave. And no one's worked longer for Ardbuckle's than me, but I couldn't care bleedin' less. I'm sixty-five next month, and I wouldn't stay, not for a bucket full of fivers. I've got me plans, Johnny. Maurice Watkins ain't goin' to starve.'

· 62 ·

John said to himself, then there were twenty-two, and went to his department. The only immediate prospect he saw for himself lay in playing his cards correctly in the election. His applications to London booksellers for a better job had not borne fruit. After the shop closed, he met Fergie, Adrian and Maimie Perkes at the Duke's Head where they agreed to invite all retail departmental heads, whom it concerned, to an electoral college meeting at John's flat.

John lived with Jane Crispin in cramped rooms which the landlord, name of Ardbuckle, designated a flat. It had been a tied cottage until the law was changed to give tenants security of tenure, a law which Blanche had celebrated by raising the rent as soon as one tenant, having been sacked, moved away to take a job in London. Even Blanche could not pretend that the flat was self-contained. Off the stairway, between the second and third floors of a typical Georgian-style Victorian terrace house, was a minuscule kitchen and a slightly larger bathroom with WC. Up the common staircase were three rooms, two of them divided by folding doors. The sitting room was not inelegant and Jane had furnished it with pieces of her own in defiance of Blanche. The adjoining bedroom took a four foot double divan and a dressing table. The meter cupboard, on the landing, functioned as wardrobe. On the other side of the folding doors was a small dining room.

Jane was having no truck with John's meeting, and was indulged because of her pregnancy. She closed the folding doors and settled to a video of *Gone With The Wind*, announcing that she did not wish to be disturbed. John's eight colleagues crammed into the dining room, most of them round a table on which their host had placed a bowl of nuts, crisps and raisins. There were only four chairs, so some sat on stools, others leaned against the sideboard. 'Jane,' John explained, as sounds of a mighty battle blared from the adjoining room, 'has a migraine.'

When he had poured glasses of blanc de blanc and red Languedoc, and after providing orange juice for Gerda Kohl who said, pointedly, that she never drank alcohol before eating, and Lord Terence had started to light his pipe until howled down by the others, John explained why he had called the meeting. 'I think there will be fewer than twenty of us by polling day,' he concluded.

'I never had a sense of power before,' said Daniel, cleverly manipulating his glass of red at the same time as helping himself to nuts with his foreshortened arm. 'Who haven't you invited, John? We are only eight.'

'I think of us as the core.' They all liked that.

'Of course, the electoral college includes grand Sir Hugh but I think of him as one of *them*.'

Lord Terence, who had certainly never thought of himself as one of *us*, looked up at them from a foot stool in the grate, and intoned, ' "Let us not stray into the paths of caste, the rights of birth" – who wrote that?'

'You probably,' said Fergus. 'This is *not* a literary quiz. It's obvious why you didn't invite Sir Hugh, or the accountant wallah and his clerk. They're part of top management.'

John reminded them that nonetheless they would be entitled to vote. 'So will little Katie Pimple. And Amy... not you, dear thespian,' to the new head of Music & Drama, 'I mean the one who brews our disgusting coffee.' Amy Thresham, far away in a world peopled by divorced stepmothers denied the final sacraments, came to and said sharply, 'I *know* I have a vote!' 'And Nell,' John continued, 'who moves the dust around so effectively.' He felt they were listening to him. 'I'm not saying they don't have their rights. But I thought a preliminary meeting of we departmental managers would be a sensible way of beginning.'

'I know it sounds elitist,' put in Fergus, 'but I agree.' They were all astonished; he never agreed with anyone. 'We must formulate policy, then attempt to impose it on others.' (While he spoke he was studying Terence Absolom's head and felt an urge to have him as a sitter.)

Daniel said he thought Fergus's a truly democratic idea. Amy Thresham looked puzzled.

'Supposing, I am only saying *supposing*,' remarked Terence, fresh from a debate in the Lords (he'd been short of the ready) 'they have different policies?'

'Then they can tell us, can't they, like they do up in your old talk shop at Westminster. But that doesn't prevent us from kick-starting the whole thing.'

'To what end, Fergus?'

'To ensure we get the director who will best look after our interests.'

John took charge again. 'I think it would be a good idea to ascertain who we favour, and also to find out who is Hugh's favourite.'

'Now you are talking,' said Adrian who felt ignored, propped as he was on a small clothes horse.

'How deliciously conspiratorial,' commented Daniel, but Maimie looked sternly at him and contributed the fact that she took the election most seriously, and supported Dean Phillips. 'He's straight. I'd trust him anywhere. And he's an experienced bookseller of the old school. Not a chain man.'

'I suppose you know', teased Daniel, 'that he comes from an old Quaker family which couldn't get a berth on the Mayflower?'

'I have a leaning towards ecumenicalism, Daniel,' Maimie replied with dignity, though little truth.

'Then I'm surprised you don't support Dickie Klute.'

A pitiable voice was heard. 'Mrs Klute was good to me when she first came here, when I was very young.' They all looked at poor Gerda, unable to imagine her at that stage of life. 'I may give my vote to her. Unless they think I must not vote because I might still be a bloody foreigner.'

Daniel said surely she'd been nationalised at about the same time as coal.

'All very witty, no doubt...' John interrupted '...but let's stick to business. Dean Phillips may not stand.'

'In that case,' Maimie said, 'I'd go for Stanley Brooke-Forster. He's an old darling. He doesn't know a thing about books but he'd leave us alone. And he's becoming quite famous in that soap – what's its name? – so that will help our image after all that striptease, which I did not hold with. I certainly would never vote for Dickie Klute.'

They interrupted themselves to reminisce about the signing which, on balance, most of them had enjoyed. More wine was poured. John discovered another packet of crisps. Tummies began to rumble. Some heads were becoming fuddled. Fergus called them to order. Jane turned up the sound on the video to drown the noise of the meeting. Then the plonk ran out.

Terence Absolom said they all needed time to decide who they plumped for. 'Why don't we go home and cogitate, then meet again at my place on Sunday? I'll get the sisters to put on a cold collation.' And, he thought, we can have some drinkable wine.

Fergus, who was unconsciously doodling a profile of Terence on a paper napkin, agreed for an unprecedented, second time but recommended they appoint a chairman and all be sworn to secrecy. From politeness, John was elected, with Terence as deputy, although Gerda said she could not respect the confidentiality since she would have to discuss her views with Alouette, her *assistante*. She stared at them defiantly. Some went to the pub after leaving John's, but not Gerda. Adrian told them, 'She'll go straight to Sir Hugh in the morning and tell him we're plotting. You can't trust krauts. I'm a historian. I know.'

Daniel told him he was pissed. 'But I don't say you're wrong.'

Maimie accused them of talking like football hooligans. 'That reminds me. Why wasn't Kim with us?'

Fergus said, 'John issued the invites. I don't think he trusts her.' He noticed the napkin which caricatured Terence in an Osbert Lancaster-upper-crust-style, and quickly pocketed it

'Yet he invited Gerda.'

Daniel broke in... 'We don't know who Sir Hugh favours.'

'I think we do,' Fergus replied. 'Aren't you aware that Dickie Klute has been installed at Ridge End?'

Maimie asked innocently, 'Has she rented Miss Ardbuckle's house?'

'No,' spat Fergus, 'she's moved in with Sir Hugh. It's his house, for Christ's sake!' Maimie took much of the night to work that one out; Gerda spent much of hers torn between loyalty to employer and loyalty to colleagues. The employer won, which was why she sought an appointment with Hugh next day.

· 63·

Hugh became so engrossed in the Blanche journals that he ceased to suffer from ruffled amour-propre. In any case, since his attraction to Dickie Klute, it no longer concerned him more than momentarily. (And he had rid himself of his mistress with the help of a large cheque.) He had not revealed existence of the diaries to Dickie when she moved into Ridge End, so a certain deception became necessary. While she was in her study writing he could read them in his with a fair degree of security but, like Jane Austen, he always kept the volume he was studying close to cover, and carried it in his brief case to and from Ardbuckle's. What occupied him, now that he had become reconciled to not being a legatee, was the identity of the person who had predated them all in Blanche's life. Cryptic references were made to him throughout the early volumes of the journal – 'Beloved A' – presumably Alphonse – 'A who means more to me than anyone else in my life' – 'A who says he could never marry me' – 'A who my parents find scintillating' – but also, 'A who my parents hope I am not taking too seriously.' Finally, 'A has been killed. My life is as good as over. I shall not mention him again. I shall cease to keep this journal.' So, who was Alphonse? Was it a coded name? And why could he never marry her?

Yet Blanche did resume the journal after World War Two, and with the poignant sentence, 'There is no one else I can talk to, least of all my child. I have therefore to talk to my diary.' What she immediately had to confide to it was mostly about the condition of the shop, the difficulty of getting staff, the dishonesty of those she could get, the shabbiness of everything, her hatred of austerity, her longing to lie in the sun, her desperate loneliness.

So there was – or had been – a child, as was being rumoured around Ardbuckle's. He made a mental note to ask John Ogglethorpe who seemed to think that the young blackguard from the *Gazette & Herald* was somehow involved. Only his obsession with the journals had delayed

Hugh's investigation of what could be an intriguing new factor. Would she, or he, just by the right of primogeniture, have a claim on the Ardbuckle estate? That was a possibility worth exploring. He returned to the journal and came upon this entry, dated New Year's Day, 1950:

So the western world is poised again for its annual ritual of seeing in the New Year, with the pathetic hope that it may be a better one, more significant than the last, bringing undreamed-of rewards. In fact it is only one more night to be followed by another, preceding one more day, etc, December turning into January, for what purpose? I lost such belief as I ever had in the therapeutic qualities of a New Year nearly a decade ago. Then I knew that the only contentment, the only motivation in my life, would be totally materialistic and hedonistic. I was cut off emotionally from this planet. The little bit of happiness I knew had vanished. I was left with health, wealth and an inordinate energy.

Somewhere, I may have a daughter. I do not know if she is healthy, deformed, or even alive. I rarely think of her. My appalling energy insists that I go on ruling other people's lives, indulging my instincts. Either that or I do myself in. But I don't wish to end it all. I don't think I'm afraid of suicide, I just prefer to live. I am healthy, wealthy, probably not wise, and have strong sexual urges. The life force propels me on. I'm not a depressive. I'll see it through.

Hugh was profoundly affected by this credo. For the first time he felt affection for the woman with whom he'd so often slept. Yet he still wished to know about Alphonse. *And* their child! Blanche had never mentioned a child to him. He read on avidly and was rewarded. Late in 1952 Blanche was recovering from flu and pitying herself:

My first illness since the child was born. I hate being ill. I nearly died when I gave birth. I was in a coma for days. By the time I recovered the child had been whisked away out of Europe because it was half-Jewish. A was forced to flee from Germany. I was taken back to England just in time.

War broke out three days later. My life was in ruins.

Hugh read this in his office at Ardbuckle's. He was still musing over it when his secretary, Gladys Little, a thin but obtrusive woman of about fifty who fussed over him unceasingly unless ordered away in Rabelaisian phrases, told him Gerda Kohl was anxious to see him. 'She has been up here four times already Mr Mattingson. Frankly, I don't like to speak ill of people but she is being unpleasant.'

'Gerda was born unpleasant. It's a trait in her which we have to forgive, rather like your everlasting fussing. Have you ever thought, dear Glad, of pretending you are a doormat and flinging yourself down in front of me as I enter the office?'

'I am not a masochist.'

'Know thyself, dear Glad.'

'I only wish to do my job and help you.'

'God defend me from the saints. Why don't I sack you?'

'I expect you will. Nobody keeps me for long.' Gladys pealed out what she liked to think of as her silvery laugh. She had her moments of realism. 'Are you going to see Gerda or not? You won't get any peace until you do.'

'March her in. Preferably in irons. Then bring me a black coffee and a small strychnine for Fraulein Kohl.'

Gerda swept in, her unironed, drab, fawn overall covering the upper part of her long, stained, grubby skirt. 'I should sit down?' she asked.

'Sit down, stand up, lie on the floor, bite the carpet, do whatever comes unnaturally.'

'I think you joke with me, Mr Hugh. You know I do not understand your jokes.'

'That is because I am a failed actor. I do not pro-JECT.'

Gerda stared at him bleakly. Why would he not be serious? She had come to assist him, to show him she was his loyal servant. Why could he not realise?

'Gerda, dear heart, explain what is on your mind. Then allow me to attend to my morning post. Pronounce, Fraulein Kohl! Don't you think I look rather fetching today?' He was wearing a Vatican Swiss guard's uniform.

'Always you are looking beautiful. But not like a bookseller. You should wear overalls.'.

'What a depressing old cow you are, Gerda.'

'Books, they are dirty. Overalls is sensible.'

Hugh regarded her benignly, wondering if that centre fang would come away if he gave it a quick tug. 'What,' he declaimed suddenly, 'is the news on the Rialto? Whose argosy hath sailed from the packing room drains with our wealth?'

'Mr Mattingson, I simply do not understand you. What is this Rialto? But I must talk with you. You are my master.'

Thank God, thought Hugh, she is not my mistress.

'THEY,' said Gerda, with vibrant intensity, clasping her hands so tightly together that Hugh considered what action he should take if they failed to come apart, 'THEY are plotting.'

'They?'

'The electoral college.'

'And which of the particular Us, or Them, are They?'

'The ones who are having the vote. But only the book department managers. Others, lower orders, were not invited to the meeting.'

'So you had a meeting?'

'At last he listens. *Ja*, at the flat of Mr Ogglethorpe.'

'And what was said at the meeting?'

'They wished it to be secret. No one should know.'

'Should I know?'

'Only if I tell you. But I do not do anything yet except to tell you they want to know for whom you vote. They will go to the castle of Lord Absolom and discuss it some more.'

'When will they go?'

'Next Sunday. I shall not go. I will be loyal. They are wanting for us to decide who shall be voted for. I think you should tell them.'

'Perhaps they wouldn't agree with me?'

'You are managing director. You should tell them.'

'I don't think, dear *Fraulein*, you quite grasp the concept of democracy. They, Them, That Lot, do not have to accept what I want. Their vote is free.'

'Surely, Mr Mattingson, you wish to influence them?'

Hugh rose. 'Gerda, you are telling me this to help me. I am grateful to you, but you should forget you have spoken to me. You are not behaving correctly.'

'Always I act correctly. I am not that sort of woman.'

'You misunderstand…'

Gerda stood up, her arms straight at her sides. 'I shall not stay. I will tomorrow formally give you my written notice. I do not like the set-up.'

This did not suit Hugh. He was confident he could always rely on Gerda's vote to be placed where he wished it to go. 'Sleep on it, dear lady, you are not a good age to find another job.'

Gerda burst into tears. 'That is a very rude thing to say to a lady. Nobody likes me. Nobody values me. I was trying to help.'

Hugh called Gladys to comfort the little woman. He asked her forgiveness.

'I did not mean to hurt you, *Fraulein*.' Believing she could be persuaded to stay, he left the two women together and took the Ardbuckle journal up to the penthouse. It magnetised him. Somewhere within it lay the answer, although the answer to precisely what was no longer clear.

August 3, 1970.
I had always had a regard for O when he came to us, as quite a young
man, after the war. I remember his rather noble nose, a Roman sort of
nose, not the type I associate with the working class. Yet I would not
call him a handsome man. Too short, too stocky. It was only his eyes
and his nose which appealed to me. I gave him a job but not, of course,
in the bookshop. He is not literate, never was, though he says he reads
war novels and Hornblower – 'Ornblower, as he calls him. It was the
anniverary of A's death, so far as I know when that exactly was. I fan-
cied him. I called him to look at a plumbing leak. I invited him to stay.
He was tender, wonderful, it was what I wanted at that moment. I
didn't want to laugh. I asked about his wife. He said she'd understand,
except he wouldn't tell her. 'Won't she guess?' I asked. 'Not once I've
'ad a barf,' he said crudely. That spoilt it. 'You'd better go home,' I told
him, but he didn't budge. I asked him to pour us cognacs, and we
talked. I told him things I've never told any of the others.

Who was this, mused Hugh. There was a degree of affection here missing
from almost every other entry. O was a longstanding employee but he
wasn't a bookseller. And he'd done some plumbing. But what was it they
had talked about so intimately? Next morning he demanded staff personal files and wages books back to 1960. Jawarharlal Deolali complained
that all but the most recent were in the archives, up in the roof.

'Then get them down, dear soul, please, NOW.'

'But, Mr Hugh…'

'NOW.'

Soon, Denis Sandlecombe came lumbering into Hugh's office, laden with
red bound Cathedral wages books. 'There are no personal files, Mr Hugh.
Mr Deolali says we've never kept them.'

'Tell him he is guilty of gross negligence.'

'Yes, Mr Hugh. Where shall I put these? My arms are breaking.'

'Dump them on the floor.'

'Mr Deolali says they are highly confidential.'

'I don't think the mice behind the skirting can read.'

'No, sir.'

'Have you been here long, boy?'

'Yes, sir. Two years. I'm Denis Sandlecombe.'

'Denis, my apologies. Two years. So you have certain rights.'

'Am I supposed to have committed some crime, sir?'

'Most of them have.' How would this youth vote? Might it not be better to get rid of him?

Denis said coldly, 'If you'd like to check the petty cash, I think you'll find it balances.'

'If it does, it will be the first petty cash ever.'

'Sir, I resent that.'

'I'm sure it's OK, Denis. Don't worry.'

He's bonkers, thought Denis. Mr Deolali had told him this was a job worth cherishing. Now he had doubts; he'd look around.

· 64 ·

Hugh fell upon the wages books and the answer soon hit him. 'Of course,' he cried aloud, 'How stupid of me.' He dialled a number on the intercom and, after three minutes of total silence, he began to shout at it. 'This is the managing director. Get Watkins at once.' Silence. Followed by more silence. He charged from the office and outside, on the corridor, came upon Katie Pimple who was scuttling past, en route for Travel, hoping not to be noticed.

'Woman! Do you work here?'

Katie gaped at the man in the colourful costume, whom she knew to be some sort of overlord. She was tongue-tied, petrified.

'Or are you a customer? In which case, can I help you?'

Katie stared at him in disbelief, the corners of her mouth beginning to crumple.

'Are you a shoplifter?' thundered Hugh.

Katie went white with terror.

'When we catch them, we hang them from the rafters.'

Katie fainted and a huge tome on modern art crashed to the floor with her. She was mildly concussed; the book was badly cornered.

'I was right!' cried Hugh.

Amy Thresham came upon them. 'Katie dear, why have you been so long... Mrs Thwaites is waiting. Oh dear! Is she ill? Has she had a seizure?'

'She seems to have stolen this book.'

'Nonsense, Mr Hugh, it's Katie Pimple. Katie, my love.' Amy slapped her cheeks. Katie came round.

'Is there any blood?' Hugh enquired.

'A nasty bruise. She must have tripped. She was bringing the book to my department. I doubt if the customer will take it now. It's badly damaged. Katie, how do you feel?'

Katie whimpered and allowed herself to be led to a cloakroom. Hugh tried to assist but she screamed when he came near her, causing Amy to come out of her genealogical trance of the moment sufficiently to ask herself if he had made a pass at the poor Pimple.

In the annexe, in Music & Drama, Mrs Thwaites, who had entered the tunnel by mistake and lost her way, while looking for Art, declared she'd never had such poor service in her life, and swept out unnoticed.

Hugh returned to his office, chastened, and dialled Watkins, this time getting through. That worthy slouched into his presence a few minutes later, out of breath from climbing many steps, shooshing heavily through his lips.

'Was there something wrong, guv?'

'Sit down, Maurice.'

'If I don't I'll bleedin' fall down guv. I was coming to see you anyway.'

'Were you? Why?'

'Retirement.'

Watkins cast his eyes over Hugh's office, relieved that he wouldn't have to decorate it again. All those twiddly bits the architect had thought up.

Hugh savoured Watkins' words. (So now they were twenty-two.)

'I'm about to be sixty-five, guv. Next month. Don't want to inconvenience you but I shan't be staying once me pension is through. I've got this little place down on the Sussex coast, near old bugger Bognor. Lovely spot. Missus is crackers about it. And I promised 'er, ages ago, "when I retire, Dot," 'I says', "that's where we'll pack up and go".'

'How will you support yourself, Maurice?'

'I ain't a poor man, Sir-Roo.'

Hugh wondered what racket he operated. He had never manned a till but he could have something going on the property side. Except that most of the tenants were too impoverished. Perhaps that was why. Protection money they paid Maurice? If so, why was he anxious to go?

Watkins interrupted his ruminations. 'I bin luckier than you might think. She give me some money years ago. By then you'd already come on the scene… and taken over.' He did one of his most prodigious winks, and Hugh realised he was being treated as a fellow bedmate of Blanche's. 'She suddenly got tired of me. Frankly, between you and me, I think she'd got bored. I didn't do nothing funny, know what I mean? I was just straight in and out. And she did like 'aving jolly chats afterwards. You probably found the same but you, being educated, and religious, and all that ole malarky, that's probably why she kept you going longer. I often thought you and 'er must have bin ideal.'

Hugh winced.

'No, come on, Sir-Roo, we've been in this together.'

'But not, I'm thankful to say, at the same time.'

'She always reckoned you was a bit of a snob.' Maurice released one of his choicer choking, phlegmy laughs. 'Never mind, too late to quarrel about 'er now. And any'ow, what I was about to say was, one night when we'd been up to a real old bit of rumpy-pumpy, she says, "That was a bit rough Watkins" – always called me Watkins, even in bed – "That was a bit rough … I don't think I'm going on with this".'

'She said that to you, did she?'

'Yeah, she never wanted to say, "I love you, my darling" and that sort of flannel – now my missus likes that – but Miss Ardbuckle just wanted the ole rumpy-pumpy, then a good giggle. But I don't find nothing funny in it. I think it's bloody marvellous. So does my old girl.'

'So why did you go to bed with Miss Ardbuckle?'

'I like a bit of a change when it's offered. Nothing against my old lady.'

'And does your old lady know?'

Watkins was affronted. 'I wouldn't tell her. We don't go in for dirty talk.'

Hugh took a chance. 'What do you know about Blanche's child?'

Watkins was astounded. It silenced him for all of seven seconds. ''Ow do you know about the child then?'

'How do you know, Maurice?'

'She told me, didn't she?'

'Told you what?'

''Ow it was took from 'er, even before she knew what sex it was. And 'ow she 'ad to be got back to England because of the war. Before the border was shut.'

'Which border?'

'The German border, I s'pose, into France. And the baby 'ad to be got out before that, when she was too ill to nurse it. And the parents, 'is parents, that is, didn't trust the British anyway.'

'Whose parents?'

'The father's. Alphonse, as she called 'im. 'Isself, 'e went to Italy. And that did him no good cos, if you remember, the bleedin' eyeties come in with 'Itler, when they saw 'ow things was goin.'

Even Hugh felt humbled by the amount of history this horny-handed son of toil had amassed.

'So 'e gets to Italy, changes 'is name. That was sensible. Don't know what 'e changed it to, but never mind. And 'e managed to get word to 'is folks who'd gone to America. They got let in, which was lucky for them, but they 'ad banking connections. Alphonse said 'e'd successfully concealed his identity but 'ad to get into the Italian army, so 'e'd 'ave to fight for 'Itler.' Maurice had a violent eruption, noxious catarrhal matter wracked him, his complexion grew purple. Hugh offered a box of tissues. Maurice spat into a few of them, then went on. 'He never saw Blanche again, poor sod, nor his child. Their child, as it was. Blanche was got back to England. Terribly ill she was. She got that skepta?'

'Scepticaemia?'

'That's it. She got that when she gave birth, and it was touch and go. But she rallied. Tough ole bird she was. What a girl! Any'ow, she recovered and come back 'ere to see Ardbuckle's through the war. She didn't tell no one about Alphonse and the baby. Then she got word 'e'd been killed fighting the Russians. The Red Cross told 'is parents in America. They 'ad the decency to let 'er know but they never told 'er nothing about the baby, and she didn't ask. Said she didn't want to know, just wanted to get on running 'er business. That's what she tole me. She was like that. But what a likeness you can see in that one who says she's 'er granddaughter.'

'Her what?'

'That one who works in lit'cher with John.'

'What's her name?

'Einstein, or something. Margitte, isn't it? Any'ow, Einstein's 'er second name. Funny you 'aven't seen 'er.'

'I've been very busy.' Hugh guffawed to cover his alarm. Blanche had never mentioned a child to him. Now there was talk of a grandchild. It might not suit his plans. 'I'm surprised no one mentioned her to me. What do you know about her, Maurice?'

'Nothin' more than what I've told you. 'Ope she won't be a problem, guv. Any'ow I just come up to say I'm goin', and 'ope you won't be inconvenienced.'

'My dear fellow, it won't be the same without you. Perhaps we should give you a party? You've been here a long time.'

'No, I'll go quietly, guv. And I won't take nothing that isn't mine. Just over a month, all right? If I've got any 'oliday pay, I'll 'ave that, please.'

'Of course, I'll see to it.'

'Every little 'elps.'

· 65 ·

That was Watkins out of the way. Another voter gone. Another lover too. He certainly wasn't making it up. Hugh grimaced. Blanche's bedmates could hardly be reckoned a select group. But there were more important considerations. He dialled John Ogglethorpe. 'Can you possibly spare me a minute?'

'Why not? My time is your time.'

John was offered tea, which he declined.

'Something stronger?'

'It's a bit early.'

'As you wish.'

'Is that sherry dry?'

'It's Tio Pepe.'

'Perhaps it's not too early.'

Hugh poured two glasses, then said casually, 'John, you've got a new girl in your department?'

'Yes. Margitte. Margitte something-stein. Goldstein, I think.'

'Not Einstein?'

'Could be. How frightening. Funny woman. She likes to pretend you're her grandfather.'

'Does she, indeed? And who was grandmother?'

'Blanche Ardbuckle, of course.'

'There seems to be a generation gap.'

'Doesn't quite fit, does it? But I had to take her on as casual labour. We were desperate. Trade is suddenly so good. She's certainly earning her keep. We'd been having the usual trouble, so Henry had to go – only been here a fortnight – and that chap from the *Gazette* was in the shop, nosing around as usual, keeping an ear open for anything he could pick up. I can't stand him. But he was useful. Said he knew someone with experience who needed a job at once.'

'And she has experience?'

'Sure. On the Continent. In Israel. She's worked all over the place. Speaks several languages.'

'Watch out you don't lose her to Gerda.'

'I'd heard she was on her way.' Hugh remained impassive. 'Didn't you know, Hugh?'

The managing director eloquently shrugged his shoulders. 'You know our rules. Perhaps it's time I altered them. It's not always convenient to have people clearing their desks at once.'

'Can't say I shall miss her.' John sipped his sherry appreciatively. Hugh topped him up, and said, 'Alouette should be able to cope. She's been here long enough.' He gave emphasis to the last two words.

'Oh yes, Hugh, she's on the electoral roll all right.'

'So this Margitte says Blanche was her grandma?'

'That's right. There is a slight resemblance. When she told me I assumed she'd come to contest the will.'

'That thought had occurred to me, John.'

'She says her attorney told her she wouldn't stand a chance. Apparently she can't prove she's an Ardbuckle because she was an illegal immigrant. Slipped past Ellis Island in a sea mist, that sort of thing.'

'Maybe I should have a word with her. But, first, there was something else… I understand you had a little meeting in your flat, John?'

'Right.'

'And you're planning to have another at Terence's *schloss*?'

'Right again. It's a democratic society, Hugh.'

'That's what I told Gerda.'

'The old kraut wouldn't understand.' Each was thinking: now Gerda's gone, that's another less.

'Is that all, Hugh?'

'I think so, John, but don't gulp that delectable sherry. Funny old set-up isn't it, one way and another?'

'Unique, I'd say.'

'Before you go, John, I should tell you that Dickie Klute is very serious about the election. Has some really sound ideas. She thinks very well of you.'

'I noticed she took a lot of interest in me at the signing.'

Hugh fabricated a resounding stage laugh. 'Seriously, John, if she wins the jackpot, I think there's little doubt you'll be on the board.'

'I'll tell them that at Chateau Terry on Sunday.'

'Get off your high horse, John. Everyone needs a break.'

'Sorry, Hugh. I'm glad Dickie thinks well of me. It's always good to have friends in high places.'

Hugh sent next for Alouette.

'Ma cherie,' he cried, as she entered his room, looking her role in wide-necked top, tapering cord trousers and high heels, her jet black hair swept back behind her ears.

'You 'ave asked for me. M'sieur. There is no one on the floor except a little junior we took on last week.'

'Are you very busy?'

'I don't know which way to turn... everyone asks for Armand de Tancarville in French... I tell them it makes no difference.'

'Alouette, I have to tell you that Fraulein Kohl has left us.'

'You think she did not say "farewell" to me? We 'ave washed the floor with our tears. And now she 'ave no job. She will starve, Monsieur. Nobody cares.'

'Please don't take it so badly. In accordance with company policy she was required to leave at once, although she has been given four week's money.'

''Ow stupid, your company policy.'

'It was laid down by Miss Ardbuckle.'

'Now she is dead, you should change it.'

'Too late. I realise it is difficult for you but I would like to offer you the job of Manager of the Foreign Languages department.'

'And I refuse. I sink you are mad. Please accept one month's notice.'

'But Alouette…'

'I can go back to Paris. And at once. I must not work my notice, as you say, *n'est pas?*'

'Company policy…' Hugh blustered.

'Then you will arrange to pay my wages at once. I am paid in cash.

'Au revoir, M'sieur.'

'Au revoir, Madame. I will instruct Mr Deolali.'

The list was diminishing with alarming swiftness, even before he had drawn up a sublist of likely voters for Dickie. He sent for Margitte Einstein.

Hugh could not believe he had overlooked Margitte. She had all the poise and sharp features of her grandmother. And her eyes, just like Blanche's, darted mischievously about. The dark hair, though, presumably came from her father, whoever he may have been.

'Miss Einstein, I wish you good morrow. We have a small problem. The Languages department is bereft of staff. I won't go into the reasons. I understand, from John Ogglethorpe, you are proficient in various European and other languages?'

'I *sprachen ze deutsche*, I *parle francais*. I have some *italiano* under my belt, a modicum of Spanish. A lotta Hebrew, some Urdu, a smattering of Japanese… I get the Hebrew through my grandfather's family.'

Hugh ignored the last remark. 'I can offer you an extra two thousand a year for your new responsibilities.'

'Better make it five.'

He inclined his head in acquiescence. 'I will tell accounts. But, Miss Einstein, why did you pretend I am your grandfather?'

'It has a kinda truth,' she said mischievously. 'And some guy had to be. Make it six thou, I'll tell you about the real one.'

'I don't believe you knew him,' said Hugh, and outstared her.
'You win.' Margitte laughed. 'But I want cash.'
'Any particular currency, you favour?'
'Sterling but in Scottish bank notes,' she replied.
'And would you like the Queen to be pictured on them wearing a kilt?'
'No, I guess I'd prefer one of her sons. That dishy one who isn't gay.'
'I have a line to the best forger in the business. I'll see what I can do.'
'You really are quite an old poppet.' Margitte walked round the desk and pecked Hugh's cheek. 'I guess, we could get along together.'
Would that, Hugh pondered, rank as incest?

· 66 ·

A contingent of Ardbuckle's middle-management presented itself, in two minicabs, at the west door of Terence Absolom's stately home on a mid-August Sunday, some while before the tourist coaches were due. Maimie Perkes was of the party, dressed in a gold, kaftan-style garment with a square neck, draping girdle, large red buckle and sequined sandals which pinched her toes. Amy Thresham, in more casual attire, found difficulty in emerging from the back seat of the Cavalier saloon, in which she had been weaving fantasies about illegitimate descendents of sheep rustlers whose blood could be coursing through her veins. John Ogglethorpe, who had been influenced by Jane's pregnancy to become chivalrous towards all women, leaped from the passenger front seat to assist her. Fergus, sketch pad in hand, Daniel, confidently facing the world with his eye unshielded, and Adrian, sporting an actual beard of his own, mysteriously coloured rodent grey, climbed from the other car which should also have carried Jim Woodstock, but he had glimpsed a red light and taken early warning. 'Mustn't be too greedy,' he had told his partner. 'All good things come to an end.' They stood a pot plant against the main door of Ardbuckle's in memory of Blanche before driving off to the affluent retirement which she had made possible.

The Absoloms, brother and two sisters, lived in the south-west wing of the Jacobean house (erroneously described, in later centuries, as a castle) which was open to visitors for much of each year. By arrangement with the National Trust, Terence, Lady Babs and Lady Theodosia, had a mere score of rooms for themselves, all carefully screened by dense shrubbery from the prying eyes of trippers. Each had a commodious en suite bedroom, the ladies had separate sitting rooms, and Terence a library/study. There were two drawing rooms, one dining room, a breakfast room, three guest rooms (also en suite), a cavernous kitchen of immense proportions, with separate pantry, still room and scullery, a cellar, numerous loos and powder closets, plus a reception hall the size of a cinema foyer. ('We just don't know where to put anything,' was Lady Babs' constant bleat.)

The Ardbuckle party was received in the gold drawing room (tapestries mentioned in Pevsner) where the walls also featured family portraits that had been awaiting restoration for umpteen generations. Sherry was served before the visitors were ushered up the monumental staircase to Terence's library, for the meeting. There, much time was passed in admiration of his Lordship's comprehensive collection of poets in first editions. (So many never made it to a second.) When interest waned Terence remarked, casually, 'Well, my friends, numbers seem to be dwindling. At the last count the electoral college was a mere nineteen, I am told.'

'Eighteen,' corrected John. 'Sandra Stokes has got her place at Leeds.'

'What I would like to recommend,' said the host, 'is that we seven should be absolutely open with one another, and declare where we stand. Good idea? Hmm?'

Maimie responded at once. 'You know where I stand. I support Dean Phillips. Or, if he's not standing, I'd vote for Stanley Brooke-Forster, for the reasons I've already given. I think it's time to make up our minds and do what we can to ensure job security. I'm for supporting the man we can trust – and he has told me categorically that he's standing – so I just wouldn't feel happy, not backing him. Yes, I'm for Dean Phillips.'

Adrian said that he, on the whole, was inclined to favour the same candidate unless anything significant occurred in the meantime to make him change his mind. Daniel observed that something significant seemed to occur about every five minutes. Terence ignored him and said, 'Phillips is certainly a most agreeable candidate but isn't his age against him?'

'So who,' asked John,' would you prefer?'

'I think it would have to be Dickie Klute. I mean, she is pretty shrewd, and she's literate, and not at all a bad novelist. Also, she does buzz awf every year and write her new book, so she wouldn't always be hovering over us…' Lord Absolom rested his case.

Amy Thresham said she'd rather have a man. ('A new experience for her,' whispered Fergus to Daniel.) '…if only for a change. And I'd go for Stanley Brooke-Forster. I think he'd do us a lot of good.' She blushed. 'And he's awfully good in that thing on the box', thus revealing that she sometimes took time off from her ancestors. 'I told you,' said Daniel. 'Something significant every minute. Well, I back Abel Farmer. He's the man of the future. Look what he's done already!'

Then Fergus threw in his usual suggestion for a management buyout.

'Is it an option?' enquired Terence.

'Could be, if we all stand together.'

His Lordship thought it raised a new issue. 'I don't say it is to be dismissed, Fergus, but is it really on the cards?'

Fergus shrugged, 'If you don't want a fight. I'm easy.' (He had decided to opt out in favour of sculpture.)

'I want to be realistic.'

'So you'd vote for Abel Farmer, would you?'

'I haven't even mentioned Abel Farmer.'

'Terry's quite right.' John Ogglethorpe had been looking for an opportunity of taking charge. 'No one has mentioned Abel, apart from Dan, but there does seem to be a feeling that Dean is the man.'

'Where does Hugh stand?' Adrian asked.

'That must be pretty obvious to most of us. We do know that he is seeing a lot of a certain person who is one of the legatees. Need I say more?'

'So you are saying, John…' Fergus positioned himself to get Terence into profile, '…that we should vote for the Klutey beauty?'

'You've called her that before Fergus, but I'm not saying anything of the sort. I'm just reminding us all of the state of the market.'

'You think Sir Hugh is really serious about promoting Dickie Klute?'

'I'm sure of it.'

Adrian said Abel Farmer would fight that.

'Of course, he will', said John. 'That's why we should decide whether we are to support Abel or Hugh. Our numbers are thinning all the time. I don't think Dean Phillips comes into it, I really do not. He's a nice chap but he's like the Libdems – he's never going to win outright.'

Maimie said that simply was not true. Lord Terence agreed. 'The consensus seems to be moving towards him. I think we should now sound out the other people in the electoral college, those who are not here. Meanwhile, we should go down to lunch. My sisters have prepared a cold collation. Do hope none of you is allergic to fresh salmon.'

'I'm vegetarian,' said Fergus, who wasn't, but wanted to see how irritation might alter Terence's physiognomy.

'Never mind, dear boy,' replied his Lordship, with total sang-froid, 'there's an ample cheese board.'

'Do the maggots in Stilton count as meat?' asked Daniel.

· 67 ·

Abel realised there would be months ahead before probate was granted. He turned his thoughts from Ardbuckle's. At the end of the summer he also thought he needed a diversion from his own business. He recalled he was a member of the MCC, thanks to an uncle who had put him up decades ago. There was a match at Lord's that day. He would take a few hours off.

Abel presented his pass at the pavilion door, was waved through and sauntered into the Long Room where he instantly felt a sense of privilege. Only members could come here. About twenty thousand plus of them, and it was as well they weren't all there at once, but never mind. He exulted, momentarily. Then, he thought, what about some cricket? He walked out of the Long Room, on to the terrace of seats in front of it, as he remembered that this was the most cherished position of all from which to watch. As he sat down the players were suddenly all running for cover. Rain had stopped play. He found himself next to some johnny who was annotating a book. He saw it was the *Legends of Arthur*. The man snorted as he read and pencilled in comments. 'Bloody marvellous!' He exclaimed. 'The moment you sit down, the heavens open. Always the same. Back to dear old Arthur.'

Abel sat awhile hoping the rain would stop. It didn't. The man reading his very tattered copy of *Arthur* sighed. 'Time for a booster. Care to join me?'

Abel was only too relieved to accept the invitation. He walked through the Long Room to the bar and stood at the counter with his new found friend, who observed, 'Don't think I've seen you here before.'

'Don't often come.'

'There'll be women soon. Bound to happen.'

'They get in everywhere,' said Abel, understanding that that was the correct response.

'Know anything about King Arthur?'

'Not much. Did it at school.'

'My latest chore for dear old Three. Now my wife would find it an absolute doddle, dear old Dickie would. She's a writer.'

'Dickie? Do you by any chance mean Dickie Klute?'

'You know her? Do you happen to have seen her lately?'

'Indeed, yes. We're co-directors of a bookshop in Rustrock Spa.'

'Ardbuckle's? Dickie told me about that. It's where we met. She's hoping to make her fortune out of it. But now, I'm told, some long lost child has emerged'

This was news to Abel. 'Ye-es', he said, and you can't get more non-committal than that.'

'Funny old set-up there. You're not the chap she's in cahoots with, are you?'

'I'm Abel Farmer.'

'Don't think that's the name. I say I probably shouldn't be saying all this to you.' They laughed. Abel asked Butch if he'd like 'the other half?'

'No thanks, old chap, it'll be a long day. Later on.'

'I don't think I'll hang around. Looks as though it's really set in.'

Abel strode quickly away from Lord's and hailed a taxi. Who was this family interloper? And what were Dickie and Hugh up to? He supposed Hugh had decided to back her for the jackpot, then muscle in on it himself. Crafty bugger. And there they were, on the spot, rallying support. Back at his office, Abel lost no time in inaugurating his own campaign. 'John,' he trumpeted down the phone in the exaggerated manner which some employ when they are uncertain what tone to adopt. 'John Ogglethorpe! How are you? How are THINGS?'

Gawd, thought John, he's already on the campaign trail, I must find him a baby to kiss. 'I'm fine, Abel, thanks. And you?'

'Me? I don't have time to even think about it. Business still buoyant?'

'It's pretty good.'

'Great. Now John, are you by any chance free this very evening?'

'I could be. Depends where.'

'At Rustrock.'

'Then, yes.'

'Could we dine?'

'Surely.'

'What about Crespini's? It's in *Michelin*. Should be all right.'

'So long as it's not AA recommended.'

'You're right. Seven… nineteen thirty, then. Bye John.'

'Cheers, Abel.' Prat, he thought.

John would have preferred La Foliage Imaginaire because, for him, French cuisine was unsurpassable, even when, as at that particular restaurant, the chef was the son of a Cumbrian peasant. However, Crespini's would be interesting. No doubt there would be a passable sea food salad, and perhaps a tasty lasagne. And there could be a delectable *dolce* to follow. John was a man who found it irksome to live, with champagne tastes, on an iced lager income.

The lasagne in fact, was not at all bad, not as good as Jane's when she was concentrating, but acceptable. And Abel was lavish with the wine although he drank little himself. He decided not to mention the New Pretender, whoever he/she was, but got down to business almost at once.

'This waiting is crucifying me.'

'It's getting everyone down.'

'Not surprising. But I haven't brought you out to dinner to whinge about that. The whole structure of Blanche's will is typical of her but I can't do anything about it. I can, though, do something for you… if you are interested.'

John sipped wine. It was chilled, which was good, tasteless, which was not, but it would have had flavour had it been brought from the fridge earlier. John took food and drink seriously. He had scarcely registered what Abel had said.

'At the Ridge End party I had a chat with your Jane.'

'She told me.'

'She hates it here.'

'She's told me that too.'

'I bet she has. When's the baby due?'

'In four months.'

'Now, John, I'm opening in Regent Street in three month's time. We're geared into a tremendously expansive groove. How would you like to be assistant general manager?'

'Not as much as I'd like to be general manager.'

'Good answer, but I already have one. There'll be other openings soon though.'

The waiter interrupted them, brandishing an obscenely large pepper mill. While he wielded it, John gained a little respite in which to think.

'It may seem to you' said Abel 'that I am going behind the backs of my co-legatees but, frankly, the way they are behaving, I think the rule book's gone out of the window.' John looked at him silently, still trying to concentrate on his food (he hated the whole concept of 'the working lunch'). 'Especially now that Hugh seems to be regarding himself as a candidate.' John remained silent. 'Of course, you'll want to discuss it with Jane. Sleep on it, and all that. I'll tell you what I have in mind salary wise.' He spoke of pensions, annual increments, accommodation, sick pay. John became less obsessed with his meal. As he took a slow, long mouthful of wine, he realised that Abel's offer was what he had been looking for in writing all those letters. Jane would be over the moon. Of course it would mean letting Fergus down, even though he'd already told the Ulsterman that he would leave if he found the right place. He had also hinted to Hugh and Dickie, both of whom he genuinely liked, that they might have his support. Under them, he would be virtually in charge of Ardbuckle's, and he'd rather work for Ardbuckle's than for a chain. But, he would also rather work for a man than a woman (the Blanche experience had biased

him) and supposing Margitte was a serious contender? He decided not to
mention her.

Abel chatted on about his expansion plans. John tried to concentrate on
the zabaglione. It was no use. 'You've made me feel like a rat, Abel.'

'You have to look after number one.'

'I have to look after numbers two and three first.'

Jane whooped with pleasure. 'When can we go? You won't turn it down? I
don't think I could have borne this place much longer.'

'I feel shitty about ratting on Hugh and Dickie.'

'They'll understand.'

When he told Hugh he blamed it on Jane. Hugh was dignified about it.
In fact, he was not all that upset. The electoral college was getting small-
er by the hour but all the candidates were losing supporters, not just
Dickie.

Fergus Welch made a show of being displeased but agreed to be taken
to the Duke's Head after work, where he said fiercely, 'You'd better make
it a double,' as he settled to sketch John's head on a beer mat.

'Now look, Fergie, you couldn't expect me to turn down such an offer.
I have Jane and the baby to think about as well. And, if Abel doesn't win
Ardbuckle's, he'll open here and bust it. Then where would I be?'

'I was relying on you,' said Fergus with an utter lack of conviction, totally absorbed as he was in sketching. 'I'll tell you what, John. I'm feeling
magnanimous. I'll forgive you, if you'll just sit still a moment and let me
draw you.'

'Suppose Abel offered you a job, also?'

'Just keep quiet will you. Hold that expression.'

'What's this all about?'

'I'd like you to sit for me, John. Would you do that?'

Fergus had made a decision. Business had picked up. Blanche was going to give him a posthumous handshake. Since Muriel had left him he was getting on reasonably with Dolly again. He'd send her out to work and he'd mind the house. The kids were at school. He'd have time to sculpt. He began to visualise Absolom, John Ogglethorpe, and even Maimie, in desperately thin Etruscan mode, with Giacometti overtones. So sod, Science & Technology. He had a sudden vision of a long, spindly Absolom turning away from an emaciated Maimie. The thinness would symbolise their impoverished minds. Or perhaps he'd do a headless Terry, with his face between his legs and something lewd protruding through his mouth. And if that didn't win the Turner, what would?

· 68 ·

Next day on arrival at Ardbuckle's Alick Tremlett asked for a word in private with Fergus. They ascended to the turret above Science & Technology where Physics & Chemistry was accommodated in an octagonal room with no windows. Here there were only skylights onto a platform surrounded by charming finials. It was that same chamber where the nude Fergus had encountered Professor Ellstein.

'You won't like this, Fergie, but I'm going.'

'I couldn't care sodding less.'

Alick was flabbergasted. He had made a great effort to face Fergus to tell him. They had been kindred spirits, efficiently running the department together, at the same time as ridiculing the mangement and developing eccentric procedures for their own amusement. Alick knew he would miss Fergus; he had supposed Fergus would miss him. 'Don't you want to know where I'm going?'

'Not really. It wouldn't surprise me if you became a fucking copper.'

'That's insulting.'

'What will you do? Throw me down the pseduo-Gothic stairs?'

'It might relieve my feelings but I don't want to get done for assault and battery.'

Fergus studied his friend's head and decided against asking him to sit, even for old time's sake. 'I'll see you tonight at the Duke, Alick, for a farewell drink.' When the other man had gone, he opened the till. Now wasn't that just his luck! It was full but there wasn't a banknote to be seen; only cheques and credit card vouchers. Had that bastard Alick got there before him? But it didn't matter. He wouldn't leave for a week or so. He was sure Blanche would have wanted him to have some remembrancer of her. He, also, had made her laugh.

So, when Abel slipped in unannounced Fergus's hand was not in the till.

'Hi, Fergus. Seen Hugh around?'

'We see very little of him, Abel.' (Here was a head he could easily resist.)

'Tell me, Fergus, have you met this new girl who's doing Foreign?'

'She's as dishy as they come. Hugh has his eye on her.'

'Who is she?'

'American, I'd say.'

'Does she have a work permit?'

'Abel, MISTER Farmer, *Sir*, you forget, I'm not actually one of you.' (His nose wasn't bad but the head, as a whole, was uninspiring.)

Alick had been offered the job of sales manager with a firm of medical publishers. He handed his letter of resignation to Hugh, who was wearing a chef's cap and apron. 'That's the second today,' he said calmly. 'I've just sacked that creature who was about to give us all food poisoning. Amy Finchingfield. After we closed last night I inspected her kitchen. She'd gone home. Salads had been prepared for today on unwashed plates and covered with sheets of grubby newspaper, under which the flies were already entering for their supper.'

'Maybe you should have given her a dishwasher. I never ate in the canteen anyway. I have two week's holiday pay due, Hugh. I'll stay for ten days if that helps.'

'That's good of you, Alick. We are a bit stretched and I'll have to relax that rule about not working your notice.

When Alick had gone Hugh set about devising plans for reducing the electoral college further. At a quick reckoning there were still about fifteen of them. As he adjusted his striped apron, an idea occurred, a bright idea, which would certainly appeal to Abel. Dickie would also agree and she would fix Stanley. Monty was in Brussels being interviewed for a job in the Olive Directorate. Dean would be outnumbered. He quickly wrote a notice and had it duplicated to all staff, telling them that Ardbuckle's, with effect from the following Monday, would become a twenty-four-hour store. There was no danger of prosecution, Hugh stated, because that was the way EC law was going. Ardbuckle's would be seen as an innovator and, once again, draw a blaze of publicity. Existing staff would be paid double time. There would be large incentives for the highest sales achieved between one and five am.

At a brief meeting with Abel, who was called away to a crisis in his own firm, he assured him Margitte's claims were bogus but that she was a useful, if temporary, addition to a depleted staff. (And, thought Abel, she doesn't have a vote.)

At the same time as writing off for other jobs, and replying to ads in *The Bookseller* and *Publishing News,* most staff agreed to the new opening hours and duties, although even Maimie demanded cash for doing so.

Hugh's venture was not a success. One financially hard-pressed assistant, not of the electoral college, was mugged at midnight, in the dimly-lit tunnel leading to the annexe, and taken to intensive care. In John Ogglethorpe's once decorous Fiction & General, there was a steady sale for sex manuals and romantic novels but a security man had to be engaged to protect the salesperson on duty. Mysteriously, lights failed on already gloomy stairways. There were accidents, broken limbs, claims. By the end of four weeks, when Mark Ampersand insisted that the new hours were counter to what the Trustees could permit, many had given notice and left: Daniel returned to north-east London to live with his adoring mum, and work in a co-operative alongside a row of seedily reputable charity shops; Fergus hacked away at stone, occasionally remembering to give the baby a bottle; the unathletic Kim, who preferred the Scrabble board to any outdoor recreation, took on an off-licence where she was allowed to chain smoke; the shaggily-bearded Adrian, now looking at least two-thirds of his age, opened a branch of Waterstone's on Skye, while Lester diversified into microchips, balancing them, he declared cheerfully, on both shoulders. Mona Darling went into partnership with Mrs Winthrop-Moore, taking a shop for the young in a neighbouring small town, stocking only books which depicted children and animals respectably clothed. Katie Pimple, who had never recovered from her encounter with Hugh, was admitted to a home for deprived persons. Jawarharlal Deolali accepted a partnership in a large corporate accountancy group, and took Denis with him, along with at least five hundred, mostly family, clients having corner shop, pharmacy and CTN affiliations. Audrey da Costa, retired on a semi-permanent basis to a health farm, accepting the suggestion of Monty Devereux, who had become roving Commissioner for Olives, to sell her 'personal' customer list to an independent London-based bookshop. The latter was a cover for spurious 'olive' branches in Andalusia receiving huge subsidies from Brussels.

Hugh then announced a 75% sale of all stock. This, at last, brought the Directors together, Monty flying in to attend from northern Sweden where he was investigating claims from an alleged olive grove owner in a region of semi-tundra.

· 69 ·

Abel Farmer, who had resolved his minor crisis, called an emergency board meeting.

'I just don't understand Hugh's motivation,' said Dean Phillips. 'I know he's eccentric but how was this to help in any way?'

'Obvious,' Abel told them, 'he's deliberately trying to ruin the business, and hoping to reduce the electoral college to a single person – himself. Then he could decide which one of us was to have the jackpot, and on *his* terms. I do blame myself for not realising sooner what he was up to.'

Monty wondered aloud who Hugh would have selected.

'Dickie, of course. Who else?'

This meant nothing to Dean who asked, 'Where is she anyway?'

'She sent apologies for absence but no explanation. She's standing by Hugh, presumably.'

'Of course he'll have to go,' Monty said.

They were agreed and sent for Hugh, who entered dressed as a diplomat about to attend a levee, and carrying a vast, bulky, plastic bag. He looked gravely at each of them in turn. 'Shall I be seated?'

'It should not take long,' Abel replied coldly.

Hugh listened, without interruption, to the allegations against him, that he had knowingly damaged the reputation of the company, used its resources recklessly and endangered the lives of staff and customers. He was ordered to resign and told some sort of compensation would be worked out by Mark Ampersand, if it was felt this was due to him. Or he might be sued.

'I shall not argue with you, gentlemen. I realise that my behaviour was inexplicable to you, and it is unlikely that you could perceive it from my viewpoint.'

'Come,' Stanley said, kindly, 'you mustn't think we are in any way biased, Hugh. We are just looking at plain facts.'

Monty sang, 'We don't want to lose you but we think you ought to go.'
The others glared him into silence.

Hugh said, 'Before you implement your verdict, as stated by Abel, I
think I should offer you one item of evidence that you are bound to have
overlooked because you had no knowledge of it.' He solemnly handed
round photographed copies of Blanche's Journals, annotated with page
numbers particularly recommended for the attention of each recipient.

'May I suggest, gentlemen, that you withhold a decision until you have
had time to peruse these journals? Call me when you have read them. In
the meantime I will undertake to stay at Ridge End... for which, I may
add, I have not received rent since Blanche's death, but no matter... and
I will not go near the shop.'

Hugh bowed elaborately, swinging the now empty carrier bag up and
down as he left.

The practical Dean Phillips enquired how many actual staff were man-
ning the shop. Abel said he would ask Margitte Einstein, who seemed to
have appointed herself temporary General Manager, then opened the formidable dossier which Hugh had handed him. 'These would seem to be
Blanche's memoirs, according to the label stuck on to the cover.' He
opened a page marked for his attention. 'I wonder what I'm to make of
this.' He read a little. 'Hm, I think we have no alternative but to give it our
attention.'

'That's me,' chortled Monty. 'I remember that day.'

'We would be wise,' Abel suggested, 'to book ourselves into hotels for the
night, to study these documents. May I arrange bookings, at the company's expense?' They nodded assent. 'I suggest we meet again tomorrow
evening for a preliminary discussion.'

Stanley said he couldn't stay because he was filming.

'Then I advise you to read this in your car, or train, or helicopter. It
looks highly relevant to our situation here.'

'I have lines to memorise, Abel.'

'It can't be worse than when you were doing weekly rep, Stanley.'

'He really is a tyrant,' the actor complained to Monty. 'I'm getting quite sick of the whole thing. *And* I haven't had a salary cheque this month yet.'

· 70 ·

The following morning Hugh Mattingson was called at home by Gordon Ruffle. 'Couldn't get you at the old emporium.'

'I'm a bit poorly. Going in later.'

'ARE you, Mr Mattingson? I got the impression you might not be going in again... at all.' Pause. 'Ever.'

Hugh was silent.

'We're running a story about Ardbuckle's this week. About all the staff who are leaving.' He made no reference to the press paragraphs that had appeared about a claimant to the Ardbuckle estate because Margitte and he were pursuing a waiting policy, not having sufficient capital to take on the legal profession, but he added a barb: 'I heard you might also be going.' 'I do not pay attention to rumour. Nor should you.' Hugh replaced the receiver.

'Right,' said Gordon, 'he's no help.' He then tried, in vain, to reach Abel Farmer, Dickie Klute (not knowing she was with Hugh, for he had not caught up with that one), Dean Phillips and Stanley Brooke-Forster. Only when he phoned Monty did he get through. Monty had had calls redirected to his hotel. 'It says, Mr Devereux, in the *Independent* this morning, that there's been a walkout of staff at Ardbuckle's.'

'That's a strange thing, Gordon.. I thought I'd read my *Indy* pretty thoroughly. I didn't notice that.' Had this wretched youth also got a copy of Blanche's diaries? 'You must excuse me, I'm very much engaged at present...'

'I suppose the name Alphonse Einstein doesn't mean anything to you?'

'Should it?'

'I'm just asking, Mr Devereux.'

'As a matter of fact, it does not. Must go. Excuse me.' He rang off, returned to the journals and, for the third time, read the marked passage about himself. He thought it showed him in rather a good light. Nowadays it might be a vote winner.

· 71 ·

The legatees gathered in Abel's suite for pre-dinner drinks. Dean was the first to arrive. 'I suppose it's going to be blackmail?'

'Publish and be damned, is my reaction. There's nothing more here than has already been implied by the tabloids. And the thing is not authenticated. Nowhere is Blanche's name on the diary, except for the label Hugh has stuck on the cover. Not that I've read it all.' Abel went on to wonder if Hugh had invented it. 'He has written a lot of books.' That had not occurred to Dean.

'Would he have had time to put all this down in longhand? Don't we have samples of Blanche's handwriting in the office?'

'I suppose we must have. Another point, Dean, is whose copyright is this? It can't be Hugh's but, if it *is* her diary, it could be ours, as legatees. In fact, it must be.'

'Have to ask Mark Ampersand.'

'I wonder if he knows about it?'

Monty arrived, still looking pleased with himself. 'I think we'll have to suppress this one, amusing though it is.' He did his screech to emphasise the point. 'Which one are you, Dean? I couldn't be certain.'

'Let's leave it that way.'

The intercom buzzed. 'Mr Abel Farmer? A message for you. I think the name is Brooke-Forster. On the outside line.' 'Abel, dear heart. Can't possibly make it. The Queen Mum has requested the Dame and me. Yes, a cameo sketch for the Royal Command show at the Pallydiddlum. The piece is still being written. The Dame and I are standing by for instant rehearsal.'

'Must be rather like an orchestra waiting for a Rossini overture.'

'Don't get that one, ducky. We couldn't refuse. It's quite an honour.'

'What did you think of the diaries?'

'Haven't had time to read them yet, dear heart, except the bit that was marked for my attention. I can't think why? Who did you say wrote them?'

Abel rang off. Over dinner the three men decided to ignore any threat of blackmail and to go ahead with sacking Hugh. They demanded his presence in the board room next day.

Abel greeted Hugh warmly. 'Thank you so much for having this entertaining document copied for us. I speak for us all when I say how much we enjoyed it. Except Stanley. He, alas, has not been able to find time to read it. Tied up with the Queen Mum, or something. But, Hughie, I think it's bound to interest some publisher or other, only it has to wait until probate has been granted, and the election is over. We can't possibly consider it until then.'

'What a pity!' cried Hugh, '*Quel pitié*. I think you'd be wise to sign a contract now. I understand a pirated edition from Taiwan is on its way.'

'Really? I'm astonished that the Far East should be so concerned with the ramblings of an anonymous English bookseller.'

'The world, Abel, has shrunk.'

'So has yours, Hugh. Shall we discuss severance?'

'I think we should wait for Dickie. She's on her way.' Hugh beamed benignly at them. He was playing the part of a minor executive today, wearing a faintly pin-striped suit over a sky blue shirt, with a plum coloured tie. It was his compromise way of merging into the background.

Dickie soon burst in, full of apologies, her loose garments flying behind her, and clutching a copy of the journals. 'Hello, darlings! Isn't this fun? I think I've recognised all of you but shall we go through it together?'

Abel said, 'Dickie, we are about to take a decision. In fact, we took one at the last meeting. Which you did not attend.'

'I was so up to here in my new book, darling. I am sorry.'

'We took a decision to ask for Hugh's resignation. I think you know why?'

'Yes, he did mention it. But, I'm afraid you can't, Abel.'

'Dickie, we have.'

'You seem to have overlooked the fact that the legatees have to be unanimous in their decisions. It was to get over that, we decided to appoint Hugh managing director. Don't you recall, darling?'

'In these circumstances, Dickie – I refer to the illegal opening of the shop and the ridiculous sale – you'd be quite irresponsible not to vote with us.'

'Sorry, darling, I think otherwise. Now, are we going to have any jolly any other business, or shall we talk about the journals?'

· 72 ·

So Hugh resumed his duties at Ardbuckle's, where his first move was to befriend Margitte Einstein whom he saw as a possible ally. As the shop closed one evening they bade farewell to the much depleted staff and went into the Duke's Head, moving to a secluded alcove where, years before, Blanche had sat with Dean Phillips and, years later, Margitte had met Gordon.

'The likeness could not be more marked,' Hugh admitted, examining the slim young brunette nursing, in two hands, the inevitable coke.

'To whom?'

'Why, Blanche, of course. Your grandmother.'

'No need for a blood test, or carbon dating? You won't have to cut off my feet and count the rings round my ankles?'

'That's for the board to decide. Tell me, dear heart, about your mother.'

'We didn't get on. We hated each other. She tried to dominate me. So I left home when I was a kid. I didn't get along with my great-grandparents either. I looked too much like Blanche. They just loathed Blanche. She wasn't Jewish, which meant her daughter wasn't either unless she chose to convert, which she didn't.

'Real happy families, then.'

'You could say that. You see, when Blanche met Alphonse... you know about Alphonse?'

'Yes,' he said, 'I think I do.'

'He was half French, half German. He and Blanche met somewhere in the Hartz mountains when she was on holiday. They just fell for each other. The parents on both sides disapproved. Well, the war was coming up. Would you wonder? But I guess it was too late. Blanche was already pregnant. Not just pregnant. She was due, for Christ's sake. Alphonse reckoned his parents should get out anyway because there was certainly Jewish blood in them. And they were liberals, didn't approve of Hitler. He was going to stay behind to be part of a plot against the Nazis. So they got across the border, and the baby was born. My grandmother, Blanche, was very, very sick. She almost died. And while she was in this Swiss hospital Alphonse's parents – my great-grandparents – played the Jewish card and managed to get to the States. I think they were in banking. I guess they would have to have been.'

Hugh admired her straightforward mind and, for once in his life, did not feel a compulsion to interrupt. He even refilled her glass of Coke.

Margitte continued; 'Blanche was gotten back to England. She never met Alphonse again. That particular plot against Hitler didn't come to anything, and he escaped to Idaly. He changed his name, obtained eye-tie citizenship, got called up. He died on the Russian front about three years later. The old folk sent a message to Blanche about that but otherwise never had any contact with her. She didn't even know whether her kid was a boy or a girl. Imagine that! And it wasn't till my mother was dying… only quite recently… we'd quarelled and I hadn't seen her for a long while… I won't go into all that… anyways, she sent for me… and that was when I learned about Blanche, and I was told I might be an heiress.'

'Which is why you're here?'

'Sure thing.'

'Let me get you another Coke.'

'Thanks. Would you like to put a little something in it? Like vodka, please. Don't know what they do to the Coke over here. Doesn't taste the same.'

'Probably it doesn't travel. Have you tried Pepsi?'

· 73 ·

The electoral college still numbered six. The only certain vote was Hugh's for Dickie, but Monty, the eternal politician, who was not expecting to be at the Olive Directorate for ever, still believed he had a chance.

Dean was being actively responsible in keeping the shop staffed because he, with Phyllis's approval, had committed himself to standing in the election, as a protest against the casual manner in which the business was being conducted. Phyllis was certain Dean would win, if some sensible senior members of staff remained.

Dean asked Abel and Monty to take spells of shop floor duty. Abel was bound to agree although he was much needed in his own firm. Dickie volunteered and was entirely obliging, setting a wonderful example, much resented by the other directors, by agreeing to work six days a week. ('Eight, if necessary!' she was heard to say.)

Monty, commuted between Brussels, Strasbourg, far-flung olive groves and Rustrock Spa, and found it all exhilarating, although most of his time was spent on airplanes… at public expense. Only Stanley defaulted. He was in work. Poor Pottersby had suffered another stroke. His former part in the soap was Stanley's for the foreseeable future.

Abel, assessing the dwindled list of voters, felt certain of none of them, even though he had promised Terence Absolom a pitch within Farmer's for his prestigious poetry department. Similarly, Dickie had only one certain vote – Hugh's, but even that was now in doubt because Mark Ampersand was investigating his eligibility on the grounds of insider interest. When Hugh was made managing director he had been given five shares in the company. The terms of Blanche Ardbuckle's will excluded anyone with a financial interest in the company from being an elector.

It, therefore, seemed advisable to Abel to eliminate some of the half-dozen remaining electors. He offered Maimie Perkes the art department at his Winchester branch, and created a genealogical mail order division, based on the same store, for Amy Thresham, who spent the length of her interview with him deep in thought about a Tudor ancestor who had converted to Protestantism while hiding up his own priest hole. Abel thought that Amy and Maimie, who had recently formed a fond relationship no longer frowned upon too heavily by some of the holy papa's advisers, would fit the ambience of the cathedral city well, even though they were not Anglicans. When Maimie, who was in no position to demand conditions, said she hoped she would be salaried, and paid monthly, he replied, 'Quarterly, if you wish.' And she agreed, subsequently spending anxious weeks awaiting her cheque, not having understood that it was quarterly in arrears.

The unenfranchised Didsbury Jackson was next to go. He had lived, since Blanche's death, in a state of hypertension and, although the carnival had run its course without a major upset, he still felt bereft of a mother figure, a sentiment which would have surprised Blanche. It certainly worried his partner who persuaded Didsbury to sell up in Rustrock and retire to their tumbledown farmhouse in the Luberon.

At about the same time Nell Pickett was heard muttering obscenities as she dirtied the shop floor with her mop. No one could be certain of her vote so, when it was discovered that she was seventy-eight, she was compulsorily retired, given a brass handshake and a leaving gift of her old rags. She was found sheltered retirement, where, for the first time in her life, she had the use of a flush toilet and a bath with running hot water. The experience killed her off within a month.

· 74 ·

This left Hugh and Lord Terence the only voters. Then Mark Ampersand pronounced Hugh ineligible. Hugh retorted by giving the five shares, which made him so, to Dickie. 'It makes no difference,' Abel told him, 'because you have not been an ordinary employee between the time of Blanche's death and *now*', an interpretation which Ampersand upheld.

Following the mass departure of such long-standing staff as had existed, there was no departmental manager left apart from Lord Terence. Margitte, by default, became overall deputy general manager, reporting to Hugh who had told her that Blanche's will was valid and that she stood little chance of challenging it successfully. On the other hand she could rely on his support to get some redress if 'his candidate', as he put it, won. He then spent much of each day researching and confirming her background with the help of his erstwhile American assistant, Ella, now a Republican senator. Every day his efforts to reach the jackpot via Dickie seemed less likely to succeed, so he was exploring another avenue. Ampersand sent in two qualified accounts clerks, at enormous expense, to handle the finances, and the five legatees took spells of duty, each spending a portion of their working time with sole elector, Terence Absolom who, for his part, saw as much of them as possible. He took his position seriously, almost as seriously as they did, arranging lengthy tête-à-tête luncheons. Each legatee made desperate efforts to be natural and at ease; behind the upper class mask of good breeding they thought they detected disquiet in Terence, and they were right. On the night before the day of reckoning he tried desperately to come to a conclusion; he was determined to be fair, although part of him wished to revert to type, and banish the lot of them. Even to cut off their heads!

The five contenders sat in a semi-circle, in Mark Ampersand's office, facing Lord Absolom, whose marked pallor had less to do with having to confront them than with his totally unexpected succession to the Dukedom of Bidborough that very morning. Mark, full of foreboding, as Terence rose to speak, sat at the secretary's desk, against one wall.

'Would you mind awfully…' began the (supposed) Lord. He had scarcely ever met the second cousin whose death, from AIDS, had dramatically elevated him to become the first ducal poet since George Villiers…'to remain seated?' He took a long drink of water. He must concentrate, forget about his own problems, concentrate on theirs. Each of them, hoped to become a billionaire; he had just become a duke, yet life's rich tapestry was looking distinctly tawdry to him.

He pulled himself together. He beamed at his colleagues. (He'd been an impoverished peer all his life; what was so different about being an impoverished duke?)

'If I stand, I'll be in danger of treating you like a public meeting. And, as we have all met frequently during the last months, I hope I may think of you as friends. Although by the time I have finished you may not think similarly of me.' (Which of them was he to choose, for God's sake!)

There was a nervous ripple of amusement, and they all said he should be seated. Terence continued. 'The reason for this meeting is somewhat bizarre, as I don't have to tell *you*. I think, I hope, we may all get through it without embarrassment. And I would ask you to remember that, although it is not easy for any of you, nor is it for me.' (His sister Babs had suggested flippantly that she should be his surrogate duchess.)

They murmured agreement, shuffled in their seats. Monty cleared his throat extravagantly. (Terence thought gloomily that dukes probably got more begging letters than lords.)

'As I said, I have come to know you all less superficially than was the case before our musical chairs left me the sole voter. May I say, very sincerely, and I hope without any hint of condescension, that you are a richly rewarding quintet. And as quintets go, you are more strings than wind...'(Except for that ghastly Devereux.)

There was polite laughter for this desperate joke, although Monty made it the occasion for a field day.

'... I have moved, in my life, mostly among poets and the gentry. Now, thanks to Blanche Ardbuckle's singular will, I have had the opportunity of many intimate talks with a leading novelist, an accomplished and popular actor, a former member of the lower house, and two distinguished booksellers, one belonging to the old school, one to the new, and both dedicated to their work.' (And both unspeakably middle-class.)

'It might well appear obvious to you that Ardbuckle's, like some other bookshops, could be run without a bookseller. There is a fashion nowadays to appoint accountants to run everything. But it will be even more obvious to you that to have an experienced bookseller take over the reins, and pull Ardbuckle's out of the quagmire into which it has regrettably sunk, might make sense.' (Given the innate snobbery of the British public, it might make more sense to appoint a duke!)

'Of the two booksellers Dean Phillips has the longer experience. His own shop, in Loamfield, also serves a major public school, and although it is somewhat smaller... indeed, much smaller... than this one in Rustrock, it could be said to belong to the same genre. I have little doubt that Dean could adapt his gifts, without any great strain, towards organising and developing Ardbuckle's. But Ardbuckle's is not just a retail book store, to use an Americanism, it is also a property company, and the sponsor of an annual book carnival dealing in antiquarian and secondhand books, and for this it is justly famous worldwide.' (Yet, he's too old, he wants to retire, I mustn't choose him.)

'Dean is undoubtedly a businessman. He must be to have stayed the course selling books in Loamfield despite much competition. And I daresay it doesn't take much, apart from commonsense, to manage a property business. Indeed, he might be the ideal person to elect from one point of view because he has expressed a marked feeling of identification with the tenants. He would, without any doubt, be a humane landlord. Nor is there any reason to suppose he could not successfully oversee the carnival, and give it new horizons.' (Terence began to feel better. He hadn't thought about the dukedom for at least ninety seconds.)

Dickie eased her buttocks. This was *worse* than being shortlisted for the Booker.

'Now let me turn to the other bookseller among you. He is both younger than Dean and into a much wider, broader way of business. He had a varied career before he launched his own group. He has a flair for publicity. His shops are constantly in, or on, the news. They are larger than most bookshops and very well stocked... some say, over-stocked...'

Abel offered the others a sickly grin. '...they have a tendency to be literary but why shouldn't a bookshop be literary? They also deal in the many non-literary -isms and -ologies which have increasingly invaded the shelves of all bookshops in recent years. Yes, Abel is younger than Dean and, within the book trade, has more of what, so I understand, is called clout. He is not afraid to take risks. He is used to delegating, and I cannot think that the property side of Ardbuckle's would prove a problem for him.' (But he's an upstart, dangerously near to thinking himself upper middle, too many pretensions; he couldn't plump for him.)

'So, those are the two bookseller claimants, if I may so describe them, and although their peers might be found in the contemporary book trade, I don't think anyone in that world is more respected and admired than are they.'

Dean looked embarrassed, Abel smirked. Both made deprecating noises.

'Now I should have said, "Ladies first". Do forgive me, dear Dickie. The only lady amongst you has already proved herself quite exceptionally capable at organising the children's department on days she has been here. She has also formulated original ideas about design, display, promotion. Her own books are increasingly popular – and we all hope, dear lady, that although you got only as far as the short list for Booker, you will actually win the Whitbread…' (But the robes! Can I afford the robes – even on loan from Covent Garden or the RSC?)

'Well said, hear, hear!' Stanley beamed at Dickie.

'Then there is the fact that Ardbuckle's was run by a woman for several decades but that, I concede, is not a very good argument, even in these feminist times.' Terence laughed mirthlessly; the others did not. 'What is a point, very much in Dickie's favour, is her growing fame. She has become a celebrity…'

So why am I not in *Who's Who*, thought Dickie, glumly. '…also I have noted that Dickie gets on well with both men and women…' (What sort of debts am I inheriting? Have inherited!)

'Whatever he means,' said Stanley in a stage whisper.

'…her relations with the staff – whenever they have remained here long enough to make it possible to have any – have been most warm. I think she would have been a very popular choice with many of those who might have had a vote. And, no doubt at all, she would confer distinction on the company. Indeed, she already has.' (But she's not tough like Blanche; she couldn't run a business herself, she'd rely too much on Hugh. No, she's out.)

'So, for that matter, would Stanley, who is rapidly becoming a household name, following several distinguished decades on the boards. He has top ratings in a popular soap. My sisters watch it avidly. Forgive me, Stanley…' (But he couldn't manage Ardbuckle's, he knows less than I do commercially; perhaps I can sell the title to some Arab?) '…for calling it a soap…'

'No, no, it *is*.'

'But not carbolic, eh?' Monty had an attack of the screeches.

'…The fact that Stanley has had little experience of retailing should not be held against him. As a young man, when the rep here sadly folded, he did a long stint at Ardbuckle's, and I have always maintained that bookselling is not something for which one needs a specialised training. It comes naturally to any intelligent, reasonably educated person, even to those of us who have suffered an – er – noble upbringing… huh, huh, huh…' (What would an Arab pay, there were no oil rights, so far as he knew?)

This is intolerable, thought Abel, and glared at Terence who said smoothly, 'I must get on but the decision I have to take is an important one, and I am bound to illustrate my reasoning. As I was saying, anyone can become a good bookseller, especially a talented actor. So, Stanley Brooke-Forster, perhaps not far off becoming, Sir Stanley, … huh, huh, … in my view, is as eligible as anyone else on the list.' He paused, cleared his throat… (Were dukes expected to entertain the royals? He felt a strong aversion to corgis…) '…but he does have a lot of engagements at present.'

Monty told himself, it's going to be me. I'm left to the last. And the others must all know it won't be them.

'Finally, there is Monty, and I could make a very good case for saying he is just the man for the job. His experience as a politician, and as a man of affairs, especially since he joined the Olive Directorate, would be of immense value to any business. And, after all, what experience does a minister of the crown have of actually running a department until he is actually appointed? He may spend two, three decades on the opposition benches, with no experience of government whatsoever…'

And when they get there, it shows, thought Abel.

'…then, suddenly, one of them finds himself Foreign Secretary, or Chancellor, or Minister for Trade. And, often, they don't make too bad a hash of it. So there are plenty of precedents for preferring Monty…'

That person preened himself.

'…and he has the advantage of coming from outside the trade. But so does Stanley, so does Dickie. However, Dickie and Stanley are actively pursuing their careers as writer and actor; Monty is free to lay down his political career, abandon his olive grove, as it were, and – do forgive me, my dear fellow – he doesn't actually have a seat at this present time, so he could give Ardbuckle's his undivided attention.' (It would be marvellous if I could offer it to an Arab, if I could wangle a passport for him... it would be great if I could sell my dukedom, but what am I to do?)

The man's mad, Abel decided, he can't be selecting Monty.

Terence looked at them all in turn, intently, solemnly, making eye contact with each of them. (No, of course not Monty. Could a politician be trusted to guarantee his poetry department?) 'How, in the face of such exemplary talent, am I to come to a decision?'

The pause that followed seemed endless. The five stuck to their seats with tension, sweat, or both. Mark Ampersand sat rivetted.

At last Terence spoke again. He cast away thought of the dukedom. He must be responsible and think of Ardbuckle's. (I'm a peer of the realm, or was.) 'The answer,' he said, 'and it is bound to disappoint all of you, is that I cannot choose. Therefore, I must abstain.'

'You can't do that,' screamed Monty.

'Can he?' Abel demanded of Mark.

Another gripping silence ensued. 'There is nothing,' said the solicitor, 'that I know of, in the terms of Blanche Ardbuckle's will, to say he can't. Such a situation she never envisaged. Nor did I.' 'So where does that leave us?' shouted Monty. 'This is absolutely irresponsible of Lord Absolom. You are not being fair to us, Terry.'

'Was it fair to ask me to decide?'

'But it wasn't our fault that you became the only one left.'

'Oh,' said Dickie, 'then who was it who pushed Hugh out?'

Abel looked straight at their tormentor and said, softly, pleadingly, 'Terry, you must name one of us.'

Lord Absolom raised his hands despairingly. 'I cannot.' (And I don't especially want to be a duke, but I do want to keep my poetry department.)

· 76 ·

After Terence had left them Mark repossessed his desk. 'I shall have to take advice, but I would think the will probably becomes null and void. Then the estate would go to Blanche Ardbuckle's nearest living relation, if she had one.'

Monty was almost apopleptic. 'And does she? DOES SHE?' He had been so near, and yet so far.

'I believe,' said Abel, 'she may have,'

'We all know she *has* had,' remarked Dickie, 'that is, if we have read our journals. The child she had in 1939 would only be in her fifties, if she has survived, and that child may have had offspring. We shall have to find out. How fascinating. Well, I never expected to win anyway.'

'And I'm quite relieved to know I haven't,' said Dean.

Stanley commented philosophically, 'It's rather like getting bad notices. You sit up all night after an opening, hoping, hoping, hoping. Then you get slated. But the following week your agent rings, and something has turned up.'

'It's all right for you.' Monty was inconsolable.

But they weren't going to play along with Monty's problems. Dean said briskly, 'So what about the shop in the meantime? Who is to run it?'

'I suppose I have to,' said Mark.

Dickie said, taking his hand affectionately, they would all help, adding, 'Hugh will be a great strength.'

'Thank you, Mrs Klute, but I think I must insist that Mr Mattingson does not interfere any further.'

'That's not very nice.' Dickie left in umbrage, following a path picked out through her new, gold-rimmed lorgnettes, a gift from Hugh. The others went too, relieved or shattered.

Mark's secretary said, 'There's a young man wanting to see you.'

'Who?'

'Gordon Ruffle, from the *Gazette & Herald*.'

'No. I can't talk to the press.'

'I think you'd better, squire,' said Gordon, who had overheard, 'you may not have news for me but I have some for you. Would you like to meet Blanche Ardbuckle's granddaughter?' (He had persuaded Margitte it was time for action.)

Mark tried to look impassive. 'I have important engagements.'

'Don't be so stuffy. Even the legal profession is in danger of entering the twenty-first century. There'll be lots of loot there.'

Mark relented. He knew the wretched reporter might be pointing to a way out of this hideous dilemma. 'Come in, Mr Ruffle. Tell me what you know.'

'Hugh Mattingson hasn't been in touch,then?'

'You could say, that we are rather out of touch. But don't.'

'So you don't know about the journals?'

'Yes, I do know about them.'

'So you're aware they contain scorching entries about your five notorious legatees?'

'Young man, try not to make every word sound like a *Sun* headline. In the first place, the legatees are not notorious. They all had affairs with Blanche Ardbuckle but that's old hat. It's been all over the media. Are you suggesting anything else?'

'Do they want those journals published?'

'You said you had something to tell me about a possible grandchild of Miss Ardbuckle's?'

'She's in the journals.'

'I know that.'

'But you don't know where she is now.'

'And you do, Mr Ruffle?

'Call me Gordon. I not only know the granddaughter, I live with her.'

'Great. I hope you're happy together. Tell me about the lady.'

Gordon improvised a quick version of the facts, playing on the pitiful plight of the orphaned Margitte whose cause he, the investigative journalist, was espousing. There was no documentation, Gordon told Mark. All was hearsay. Even in investigative journalism at this level, you had to take things on trust but his story, he insisted, was basically true.

'In law, we must have proof,' said Mark. 'Does she have a birth certificate for instance?'

Gordon groaned. It was always the same with lawyers. 'I didn't have time to go in for that sort of thing, but I'll ask her.'

'I'm sorry, but I cannot accept your story without actual evidence.'

'If everyone took your attitude, no newspaper would ever get published.'

Mark savoured the benefits of such a situation.

As he left, Gordon said, 'I didn't mention that this granddaughter, Margitte, is working at Ardbuckle's now.'

· 77 ·

Counsel's opinion supported Mark Ampersand in confirming that the Ardbuckle estate should go to the next of kin but recommended that those who had been named in the now null and void will should be awarded the sums promised to them at the time it was read, some of which had already been paid. Abel Farmer's counsel did not agree. He thought the five legatees should go to the European Court to demand greater compensation. This might take several months, even years.

Advice received from others was highly contradictory, also costly, so at Abel's suggestion, they agreed to wait and see if a next of kin emerged. Mark kept his information to himself, pending verification, so did Hugh. He had not even told Dickie, but Margitte, herself, had informed the new Duke of Bidborough, whose elevation was now public knowledge. And

Margitte, urged by Gordon, sought an interview with Terence who invited the young couple to the Towers.

As he awaited them, in his study, the new Duke was sufficiently honest with himself to admit that the advice he intended to give was far from being disinterested. His enhanced rank, to his immense relief, brought no new debts and few responsibilities. His predecessor, whose uncle had sold out to Blanche and Hugh, had lived on an annuity which had died with him. All that remained to his descendant was the title. Terence was not displeased with that; he was accustomed to being an aristocrat. But over and above, he wished to retain his poetry department, so his advice to the young people, although sound, would not be entirely objective.

The butler showed Margitte and Gordon into Terence's study where they compared notes about what the various experts had pronounced on the Ardbuckle situation. 'Thousands of pounds worth of advice. Young man, you should become a lawyer and make your fortune.'

'I'm thinking of becoming a bookseller and publisher. I'm over the brash young man stage. Margitte has been a tonic for me. We're getting married.'

'There's an old fashioned streak in us all,' said Terence.

'This business of going to the international courts and so forth will surely hold things up forever, won't it, your Grace?'

'Do call me, Terence. I couldn't agree with you more. Avoidance of litigation, Gordon, has been a lifelong rule for me. But what is crucial is for you, Margitte, to prove your claim to your grandmother's estate. That should not take so long. Then come to terms with the legatees, as we call them. Be as generous as you can. They have entertained expectations, they have suffered enormous publicity. It would be a gesture on your part, Margitte. You will have the property as well as the shop, and the land on which the carnival is held. That did well even this year. No reason to give it up. That funny little Didsbury Jackson managed it pretty well before he went off with his friend. He's quite a loss. I'm not sure we shouldn't try to attract him back.'

Gordon noted the 'we'. His Grace, or rather Terry, identified closely with Ardbuckle's. He would need to watch that.

'I'd just adore to be in charge of the actual shop,' said Margitte, who also wondered what it might be like to become a real live Duchess, 'I really do have ideas about it. And Gordon is very keen to promote the carnival.'

'What an opportunity for you if all goes as planned.'

Gordon said, 'We may publish the journals if the lawyers approve. Hugh came unstuck on that one.'

'Can't advise there. Haven't seem them. I don't think I feature?'

'Just a passing reference. Not very flattering. We can cut it.'

'What did she say about me?'

'I'll show you. I've got a copy at home.'

Terence pretended indifference. 'Let me pour you a sherry.' He walked to a wall cabinet and took out exquisitely thin glasses. 'Queen Victoria is said to have drunk from one of these.'

'And did Queen Elizabeth sleep here?' mocked Gordon.

'The Towers is Jacobean.' Terence smiled condescendingly.

'Sorry, I've never been good at dates.'

'Let us drink to your venture. There is just one thing.' Terence beheld them unemotionally, kept his cool, although he knew the answer to his request would break or make his life style. 'You're well aware of my interest in the poetry department. Without being unduly immodest, I think I can claim it as my creation. I hope it may help you if I continue to administer it.'

'Terry!' cried Margitte. 'We just couldn't get on without it. Or you! How do we stop you sloping off when we're not looking?'

Superior bastard,' said Gordon, as they drove away..

'He's great. A real genuine English gentleman. And a Dook, to boot.'

'Don't give me that shit.'

'And don't you talk like that to me.' Something of the spirit of Blanche Ardbuckle was beginning to surface in Margitte. 'Now watch it!'

Gordon didn't like it but said nothing more for the moment. He had *his* plans for Ardbuckle's. When they were at home, after Margitte had supplied a quick omelette for supper, he returned to the attack. 'We don't want that mother-fucking Didsbury back.'

'Is he a mother-fucker? How would you know that?'

'What's come over you?'

'What have you got against Didsbury? In any case, all you gotta say is, you think there could be a better arrangement, and you want to run the carnival yourself. There's no need to be so crude.'

'Oh, for Christ's sake!' Gordon threw what was left on his plate at the wall, making a greasy stain. Margitte ran to him, instantly contrite. 'Darling, I'm sorry.' He repelled her, pushed her against the wall. She fell to the carpet, on to the messy remains of the omelette. 'Let's get this straight, Marg. We're a partnership but I'm boss.'

'You're a lousy pig!'

'You know you want me.'

'I hate you.' She rose, tried to get past him to the door. He began to throw everything in sight – cutlery, vases, fruit bowls, anything in his path. Then he hurled himself out of the flat.

When she had cleared up she began to miss him; he was abrasive but he was also warm, cuddly, and good in bed. She was in love with him, or thought she was. She wanted him. She seemed cursed with her grandmother's sexual appetite, she just couldn't help it. Once she had powdered her face she recovered her composure. She might have Blanche's sexual needs but she also had some of her toughness. 'He'll come back on my terms,' she declared to the mirror, 'I could get over him, if I tried hard enough... I reckon.' She stuck out her tongue at herself.

He didn't return for a week. Then he phoned and asked forgiveness. He apologised for his temper, said it wouldn't happen again – all the usual things. She gave permission for him to visit. She had been missing him, unbearably. Every other man she'd looked at seemed colourless.

Gordon arrived with a bottle of Spanish champagne. More apologies followed. 'God! I've missed you, Marg.'

'I've missed you, Gordon.'

They made love on the settee. Afterwards, she said, 'I have to tell you that I've written to Didsbury. And I've also offered the carnival to Hugh Mattingson.'

'That old fart!'

'Gordon!'

'Well he is. Look what he did to the business. He was trying to ruin it. If it hadn't been for Terence there would have been nothing left.'

'And me.'

'You couldn't have run it without Terry.'

She swallowed that one. 'But I don't want Didsbury, or Hugh, to *run* the carnival for me. I want one of them to *buy* it.'

'But I want it.'

'I shall need your help with the shop, and the publishing.'

'I don't care a fuck about publishing. I want the bleeding carnival. Is that understood?

This time she threw the first plate.

· 79 ·

Each of the legatees made a private attempt to persuade Terence that his abstention was no sort of decision. He argued that it was. He also told Dickie, who knew from Hugh about Margitte, that it was quite the best solution because it would allow for Ardbuckle's to be owned and run by Blanche's granddaughter. And Margitte had offered, not unprompted by himself, generous terms to all legatees, who would receive not one penny less than if they had been unsuccessful for the jackpot. The young woman had received, from the States, with the help of Senator Ella, proof that she was Blanche's granddaughter and next of kin, and, although Hugh's part in this proved counter-productive to him, he had not really expected Dickie to win, and was formulating other plans. Dickie, also, accepted the compromise and was, anyhow, euphoric. She had finished both her book and her play and had moved in permanently to Ridge End, having sold Piddletrenthide. She had let her Aegean villa for a year, and parted with her rights in the St John's Wood house to Butch who, she said to Terence, wouldn't actually notice she wasn't there any longer. 'When I was, Butch would be with his epics. We hadn't been together for years, in *that* sense.'

She spent some time cooing over Terence's library, hoping to find something of hers on his shelves, if only the slim volume of verse. When he realised what concerned her – because he was, after all, a bookseller, and not just a duke – Terence withdrew the slender book from a shelf, and asked her to autograph it. He also presented her with a signed copy (they all were) of his *Exterstices*.

'But, it's a nuisance,' said Dickie, as she left, 'that that frightful Monty is threatening to ruin the whole settlement. He truly believes he can win if he goes to Brussels, or the Hague, or wherever.'

'I've done my best to explain how costly that would be. Lawyers are absolute locusts. He ought to know, being in that olive business. It could take years.'

'Politicians live on false hopes. They're actually as bad as lawyers.'

'Most of them are both. You will simply have to put it to a vote, Dickie.' Which was what happened, one morning a week later, in Mark's office.

'Is a majority decision binding?' Monty demanded fiercely. 'It wasn't when Dickie didn't agree.'

'Morally,' said Dean, 'it must be.'

'I'm not interested in the morality of it.'

'That will look good on your next election manifesto. May we quote you... Montelimar?' asked Abel.

Monty, hearing his full name, paled. 'I hope this is confidential.'

'You pathetic innocent. Things do have a way of leaking out. Ask the editor of the *Guardian*. Where would he be without leaks? There are twelve pairs of eyes in this room, and six tongues, and how can we be sure there is no one with an ear to that door? Or that one? Or that other one? Or the fourth over there? Stanley! What a splendid setting for a farce.'

'I hope no one intends to debag me,' replied the actor.

Dean impatiently pointed out that there had been no ruling on the majority decision. 'Supposing this were to go to the Lords and the five Law Lords put their great collective minds to it, and three of them said, yes, but two said, no, would the majority prevail?'

'I believe it would,' said Mark.

'There's always a right of appeal,' said Monty, and screeched.

Mark became desperate. His father had recently died and left him comfortably off. He wanted to sell his practice and take his wife round the world, then retire to a life of strenuous leisure. He knew he should not risk his professional integrity but he was human. 'Whether or not it is, what I do know is that every hour, and every day, you delay taking a decision, your capital will be diminished by legal fees which will not be balanced by interest earned on the capital needed to pay them.' He looked sternly at Monty. 'I would ask you, Mr Devereux, on behalf of everyone here, to accept the majority verdict. Miss Einstein has given us authority to write you all cheques this very day. Or you could do what the Duke did. You could abstain.'

This masterly compromise appealed to the politician who declared loftily that he certainly didn't wish to be anti-social. Nor did he wish to be called Montelimar. 'I shall continue to have my thoughts but I daresay...' He smiled, villainously, ingratiatingly '... when I receive my cheque I shall banish them...'

The collective sigh of relief caused a priceless ceramic item – from a tat-shop near Ravello – to crash to the floor and splinter.

Matters proceeded apace. The ex-legatees dispersed to their bookshops, theatres, word processors, potential constituents. The bond which had held them together was broken. No more secret telephone calls, confidential leaks, engineered alliances, soliciting of staff. For the first time in his professional life, Stanley Brooke-Forster had no financial worries. Dickie had a new home and a new man. Monty went in search of a European seat ('the money is better'); one of the booksellers made plans for retirement, which would also embrace social work on behalf of the Rustrock slum dwellers, the other dreamed, Puck-like, of a chain which would encircle the globe. Of the five, the latter, Abel Farmer, was the only one who would have any bearing on the future of Ardbuckle's.

· 80 ·

Margitte announced her intention of 'living over the shop', just as her ancestors had. She also applied for naturalisation. Scarcely had she installed herself, and put into effect her modernisation programme, than Terence Absolom urged her to soft pedal. The next crisis was looming. 'It's wiser to take a step at a time.'

What crisis, she thought. Was he going to propose? Pity she didn't actually fancy him because she'd quite like to be a duchess. Perhaps some compromise could be arranged? Aloud, she said 'I want to be out of the *fourteenth* century, before we reach the twenty-first.' Forty-eight hours later she learned, from a Rustrock estate agent, that the former Ritz site, one of the few in town not owned by Ardbuckle's, had been bought by the country's leading academic bookseller. Competition, for the first time in Ardbuckle's history, had arrived.

Abel read the news in the trade press and called Margitte. 'Join my group,' he said. 'It's your only chance of salvation.'

'But I like my independence. I'm just getting used to it .'

'All my managers enjoy wide autonomy. You knew John Ogglethorpe? Well, I've just appointed him to look after Wimbledon. If he wishes, he can have anything he wants, even a grass court on the first floor, if it brings the customers in. Did I tell you, Jane had a baby daughter? They've called her Blanche. Come in with me and you'll be able to compete with Blackwell's. There'll be room for us both.'

He convinced her, but only after agreeing to Terence's department becoming a separate company in which his Grace owned fifty-five percent of the shares. She just couldn't get over knowing a real live 'Dook, for Chrissake!'

'I never interfere with what is working well, Margitte,' Abel insisted.

'Terence's department is a gold mine. If we lost him, it would only do us harm.'

'It's *us* already?'

'If you don't want it to be *them*.'

Margitte then asked if Abel knew who had let in the competition.

'No. Do you?'

'Sure. Gordon – that shitty ex of mine. He's given up journalism. Murdoch wouldn't accept his offer to edit the *Sunday Times,* so he's gone into real estate. He's with Upperton & Langley, and they've taken on Hugh Mattingson as an adviser. *And,* did you know that he and Stanley Brooke-Forster are refurbishing the theatre – which I leased to them before I knew Hugh was into property – *And* they are planning to open it with a play written by Dickie Klute. The first night is to coincide with publication of her new novel, which is said to be all about Hugh. I do wish I hadn't sold the carnival site to him.'

'Don't worry. Diversification is the current thing, but fashions change. All the newest, poshest bookshops now have coffee bars and spaces with tables where customers can copy out of books without having to buy them. And soon we'll have a sculpture arbour with displays of that dreadful Fergus Welch's latest work… did you know he's up for the Tate-Turner thing?'

'However, in ten years, diversification will be out. Bookshops will be in high streets again, crammed into former building society premises. But meantime, it's big time, and we're going to make a pile. We've got publishers on the run.'

So Margitte was encouraged by Abel to flex her muscles and express her ideas. She changed her name to Margaret Ardbuckle and he had the wisdom not to change the name of her shop to Farmer's. He found her good staff, he exploited the possibilities of the Gothic-style frontage and spent more and more time himself at Rustrock Spa, although mindful of the need to attend to his ever-expanding business. He rationalised his behaviour by saying he was entitled to a day off each week, apart from Sundays (when all his shops were open) and that Rustrock was a good place for a rest day. Sundays, he offically spent with his family, who had long since adapted to his absence, so it was only a matter of time before Margaret invited him to the flat above the shop. At first they had tea. On the next occasion, it was drinks. Then there was a working lunch. Finally...

As Abel and Margaret, now resigned to life without a coronet, settled into the new four poster which she had purchased, he murmured, contentedly, 'I have been here before.'

Down on the carnival site Hugh, clothed in impeccably cleaned and pressed denims and hobnail boots, plus a hard hat, was informing the agents for a mighty American bookselling group that he had outline planning permission to build a shopping complex which would relieve traffic congestion in the centre of Rustrock Spa.

Biographical note:

Ian Norrie, born Southborough, Kent, 1927, was a journalist at Eastbourne before becoming a bookseller. From 1956-1988 his main occupation was as manager, later proprietor, of Hampstead's High Hill Bookshop, but he also wrote and edited many books, contributed book reviews to various newspapers and magazines, was a book trade columnist and dabbled in publishing. He was Hon. Secretary, then Chairman, of the Society of Bookmen, served on the executive of the National Book League (now Book Trust) for thirteen years, on the management committee of the Booker Prize for three, was a director of the Book Trade Benevolent Society for four, and is an adviser to the National Life Story Collection's Book Trade Lives Project, administered by the British Library. He and David Whitaker recently formed The Graveyard Press which will publish corrected and amended obituaries od eminent publishers and booksellers. He is a widower, with two children and four grandchildren, and lives in Barnet, Hertfordhire.

First published in Great Britain by
ELLIOTT & THOMPSON LIMITED
8 Caledonia Street
London N1 9DZ

© Ian Norrie 2002

The right of Ian Norrie to be identified as the author of
this work has been asserted by him in accordance with the
Copyright Designs and Patent Act 1988.

All rights reserved

First Edition

ISBN 1 904027 02 4 (Hardback)
1 904027 03 2 (Paperback)

Book design by Brad Thompson
Cover photography by Alice Rosenbaum
Printed in Malta by Interprint